Bottled Hell

It had control of the air. I couldn't tell what it meant to do, but something bad was a good bet. Air's heavy – it weighs several pounds per square inch. Increasing density can crush anything in its path.

I blocked, drawing heavy oxygen out of the elevator cage and slamming it together in a tightly packed ball between my spread hands. Rahel backed away, looking down at the swirling grey-blue mass I was holding.

I set it on fire with a spark from the electricity still crackling around in the air, and wrapped the whole thing in a shell of carbon dioxide, and lifted that bowling-ball-sized inferno in one hand and held it there. Hell in a bottle.

'Bring it on!' I yelled to the empty air. Voices didn't carry in the altered atmosphere, but it didn't matter, I knew it was getting the point. 'Get your ass out here, you coward! Show yourself!'

The elevator shuddered to a halt.

Something black manifested itself in the corner as a shadow, then a stain, then a liquid-soft presence.

It wasn't a Djinn. I didn't know what it was, but evidently Rahel did. She lifted her left hand and pointed it at the thing, and her fingers sprouted claws – long, wickedly pointed things that gleamed harsh crystal in the overhead lights.

'*Ifrit*,' she hissed.

Heat Stroke

Heat Stroke

Book Two of the Weather Warden series

RACHEL CAINE

First published in Great Britain in 2008 by
Allison & Busby Limited
13 Charlotte Mews
London, W1T 4EJ
www.allisonandbusby.com

Excerpt from 'Heart and Mind' on page 11 from
Collected Poems © Edith Sitwell, published by
Duckworth Publishers. Used by kind arrangement
with David Higham Associates Ltd.

A CIP catalogue record for this book is available from
the British Library.

First published in the USA in 2004.

10 9 8 7 6 5 4 3

ISBN 978-0-7490-7921-5

Typeset in 10.5/14pt Sabon by
Terry Shannon.

The paper used for this Allison & Busby publication
has been produced from trees that have been legally sourced
from well-managed and credibly certified forests.

Printed and bound in the UK by
CPI Bookmarque Ltd, Croydon, Surrey

RACHEL CAINE is the international bestselling author of over thirty novels, including the *New York Times* bestselling Morganville Vampires series. She was born at White Sands Missile Range, which people who know her say explains a lot. She has been an accountant, a professional musician, and an insurance investigator, and still carries on a secret identity in the corporate world. She and her husband, fantasy artist R. Cat Conrad, live in Texas with their iguanas, Pop-eye and Darwin, a *mali uromastyx* named (appropriately) O'Malley, and a leopard tortoise named Shelley (for the poet, of course).

www.rachelcaine.com
www.myspace.com/rachelcaine

Available from
ALLISON & BUSBY

The author wishes to thank:

Cat Conrad
Joanne Madge
P.N. Elrod
Kelley Walters
Annie Wortham
Leah Rosenthal
Sharon Sams
Glenn Rogers
Michael Shanks
Joe Bonamassa
Kenny Kramme
Eric Czar
ORAC
SDJ
Lucienne Diver
Laura Anne Gilman

...not that she personally knows all of them.
But they're deserving of gratitude anyway.

Said the Lion to the Lioness – 'When you are amber
    dust –
No more a raging fire like the heat of the Sun
(No liking but all lust) –
Remember still the flowering of the amber blood and
    bone,
The rippling of bright muscles like a sea,
Remember the rose-prickles of bright paws
Though we shall mate no more
Till the fire of that sun the heart and the moon-cold bone
    are one.'

Said the Skeleton lying upon the sands of Time –
'The great gold planet that is the mourning heat of the
    Sun
Is greater than all gold, more powerful
Than the tawny body of a Lion that fire consumes
Like all that grows or leaps…so is the heart

More powerful than all dust. Once I was Hercules
Or Samson, strong as the pillars of the seas:
But the flames of the heart consumed me, and the mind
Is but a foolish wind.'

EDITH SITWELL, 'HEART AND MIND'

Previously...

My name is Joanne Baldwin, and I used to control the weather.

No, really. I was a member of the Weather Wardens. You probably aren't personally acquainted with them, but they keep you from getting fried by lightning (mostly), swept away by floods (sometimes), and killed by tornadoes (occasionally). We try to do all that stuff. Sometimes we even succeed.

But I ran into something bad – something that threatened to destroy me from the inside out – and when the Wardens turned against me too, I ran for my life. I spent a memorable week looking for a man named Lewis Levander Orwell, who I thought just might be able to save my life. I picked up a friend named David along the way, who turned out to be way more then he seemed.

I found Lewis. It didn't help. I died.

Luckily for me, David didn't let it end there. But now I'm still on the run – only now I'm one of *them*. A Djinn.

At least I still have a really fast car...

Chapter One

There was a storm brewing over Church Falls, Oklahoma. Blue-black clouds, churning and boiling in lazy slow motion, stitched through with lightning the colour of butane flames. It had a certain instinctual menace, but it was really just a baby, all attitude and no experience. I watched it on the aetheric plane as the rain inside of it was tossed violently up into the mesosphere, frozen by the extreme cold, fell back down to gather more moisture on the way. Rinse and repeat. The classic recipe for hail.

Circular motion inside the thing. It was more of a feeling I had than anything I could see, but I didn't doubt it for a second; after years of overseeing the weather, I vibrated on frequencies that didn't require seeing to believe.

I gathered power around me like a glittering warm cloak, and reached out for—

'Stop.'

My power slammed into an invisible wall and bounced off. I yelped, dropped back into human reality with a heavy *thud* and realised I'd almost driven Mona off the road. Mona was a 1997 Dodge Viper GTS, midnight blue, and I was driving her well the hell in excess of the speed limit, which was just the way I liked it. I controlled the swerve, glanced down at the speedometer and edged another five miles an hour out of the accelerator. Mona's purr changed to an interested, low-throated growl.

'Don't *ever* do that when I'm breaking a century on the interstate,' I snapped at the guy who'd put up that wall I'd just slammed into. 'And jeez, sensitive much? I was just giving things a little push. For the better.'

The guy's name was David. He settled himself more comfortably against the passenger side window, and said without opening his eyes, 'You're meddling. You got bored.'

'Well, yeah.' Because driving in Oklahoma is not exactly the world's most exciting occupation. 'And?'

'And you can't do that anymore.' *That* meaning adjust the weather to suit myself, apparently.

'Why not?'

His lips twitched and pressed a smile into submission. 'Because you'll attract attention.'

'And the fact I'm barrelling down the freeway at over a hundred...?'

'You know what I mean. And by the way, you should slow down.'

I sighed. 'You're kidding me. This is coasting. This is little old lady speed.'

'NASCAR drivers would have heart attacks. Slow down before we get a ticket.'

'Chicken.'

'Yes,' he agreed solemnly. 'You frighten me.'

I downshifted, slipped Mona in behind an eighteen-wheeler grinding hell-for-leather east toward Okmulgee and parts beyond, and watched the RPMs fall. Mona grumbled. She didn't like speed limits. Neither did I. Hell, the truth is that I'd never met any kind of limit I liked. Back in the good old times before, well, yesterday, when my name was still Joanne Baldwin and I was human, I'd been a Weather Warden. A card-carrying member of the Wardens Association, the international brotherhood of people in charge of keeping Mother Nature from exterminating the human race. I'd been in the business of controlling wind, waves, and storms. Being an adrenalin junkie goes with the territory.

The fact that I was *still* an adrenalin junkie was surprising, because strictly speaking, I no longer had a real human body, or real human adrenalin to go with it. So how did it work that I still felt all the same human impulses as before? I didn't want to think about it too much, but I kept coming back to the fact that I'd *died*. Last mortal thing I remembered, I'd been a battleground for two demons tearing me apart, and then I'd – metaphorically speaking – opened my eyes on a whole new world, with whole new rules. Because David had made me a Djinn. You know, Arabian Nights, lamp, granter of wishes? That kind. Only I wasn't imprisoned in a lamp, or (more appropriately) a bottle; I was free-range. Masterless.

Cool, but scary. Masterless, I was vulnerable, and I knew it.

'Hey,' I said out loud, and glanced away from the road to look at my travelling companion. Dear God, he was gorgeous. When I'd first met him he'd been masquerading as a regular guy, but even then he'd been damn skippy fine. In what I'd come to realise was his natural Djinn form, he was damn skippy fine to the power of ten. Soft auburn hair worn just a little too long for the current military-short styles. Eyes like molten bronze. Warm golden skin that stretched velvet soft over a strong chest, perfectly sculpted biceps, a flat stomach... My hands had a Braille memory that made me warm and melty inside.

Without opening those magical eyes, he asked, 'Hey, what?' I'd forgotten I'd said anything. I scrambled to drag my brain back to more intellectual pursuits.

'Still waiting for a plan, if it doesn't disturb your beauty sleep.' I kept the tone firmly in the bitchy range, because if I wasn't careful I might start with a whole breathless I-don't-deserve-you routine, and that would cost me cool points. 'We're still heading east, by the way.'

'Fine,' he said, and adjusted his leaning position slightly to get more comfortable against the window glass. 'Just keep driving. Less than warp speed, if you can manage it.'

'Warp speed? Great. A *Trek* fan.' Not that I was surprised. Djinn seemed to delight in pop culture, so far as I could tell. 'OK. Fine. I'll drive boring.'

I glanced back at the road – good thing, I was seriously over the line and into head-on-collision territory – and steered back straight again before I checked the fuel gauge. Which brought up another point. 'Can I stop for gas?'

'You don't need to.'

'Um, this is a Viper, not a zillion-miles-to-the-gallon Earth Car. Believe me, we'll need to. Soon.'

David extended one finger – still without cracking an eyelid – and pointed at the dial. I watched the needle climb, peg out at full, and quiver. 'Won't,' he said.

'O-K,' I said. 'East. Right. Until when?'

'Until I think it's safe to stop.'

'You know, a little information in this partnership would really help make it, oh, say, a partnership.'

His lips twitched away from a smile, and his voice dipped down into octaves that resonated in deep, liquid areas of my body. 'Are we partners?'

Dangerous territory. I wasn't sure what we were, exactly, and I wasn't sure I wanted him to tell me. He'd saved me; he'd taken the human part of me that had survived an attack by two demons, and transformed it into a Djinn. I hoped that didn't make him my father. Talk about your Freudian issues. 'OK, genius, I don't know. You define it. What are we?'

He sighed. 'I'd rather sleep than get into this right now.'

I sighed right back. 'You know, I'm a little freaked out here. Dead, resurrected, got all these new sensations – talking would be good for me.'

'What kind of new sensations?' he asked. His voice was low, warm, gentle – ah, sensations. I was having them, all right. Loads of them.

I cleared my throat. 'First of all, things don't look right.'

'Define right.'

'The way they—'

'—used to look,' he finished for me. 'You've got different eyes now, Joanne. You can choose how to look at things. It's not just light on nerves anymore.'

'Well, it's too...bright.' Understatement. The sun glared in through the polarised windows and shimmered like silk – it had a liquid quality to it, a real weight. 'And I see way too much. Too far.'

Everything had...dimensions. Saturated colours, and a peculiar kind of *history* – I could sense where things had been, how long ago, where they'd come from, how they'd been made. A frightening blitz of knowledge. I was trying to shut it down, but it kept leaping up whenever I noticed something new. Like the gas gauge. Watching that quivering indicator, I knew it had been stamped out in a factory in Malaysia. I knew the hands of the person who'd last touched it. I had the queasy feeling that if I wanted to, I could follow his story all the way back through the line of his ancestors. Hell, I could trace the plastic back to the dinosaurs that had died in the tar pit to give petroleum its start.

David said, 'All you have to do is focus.'

I controlled a flash of temper. 'Focus? That's your advice? News flash, Obi-Wan, you kinda suck at it.'

'Do not.' He opened his eyes, and they were autumn brown, human, and very tired. 'Give me your hand.'

I took it off the gear shift and held it out. He wrapped warm fingers over mine, and something hot as sunlight flashed through me.

The horizon adjusted itself. Sunlight faded to normal brightness. The edges and dimensions and weight of things went back to human proportions.

'There.' He sounded even more tired this time. 'Just keep driving.'

He let go of my hand. I wrapped it back around the gearshift for comfort and thought of a thousand questions, things like *Why am I still breathing?* and

If I don't have a heart, why is it pumping so hard? and *Why me? Why save me?*

I wasn't sure I was ready for any of those answers, even if David had the energy to tell me. I wasn't ready for anything more than the familiar, bone-deep throb of Mona's tyres on the road, and the rush of the Viper running eagerly toward the horizon.

I had another question I didn't want to ask, but it slipped out anyway. 'We're in trouble, aren't we?'

This time, he did smile. Full, dark, and dangerous. 'Figured that out, did you?'

'People say I'm smart.'

'I hope they say you're lucky, too.'

'Must be,' I murmured. 'How else do I explain you?'

Brown eyes opened, studied me for a few seconds, then drifted shut again. He said, just as softly, 'Let's pray you never have to.'

The car didn't need gas, and I discovered that I didn't need sleep – at least not for more than twenty-four hours. We blew through Tulsa, hit I-70 toward Chicago, bypassed Columbus, and eventually ended up on a turnpike in New Jersey. David slept. I drove. I was a little worried about mortal things like cop cars and tollbooths, but David kept us out of sight and out of mind. We occupied space, but to all intents and purposes, we were invisible.

Which was not such an advantage, I discovered,

when you get into heavy commuter traffic. After about a dozen near misses, I pulled Mona over to the side of the road, stretched, and clicked off the engine. Metal ticked and popped – Mona wasn't any kind of magical construct, she was just a plain old production car. OK, the fastest production car ever made, with a V10, 7990 cubic centimetres, 6000 RPM, and a top speed of over 260 miles per hour. But not magic.

And I'd been pushing her hard.

I rolled down the window, sucked in a breath of New Jersey air laden with an oily taste of exhaust, and watched the sun come up over the trees. There was something magical about *that*, all right – the second morning of my new life. And the sun was beautiful. A vivid golden fire in the sky, trailing rays across an intense, empty blue. No clouds. I could feel the potential for clouds up there – dust particles and pollution hanging lazily in the air, positive and negative charges constantly shoving and jostling for position. Once the conditions came together, those dust particles would get similar charges and start attracting microscopic drops of moisture. Like calls to like. Moisture thickens, droplets form, clouds mass. Once the droplets get too heavy to stay airborne, they fall. Simple physics. And yet there was something seductive and magical about it, too, as magical as the idea that chemical compounds grow into human beings who walk and talk and dream.

I watched a commercial jet embroider the clear

blue sky, heading west, and stretched my senses out. There wasn't any limit to what I could know, if I wanted... I could touch the plane, the cold silver skin, the people inside with all their annoyances and fears and boredom and secret delights. Two people who didn't know each other were both thinking about joining the mile high club. I wished them luck in finding each other.

I sucked in another breath and stretched – my human-feeling body still liked the sensation, even though it wasn't tired, wasn't thirsty or hungry or in need of bathroom facilities – and turned to David...

Who was awake and watching me. His eyes weren't brown now, they were sun-sparked copper, deep and gold-flecked, entirely inhuman. He was too beautiful to be possible in anything but dreams.

The car shuddered as three eighteen-wheelers blew past and slammed wind gusts into us – a rude reminder that it wasn't a dream, after all. Not that reality was looking all that bad.

'What now?' I asked. I wasn't just asking about driving directions, and David knew it. He reached out and captured my hand, looked down at it, rubbed a thumb light and warm as breath across my knuckles.

'There are some things I need to teach you.'

And there went the perv-cam again, showing me all the different things he probably didn't mean...

'So we should get a room,' he finished, and when

he met my eyes again, the heart I didn't really have skipped a beat or two.

'Oh,' I breathed. 'A room. Sure. Absolutely.'

He kept hold of my hand, and his index finger traced light whorls over my palm, teasing what I supposed wasn't really a lifeline anymore. The finger moved slowly up over the translucent skin of my wrist, waking shivers. *God.* I didn't even mean to, but somehow I was seeing him on the aetheric level, that altered plane of reality where certain people, like Wardens and Djinn, can read energy patterns and see things in an entirely different spectrum.

He was pure fire, shifting and flaring and burning with the intensity of a star.

'You're feeling better,' I said. No way to read expressions, on the aetheric, but I could almost feel the shape of his smile.

'A little,' he agreed. 'And you do have things to learn.'

'You're going to teach me?'

His voice went deep and husky. 'Absolutely. As soon as we have some privacy.'

I retrieved my hand, jammed Mona into first gear, and peeled rubber.

We picked an upper-class hotel in Manhattan, valeted Mona into a parking garage with rates so high it had to be run by the Mafia. I wondered how much ransom we were going to have to pay Guido to get her back. We strolled into the high-class marble and mahogany lobby brazenly unconcerned by our lack of luggage.

'Wow,' I said, and looked around appreciatively. 'Sweet.' It had that old-rich ambiance that most places try to create with knock-off antiques and reproduction rugs, but as I trailed my fingers over a mahogany side table I could feel the depth of history in it, stretching back to the generations of maids who'd polished it, to the eighteenth-century worker who'd planed the wood, to the tree that stood tall in the forest.

Nothing fake about this place. Well, OK, the couches were modern, but you have to prefer comfort over authenticity in some things. The giant Persian rug was certainly real enough to make up the difference.

The place smelt of that best incense of all – old money.

David waited in line patiently at the long marble counter while the business travellers ahead of him presented American Express cards and listened to voicemail on cell phones. A thought occurred to me, and I tugged at the sleeve of his olive drab coat. 'Hey. Why—'

'—check in?' he finished for me. 'Two reasons. First, it's easier, and you'll find that the less power you use unnecessarily, the better off you are. Second, I don't think you're ready to be living my life quite yet. One step at a time.'

He reached into his pocket and came out with an American Express card. I blinked at it. It said DAVID L PRINCE in raised letters. 'Cool. Is that real?'

I said it too loudly.

His eyes widened behind concealing little round glasses. 'Not a great question when we're about to use it to pay for the room, is it?'

Oh. I'd been figuring we were still in some unnoticeable fog, but clearly not; the guy in line ahead of me was distracted enough from the cell phone glued to his ear to throw us a suspicious look. True, we didn't have the glossy spa-treated look of the rich, or the unlimited-expense-account confidence of the corporate, but we weren't exactly looking homeless, either. I shot him a sarcastic smile. He turned back to his business.

'Sorry,' I said, more softly, to David. 'Obviously, yes, it's real, of course. I mean – hell, I don't know what I mean. Sorry. Um...where do they send the bills?'

'Not to me.'

His smile made my train of thought derail and crash. Cell Phone Guy in front of us picked up his room key and got out of line; David and I moved up to the counter, where a highly polished young lady too nice for New York did all the check-in things, issued us plastic key cards, and fired off amenities too fast for me to follow. A uniformed bellman veered out of our path when he saw we were bag-free and gave us a look that meant he was no stranger to couples arriving for short, intense bursts of time.

David took my arm and walked me to the elevators, across the huge Persian rug, past a silent piano and a muted big-screen TV that was showing some morning show with perfect people interviewing more perfect people. We rode the elevator with Cell Phone Guy, who was still connected and chatting about market share and a corporate vice president's affair with the wife of a global board member. The latter sounded interesting. As it happened, we were both on the same floor – twelve – and he looked at us like we might be after his wallet or his life, but before long he peeled away to a room and we continued on, down a long hallway and to a bright-polished wooden door with the number 1215 on it.

David didn't bother with the key card. He touched the door with his finger, and it just swung open.

I looked at him. 'What happened to "the less you use, the better"?'

He scooped me up in his arms and carried me over the threshold. Gravity slipped sideways, and I put my arms around his neck until he settled me down with my feet on the carpet.

'What was that for?' I asked. He felt fever-hot against me, and those eyes – God. Intense, focused, hungry.

'Luck,' he said, and kissed me. I felt instant heat slam through me, liquefying me in equal proportion to how incredibly real he felt against me, and I felt a feverish urge to be naked with this man, *right now*, to be sure that all of this wasn't just a particularly lovely dream on the way to the grave and oh *God* his hands burnt right through my clothes like they weren't there.

And then, as his palms glided up my sides, wrinkling fabric, the cloth melted away and disappeared, and then it was just flesh, and fire, and the taste of David's lips and tongue. I felt myself burn and go faint with heat stroke, revived with the cool relief of his skin.

And if it was a dream, it was the best I'd ever had.

In the morning, we got down to the work of teaching me to be a Djinn.

I'm not what you could call spiritual, so learning how to *be* spiritual – in the true spirit sense of the word – was a challenge. Sure, I'd been a Warden, but calling the wind and calming storms was all about science for me. I understood it in the way a child of the atomic age would, which meant subatomic particles and chaos theory and wave motion. Hell, I'd been a weather-controlling *bureaucrat*, when you came right down to it. Nothing that you might call preparation for being granted power on a legendary scale.

David started me out with that night of incredible, unbelievable sex, and the next morning when I woke up it felt like it was still going on. I mean, senses locked wide open. Chakras at full power. Every touch, every taste, every random sensation echoed through me like a struck bell. It was fun at first.

Then it got to be painful.

'Turn it off,' I groaned, and hid my head under a down pillow. David's fingers traced the bumps of my spine, dragging down the sheet in slow, cool increments. 'Oh, God, please, I can't stand it!'

He made a sound, low in his throat, and let his touch glide down over my buttocks, down the backs of my thighs. 'You'll need to learn how to shut off your senses,' he said. 'Can't walk around like this all the time, can you?'

I knotted my fists in the pillow and screamed into the mattress. Not that he was particularly trying to drive me nuts, it was just part of the overload. *Everything* was sexual. The sheet, sliding over the backs of my legs. His fingertips firing nerves. The smell of him, the taste of him still tingling on my lips, the sound of his breath in my ear.

'I don't know how,' I whispered, when I'd stopped shaking. 'Tell me how.'

'You have to learn how to choose what level of sensation and perception to use,' he said. 'To start with, I want you to meditate and block out what's around you.'

'Meditate?' I took my head out from under the pillow, shook dark hair back from my face, and rolled over on my side to look at him. 'Excuse me, but the closest I ever got to having a spiritual awakening was dating a yoga instructor. Once.'

David propped himself up on one elbow, looking down at me. No mistaking it; he was enjoying this a little too much. And I was enjoying the bird's-wing graceful sweep of his pecs. 'You're underestimating yourself. You're highly spiritual, Joanne. You just don't know it. Just clear your mind and meditate.'

Meditate. Right. I took a deep breath and tried to relax muscles I no longer actually had. Which was more than a little confusing, even in the abstract.

'Focus,' David's voice said next to my ear, and of course, it was instantly impossible to stay anything like on track. His voice got inside me in places that nice girls don't mention. His breath stirred warm on my skin, and there went that potential orgasm thing again, a little earthquake of sheer pleasure that completely sabotaged any chance of achieving my centre.

I didn't open my eyes, but I said, 'I could focus a lot better if you were somewhere else.'

'Sorry.' He didn't sound sorry. That velvet-smooth tenor sounded smug. 'I'll be quiet.'

He was. I concentrated on visualising something calming – in my case, it was the ocean – but the whole wave-and-surf vibe fell apart when I heard him rustling pages. I sighed and opened my eyes, propped myself up on my elbows, and looked over at him.

He was lying next to me in bed, propped up, reading the newspaper.

'You're kidding,' I said. He gave me one of those *What?* looks and went back to the Metro section. 'I'm trying to meditate here! Give me a break. At least *help*.'

'I am helping,' he said. 'I'm distracting myself so I don't distract you.'

I glared. It had absolutely no effect. He sighed, put the paper at half-staff, and looked at me gravely over newsprint. 'Fine. What would you like me to do?'

'I don't know! Something!'

'I can't meditate for you, Joanne.'

'Well, you can...encourage me!'

He folded the *New York Times* and put it down on the side table. 'Oh, I'd *like* to encourage you. I just don't think it would help you focus. Unless...'

'What?' I asked. He turned on his side and reached out, trailed a single fingertip over the curve of my shoulder and down my arm. Little earthquakes, building to a major seismic event inside...

'Never mind.' It wasn't nothing, I could tell. He wasn't trying to distract me, he really *was* trying to distract himself. From me. 'Meditate for another half hour, and I'll tell you.

My entire attention fixed on the square half-inch of skin his finger was touching. 'Half an hour?'

'Half an hour.'

'I can do that.'

Sheer bravado, but now I was motivated. I flopped back flat on the pillow, closed my eyes, and concentrated hard on that ocean…blue-green waves rolling in from a misty horizon…churning to pale lace as they crashed on the shore…whispers of mist cool on my skin…a fine, endless white sand beach that glittered in sunlight…

I felt like I was actually achieving something – clearing my mind of the idea of him lying beside me, anyway – when he blew it for me by talking again.

'Joanne,' he said. 'Quit hovering.'

I opened my eyes and realised I was looking at the motel room ceiling. White spackled moonscape broken up by a dusty ice sculpture of a light fixture two inches from my nose.

Oh. When he said hovering, he meant *hovering*. As in seven feet above the bed.

'Crap,' I said, and looked over my shoulder. 'I went all *Exorcist*.'

'Actually, it wasn't a bad try. I felt you go quiet for a few minutes.'

'How many minutes?' I rotated myself in mid-air to face him. *Ha!* Managed it gracefully, in a controlled weightless spin, which was nice; control had been kind of a problem. Obviously. My hair spoilt the effect by flopping forward, and I tried shoving it back over my shoulders. It repeated the flopping thing.

'Let's call it…thirty.' David's smile turned

dangerously amused, and he reached down and pulled the sheet away from the rest of him. I stopped messing with my hair and lived for the moment, because like me, David hadn't bothered with pyjamas. He patted the Joanne-shaped hollow in the bed next to him.

I tried to get down. Really. But whatever switch I'd thrown to get up here, I couldn't seem to find it again. I kept hovering. 'Um, not that I'm not motivated, but…'

'You're stuck.'

'Kind of a yes, bordering on an *oh, crap*.' I tried to make it funny, but truth was, it scared me. All this power, none of the control I so obviously needed just to get through what was for David nothing but an autonomic function. 'You forgot to tell me about the gravity-being-optional part of this exercise.'

He levitated up, an inch at a time, and when he was still a foot away I felt the summer heat of his skin. He smelt like warm cinnamon and peaches, and it made my mouth water and my body go golden.

He stopped with a cool two-inch cushion of air between us.

'I didn't forget,' he said. 'I just didn't think you'd be able to do this for a while. Don't worry, it's normal.'

'Normal? I'm halfway into the bed of the guy upstairs!'

'I'd rather you were more than halfway into the bed down here.' That look on his face – naked, powerful, proprietary – sent a pulse of sheer need through me.

'Tease,' I said. He made a sound in his throat that wasn't quite a laugh.

'Come back to bed and we'll see.' He lowered himself by a couple of inches. I tried to follow. Failed. He drifted back up. 'Want me to help you?'

'No. Yes. Hell. I don't know, what's the right answer?'

His hand touched my face and drew a slow line of fire down my neck to my collarbone. 'You have to learn to stay in the body, Jo. We can't exactly do this out in public.'

'News flash. You do this out in public and you draw attention for more than defying gravity.' I tried to sound nonchalant, but it was tough with all the combustion inside me. *God*. I couldn't seem to get used to the hypersensitive nature of being a Djinn. It was the little things that got me – the sharp-edged beauty of how things looked, the intensity of how they felt, tasted, smelt, sounded. The human world was so *real*. Sometimes it was so real it made me weep. I couldn't decide if it was like living in a perpetual state of orgasm, or being perpetually stoned; maybe both.

The casual touch of David's fingers on my skin was enough to start chain reactions of pleasure deep inside, and I caught my breath and closed my eyes as his touch moved down, glided over the curve of my breast.

'Come back to bed,' he murmured, and his lips brushed mine when he spoke.

'I can't.' Literally.

'Maybe it's that you don't want to.'

'Oh, believe me, that's so very not the problem.'

His warm lips melted against mine like silk in the sun, and his hands did things that ought to be illegal, and mandatory for every woman in the world to experience daily. Suddenly we were skin to skin, and my mind whited out.

He slowly rotated us until gravity was cradling my back. 'You need to learn to stay in the body, no matter what happens. Think you can do that?'

'Try me.'

Oh, that smile. It could melt titanium. 'I intend to.'

He kissed me again, and this time there was nothing sweet and nice about it; this was dark and serious and intense, full of hunger and need. Oh yeah, this was the difference between human and Djinn.

Intensity.

I felt my whole body catch fire, responding, and arched against him. It felt so right, so perfect, and he held me to him with one hand on the back of my head, one in the small of my back as he dropped burning kisses on my neck, my breasts, the aching points of my nipples.

Oh, God.

He whispered something to me in a language I didn't know, but it didn't matter; some languages are translated in the skin, not the mind. If living as a Djinn is like being in a perpetual state of orgasm, you can imagine how much better it gets when you approach the real thing.

I found the switch, and we fell back to the bed with a solid, vibrating thump that rattled the headboard.

It was a good start.

And on the fifth day of my new life, I had a lovely funeral.

Well, it wasn't really a funeral – you need a body for a funeral, preferably an open casket, and the fire hadn't left a whole lot for reconstructive purposes. The Wardens Association was too discreet to hold the service in the UN Building – the corporate offices – so they rented a nice big ballroom over at the Drake Hotel and sent out invitations to three or four hundred Wardens. I heard about it because David heard about it, through whatever arcane grapevine the Djinn had in place.

'—but you're not going,' he finished, as we split a small pot of room service coffee. Some vices never go away, even after death. Coffee. Sex. Alcohol. Hell, if I was a smoker, I figure I would've still been lighting up and griping about the price of a carton.

I stirred cream into my coffee. David disapproved of cream; it was obvious from the concerned frown that formed between his eyebrows. 'I'm not going?' I echoed it mildly, but his attention immediately shifted from my poor coffee etiquette to what I was saying.

'No,' he said. 'And we're not going to fight about that, right?' His eyebrows went up, then down.

'Of course not,' I said, and smiled as I blew gentle ripples on the au lait surface. We were sitting cross-legged on the bed, sheets draped over sensitive bits more because of hot coffee prudence than modesty. 'That's a classic guy mistake, by the way.'

'Excuse me?'

'Sleeping with me, then thinking you can tell me what to do.'

Those eyebrows, so expressive. They pulled together again, threatened to close ranks across his forehead. 'I didn't—'

'Did.'

'—sleep with you. In fact.'

'Common usage. Did too.'

'Didn't.'

'Did too.'

He held up one hand, palm out. 'OK, I didn't mean it that way. I just meant that it's too dangerous for you to go out among humans right now. Especially Wardens.'

'And therefore, according to you, I'm not going. Because it's too dangerous.'

'Therefore,' he agreed. We sipped coffee. There's something oddly relaxing about the smell – rich, nutty, the very essence of the earth – and I breathed it in and just savoured the moment. Another great advantage of being Djinn – I didn't need a shower. No dead skin cells needing to be sloughed, no bacterial processes breaking them down and creating stink. Djinn are clean and whatever smells we have are something we choose, on some subconscious level. Mine, I figured, was a kind of jasmine. Something pale and fragrant, with an undertone of obsession.

David finally sighed and set down his cup with a well-bred tinkle of china. 'So therefore you're going to completely blow off the warning and go anyway, no matter what I say, right?'

I tried to be sober, but my mouth wouldn't obey me; it curved into a provocative smile. 'Figured that out all by yourself?'

He was frowning again. God, he was *cute* when he frowned. I wanted to lean over and kiss away that crease between his eyebrows. 'Please listen to me. I'm serious. It's too dangerous.'

'Yeah, I got that from the part where you said it was too dangerous.'

'And?'

'And…it's still my choice, unless you're planning on attempting to run my life for the rest of eternity, which I don't think either of us would like. If you don't want me to go, you'll have to be a lot more specific than "It's too dangerous." Everything I've done since I was born has been dangerous.'

He *had* saved my life, and there was this very definite relationship forming between us, but I felt it was important to get the ground rules straight. I took a mouthful of rich hazelnut-flavoured brew, softened with that creamy edge, and swished it around my tongue. Intense. I felt like if I concentrated, I could follow the beans all the way back to the rich Colombian ground that nurtured them – back to the plant that bore them – back through time, all the generations. Same with the hazelnuts, the water... Even the china cup had memories attached. Good, bad, happy, frightening. I didn't have to concentrate to sense them swirling like the cream in the coffee.

So much history in the world. So many possibilities for the future. Why was it that as a human I'd never understood any of it?

'Jo?' David. He was staring at me with those rich orange-flecked brown eyes. Had he been talking? Yeah, probably. I'd spaced. 'I'm not talking about physical danger. There's little that can hurt you now, but just being strong isn't everything. You have to learn how to use that strength. And until you do, it's not a good idea for you to put yourself in situations where you might have to...'

'Act like a Djinn?'

He looked relieved. 'Exactly.'

'What if I just act like a normal person?'

'Not a good idea.'

'Because?'

He got up and walked over to the windows. As he eased aside the curtain, a shaft of sunlight speared in and glittered on his skin; he pulled in a deep breath that I heard all the way from the bed and stood there, staring out, for a long time.

My turn to give him a worried prompt. 'David?'

He half turned and gave me a sweet, sad smile. 'In case you haven't noticed, you're *not* a normal person. And if you get yourself into trouble, you could give away what you are. Once that happens, you're no longer safe.'

'Because I could get claimed.'

The smile died and went somewhere bad. 'Exactly.'

David had been claimed twice that I knew about. Neither had been pleasant experiences. His last owner and operator had been…well, a former friend of mine – and before that he'd been at the mercy of a sweetheart of a guy named Bad Bob Biringanine. I knew from personal experience that David had done things in Bad Bob's name that would turn anyone's stomach. He'd had no choice in that. No choice in anything.

It was the horror he was trying to warn me about.

'I'll be careful,' I said softly. 'Come on, if you had the chance to see your own funeral, wouldn't you take it?'

'No,' he said, and turned back to whatever view there was outside of that window – being New York

City, probably not a hell of a lot other than buildings. The sunlight loved him. It glided over planes and curves, over smooth skin, and glittered like gold dust on soft curls of hair. He reached out and leant a hand against the window, reaching up toward the warmth. 'Your human life's over, Jo. Let it go. Focus on what's next.'

There were so many people I'd left behind. My sister. Cousins. Family-by-choice from the Wardens, like Paul Giancarlo, my mentor. Like my friend Lewis Levander Orwell, the greatest Warden of all, whose life I'd saved at the cost of my own. We had a long and tangled history, me and Lewis – not so much love as longing. One of the great precepts of magic, that like calls to like. We'd gravitated together like opposite magnetic charges. Or possibly matter and antimatter. If not for David…

I realised, with a jolt of surprise, that I wanted to see Lewis again. Some part of me would always long for him. It wasn't a part I ever wanted David to know about.

'What's next is that I let go of that life,' I said aloud. 'Which I can't do without some kind of…goodbye. It's as much a memorial *for* me as *of* me, right? So I should go.'

'You just want to eavesdrop on what people are saying about you.'

Duh, who wouldn't? I tried bribery. 'They'll probably have cookies. And punch. Maybe a nice champagne fountain.'

It was tough to bribe a Djinn. He wasn't impressed. He kept looking out, face turned up toward the sun, eyes closed. After a few moments he said, 'You're going with or without me, aren't you?'

'Well, I'd rather go with you. Because, like you pointed out, it might not be safe.'

He shook his head and turned away from the window. I could almost see the glow radiating off of him, as if he'd stored it up from the touch of sunlight. The fierce glow of it warmed me across a small ocean of Berber carpet, through a white cotton duvet of goosedown.

I felt the surrender, but he didn't say it in so many words. 'You can't go out like that,' he said, and walked over.

'Oh.' I blinked down at myself and realised I hadn't the vaguest idea of how to put my own clothes on – magically speaking. 'A little help…?'

David put his hands on my shoulders, and I felt fabric settling down over my skin. Clothes. Black peachskin pants, a tailored peachskin jacket, a discreet white satin shirt. Low-heeled pumps on my feet. He bent and placed a warm, slow kiss on my lips, and I nearly – literally – melted.

When I drew back, he was dressed, too. Black suit, blue shirt, dark tie. Very natty. The round glasses he wore for public consumption were in place to conceal the power of his eyes, even though he'd dialled the colour down to something more human.

David was very, very good at playing mortal. Me…well, there was a reason I hadn't tried to dress myself. I wasn't even good at playing Djinn yet.

He produced a pair of sunglasses and handed them over. I put them on. 'How do I look?'

'Dangerous,' he said soberly. 'OK. Rules. You don't talk to anyone, you don't go off on your own. You do exactly what I tell you, when I tell you to do it. And most of all…'

'Yeah?'

'Don't use any magic. Nothing. Understand?'

'Sure.'

He offered his hand. I took it and unfolded myself from the bed, setting the empty coffee cup aside on the mahogany nightstand.

'This is such a bad idea,' he said, and sighed, and then…

…then we were somewhere else.

Somewhere dark. It smelt of cleaning products.

'Um—' I began.

'Shhh.' Hot lips brushed mine, delicate as sunlight. 'I'm keeping us out of their awareness, but you need to stay out of the way. People won't see you. Make sure you don't run into them.'

'Oh. Right.'

'And don't talk. They can still hear you.'

'Right.'

'And don't touch anything.'

I didn't bother to acknowledge that one. He must have taken it as a given, because the next second there was a crack of warm lemon yellow light, and a door opened, and we stepped out of a janitor's closet onto a mezzanine. Big, sweeping staircase to the right heading down to an echoing marble lobby – a vast expanse of patterned carpeting that cost more than the gross national product of most South American countries. Lots of rooms, discreetly nameplated in brass. Uniformed staff, both men and women, stood at attention. They had the brushed, polished, pressed gleam of being well paid in the service of the rich.

David walked me across a no-man's-land of floral burgundy. Past the Rockefeller Plaza Room and the Wall Street Board Room and the Broadway Room. At the end of the lobby, a narrow hallway spilt into a larger ante-room. Burgundy-uniformed security guards to either side. The babble of voices rising up like smoke into lightly clove-scented air.

Suddenly, I had a desire to stop and reconsider this plan. Suddenly it was all very...real.

'Oh man,' I murmured. David's hand on my arm tightened. 'I know. No talking.'

'Shh,' he agreed, lips next to my ear. I swallowed, nodded, and put my chin up.

We strolled right in between the two guards, who stayed focused somewhere off into the distance. David had explained to me once how much easier it was to just redirect attention than to actually become invisible; he'd demonstrated it pretty vividly once, in a hot tub in Oklahoma City. I wished I knew how he did it. Just one of the thousands of things I still needed to learn about being a Djinn.

The ante-room was large enough to hold about a hundred people comfortably, and it was at capacity. At first glance it looked like an office party, only people wore more black and the noise level was two decibels lower than normal. Big floral display at the polished mahogany doors at the end of the room, chrysanthemums and lilies and roses. A guest book next to them. Lots of people standing in line to sign.

David steered me expertly out of the path of a tall, thin woman in black I barely recognised – Earth Warden, Maria something, from the West Coast. She was talking to Ravi Subranavan, the Fire Warden who controlled the territory around Chicago.

Everywhere I looked, people I knew. Not many were what I'd call friends, but they'd been co-workers, at least. The cynical part of me noted that they'd shown up for free booze, but the truth was most of them had needed to make arrangements to be here – naming replacements, handing over power, enduring long drives or longer plane rides. A lot of hassle for a free glass or two of champagne, even if it was offered at the Drake.

I kept looking for the people I was hoping to see, but there was no sign of Paul Giancarlo or Lewis Orwell. I spotted Marion Bearheart sipping champagne with Shirl, one of her enforcement agents. Marion was a warm, kind, incredibly dangerous woman with the mandate to hunt down and kill rogue Wardens. Well, killing was a last resort, but she was not only prepared to do it, she was pretty damn good at it. Hell, she'd almost gotten me. And even with that bad memory, I still felt a little lift of spirits seeing her. She just had that kind of aura.

She looked recovered – well rested, neatly turned out in a black leather suede jacket, fringed and beaded. Blue jeans, boots. A turquoise squash blossom necklace big enough to be traditional in design, small enough to be elegant. She'd gotten some of the burnt ends trimmed off her long, straight, greying hair.

Shirl had cleaned up some of her punk make-up and gone for an almost sober outfit, but the piercings had stayed intact. Ah well. You can take the girl out of the mosh pit... No sign of Erik, the third member of the team who'd chased me halfway across the country. Maybe he wasn't feeling overly respectful to my memory. I'd been a little hard on him, now that I thought about it.

David reversed course in time to avoid a collision with an elegantly suited grey-haired man, and I realised with a jolt that my little shindig had drawn the big guns. Martin Oliver, Weather Warden for all of the continental US. *Not* a minor player on the world stage. He was talking to a who's who: the Earth Warden for Brazil, the Weather Warden for

Africa, and a guy I vaguely recognised as being from somewhere in Russia.

My memorial had become the in place to be, if you were among the magical elite.

David tugged me to the right to avoid a gaggle of giggling young women eyeing a trying-to-be-cool group of young men – did I know these people? Weren't they too young to have the fate of the world in their hands? – and we ended up walking through the mahogany doors into a larger room, set up with rows of burgundy chairs.

My knees threatened to go weak. All the place needed was my coffin to complete the scene, but instead they had a huge blown-up picture of me, something relatively flattering, thank God, on an expensive-looking gold easel. In the photo I looked…wistful. A little sad.

She's dead, I thought. *That person is dead. I'm not her anymore.*

There were so many arrangements it looked like a flower shop had exploded – lilies were a theme, and roses, but it being spring I got the rainbow assortment. Purple irises, birds of paradise, daisies of every shape and size.

It hurt and healed me, thinking of all those people laying out time and money for this incredible display.

We weren't alone in the room. Two people were sitting at the front, heads bowed, and I squeezed David's hand and let go. I walked up the long aisle toward the eerie black and white photo of myself, and the two men I'd come to see who were seated in front of it.

Paul Giancarlo was sitting bent over with his head cradled in big, thick-fingered hands. Not crying – men like Paul didn't cry, it was against the whole tough-guy code of ethics – but he was rocking back and forth, chair creaking, and I could feel his distress like heat from a stove. He wasn't fat, but muscular, and he stressed the structural limits of the sharp hand-tailored suit he was wearing. I'd never seen him in a tie before. It was strangely sweet. I wanted to put my arms around as much of him as my embrace could reach. I wanted to sink into his bear-hug warmth and never come out again, because one thing about being with Paul, he made you feel safe.

Funny, considering his heritage was something straight out of *The Godfather*.

'Should've done something.' His words were muffled by his hands, but he was talking to the man who sat next to him. 'You fucking well should have done something, Lew. What's the use of being the biggest swinging dick around if you can't save the people who matter? Answer me that!'

He slapped the question at Lewis Levander Orwell. Lewis might actually be the most powerful human on the planet, but next to Paul he looked like wallpaper. Tall, rangy, with puppy-dog brown eyes and a reasonably handsome face, he could have fit the part of an ad executive, or a lawyer, or any of a hundred normal white-collar jobs. He didn't look like a guy who could command the weather, fire, and the very power of the earth itself. But the things I'd seen him do, the sheer force I'd felt him wield…incredible. Humbling.

'Being the biggest swinging dick around? It's not much use at all,' Lewis said. He had a low, warm tenor voice, just a hint of roughness around the edges. He was staring down at his hands – long sensitive fingers, the hands of a pianist or a sculptor – as they pressed down on his thighs. His suit was not nearly as nice as Paul's – serviceable, generic, forgettable. He never had been much of a fashion plate. 'I tried to save her. You have to believe I tried. It was just…too much.'

'I guess I don't have any choice but to believe you, right? No witnesses.' Paul sucked in a breath and sat up. His face hovered on the border between brutal and angelic. Grey salted his temples these days, which I hadn't noticed before. He was ten years older than me, which put him close to forty, but the grey in his hair was the only indication he'd aged a day since I first saw him. I'd been eighteen, scared and irrationally arrogant; he'd been twenty-eight, and arrogant for damn good reason. He'd saved my ass then, when Bad Bob Biringanine had tried to stop me from becoming a Warden.

I couldn't believe he was blaming himself for not saving my ass five days ago. I wanted to smack him one and tell him it was OK, I was right here, that the Joanne he'd known might be gone but most of her – maybe the best of her – lived on. I actually did reach out, or start to, but then Lewis's eyes focused on me.

Unmistakably seeing me.

Oh. Well, of course he could, he'd seen me before, at Estrella's house, when I was new-born into Djinn-hood. Lewis could see, well, *everything* when he wanted to. Part of the legacy of who and what he was.

I shaped a silent *hi.* He half closed his eyes and smiled. Not surprised to find me here at all. *Hi yourself,* he mouthed, and the warmth in his expression made me tingle all over. Yeah, it's like that between us. Always. Nothing either of us could control, no matter how much we wanted to.

Holding the stare, Lewis said, 'She's OK, Paul. Believe me. She's in a better place.' About three feet to his left.

'Yeah? You got a fuckin' pipeline to heaven these days? I knew you were supposed to be some kind of god, but I didn't know you had the all-access pass.' Paul's bitterness was scorching. He wiped his face and sat back with another creak of the chair. 'Whatever. Look, she never said so, but I know she had a thing for you.'

Lewis broke eye contact with me to blink at Paul. 'She what?'

'Had a thing.' Paul shrugged. Only Italians could

put so much into a shrug. 'One night we got drunk and she told me…about college. That time.'

'Oh.' Lewis looked thrown, but not as thrown as I felt. I'd *told Paul*? About me and Lewis doing it on the floor of the Storm Lab one rainy afternoon when I was a freshman? I'd told Paul about Lewis being my first guy? No way. Although I dimly recalled a night four or five years ago, with blue agave tequila and strip poker…hmmm. Maybe I had. Wouldn't be the first indiscreet thing to pass my lips.

Paul was still talking. 'So she wouldn't want you to be here.'

I wouldn't?

'Given the circumstances,' he finished.

What circumstances?

Lewis glanced at me. I shrugged to indicate I had absolutely no idea what Paul was talking about. 'Don't worry, I'm not going to stay,' he said, as much to me as to Paul. 'Seeing that the Wardens Council and I had that little disagreement about my Djinn. As in they wanted them back. So low profile seems to be the dress code.'

The Wardens Council, unhappy with Lewis? About Djinn? Oh. That. There had been a time a few years ago when Lewis had busted out of confinement by the Wardens, and stolen three bottles of Djinn on the way. Why three, I don't know; I don't even know if he had a particular reason to take the three he did. But whatever the case, it hadn't made him popular with the Wardens. In fact, he'd kind of been on a most-wanted list ever since. I'd figured that they'd kissed and made up, since the last time I'd seen him he seemed pretty buddy-buddy with Martin Oliver, but maybe I'd overestimated the prodigal son factor. Evidently, they still wanted Lewis to return the Djinn he'd taken. Which I knew he couldn't – and wouldn't – since he'd set all three free.

Which made, what? A stand-off? Lewis versus the entire Wardens organisation? Not that it wasn't even odds…

Paul grunted agreement. 'Steer clear of Marion and her gang. They're still under orders to bring you in for questioning.'

'Thanks. I will.' Lewis started to get up. Paul reached out and grabbed his arm, pinning him in place. Lewis looked pointedly at the offending hand, and continued, 'Unless you want credit for bringing me in yourself…?'

'Don't flatter yourself. I don't give a damn whether you stay out in the cold or make yourself emperor of the world. I got something to say before you go.'

'Go ahead.'

It took him a few seconds to work his way up to it, and then he said, bluntly, 'She loved you. I knew that even if she didn't. And you were a fucking idiot not to realise it when you still had the chance.'

Lewis deliberately didn't look my way. There was

a bitter sadness in those dark-chocolate eyes. 'Oh, I realised,' he said. 'What do you want me to say? That I loved her back? What difference does it make now?'

Shit. Djinn or not, that hit me in undefended places. If he'd said that even two weeks ago, things would be different now. Far different...

I felt David react, even across the room, and shifted my attention away from Lewis and Paul back toward the entrance, where David was standing. Still in human disguise, still gorgeous, but with the flaring powerful aura of a Djinn spreading around him like wings of fire. At first I thought it was a response to what Lewis had said, but no... There was somebody walking in front of him, drawing the full fury of his stare.

Not a Djinn, a woman. I didn't know her. She was tall, leggy, wearing a dress that met only the most lax funeral style conventions – it was at least black – but I was pretty sure that not even I would have worn a low-cut, high-slit lace dress to somebody's memorial service. I seriously envied the stiletto heels, though. They looked lethal.

Apart from that, she had cinnamon hair worn long and in loose waves, the kind of satiny sheen to it that you only get in commercials and very expensive salons. A face that blew past pretty on the express-way to beautiful. Wide-set eyes and a full-lipped, pouty mouth outlined in pearl pink shine. Her only jewellery was a diamond pendant that flashed to the power of at least a carat.

David looked ready to kill. In fact, I thought for a second he wasn't going to drift out of her way as she walked forward – *that* would have been quite a shock for her, running into something that wasn't there – but he moved at the last second and pivoted to follow her with eyes so bright and focused they should have set her hair on fire.

I didn't need to make any pantomime to Lewis; he'd already seen the newcomer, and his face had gone...still. Expressionless. Paul turned to look, too.

'Gentlemen,' she said, and she had a soft Southern accent, made the word into a complicated, caressing drawl. 'I was hoping to catch up to you, Paul.'

'Having a private moment here,' Paul said. His voice was flat, cold, not at all the warm purr he usually reserved for beautiful women. 'Wait outside, will you?'

She was tough, I had to give her that. The warm, inviting smile didn't waver. The big doe eyes – up close, they were a particularly interesting shade of moss green – took on a brighter shine. 'All I want is a minute, Paul.'

'Can't have it right now. Out.'

Lewis said, 'I don't believe we've been introduced.'

'And you're not going to be,' Paul said flatly. 'Yvette. Out.'

She held out a delicate, perfectly manicured hand

to Lewis and notched the smile up another few degrees on the seduction scale. 'Yvette Prentiss,' she said. 'I work with Paul.'

'No, she works *for* Paul, and she's not going to be working for Paul much longer if she doesn't turn her ass around and march out of here.' Paul's tone had gone dangerously dark, with a hard New York edge. 'Get the point?'

'Sure.' She let her eyebrows form a comment, lowered her hand and held the smile – and eye contact with Lewis – ten seconds too long for my comfort. 'I'll be outside, then.'

The two men watched her walk away, hips swaying, graceful and sleek and sexy. Paul's expression was murderous. Lewis's was still blank, like he'd been hit by a very large truck.

She passed within two inches of David, and I could see the effort it took him not to reach out and do something fatal to her.

Lewis asked, 'Who the hell was that?'

Paul sighed. 'Trust me. You *really* don't want to know. And you *really* need to get the fuck out of here before somebody who knows your face takes a look in here. You're just lucky she hasn't got a frickin' clue who you are. Believe me, there are black widow spiders, and then there's Yvette. She might be totally fuckable, but you probably wouldn't survive the night.'

Guy talk. Jeez. What I'd missed when I'd been corporeal.

Lewis nodded, stuck his hands in his pants pockets, and walked toward me. I stayed in his way, willing him to say something, anything. He adjusted course to miss me by an inch or so.

As he passed, he whispered, 'Find me. We need to talk.'

I could tell you about the memorial service, but really, you know how it went. People got up, in varying degrees of discomfort, and said nice things about me. Some of them were actually heartfelt, like Paul's; some were political correctness gone wild. I mean, to hear some of these people talk, I made Mother Teresa look self-centred. Truth was, I'd never been what you could call a saint – mouthy attitude-challenged, headstrong, and with a love of the bad-girl side of life. Give me a choice between serving at the soup kitchen and a night slamming down tequila shots with hard-bodied guys, and I'd be reaching for the salt and lime every time.

About the time I heard the fourth person I barely knew use words like *heroic* and *selfless* I had to take a walk outside to clear my head. A few people were still milling around the reception area, gobbling up the rest of the shrimp and ladyfingers. One of them was the walking hormone factory who'd introduced herself as Yvette Prentiss. She wasn't wasting her time listening to the fictional story of Joanne Baldwin; she was bending the ear of a middle-aged, very rich-looking gentleman with a London suit and an Eastern European accent.

David appeared next to me. Literally appeared. I almost knocked over a spindly-legged table holding a discreet black-bordered stand announcing that my memorial service was By Invitation Only.

I put my lips close to his ear and whispered, 'So? How do you know her?'

He shook his head. 'Later.'

'Uh-uh. Now.'

He gave me a resigned look and guided us to a small alcove near the back, where we'd be out of the way of foot traffic. Also well away from any potential eavesdroppers, who might have found a conversation coming out of empty space disturbing.

The fire had faded out of his eyes, but he was still wired; I could feel it coming off of him in waves of static. He said, 'Her name is Yvette Prentiss.'

'Heard that the first time. Evidently there's more to the you-and-her than introductions.'

'A little.' He looked past me, toward her, then quickly away. 'She was a friend of Bad Bob's.'

David's former sick, demented master. OK, I could believe that, and it didn't raise her in my estimation. 'How good a friend? The come-on-over-and-watch-a-movie kind of friend, or the come-on-over-and-sweat-up-the-sheets kind?'

David avoided my eyes. 'Let's just say they had appetites in common.'

'Let's say a little more than that.'

'Why?'

'Because it's creeping me out that she's in mourning and I've never met her.'

He focused back on her with that scary intensity. 'Oh, she's not in mourning.' Which I could believe, seeing her flirt and tease at the other end of the room. She was currently sucking sauce off of a shrimp, to the delight of the middle-aged guy hovering near her like a bee on a flower. 'She's hunting. Bad Bob paid her bills. She's looking for a new source of income.'

'David.' I drew his eyes back to me. 'What's with the two of you?'

'There are things I don't want to remember about my time with him. She's one.'

That sounded dry and uninformative, but he was shaking. *Shaking.* 'David?'

He reached for me and captured my face between his hands, leant his forehead against mine. Lips close enough to taste. 'You're an innocent,' he said. 'I want you to stay that way. Don't let her near you, and whatever you do, *don't* let her know you're Djinn. There are things – I can't tell you. And I hope you'll never know.'

Across the room, Yvette Prentiss laughed. She had a sweet little-girl laugh that no doubt charmed the pants off of rich old guys arrogant enough to believe she loved them for their personalities. Maybe it was my imagination, but I thought there was a deep, midnight black thread of darkness in it.

I felt the laugh rip into David like a claw, and did the only thing I could.

I said, 'Let's blow this place and go home.'

Two days passed. Nice days. There's nothing bad about lazing around a fancy hotel room with the sexiest guy in the world and unlimited pay-per-view movies.

Not that it was all fun and games. I was learning things, like the physics of being a Djinn. They were entirely different than the physics I'd learnt as a human being, and believe me, I'd been a specialist. Handling the weather with any degree of skill requires an absolute knowledge of little rules like conservation of energy, and it was full of detail work. I can't even count how many times disarming hurricane-force winds boiled down to something as simple as turning down the subatomic thermostat, changing the world one whirling atom at a time.

But operating as a Djinn was the difference between a two-dimensional game of tic-tac-toe, and a three-dimensional Rubik's Cube of consequences. There were still scales, and they still had to balance – if I wanted to control the weather, I could still reach up into the aetheric and create a little warm air cushion moving counter to the cold-air mass streaming in from the sea, and voila, rain. In human terms, that would have cost me personal energy.

As a Djinn, I had to balance the physical world, the aetheric, and about ten other planes of existence to create that rain, all without pulling anything out of my own essence. Because, as a Djinn, I didn't *have* any essence, really. I drew power from the earth, the sun, the life around me. It was surprisingly difficult to do.

And, I discovered, I was pulling power from David. Lots of it. A big silvery conduit of it, flowing from him into me up on the aetheric plane, like a sleek, barely visible umbilical cord.

'It's nothing,' he said, when I brought it up. 'Training wheels. Once you start feeding yourself from other sources, it'll stop.'

It was a *lot* of power. I wondered how hard he was having to work to keep himself strong. The image of a transfusion kept occurring to me – blood flowing out faster than the body could replenish it. Juice and cookies probably wouldn't be enough, not when he kept bleeding like that.

All this learning was tiring. And Djinn, I found, really did need sleep – not as much of it as humans, or in the same physical ways, but the pull still existed, and on the seventh evening I fell asleep in David's arms to the comforting flicker of Jay Leno telling political jokes. It was the first time I'd slept since I'd died.

I woke up with a shock, jerking myself out of a dream. Nightmare. A burning house, pain, screaming, my soul being shredded and consumed...

'Shhhhh.' David turned on his side and raised up

on an elbow to look down on me. It was dark in the room, although I could see grey fingers of light curling around the edges of the blackout curtains. Dawn, it looked like. How long had I been asleep? 'You're dreaming.'

I blinked and focused on him, wondering how he knew. I had a heartbeat – or at least, I did because I believed that I did – and maybe that was it, maybe he could feel the fast, panicked tap of my pulse in my skin. Or maybe he knew because he just *knew*. I had no idea really how powerful David was; I was barely starting to realise how powerful I was, come to think of it. Or, to be more accurate, how helpless, at my level of development.

'Dreaming,' I repeated, and had a surprising thought. 'Djinn dream?'

'Sure.' His eyebrows arched, thick and expressive. 'Why wouldn't we?'

'Oh, I don't know... You don't really have brains?'

'We,' he corrected. Yeah, I kept forgetting that Djinn included me, now. 'Dreaming isn't a function of an organ – or of the body. It's a function of the soul. Like...' He moved the sheet and put his palm flat over my heart, but he never looked away from my eyes. 'Like this,' he finished. 'Understand?'

'No.'

'Let go.' I wasn't holding anything. I opened my hands anyway. He shook his head. 'No, let go of your body.'

'Um...OK...' I'd just spent the last seven days learning how to stay *in* my body. 'Hang on a second...'

He dissolved into mist before I got the last word out of my mouth.

I could still feel his hand warm on my skin.

I slowly relaxed my grip on the world and let it blur around me, let myself slide up into the aetheric, where the world took on different spectra and realities and possibilities. I was real here, too, but different.

David was still with me, still holding his hand on my chest, but neither of us were flesh.

Understand? he asked again. Not a physical voice, not a mental one – kind of a vibration that translated itself into words somewhere in my head. It was dim and distant, but I could still understand it. Oddly, it felt like it was vibrating through that silver power connection between us.

How can I feel that without having—

—a body? I couldn't see him, but I could still sense him, and what I sensed translated to me as a smile. *You always have a body. Come on, Jo, you know physics. Matter into energy. Matter exists in three states...*

Solid, liquid, gas.

At least in the physical world. And does the form of the matter make matter less real?

That doesn't explain how I can feel you touching me.

You think touch is a sense that's hardwired into nerve endings? He did highly inappropriate things to areas of my body that didn't exist in any corporeal way. I still felt heat inside, felt parts of myself that no longer strictly existed start to ache and need. *You think any of this has anything to do with bodies?*

Well, I don't think I'm ready for making love with you as a gas.

Too bad. His voice – or my interpretation of it – vibrated inside me, intimately. *What about liquid? Want to get wet?*

You're a very bad influence, did you know that?

I felt his smile like lips against my skin. *It's been said.*

Would you stop that?

Stop what? If you don't have nerve endings...

All right, I get the...the point... How can you gasp for breath when you aren't breathing? *Can we go back now?*

I was starting to adjust my senses to the aetheric; it wasn't that I could *see* him exactly, but I still sensed him. It was a little like night vision – an outline that glimmered in a there-not-there kind of fog, in silvery shifting layers. Beautiful. Ghostly. I'd spent a lot of time on the aetheric level as a human, and I'd never seen anything like him up here. But then maybe my eyes – even my eyes in Oversight – hadn't been equipped to view the spectra on which the Djinn radiated.

Speaking of which, the plane stretched on, unbroken to the limits of perception, and it was...beautiful. Even more beautiful than before. Where, as a living breathing girl, I'd seen things in Kirlian outlines of reds and greens and blues and golds, in Djinn-sight the aetheric was deeper, richer, and more complex. Layers of colours, swirling together like oil on water. Outlines were both more and less distinct – still familiar, but more difficult to recognise because of their depth. I wasn't seeing the skin of things anymore. I was seeing the skin, the muscles, the bones, the organs. The very heart of life.

Humans displayed as flickering ghosts, pale and transparent; some glowed hotter than others, and those, I understood, were probably Wardens. People with power over the various elements. Hundreds of thousands of them crowded the place in confusing eddies, drifting and pulsing, combining, melting into each other, giving and taking. I was watching the entire flow of life on the spiritual plane.

It was breathtaking. Humbling.

Circling in and around them were the multi-layered fogs of Djinn. I couldn't really focus on them – they tended to disappear when I tried to zoom in – but I had the unnerving sensation of them being *everywhere*. *Jeez*, I breathed, virtually speaking. *How many of them – us – are there?*

He didn't answer me, which was odd; I couldn't

see his face, of course, but I had the sense somehow that his attention had shifted away from me. Watching...focused somewhere else.

What the hell is that? he asked absently.

What?

He stretched out a – hand? – and brushed it through empty air. I didn't see anything. No, wait, I did...just the faintest glimmer of light. You know that cold phosphorescence that fish have, in the deepest black of the ocean? A kind of cold light, in tiny little blue specks.

It was like that. An insubstantial fairy glitter of blue, few and far between.

And I felt a sudden rush of tension from him. *Can you see that?*

Sure. What is it?

I don't know. From the tone behind that, he obviously hadn't run across anything like it before, and it was worrying him. *I can't feel it.*

I reached out and experimentally tried it, too. Where I touched, there was a phantom coldlight sparkle, just a few tiny lights firing. *Huh. I don't feel anything.*

Exactly. Energy is being expended, or it wouldn't show up as light. Yet we don't feel it.

*That's...*I tried a half dozen thoughts on for size and discarded most...*interesting?*

Yes. Interesting-bad, I presumed, from his tone. He did something I didn't quite see, created a clear bubble of energy. Inside of it, some of those coldlight sparkles twinkled like fireflies. He studied it, moving closer. *Shit!*

The fireflies had flown through the globe like it didn't even exist. David pulled back, took me with him, to a healthy distance. The sparkles faded into darkness.

Are they still there? I asked.

Don't know. He didn't seem inclined to check, either. *That shouldn't happen.*

What?

Any of that.

Oh. I waited for inspiration. Nothing arrived. *What now?*

We leave, he said, and I felt a sudden hard tug that, if I'd still been flesh, would have tipped me off balance. As it was, it felt like the fog that made me up flew apart and settled back together.

Had I thought we were moving fast before? No. We dropped out of the sky, heading straight back down at supersonic jet speeds, and I couldn't control a squeak of alarm. Not that impact with anything would hurt me, in my present state, but instincts are hard to overcome.

David braked us with professional ease, and we drifted the last two feet down to the bed.

This was where being a Djinn really differed from my experience as a human. I'd walked the aetheric before – lots – as a Warden, but I'd always had a body to anchor myself to. The Djinn didn't have that. Their – *our* – bodies are made of potential energy, so it required a state change to enter the real world again.

It took me a couple of minutes to figure out how to do that. I understood *how*; that was knowledge that seemed to come as standard equipment with entering the Djinn lifestyle. What I didn't quite have yet was the muscle memory, the instinctive control. Like a baby learning to walk.

I built myself from the inside out. Cell by cell. Bones, complete to the delicate honeycombed structure of the marrow; then a complex interweaving of nerves and muscles and blood vessels, organs, tissue; then, finally, I wrapped it all in skin and stretched.

Ah. Not bad.

When I opened my eyes, David looked deeply unsettled.

'What?'

'You have...no idea how that looks,' he said.

'Yeah, well, it's pretty damn weird from this side, too. Crap!' I dragged a handful of my hair closer to look at it. 'That's not right.'

My hair had always been straight. Dark, straight, worn long. For some bizarro reason, I was now blessed with curls.

'No, I like it.' He wrapped a curl around his finger and brushed it with his thumb. 'Think of it as an unexpected appointment at the salon. Look, we'll get into the finer points of personal grooming later. I need to find out more about what's going on up there.'

'With the sparklies. Yeah, they looked *real* dangerous.'

He frowned at me. 'They shouldn't even exist. That's dangerous enough for me.'

'So? What's the plan, Sherlock? We stick them in a test tube and start experimenting?'

He stepped away from me and turned to pace the room restlessly. He was no longer entirely comfortable, I could see that; in addition to the change in body language, he'd put on a pair of blue jeans and a loose, worn grey T-shirt with the logo of some university faded almost to invisibility. As I watched, he formed a blue-and-white checked shirt, buttoned halfway.

No shoes, yet. He wasn't quite ready to go. 'I have to talk to someone,' he said. 'Can I trust you to stay here for a while?'

'Can't I go with you?'

He focused on me for a second, then moved his gaze away. 'No. That wouldn't be a...good idea.'

'Who are you going to see?'

'You don't need to know.'

OK, this was starting to piss me off. 'Sorry, is my new Djinn name *Mushroom*? Because I don't like being kept in the dark and fed bullshit, David. Just so you know.'

I expected him to snap a comeback, but instead he smiled and paused in his pacing. 'Are we having our first quarrel?'

'No, I recall a hotel room back in Oklahoma where you tried to make me claim you as a Djinn slave. *That* was our first quarrel.' It had been a doozy. The apology sex had been even better.

'Right.' He locked his hands behind his back and wandered to the windows to look out. 'Something's wrong up there. I don't know what it is, or what caused it. I don't even know if it's dangerous, but…it doesn't feel right. And that's as much as I know, Jo. I need to ask around, see if anybody else has noticed anything. This could be very important.'

'Or it could be leftovers from the big New Year's Eve party up on the aetheric.'

He shrugged and folded his arms across his chest as he stared out. 'As party favours go, those are pretty persistent.'

He really *was* worried. I sat down on the bed and pulled a sheet over myself, kind of a wrinkled toga, nothing elegant but at least a covering. 'So go, then,' I said. 'If it's that important.'

He turned to look at me, and I read a flash of gratitude, just before the phone rang.

We froze. His copper eyes swirled darker.

'Wrong number?' I asked.

'Let's find out.' He crossed to it, picked up the elegant little handset, and angled to watch me. 'Hello?'

Not a wrong number. His expression went blank and stiff.

'Not over the phone,' he said. 'We need to do this in person. Where do you want to meet?' Another pause. 'Yes,' he said. Pause. 'I know where it is. Yes.'

He hung up. In the same motion, his favourite olive drab wool coat formed around him, long and deceptively elegant. When he turned to look down at me, he'd also added the round disguising glasses that I remembered so well from the first time we'd met. They made his angular face look gentle, and behind them his eyes had gone a warm brown instead of Djinn copper.

'We've got to go.'

I didn't like the way he said it. I didn't like the sudden tension in his shoulders, either. 'Trouble?' I asked.

He smiled slightly. 'It's still your middle name, isn't it?'

'Who was on the phone?'

'Later.'

'Come on, remember the whole mushroom thing? Who called?'

He gave me a long, unhappy look, but he must have known he couldn't just drag me around like a suitcase. 'Lewis.'

'Lewis?'

'He wants to meet you.'

'Oh. Right. He...mentioned that, back there – you know, at the funeral.' I gestured vaguely over my shoulder in a direction that probably didn't indicate the Drake Hotel. 'Something on his mind.'

He didn't look any happier at that revelation. 'Joanne, you have to—'

'—leave my mortal life behind, yeah, I know, but it's *Lewis*. You know?'

He did. And once again, no spikes on the happiness meter. I let the sheet fall away, looked down at myself, and frowned. Oh, the skin looked OK; evidently, I had the knack, just not the expertise yet to do it fast. No, I was thinking about clothes. As in the lack thereof.

'Um…' I pointed at my breasts. 'Don't think they let me go out in public like this.'

David crossed his arms across his chest and looked, well, obstinate. Cute, but obstinate. 'You expect me to do everything for you?'

'No. Just dress me. Please.'

'And what if I don't?'

Ah, he'd figured out a way to keep me out of trouble. Or so he thought. I gave him a warm, evil smile. 'Then you'd better hope I can master that not-being-noticed thing really quickly, because otherwise me and the NYPD are going to have a beautiful friendship.' I swung my legs out and stood up, and started walking for the door. He stepped back, looked down at his crossed arms, then up and over the top of his glasses. Effective. He *must* have known how gorgeous he looked doing that.

'Seriously,' I said, and clicked back the privacy lock. The hotel air-conditioning whispered cold over my skin in places that didn't normally get to experience a breeze; I shivered and felt goosebumps texturing me all over. 'Going outside now. Clothes would be a plus, but whatever…'

OK, I was bluffing, but it was a really, really good bluff. I swung the door open, hoping there wouldn't be some society matron with her poodle-dog in the hall, and stepped out with my naked feet on the plush carpet. Expecting clothes to materialise around me.

They didn't.

It wasn't *that* good a bluff, apparently. David raised the stakes.

The door slammed shut behind me, slapping me like a barely friendly smack on my bare butt. I yelped, crossed my arms over my breasts, then dropped one hand down to make a totally inadequate privacy panel. Shifted from one foot to another and pressed my back against the wood and said, 'Fun-ny, David! Come on, help me out here.'

He didn't sound amused. 'You need to learn how to dress yourself.'

'I will. I swear. Just – not right now, OK?'

'Not OK. Either you admit you're not ready and come back inside, or put your own clothes on. Out there.' Not a drop of sympathy in David's disembodied voice. I pulled in a breath, leant against the door, and struggled to concentrate. Clothes are tricky, when you have to create them out of air and energy and make them look, well, *good*. Although frankly at the moment, I figured I'd better settle for fast and ugly. Wal-Mart was OK by me.

I squeezed my eyes shut and focused. Seconds ticked away. I started to feel the burn of panic because my mind was completely, utterly—

'Any time,' David advised. His voice didn't come from behind the door, it was in front of me. I peeked and saw him leaning against the opposite hall wall. No way to classify that particular smile except as sadistic – cute, but sadistic. He checked his watch. 'It's a high-traffic area. I give you…two, maybe three minutes, if you're lucky, before someone comes along.'

'Bastard,' I muttered, and went back to concentrating. When I had the image in my head, I opened my eyes wide and stared at him as I started building my new wardrobe. And yeah, OK, I was trying to get back at him.

But still, it was so cool.

I added pieces the same way I'd constructed my body, from the inside out: boy-cut panties first (lacy), bra (sheer), stockings (thigh high), knee-length leather skirt (black), lime green midriff-baring shirt (polyester). David leant against the wall and watched this striptease-in-reverse with fabulously expressive eyebrows slowly climbing toward heaven. I finished it off with a pair of strappy lime green three-inch heels, something from the Manolo Blahnik spring collection that I'd seen two months ago in *Vogue*.

He looked me over, blinked behind the glasses, and asked, 'You're done?'

I took offence. 'Yeah. You with the fashion police?'

'I don't think I'd pass the entrance exam.' The eyebrows didn't come down. 'I never knew you were so...'

'Fashionable?'

'Not really the word I was thinking.'

I struck a pose and looked at him from under my supernaturally lustrous eyelashes. 'Come on, you know it's sexy.'

'And that's sort of my point.'

Oh yeah. We were going to see Lewis. I chose not to think too much on what that revealed about my motives. Too late now. I walked past him, head high, heading for the elevators.

'Coming?' I asked. He fell in step with me.

'Considering I'm the only one of us who knows where he said to meet him, you'd better hope.'

'I'm surprised you're so eager.' Not that he and Lewis didn't get along, or hadn't, anyway... 'Oh. You're hoping he's got some idea about your little sparkly things.'

I got another frown for that one. 'I hope that's what they are.'

'Instead of...?'

'Something else. I just get nervous when the universe doesn't obey its own laws.'

'Welcome to my world,' I said. 'Having kind of

a weird life experience these days.'

I hadn't been out of the room except to travel the aetheric – and that somewhat queasy trip to the Drake Hotel – since we'd checked in; the elegance came as a shock. First, the carpet – a blue-and-gold riot of French Provincialism. Next, the genuine Louis-the-whatever gilt tables with chunky glass vases of silk flowers.

No, I definitely hadn't dressed to fit the room.

I stopped in the full force of a patch of sunlight in the lobby window and let my skin soak up the energy. I hadn't realised I needed it until it reached inside and stilled me in a way that only David's touch had been able to achieve.

David didn't speak for a moment, just stood with me in that hot golden patch of warmth. When I looked over at him, his eyes were closed, his face rapt in a kind of worship. I took his hand. He looked over at me, smiled, and pushed the DOWN button on the panel for the elevator.

'Why does that feel so good?' I asked. 'And don't tell me it's because we've been shut in a room for days.'

'Like calls to like,' he said. 'You're made of fire now.'

'So I'm going to feel like this every time I pass an open flame? Great. Firegasm.'

'Remember that focus thing we were talking about? Learn to practice it.'

The elevator dinged and yawned open. Nobody

inside. We entered and David touched the button for L.

'You haven't told me where we're heading.'

'No,' he agreed.

'And you're not going to?'

'Right.'

'So much for the partnership.'

He was still facing the control panel, deliberating not looking at me. 'I'm responsible for your safety, Jo. You have to let me make the decisions about what's too dangerous.'

'What's dangerous about letting me know where we're going?'

'Nothing. But you need to keep in mind that whatever Lewis is going to talk about, it's to do with the mortal world. You need to be very, very careful right now about keeping separate from it.'

'So whatever Lewis wants, we're going to say no, unless it has to do with the Djinn.'

'Yes.'

'Does he know about that? Because if he does, I'm pretty sure he wouldn't bother wasting the—'

The elevator hadn't stopped, and I was sure it had been empty when we'd gotten inside, but all of a sudden a third voice behind me said, 'Ah, there you are.'

I yelped and went south until I collided with an elevator wall; my body threatened to break up into mist, but I held it together. There was another Djinn in the elevator with us, leaning casually against the back wall. I knew her instantly, if nothing else for her neon-bright wardrobe. Today's was a kind of electric eye-popping blue: flared pants, low-cut vest with no shirt beneath, beautifully tailored jacket. Blue was a good colour on her. It accented the rich dark-chocolate shade of her skin. Her elegantly tiny shoulder-length braids were plaited with matching neon blue beads, which clicked like dry bones when she tilted her head.

Rahel had always known how to accessorize.

Djinn, I was coming to understand, had a flare for the dramatic, so popping in unannounced wasn't necessarily threatening. Rahel had done this to me before, in the days when I still had a pulse and a human lifespan. The first time I'd met her, she'd blipped into existence in the passenger seat of my car, which had been doing seventy at the time. I'd barely kept it on the road.

She'd enjoyed the joke then, and she was clearly enjoying it now. She crossed her arms, leant back against the elevator wall, and took in the reaction with a smile.

Unlike me, David didn't seem surprised at her sudden appearance. He slowly turned to face her, and his expression was a closed book. 'Rahel.'

'David.'

'Not that I'm not happy to see you, but...'

'Business,' she said crisply.

'Yours or mine?'

'Both. Neither.' Not really an answer. 'You know whose business it is. Don't you?'

No answer from David. Rahel hadn't paid the slightest attention to me, but now her vivid gold-shimmering eyes wandered in my direction and narrowed with something that might have been amusement, or annoyance, or disgust. 'Snow White,' she said. '*Love* the perm.'

Defending my hairstyle was the least of my worries. 'Rahel, what the hell is going on?' Because there was no question that trouble was brewing. No coincidence that Lewis was trying to get me, and then Rahel popped in with urgent business. I could feel the gravity, and we were right in its centre.

She didn't answer, not directly. She turned her attention back to David and shrugged. 'Tell her.'

David shoved his hands in his coat pockets and leant against the wall, considering her. 'Oh, I don't think so. If Jonathan wants to see me, let him come find me. I don't come running to him like a kid to the principal's office.'

'Do you imagine I'm giving you a choice?' she asked, silky as the finish on a knife. The tension already swirling in the air between them turned thick and ugly.

'This is a bad place for you to fight me, David. And a very bad time, don't you agree? He wants to see you. It's not an invitation you refuse, you know that.'

The elevator dinged to a stop on the third floor.

Doors rumbled open. Outside, a middle-aged couple waited with impatient 'tudes. Anybody with a grain of sense would have known not to get in that elevator, given the body language of the three of us already inside, but these two were clearly self-absorbed to the point of impairment. The woman – fat, fifties, fabulously well kept – was complaining about the quality of the preserves on the breakfast tray as she petted a white rat of a dog. She crowded in. Hubby rumbled across the threshold after her.

'Excuse me,' the matron said to me, clearly expecting me to move back and give her royal personage more breathing room. She raked me with a comprehensive fashion-police inspection from head to toe, then Rahel. 'Are you guests here?' With the strong implication that we were working the hotel by the hour. Rahel shot me a glance out of eyes that had moderated themselves to merely amber. Still striking, but in a human fashion-model kind of way. She showed perfect teeth when the woman glared at her, but it wasn't a smile.

'No, ma'am,' Rahel said equably. 'Hotel security. May I see your room keys?'

The matron huffed and fluffed like a winter sparrow. Hubby dug a key card from his pocket. Rahel took it in inch-and-a-half-blue-taloned hands, studied it intently, and handed it back. 'Very good. Have a nice day.' For some reason, I had the strong impression that key card wouldn't be working the next time they tried it.

Another musical *ding*, and the elevator doors parted like the Red Sea. The couple stalked haughtily out into the arched marble foyer. I started to get out, too, but the doors snapped shut in front of me – fast and hard, like the serrated jaws of an animal trap.

David's eyes flared back to copper. Rahel's flashed back to bitter, glowing yellow. There was so much power crackling in the air it stung my skin.

'OK, can't we just talk this over?' I asked, and then the elevator dropped. I mean, *dropped*. Fell straight down. I yelped and grabbed for a handhold, but there was no need; my feet stayed firmly on the carpeted floor. Neither David nor Rahel flinched, of course. I hated not being the coolest one in the room.

'Don't make me do this,' David said, as steadily as if we weren't in free fall. 'I don't want to fight you.'

'Wouldn't be much of a fight,' Rahel replied, and at her sides, her fingernails clicked together in a dry, bony rhythm. They were changing colour, from neon blue to neon yellow. The pantsuit morphed to match. I knew, without quite knowing why, that these were Rahel's natural colours, that she was pulling power away from fripperies like outward manifestations to focus it inside. She was gathering her strength. 'We both know it, and I have no wish to hurt you worse than you've already hurt yourself.'

The downward drop of the elevator slowed, but there was no way any of this was natural. Even if we'd been headed for the basement, I didn't really believe that it was fifteen floors down from the lobby. No, we were well into Djinn geography now. Human rules applied only as a matter of politeness and convenience. The elevator was a metaphor, and we were arriving at another plane of existence. Dangerland, next stop. Ladies' lingerie and life-threatening surprises.

'I'm not taking her to him. Not yet.' David again, this time very soft, deceptively even.

Rahel grinned. 'Who are you afraid for, David? Snow White, or yourself?'

'She's not ready.'

'Then sistah girl better *get* her ass ready. You broke the law, David. Sooner or later, you knew you'd have to explain yourself.'

Broke the law? I blinked and dragged my eyes away from Rahel's glittering, neon-bright menace, and saw that David had gone very still. I'd seen that look before, when he'd been faced with slavery and death – it wasn't acceptance, it was a kind of insanely peaceful courage. 'Then I'll see him alone. There's no reason to involve her in this.'

Rahel clicked her talons dismissively. 'You know better. She is the corpse at the murder scene, David. The crime, in the flesh. She comes.' This time, when she bared her teeth, they took on a needle-sharp ferocity. 'Unless you want to leave her orphaned in this cold, cruel world. How long would she last, do you think?'

'Hey! Don't talk around me, OK?' I barked, and stepped in between them. Rahel actually looked surprised at my outburst. 'One of you had better start explaining to me what's going on. Now.'

For a second, neither of them looked ready to spill the beans, but then the elevator came to a smooth gliding halt, and the bell rang.

David finally said, 'We're going to see Jonathan.'

'And I'm supposed to know who he is because...'

'Because he is the one true god of your new existence, little butterfly,' Rahel said. She wasn't smiling anymore. 'He is the Elder who was born at the first turning of the world. He is fire made flesh. And you *really* don't want to piss that man off.'

The elevator doors cranked open. I don't know what I was expecting – some cheesy B-movie interpretation of hell, maybe – but what I saw was nothing but a clean white hallway stretching off into the distance.

Rahel said, 'You *will* do as Jonathan requests. Your choice, David. If you do force me to fight, you know the outcome.'

'Do I?' His intensity was scary. So was the little half-smile on his lips. 'Maybe I could surprise you.'

She tilted her head to one side. The beads in her dreadlocks clicked and whispered. No other answer.

David pushed away from the wall and stepped

out of the elevator into the hallway. I followed, pulled even with him, and felt a bubble of panic threatening to rise somewhere in my not-entirely-solid throat. 'We're in trouble, right?' I asked. I glanced back. The elevator doors were sliding closed. Rahel was nowhere in sight.

'Not...exactly.' He stopped, put his hands on my shoulders and turned me to face him. 'Jo, you have to listen to me now. It's important. When we get in there, don't say *anything*. Not even if he asks you directly. Keep your eyes down, and your mouth shut, no matter what happens. Got it?'

'Sure.' He didn't look convinced. I searched his face for clues. 'So how bad is this for you?'

Instead of answering, he ran his fingers slowly through my hair. Weirdest sensation: I could literally *feel* it relax, the curls falling out of it into soft waves.

His touch moved down, an inch at a time, teasing it straight. It felt so warmly intimate it made me feel weak inside.

'David—' I whispered. He put a finger on my lips to hush me.

'Your eyes,' he said, leaning closer. 'They're too bright. Dim them down.'

'I don't know how.' His lips were about three inches from mine, close enough that I could taste them. 'What colour are they now?'

'Silver. They'll always be silver unless you change them.' He had autumn brown firmly in place, looking human and mild as could be. 'Try grey.'

I thought of it in my head, a kind of smoky soft grey, gentle as doves. 'Now?'

'Better. Focus on that colour. Hold it there.' His hands moved out of my hair and caressed my face, thumbs gently skimming my cheekbones. 'Remember what I said.'

'Eyes down. Mouth shut,' I confirmed.

His lips quirked. 'Why am I not convinced?'

'Because you know me.' I put my hands over his, felt the burning power coursing under his skin. Light like blood, pumping inside him. 'Seriously. How bad is this?'

He pulled in a deep breath and let go of me. 'Just do what I told you, and we'll both be fine.'

There was a door at the end of the hall marked with a red EXIT sign. David stiff-armed it without slowing down, and I followed him into a sudden feeling of pressure, motion, intense cold, disorientation...

...and somebody's house. A nice house, actually, lots of wood, high ceilings, a kind of cabin-ish feel while still maintaining that urban cachet. Big, soaring raw stone fireplace, complete with wrought iron tools and a big stack of logs that looked fresh-chopped. The living room – which was where we were – was spacious, comfortable, full of overstuffed furniture in masculine shades. Paintings on the walls – astronomy, stars, planets. I caught my breath and braced myself with my hand on the back of a sofa.

The place smelt of a strange combination of gun oil and aftershave, a peculiarly masculine kind of odour that comforted me in places that I hadn't known were nervous.

There was a clatter from what must have been the kitchen, down the hall and to the left, and a man came around the corner carrying three dark brown bottles of Killian's Irish Red.

'Hey,' he said, and tossed one to David. David caught it out of the air. 'Sit your ass down. We're gonna be here a while.'

I stared. Couldn't quite help it. I mean, with all the build-up, I'd been expecting a three-headed Satan breathing fire and picking his teeth with a human rib. This was just – a guy. Tall, lean, with a built-in grace that reminded me of animals that run for a living. He looked older – forty-five? fifty? – and his short hair was a kind of sandy brown, thickly salted with grey. An angular face, one that bypassed handsome for something far more interesting. Lived-in. Strong. Utterly self-assured.

He was wearing a black T-shirt, khaki cargo pants, some kind of efficient-looking boots, maybe Doc Martens. He settled himself down in a sprawl on the couch, all arms and legs and attitude, and finally held out the other beer toward me. I leant forward to take it, and his eyes flicked over and fixed on mine.

I froze. Just…whited out. I thought nothing, felt nothing until the cold sweating bottle slapped my palm, and then I looked down and focused on it, blinking. I couldn't have said what colour his eyes were, but they were incredible. Dark. Intense. And *very* dangerous.

David had eased himself down to a sitting position on the edge of a brown sofa with worn spots on the arms. He held the beer between his palms, rolling the bottle slowly back and forth, and now he glanced at me and I saw something unsettling in his eyes.

It might have been fear.

'Jonathan,' David said.

'David. Glad we're still on a first-name basis,' Jonathan replied, with a half-inch nod that conveyed nothing. His eyes flicked to me, then away, so brief you couldn't even call it a look. 'You. Sit your ass down.'

I did, feeling gawkish and stupid and so much like an intruder it stung. There was something between these two; it was so powerful that it warped space around them, tingled in my skin like electric shock. Love? Hate? Bitterness? Maybe it was all that. Certainly it wasn't a passing acquaintance. It had the ancient feel of something long-term and deep as the ocean.

Jonathan took a swig of beer. 'Well, she's pretty,' he said to David, and jerked his head at me. 'You always did like the dark-haired ones.'

David raised his eyebrows. 'Is this the part where you try to embarrass me in front of her?'

'Enjoy it. This is as fun as it's likely to get.'

The fire popped like a gunshot. Neither of them flinched. They were locked into a staring contest. David finally said, 'OK. I'm only here as a courtesy. Tell me what was important enough to send Rahel around after me like your personal sheepdog.'

'Well, you don't call, you don't write...and you're offended on Rahel's behalf? That's new.' Jonathan waved it away, tipped his bottle again and swallowed. 'You know what's so important. I've never seen you do anything so...incredibly, brainlessly stupid. And hey. That's saying something.'

God, it all looked so *real*. I knew that the room around me had to be stage dressing, built out of Jonathan's power, but it felt utterly right. The pop and shimmer of the fire in the hearth. The woodsy smell of smoke and aftershave. The texture of the slightly rough couch fabric under my fingers. There was even frost on the windowpanes, and a localised chill from that direction – it was winter here, deep winter. I wondered if that was any indication of his mood.

David said lightly, 'You're keeping score of my screw-ups? Must get boring for you down here, all by yourself. But then that's your choice, isn't it? Being alone.'

A flash came and went fast in Jonathan's eyes, and sparked something in response in David. Silent communication, and very powerful. Ah. Whatever was between these two wasn't hate. It looked a lot – uncomfortably – like love.

Jonathan let that flash of emotion fade into a still, empty silence, set his beer aside, and leant forward with his hands clasped. 'Don't try to change the subject. What you did wasn't just selfish, it was nuts. You put us in danger.' Jonathan's eyes were changing colour, and I looked down, fast. I knew, without anybody telling me, that it wasn't safe to be facing that particular stare. His voice went quiet and iron hard. 'Do I really have to tell you how serious this is?'

'No,' David said. 'Let's just get on with it.'

'You want to at least explain to me why you did it?'

David's voice was warm, intimate, almost compassionate. 'Jonathan, I don't have to explain a damn thing. You already know everything I'm going to say. You always have.'

'Not true. You were always full of surprises.'

'Good ones, occasionally. Maybe this will be one of them.'

'Oh, you'd so better hope.'

It was a very heavy silence that followed. I listened to the crack and pop of logs on the fire and focused on the smooth pebbled leather of my skirt. *Eyes down. Mouth shut.* I could do that.

Jonathan sighed and stirred. 'You gonna drink that beer or what?'

'No. You know I hate the stuff.' David held out the untouched bottle.

Jonathan leant across the empty space and took it. 'How about you, Snow White? You drinking?' He was talking to me. I'd almost forgotten about the sweating cold Killian's in my hand, except as something to hold on to; I took a fast, mute sip and glanced up.

Mistake. He was staring at me. I fell into those eyes, like Jonathan had his own dark gravity, and for a few seconds I *knew* him. Old. Wise. Limitlessly powerful. Funny. Sarcastic. Cold. Merciless. Sentimental. Sad. Lonely. I could see history stretching back to a dizzying distance, just a blur of days…

But the door swung both ways.

I knew him.

He knew me, too.

There was nothing, *nothing* he didn't touch inside of me, and yet it wasn't like the raping intrusion you'd think. I had the sense of compassion, of amusement, and a kind of strange gentleness as he gathered me in, learnt me, lived in me.

'Jonathan! Dammit, stop!' I heard David's shout, but it was too far, too far to travel to answer. Was it possible to be consumed like that, and still be whole? I felt like I was unravelling, spreading thinner, thinner…there was no pain, but a vast sense of *becoming*…

Something sliced across that connection like the blade of a knife, and I felt the bottle in my fingers sliding free, out of control, heading in frozen ticks of time for the floor.

David caught me as I fell. I heard the bottle hit the floor. Every nerve in my body fired as if a bolt of lightning hissed up from the ground, down from the clouds, caught me in its current and burnt me into nothing.

The bottle shouldn't have broken, but it did, it shattered into a million glittering pieces. I felt myself breaking, too.

I heard Jonathan say, 'You should know better, David.' He was still sitting on the couch at ease, watching the two of us. 'They're too fragile. You're working with flawed material. Talk about your lost causes—'

'Leave her alone!' David yelled. He lifted me in his arms, and I felt the solid weight of him, the flaring pale beauty of fire reaching out to wrap me close. 'Jonathan, please *stop*!'

'No. *You* stop me.' Jonathan wasn't just a guy on a couch now, he was more than that, he was a vast power moving through the aetheric, a shadow on the wind, a storm on the air. 'C'mon, David. Stop me. It's easy, you've done it a thousand times. No big deal.'

I was...unravelling. Breaking apart. Being subsumed into something vast and unknown and deep as space, sweet as pure cold mountain air...

I felt David grabbing for me on the aetheric, struggling to hang on, but it was like trying to hold sand in the wind.

Stop me, Jonathan said, in the aetheric, in the world, in that other place I couldn't even name yet. *Come on, David. Just do it.*

'I can't!' David's raw scream of rage sounded torn out of him with pliers. 'Jonathan, I'm begging you, *please stop*!'

And Jonathan let go. I fell back into flesh, into David's arms, into pain. Oh, *God*, that hurt. Everything too bright, too sharp, too cold, too hot. For a few aching seconds I wanted to go back to that place where Jonathan had taken me, the place on the edge of nothing. I wanted oblivion with an intensity that scared me.

Jonathan picked up a beer bottle and took a long, throat-working gulp, put the empty down, and sat back with his arms crossed. Looking at the two of us. I couldn't tell anything at all from his expression. Had all of that, all of *me* meant anything to him at all?

'So, did you tell her?' he asked. No answer from David, but I could feel the trembling of his muscles. 'Of course you didn't. Look – what's your name? Joanne? – Djinn live by rules, and one of the rules is that humans die while we go on. Like it or not, there's nothing we can do about that.' His dark, dark eyes moved to David's face. 'We can't create energy, all we can do is translate it from one form to another. The demons that killed you ate the energy that kept you alive, and you died. So David stole life energy from another source to bring you back.'

David let me slide down to stand on my feet, but he kept a hand on my arm, steadying me. I felt sick, light-headed. 'What?' I whispered.

Jonathan sighed. 'He stole life energy and gave it to you.'

'Stole it?' *Oh, God, don't tell me he killed someone else. Don't tell me that.*

Jonathan's eyes flicked past me to David, who said, 'I didn't steal it. I took it. From myself.'

Jonathan nodded. 'Yeah. David ripped out half of his life and gave it to you. Which means...what exactly does that mean, David? Enlighten us.'

'Nothing.'

Jonathan rolled his eyes, reached for David's untouched beer, and took a swig. 'You know, you've got one hell of a martyr thing going, maybe you ought to drop by and try it out on the pope. *Nothing.* Bullshit. You're committing suicide by girl.'

David cut in, sounding very reasonable. Too reasonable; I could feel the wire-fine tension still singing in his muscles. 'You're overstating things, Jonathan. I'm not committing suicide. So I went from the second most powerful free Djinn to a middle-ranked spear-carrier. So what?'

'Oh, for crying out loud...*so what?*' Jonathan

squinted, rubbed his forehead, and stood up to pace. Back and forth, restless energy crackling like the fire that wasn't really burning in the fireplace, on creaky floorboards that didn't really exist in any way that humans could understand. 'That's like saying giving Albert Einstein a lobotomy wouldn't matter because he still had a pulse. *We need you.* And we need you full strength. *We're at war, David!* I have to remind you of that?'

David didn't answer. His hand on my arm was tight enough to hurt.

Jonathan stopped pacing to stand right in front of me, glaring. 'What David did was about as smart as ripping his heart out with his bare hands and calling it organ donation. It's *possible* to do what he did. It's just pathetically stupid.'

'I'm fine,' David said.

'You're *not*!' He rounded on him and levelled a finger at David's face. 'Don't even start with me. You're bleeding energy all the hell over the place. You tell me...can you stop it? Or are you just going to bleed yourself dry to keep her alive? It's like trying to fill a dry lake with a teaspoon, David. You can't do it. You can't make a human into a Djinn because they don't goddamn well *work that way*!'

David didn't answer. Jonathan's face tightened up.

'And you don't give a crap what I say,' he said, resigned. 'Well, that's kind of what I thought.'

He turned away, walked to the fireplace and

picked up a vicious-looking black poker that he used to jab at inoffensive logs. Flames crackled, popped, and swirled. I looked back over my shoulder at David, who was quiet, steady, focused.

'Is he right?' I asked.

'No,' David said. 'I've been losing some energy, the same way a human might lose blood from an injury before it heals. It's nothing.'

Jonathan whirled and tossed the poker back in the wrought-iron holder with a sharp clang of metal. 'It's been *seven days*.' Jonathan's dark eyes were fierce with emotion. 'I've sat here and watched you bleed into the aetheric for *seven damn days*! I'm not sitting on my all-powerful ass while you die.'

'Not your business.'

'David—'

'*Not your business*, Jonathan!' David's copper eyes were blazing, furious, molten. Jonathan's were as black and cold as space. Neither one of them moved, but I felt defences snapping into place, and my whole essence screamed at me to get the hell out of the middle.

Not that I ever listened to sensible advice anyway.

I rounded on David. 'What cheap-ass archetype hero myth did you step out of? I didn't ask you to kill yourself for me! I would *never* ask for that! You can't just make me a Djinn and *die*, dammit! Hear me? You can't!'

Jonathan laughed. 'Please. He didn't make you a Djinn, don't you get it? He made both of you *half* a Djinn.'

I felt my hair start to curl again as my concentration slipped. I lost that dove grey focus David had tried to get me to keep, and felt my eyes change – flare – go silver. 'Half?'

'Half. As in, two halves make a whole.' Jonathan's mouth twisted into bitterness. 'A whole what, I have no idea. Probably an idiot.'

'Fine. Then fix it,' I said. 'Undo it.'

'No!' David again, and this time he moved, took me by the shoulders and physically moved me out of the way. Sat me down on the couch with a decisive shove. 'You don't understand. I *told* you to keep quiet.'

'Hey, she asked nicely,' Jonathan said, and pointed at me.

'No!' David flung out a hand, palm out, pushing Jonathan away even though Jonathan hadn't taken a step in our direction. He stepped forward, sank down on one knee in a puddle of olive drab wool coat, and took my hand in his. Warm skin on skin, truth shining in his eyes. 'Joanne, this is between me and him. Let us solve it.'

Jonathan upended his beer, drained it, and tossed the bottle into the fireplace. The crash of glass was lost in the roar of flames as the fire leapt up, eager as a pet. '*Fuck*. Heart-warming as this is, David, it's totally screwed. You can't make her one of us. You can keep her alive, you can give her power, but the price is too damn high. You really think I'm going to stand by and let you do this?'

David smiled, but I could tell he wasn't smiling at me. This was bitter, private, and painful. '"Behold, thou art fair, my love, behold, thou art fair…"'

'Hey! *Don't* quote that to me. You know I hate that.' Jonathan stalked back over, stared down at the two of us. After a long, silent moment, something melted out of him. The anger, maybe. Or the determination. 'You'd really do this.'

David's fingers tightened around mine. 'It's already done.'

'You'd die to give her life.'

'I don't think I'll have to, but if it comes to that, yes, I'm not afraid.'

Something inside me went still. Very, very still. Focused on him, on his eyes, on the power pouring out of him into me.

Power I now understood was sustaining me.

'Please.' David's voice had gone soft, low, resonant in the back of his throat. '*Jonathan*. Please. It's my choice.'

He put emphasis on the last word, and I saw it hit home in the other Djinn, who folded his arms across his chest and looked away. Covering up pain.

So much between these two I didn't understand, and knew I never could. I hadn't even known him a week; they'd had half of eternity together. No wonder Jonathan had that hard, hurting edge to him. And no wonder he wanted me dead. I'd have the same impulse, if somebody showed up to rip apart a friendship that had that kind of history.

'Your choice,' Jonathan repeated. 'Oh, you're good. If I take away your choices, I'm no better than the last asshole who held your soul in a bottle. Is that what you're getting at?'

He was staring out the windows of his house. Before, it had showed a frosted white landscape, a washed blue sky. Now it looked out on a city street, masses of humanity moving like corpuscles in a concrete artery, every one of them alone. Grey sky, grey buildings, grey exhaust belching from the tailpipes of passing taxicabs.

He said, 'You know how I feel about them. They're like a plague of locusts out there, consuming everything. And now you want to open up our world to them, too.'

'Not *them*. She's a person. One person.'

'One mortal,' Jonathan corrected. 'And there are days when every single one of them deserves to be wiped off the face of the earth.'

It didn't sound like idle conversation. Jonathan turned back to face us, looking at the two of us. 'But you're not going to listen to me. You never do. Even if this works, one of *them* will find you, just like last time, stick you in some damn bottle and make you a slave. You won your freedom, David. It's a precious gift. Don't waste it like this.'

'I'm not wasting it,' David said. 'I'm spending it on what really matters.'

Jonathan took that like a knife, with a soft grunt of breath and a flinch. He went back to the window, staring out, and suddenly I had a sense of something I'd missed before. All this power, all this massive ability – and he was trapped. Trapped here, in this house, in whatever reality he'd created for himself. Staring out at the world through those safe, distancing panes of glass.

And maybe, being what he was, being as powerful as he was, he didn't have a choice, either. *He is the one true god of your new existence, little butterfly*, Rahel had said.

A god who didn't dare leave his heaven.

'What if I die?' I asked. I must have surprised both of them; I felt David's reaction, saw Jonathan's as his shoulders bunched up, then relaxed.

'You're Djinn,' David said. 'You won't.'

'According to him, I'm only half. So I can, what, half die?' I cleared my throat. 'If something happens to me, does David get his energy back?'

'Nothing's going to happen to you,' David murmured.

'Not talking to you right now.'

'Yeah, well, you shouldn't be talking to *him*.'

Jonathan answered my question. 'Depends on whether or not he's stupid enough to die with you, or let you go. But yeah, if he let go...he'd be himself again.'

'So what you're talking about, when you say you want to fix him, is that you want to kill me.'

Silence, from both quarters. Jonathan didn't deny it.

'Wouldn't advise you to try. I may not look it, but I'm pretty tough to kill,' I said. 'You can ask around. How many people you know survived having two Demon Marks?'

Jonathan half turned and gave me a sarcastic, one-sided smile. 'Half a Djinn, and she's already giving me grief. Must be your influence.'

'Not my fault. Like this when I met her.' David's smile was delighted, warm, proud. 'You'll like her, Jonathan. Trust me.'

The flickering response – so close to being love – died in Jonathan's eyes. 'I did trust you,' he said. 'Look what it's gotten me.' He turned back to face the window. 'You broke the law, David. You brought a human into our world. That means you have to pay the price. If the price isn't giving her up, then it has to be something else.'

The fire suddenly flared and died to dead, black ashes. Light faded outside to a cold grey. When Jonathan turned around, he was no longer masquerading as a regular guy. The house morphed around me. Couches disappeared. The homey wooden walls changed to unyielding marble.

And Jonathan became something so bright, so powerful that I turned away, eyes squeezed shut, and struggled to control a surge of pure fear.

He is the one true god of your new existence.

I didn't realise that Rahel had meant it literally.

I felt David go down on his knees, and I followed, kept my head down and my mouth shut. *This* was what David had been warning me about. This was the Jonathan you didn't argue with. I felt power surge through the room, as bright and vivid as lightning, and wanted to make myself very small. I couldn't. Whatever powers I had were frozen in place, helpless. I couldn't even get myself up off my knees.

'David, will you let this woman die?' It wasn't a voice, not really. It was thunder, it was a dark, silky wind wrapping around us. Too big to be sound, to have ever come from anything like a human body.

'No.' David's voice was just a raw rasp, barely audible. I couldn't imagine how he was able to talk at all, given the pressure on us.

'Will you let her die?'

'No.'

'I ask a third time: Will you let this woman die?' He was asking it in the traditional Djinn way. The answer David gave now would be the truest one, the reflection of his heart and soul. He wouldn't be able to lie, not even to himself.

From David, a hesitation. I couldn't help it; I forced my eyes open and saw him struggling back to his feet. Standing tall, lonely, defiant.

'No,' he said. 'Never.'

The light sighed. 'Yeah,' it said. 'Figures. Well, I had to ask.'

The incredible brilliance died and left me blind. I heard footsteps. As I blinked away darkness, I saw the temple morphing again, turning back to cabin walls, tapestries, overstuffed comfortable couches. No pressure now. I forced myself shakily back upright, holding on to the back of the couch for support. Fabric dragged at my fingers, real, so damn real. All of it, so real.

Jonathan stood in front of me, back to merely human again, shoulders strong and tensed under the black shirt, eyes as dark as space. He glared at us, locked his arms across his chest, and said, 'If you won't let go of her, the only way to get rid of her is to kill you, too. But you already know that.'

'Yeah. I know.'

The glare continued full force. 'Crazy son of a bitch.'

David's luminous smile warmed the air around all of us. 'And you already knew that.'

Jonathan's fierce look softened. 'So I did.' They looked at each other for a few long seconds, and then Jonathan dragged himself back to dad mode with a visible effort. 'Here's what I've decided. I'll give her a week to learn to live on her own. One week, counting from now. Then I cut the cord. If she can't draw power on her own, she'll go the way of the dinosaurs. Maybe you'll die with her, maybe you won't. I'm not making that decision for you. I'm making one about her. Got it?'

He did, and he didn't like it. David frowned.

'Jonathan, a week's not long enough—'

'It's what she's got,' he interrupted. 'Be grateful. I don't even have to do that much.' He turned to me, and I found myself standing straighter. 'You. You understand what I just said?'

'I have a week to figure this out or I die. Got it.'

'No, you don't,' Jonathan corrected. Those dark, cold eyes weighed me and found me wanting, again. 'David's just said that he won't let go. If I cut the cord and he doesn't release the hold, you both bleed to death up there on the aetheric, and nobody can help you. Not me, not anybody. Get it?'

I swallowed hard. 'Yeah.'

'This is on you now. You fix this, or you might take him with you.'

David, dying for me because I dropped the ball? No way in hell. 'I will,' I said. 'I promise.'

'Good. Glad we're in agreement.'

I wasn't prepared for it, so when hands closed around me from behind and yanked me into an iron-hard embrace, I squeaked like a field mouse instead of fighting back. The hands that held me were feminine, perfectly groomed, with fingernails glossed in bright neon yellow.

'Don't fight me,' Rahel's voice whispered in my ear. 'Neither one of us has a choice in this.'

David whirled to face us, but Jonathan held out a hand and instantly David was frozen, unable to move. His face was chalky and strained, his eyes molten, but he was helpless.

'Here's the deal,' Jonathan continued. 'I need David with me right now, Djinn business that can't wait. So you're going to have to go to boarding school. No boyfriends to coddle you, no special favours, you get to earn your place with us the hard way. Understand?'

I didn't, but I discovered that I couldn't say a word, anyway. I threw a desperate look at David, and found him just as horrified, if not more. I could practically feel the *no!* vibrating the air between us.

'Master,' Rahel said. 'Where do I take her?'

Jonathan's narrow dark eyes swept over me one last time. Judging me like a drill sergeant assessing a particularly scrawny new recruit.

'Patrick,' he said. 'Take her to Patrick.'

David let out a strangled cry of protest, but it was too late. The world – Jonathan, David, the cabin – disappeared around me as Rahel took me out of the world.

And then, with no sense of transition at all, we were standing in an alley in Manhattan. Well, Rahel was standing in an alley in Manhattan; I was drifting around like Pigpen's dirt cloud trying to figure out how to put my skin on again. *Crap*. I'd never get the lime green Manolos right.

Rahel crossed her arms and stared at the not-space where I was. Amused. She inspected her flawless fingernails and evidently decided that neon yellow was no longer the colour of the day; her pantsuit morphed to a hot tangerine, and her nails took on a rich sunset blend of orange, gold, and blue. Even the beads in her hair changed to amber and carnelian.

'Still waiting,' she said, and wiggled her fingers to inspect the effect. Evidently it wasn't impressive enough; she added some rings, nothing too flashy, then turned her attention back to me. 'Come on, Snow White, we don't have all week.'

Keep your pants on, I thought at her. She must have heard it, because she raised one eyebrow in a very Spock-like gesture of amusement.

'The issue, I think, is *your* pants, not mine.'

I slowly formed myself, inside out. Faster than before. By the time the skin came on, I was already moving on to the clothing, adding it rapidly from the templates I'd created earlier. Zip, zoom. Maybe five seconds. Not so bad.

The shoes looked good. I leant over and admired them, decided I really needed toenail polish, and went for matching lime green.

When I looked back up, Rahel was smiling. The friendly expression disappeared as soon as I noticed it. 'What?' I asked.

She shook her head, beads tinkling in her braids. 'Nothing. It's just that your personal style might even be more untraditional than mine. Quite a feat, little one.'

'We going to stand in a stinky alley all day talking fashion?'

'Not that we couldn't, but perhaps it isn't the best plan.' She started walking toward the mouth of the long brick tunnel, where a bright New York morning flowed past in the form of anxious-looking pedestrians, none of whom looked our way. 'Do try to keep up.'

I clumped along after her – if one could be said to clump in shoes this fabulous. I picked my footing carefully, avoiding the puddles of God-knew-what and the shapeless heaps of God-didn't-even-want-to-know-what. Rahel reached the end of the alley, took a sharp right and fell into the traffic flow. I hurried to keep up with her long-legged strides. It really was a beautiful day; the sun caressed my skin, covered me in a sweet warm blanket of energy that I sucked in greedily. Around us, a constant symphony of honking cars, sirens, loud voices – energy to spare.

You gotta love New York City. Kick the crap out of it, and it just rolls over and comes back for more. Me and the Big Apple had that in common. That and a certain brash, trashy style.

'So who's Patrick?' I asked eventually. 'Friend of yours?'

Rahel's snort was rich with disgust. 'No. We don't travel in the same circles.'

Wow, even in the world of the Djinn, you could be unpopular. Who knew? 'So what's wrong with him?'

'Nothing. We're only very different.'

'Yeah? How? He into the business casual look?'

I earned a narrow, amused look from beast gold eyes. 'He thinks the best way to learn to be a Djinn is to learn to be a slave.'

I missed a step. Rahel kept on walking, but slowed enough to let me catch up. 'And this is the guy you're taking me to?'

'Neither of us has a choice,' she pointed out. 'I am bound to obey Jonathan's orders. So are you.'

'Yeah, speaking of that, why?'

She shot me a wide-eyed look, and her hot amber eyes were nearly human in their surprise. 'Why what?'

'Why do you obey him?'

She shook her head gently. 'I do not have the time or energy to teach you all of Djinn history in a day, but Jonathan commands our loyalty for a reason. If Patrick is the place you've been directed to go, I will deliver you, and there you will stay. That ends it.'

Maybe for her, but I wasn't used to taking orders without the chance to argue about it first. Still, no point in arguing with Rahel. I knew from experience that she could crush me like an ant. 'So where is this guy?'

She pointed. I blinked.

'You're kidding,' I said. Straight ahead, at the end of her pointing finger like she'd conjured it up out of the ground, stood the huge stone and steel tower of the Empire State Building. Well, the blurry outlines of it. We were a long walk away. 'Do these look in any way like LL Bean hiking boots to you?'

Rahel flashed me a blinding, sharp-toothed smile. 'Then put on comfortable shoes.'

I sighed and fell into step with her. Some days, it just doesn't pay to have fashion sense.

New York is interesting on every level, but especially on the aetheric. In the physical world it's layered like a wedding cake, history on history; dig far enough down in those sandhog tunnels and you'd find graffiti left by the original Dutch settlers, and by the long-ago-evicted Indians before them. In Oversight, New York isn't about bricks, cement, and streetlights – it's all about perceptions and energy. One enormous storage battery, stuffed with good, evil, rage, peace, fury, love, hate, and ambition. It shoots up into the aetheric for miles, a fantasyland of constantly changing illusions.

It was brighter today than it had been the last time I'd seen it, a kind of fierce pride spiking from every structure, even the tenements tainted by anger and despair.

The Twin Towers still existed on the aetheric plane. When we came into a space where the buildings would have once been visible, I stood and gaped, feeling cold prickles all over my not-quite-human skin. The ghosts of the two buildings rose like glittering ice into the grey sky.

'How?' I stuttered, but I already knew. It was there because it lived in the hearts and minds of millions, maybe billions of people, and until that faded, it would remain in the aetheric. 'Because we remember.'

Rahel nodded soberly and said, 'Humans have power. Creating, destroying, remembering...all acts of great power. Greater than any of them know.'

There was something humbling about it. I could sense the incredible force of power even from where I stood. 'Can we go there? Take a closer look?'

'Not you,' she said. 'Too young. Too much power. For you, it would be like standing in the heart of a sun.'

She shooed me on. We moved at the fast pace of foot traffic. This time of day, rush hour was in full swing – people striding to work, women in business suits and Air Jordans, bike messengers weaving in and out of the honking, stinking, creaking flow of traffic next to the sidewalk. Every other car was yellow, with rates on the side. Everybody seemed to have a big purse, a backpack, or a briefcase. Half of them were on cell phones.

'*So I said to him...*'

'*...bitch, back up off of that before I slap you stupider than you look...*'

'*...I mean, how dumb can you be? Obviously, it's a chicken!*'

I wondered if any of them realised how their personal lives sounded to the rest of the world. Or cared. I wondered if anybody had been listening to us. If they had, nobody cared. Just another day in New York, apparently.

We weren't moving as invisible, but that didn't stop people from barrelling ahead into our space at frightening rates. Rahel dodged to avoid a particularly focused blonde woman in an Ann Taylor jacket and a Kmart skirt. She had a cell phone headset over her bleached hair, smart-girl glasses perched at the end of her nose, and wasn't taking crap from anybody. I recognised the type. Black belt in shopping, no kids, no dogs, no husband, money market account diversified into international growth and mutual funds. Probably lived in a pricey but tiny closet on the Upper West Side and worked at Citibank or Chase.

She noticed us, and even for New York we were clearly not the usual sight. For just a second her grey eyes touched Rahel and locked on like missiles, and then she swerved and blasted past us, back to talking tensely about the latest slide of the Dow Jones. Rahel smiled. 'Sometime tonight, she'll have a dream. A dream about flying, or falling, or monsters. And she won't know why.'

'You did that?'

'No,' she said. 'They do it to themselves. We are not safe to look on for long, you know. Not for them.' She glanced over at me, and frowned. 'Or perhaps she'll just have a nightmare about your hair.'

'What about my—' I caught sight of it, reached up and dragged a tight curl down to focus on it. 'Dammit. I'm Shirley Temple again.'

Rahel pulled me to a stop and over to the side, under the shelter of a red-and-white striped awning in front of a dusty shoe store. The pavement was spotted with pigeon poo and ages of tobacco stains. She stood in front of me, blocking me from bystanders, and brushed her long-nailed fingers gently over my head. I felt the curls relaxing. 'There,' she said. 'Remember that feeling. Just reach for it when you need it.' She studied me more closely. 'Your eyes.'

I neutralised them to the serene dove grey that I'd managed earlier. She nodded.

We waded back into foot traffic again, and had a nice twenty-minute walk. I don't recommend that in cool shoes.

At the end of what I was coming to think of as the Manhattan Death March, the big foursquare bulk of the Empire State Building loomed over us, cool shadows rich and deep with history. 'Aren't we taking the tourist thing a little far?' I asked, staring up. The building was awe-inspiring in its achievement; I wanted to take a look in Oversight, but I knew that if I did I'd never get my hair and eyes straight again. Better to stick to the simple things, for now.

'Inside,' Rahel said, and pushed me to the big revolving glass doors. I pushed, shuffled, and emerged into the big genteel lobby, under the steely gaze of a phalanx of security guys in snappy blue sport coats. The place smelt of fresh paint and old wood, and there was so much to see, even without resorting to Oversight or rising into the aetheric. Gorgeous deco touches, a sense of weight and history to the place that made me want to sit down and soak it in. So many people had come through here, over the years, bringing with them their fears, their loves, their hopes and dreams.

I could feel the echoes of them trapped in every tile on the floor, in every steel beam of the structure. It felt…deliriously weighty.

Visitors were queuing up behind a maroon velvet rope next to a sign that said TOURS. There was a metal detector involved, and I was sure the German shepherd sitting pretty in the corner wasn't there for his health.

'Walk through the detector,' Rahel said. 'Don't touch anything.'

'Um, people in line—'

'Go around them.'

I did. Nobody glanced my way. Now that I concentrated, I could feel something hanging around me – a kind of grey veil, a *don't-see-me* that wasn't quite invisibility. Rahel's doing. I was getting better at figuring that out, anyway; I couldn't even sense it before. I waited until there was a pause in people going through the detector and darted in, zipped through, and felt the weirdest sensation, a kind of burn deep inside. *Whoa*. Weird.

The dog was looking at me. At first I thought he was just staring in my direction, but he watched me as I walked across the lobby, and as Rahel joined me I nudged her and jerked my chin in the direction of our furry friend.

She nodded. 'Animals see us as we are,' she said. 'Dogs don't feel threatened, but beware of cats. They can be unpleasant.'

'O-K.'

She pressed the button. We waited. Eventually a likely candidate arrived, and we crowded in fast, cutting off the flow of tourists with a fast-closing door. Rahel pressed a button – which floor, I didn't see – and then turned and stared into the empty corner of the metal box.

'Um…' I was at a loss for words, for once. 'Is there something…'

'Quiet,' Rahel snapped. 'I'm thinking.'

I was quiet. I listened to the creak of the elevator, the hiss of cables as they hauled us up toward heaven. Distant voices dopplered past one floor at a time, snippets of conversation that wove in and out too fast to catch.

I became aware of something else. A low-level hum somewhere in the far corner of the elevator, a sound where there should be no sound. No presence.

'What's that?' I asked, but before I got more than the first word out, Rahel was *moving*. Spinning away from me, slamming into the empty space of the corner, grappling with something that was shadow and darkness and then…

And then I saw it. Definitely not human. Black, fluid, like a spilt shadow, a stain on the world. Rahel was trying to hold it, but it slid away from her like oil, oozing past her, flowing toward me.

'Go up!' she shouted to me, and her talons changed colours from neon orange-yellow-blue to diamond, and she slashed at the thing between us, tearing deeply. I heard it scream in a high, metallic, screeching voice. 'Idiot! *Go up!*'

She meant up to the aetheric. I let go of my human form and went instantly into fog, vapour, mist...into nothing that could be gotten hold of. But that meant I went up into the next plane of existence, and there, the battle was *really* going on.

Rahel – fog and fire in the aetheric, a bright glowing ghost – was inside of a black, crackling cage of fire. As I watched, she howled and slashed at it, but the wounds she made faded within seconds.

It was...it was *eating her*. Consuming her, bleeding off power, feeding it through that cage of fire and into something else, something that I couldn't even see for the darkness. *God*. The thing was looking at me, not at her. I could feel its hunger vibrating the world between us.

I didn't think. I just reached out and grabbed hold of that black cage of fire. I guess I intended to rip a hole in it big enough for Rahel to escape, but that wasn't what happened. The second I touched it, it bonded to me, made me a circuit in that huge flow of current. I was locked in place.

'Joanne!' Rahel shouted, and I felt her reach through the bars that separated us and touch me.

'Draw on David! Fight!'

I didn't have a choice. The sensation of being sucked dry was so overwhelmingly revolting that I would have used anything, anybody to pull away. I grabbed hold of that silvery cord that connected me to David and felt power cascade into me, heady, brilliant, hot, *pure*. It was like introducing a circuit breaker into the flow. The cage around Rahel fell apart into writhing black spikes of energy, and I reached to pull her free. When I touched her, I left silvery contrails of power behind. She grabbed hold and dragged me down, through aetheric, rocketing back into the real world. We slammed back into the elevator cage with enough force to rock it on its cables, and Rahel didn't waste any time with niceties; she took over for me, creating flesh and form in less than a flicker of a second, and when I opened my eyes her neon yellow ones were staring into mine from less than a foot away.

'What the hell was—'

'Hold on!' she shouted, interrupting me, and I felt the power surge around us. Not from her, not from me, from that *thing*.

I didn't think, I reacted. I reached out and slapped it down, hard. The resulting concussion of force erupted in sparks and blue-white flashes as energy turned to electricity, seeking the ground.

Ah, *this* was something I could handle. I reached out on the subatomic level and quickly dispersed the field, bleeding it off into a million tiny jolts through the steel frame of the building. All over the place, people would be picking up static charges from carpet, shocking themselves on doorknobs, feeling prickles on the backs of their necks.

'No!' Rahel said, and grabbed me by the shoulders. 'We can't fight here! Too close!'

Not that we had any choice. The thing was still coming at us, hard and fast, and I ignored her to reach out through the aetheric and read what was going on.

It had control of the air. I couldn't tell what it meant to do, but something bad was a good bet. Air's heavy – it weighs several pounds per square inch. Increasing density can crush a human – or even a humanoid – body like an empty beer can.

I blocked, drawing heavy oxygen out of the elevator cage and slamming it together in a tightly packed ball between my spread hands. Rahel backed away, looking down at the swirling grey-blue mass I was holding. Her eyes went wide.

I set it on fire with a spark from the electricity still crackling around in the air, and wrapped the whole thing in a shell of carbon dioxide, and lifted that bowling-ball-sized inferno in one hand and held it there. Hell in a bottle.

'Bring it on!' I yelled to the empty air. Voices didn't carry in the altered atmosphere, but it didn't matter, I knew it was getting the point. 'Get your ass out here, you coward! Show yourself!'

The elevator shuddered to a halt.

Something black manifested itself in the corner as a shadow, then a stain, then an oil-slick presence.

It wasn't a Djinn. I didn't know what it was, but evidently Rahel did. She lifted her left hand and pointed it at the thing, and her fingers sprouted claws again – long, wickedly pointed things that gleamed harsh crystal in the overhead lights.

'Ifrit,' she hissed. She looked savage. 'Leave this place.'

There were eyes in the shadows; I could feel them even if I couldn't see them. Dark eyes. And a darker amusement. The ball of fire I'd made was starting to get hot, even through the layering I'd put around it. I tossed it from one hand to the other, looking casual and – I hoped – deadly.

The Ifrit purred, 'Peace to you, my sisters.'

'War, my sister,' Rahel answered softly. 'Who lets you hunt here?'

'Sweetmeat, I hunt where I choose,' the thing said. It had a voice like darkest velvet, and even though the air was too thin to hold a smell I could *taste* it, like rotting meat in the back of my throat.

'Not here. Not now.'

I don't know how it did it, but it smiled. Grinned, actually. Maybe it was just that my eyes were getting accustomed to the lack of features in its face, and added some imaginary ones, but I thought

I saw a flash of teeth. 'This creature cannot survive,' it said, and pointed toward me. 'Think you I will allow its energy to be wasted?'

The Ifrit was talking about me. 'Who you calling a creature?' I shot back.

'Hush,' Rahel said absently. She was staring at the Ifrit with a frown now, no longer afraid. 'Get rid of that fireball before you hurt someone.'

Oh. The fireball. I killed it by the simple expedient of cracking the carbon dioxide shell and instantly supercooling the molecules as they tried to hurtle out and fry us alive. By the time the snapping sound echoed through the elevator car, all that was left was a faint smell of ozone and a wisp of smoke that I left, just for effect.

'Now,' Rahel said, and slowly lowered her hand. 'Who sent you, my poor sister?' I wondered what had made the attitude change. *My poor sister?* The thing didn't look either poor or related. Or even vaguely female.

Right on cue, the elevator dinged and the cage shuddered to a stop. The doors slowly creaked open on a spacious but faded hallway, an expanse of not very new business-class carpet…and Santa Claus. Really. Big, burly, tall, with thick bushy white-blond hair, twinkling Caribbean blue eyes… He was wearing a blue velour jogging suit, Nike cross-trainers, and little narrow Claus-friendly glasses perched on the end of his nose.

'Actually, she's mine. Sorry for the inconvenience,'

he said. He stuck his hand out sideways for me to shake. I stared at it, at him, at Rahel, at the Ifrit who was now lounging against the elevator wall as if it didn't have a care in the world. The air still smelt of fear and ozone.

'Joanne Baldwin, I presume,' he said, with that same devil-in-the-details smile.

'Who the hell are you?' I blurted. Rahel sighed, shook her hands and inspected her restored nail polish critically.

'His name is Patrick,' she said. 'And I regret to say that he's your new instructor.'

The Ifrit vanished while I wasn't looking, but I had the strong impression that it hadn't gone far. Patrick and Rahel exchanged long looks. On Patrick's side it was cute and twinkly and frankly lecherous; on Rahel's it was pained, long-suffering, and repulsed.

'Don't,' she said when Patrick opened his mouth. He looked hurt. 'I have no need for intercourse with you, social or otherwise. Now. You're expecting her, I presume.'

Patrick nodded and slapped a hand out to stop the elevator doors from closing between us. He gave us a grand, sweeping gesture that included a comic-opera bow. Rahel ignored him and pushed past. I followed, and I had the strong impression that while he was down there bowing and scraping, he was checking out my ass.

Patrick let go of the doors and offered me his

arm, which I didn't take. Rahel watched the pantomime impatiently. 'Let's get on with this,' she snapped. 'I do not appreciate your little joke.'

'What, my Ifrit? Please. As if you could possibly have been hurt by her, Rahel. Nice theatre, though, very nice, I very much liked your screaming. I presume Jonathan told you there might be some excitement along the way?'

'He neglected to mention it. I assume you were testing our new friend?'

'Of course.' He offered Rahel his elbow this time; she looked at it like something fished out of a sewer line and kept walking. Patrick darted ahead down the hallway, presumably leading us somewhere as he talked over his shoulder. 'No offence, my dear, but I do like to know that she won't curl up and die before I even work up a good sweat. I thought with you here, she might expect you to save her, but that was quite a nice surprise. Got backbone, this one. No brains, but backbone.'

'Hey!' I snapped, and walked faster to catch up. They had pulled ahead of me by at least ten feet, taking long strides that my high heels, no matter how kicky, weren't appropriate for matching. 'So that was some kind of test?'

Patrick threw Rahel a bushy-eyebrows-raised look. 'Oh, she's quick, isn't she?'

'Very.' For the first time, they were on the same wavelength.

We came to a halt in front of a narrow office

door, unmarked except for a number and a weathered sign that read PLEASE KNOCK. Patrick twisted the knob, swung the door wide, and stood aside to let me precede him. I took a tentative step in and found a not-very-comfortable waiting room, the standard for HMO doctors and low-cost dentists – industrial furniture, magazines that looked vintage, a crappy, out-of-register TV playing silently in one corner. No receptionist visible, nothing but another door, this one unmarked.

'That way.' He nodded toward the other door. I crossed the empty waiting room and reached to open it...and it silently drifted open before I touched it.

'Don't mind that. My Ifrit's a little bored, and really, you *are* remarkably beautiful, my dear. She's drawn to that sort of thing.'

I'd never been leered at by Santa before. It was unsettling.

'Patrick,' Rahel said reprovingly. 'Behave.'

Santa – Patrick – put on an injured, kicked-puppy expression. He had a smooth tenor voice, buttery soft, with an accent I couldn't quite pin down hovering around the edges – not American, maybe antique European. 'I'm extremely well mannered,' he huffed. 'I'm also very well qualified, in case you're wondering, my sweet little peach. You see, I'm the only living example of what David's trying to do with you. I'm the only human ever to survive being made into a Djinn by another Djinn.'

I needed to sit down, suddenly. There was a lot implied in that simple statement – one, this had been tried before, and two, it had only happened once successfully. *Not* the news I was hoping to hear.

Patrick must have sensed it, because he waved a hand and suddenly there was a guest chair behind me, of the same industrial discomfort as the waiting room furniture. I sat. Rahel put a hand on my shoulder, and between that and the friendly, heavy weight of Patrick's stare, I felt somewhat anchored again.

'When I was forty-two, I contracted a fatal disease,' Patrick said, and settled back behind his desk with a protesting creak of chair springs. He steepled his fingers on the curve of his stomach. 'I had been, to that point, what you would call a Fire Warden. When I died, my Djinn—'

'Sara,' Rahel said quietly. They exchanged an impenetrable look.

'—my Djinn, Sara, made me into the man I am today.' He smiled brightly. 'Which isn't a man at all, of course. So therefore Jonathan feels that I am well qualified to teach you how to become a Djinn. You do understand you're not one now?'

'Jonathan was pretty clear on that,' I said.

'You should believe it.' Patrick's smile disappeared like he'd pulled the plug on it. 'You'll die, and take David with you, unless you learn how to survive without the life support he's providing you. Do you understand that?'

I swallowed. 'Yes.'

'Then forget everything David has taught you already. We're starting over. The problem is that natural-born Djinn have no idea what you need to learn to survive – and it is completely different from what they think you need to know.'

'That's what the thing in the elevator was about?'

'Not at all. That was just a bit of fun.' Patrick had a naughty grin. 'Rahel and I have quite a history, don't we, my sweet? And I'm sure she enjoyed a little challenge.'

Rahel didn't look as if she'd enjoyed any of it, and this little conversation still less. 'If you're done with me...' she began.

Patrick's turquoise eyes flicked toward her, and there was power there, all right, power as great or greater than Rahel's. 'Yes, love, I'm done. Why don't you get on about your master's business like a good little doggie?'

The chill in the air between them deepened to an arctic storm front. Rahel's smile wasn't at all friendly. Neither was Patrick's.

Rahel said softly, 'I release her in your care, Patrick. One warning. Jonathan will not take it well if you allow anything to happen to her.'

'You're so sure of your master's voice in this matter? Because I wasn't under the impression that Jonathan had formed any special attachment to this girl. None at all.'

Her eyes narrowed to burning gold slits. 'Very

well. *I* won't take it well if you allow anything to happen to her.'

'I thought she was David's bit of mischief. Or is she yours? I do so *love* a girl who's flexible, you know. Perhaps I might join the fun...?' He held on to an annoyingly bright smile as she hissed and stalked away. The door silently swung open as she approached, and shut when she departed.

I listened for any sense that she was going to hang around, watch out for me. All I sensed was that vast, quiet weight of Patrick's power, and the dark shadow of his Ifrit sliding around the edges of my consciousness.

'Alone at last,' said Santa Claus, and gave me a particularly unsettling smile.

'Mind if we go to my place?'

Patrick had a loft apartment on West Seventy-third, big and horribly expensive and decorated with as much abandon as a Djinn's imagination and apparently limitless budget could provide.

It was a disaster.

His 'office' had been impersonal, deliberately bland, but his home didn't share the same flaws. Carpet in a colour that even Rahel wouldn't have worn – aggressive, eye-hurting blue – competed with neon yellow leather couches and shiny green occasional tables. Those damned Warhol Marilyn prints on the wall. Tasteless plaster copies of naked Greek statues, the lewder the better. He liked smiley faces, too. The bathroom was decorated in them, complete to see-through toilet seat with little yellow happy faces floating inside.

There was, demonstrably, no Mrs Claus.

Patrick handed me off to the care of the banana yellow leather sofa, which was a lot more uncomfortable than it looked, and disappeared into the kitchen. He came back with two tumblers of something that looked alcoholic but in far too generous a portion for safety. He handed me one. I put mine down on the table, and he hastily dealt me a round coaster that featured an underwear-clad Bettie Page being spanked with a hairbrush.

'So.' He beamed at me, and dragged a chair closer to plump himself down. 'You're wondering how this works.'

'A little.'

'Very simple,' he said, and steepled his fingers under his chin. Those eyes – warm and deep as a tropical ocean. Deceptively peaceful. 'Do you know what an Ifrit is?'

'Met one. Didn't like her.'

'So you did.' Patrick looked past me, and I sensed something dark and shadowy lurking over my shoulder. I didn't turn. 'She is what you could become, if you don't do this right. She is a fallen Djinn. She can't reach the power of the universe itself, she can only consume it through others.'

'I thought that was what Djinn did. Consumed it through others.'

'No, no, I told you to forget everything David told you.' He waggled a finger at me. 'I grew up in an age of alchemy, so I will put it to you in alchemical terms. We *transmute* the essence of a thing. We have power of our own, that we draw from the world around us, but to do the great things, the miracles the Djinn are famous for, we draw from the life energy of humans. We can only do that if we're claimed.'

'You mean slaves.'

Patrick shrugged. 'I prefer to think of it as being in public service. In any case, you're not ready for such a step just yet. First, you have to learn how to live without a power source, such as a human or another Djinn.'

'That's why I'm here.' I chanced a sip of the drink he'd poured me. *Yowza*. The good stuff. Apparently, Patrick's bad taste didn't extend to his palate.

'Exactly. You must learn to feed from what's all around you, change its form and consume the excess energy produced. My poor Ifrit there exists as a kind of vampire, stealing the souls of others because she cannot touch the forces of life herself. Yes?'

I wanted to shudder, but I didn't want him to see me do it. I just raised my chin and stared. Patrick smiled.

'Tell me something about yourself.'

'I'd rather save the small talk.'

'There's no need to be rude, child, and believe

me, I'm asking for a reason. Tell me something about yourself. Anything.'

'I'm twenty-eight...'

He rejected that one out of hand. 'Something personal. Something...interior. Tell me something you love.'

I thought about it for a long few seconds, then said, 'Ralph Lauren's summer line this year. Not the spring collection, which was way too pastel, and the winter was really crappy, all bland browns and greys. But he's got some good fabrics this summer, kind of a hot tangerine matched with dull red. Only the skirts, though. His Capri pants are for shit. Pockets? Who wants pockets on Capri pants? What woman in her right mind puts extra fabric on her hips?'

There was a long and ringing silence. Patrick's eyes were wide and rather frightened. He finally cleared his throat and said, 'Anything else apart from fashion?'

'What do you want me to say? Puppies? Fluffy kittens? Babies?'

'Let's try something simple. Your favourite food.'

I rolled my eyes. 'Chocolate.' *Duh*.

Patrick went to the kitchen and came back with...a cup of sugar. He set it down in front of me. I eyed the white crystals. 'Um...not really that hungry. Or that desperate.'

He settled in a bright red armchair with a creak of leather. 'No. Make it chocolate.'

I gave him a blank stare.

'Alchemy,' he reminded me. He reached into a candy dish and took out a silver-wrapped Hershey's Kiss, shelled it and set it down next to the sugar. 'There's your exemplar. Transmutation. You alter the chemical formula of the sugar and take the resulting energy into yourself. Also, if you'd like, the chocolate, of course.'

He reached into the sugar and dipped out a handful of granular white, put it in the palm of his hand, and waggled his eyebrows theatrically. The sugar thickened, darkened, and morphed into a small, perfect Hershey's Kiss. He popped it into his mouth and sucked with lascivious delight.

'It's not necessarily proportional,' he said, smacking on the chocolate. 'It depends on how much power you want to pour into it. But you will need at least something to work from. That's not usually difficult – most things you need are all around you. Once you get proficient enough, you'll be able to draw the raw material without it being necessarily in a similar form, but we'll start with the easy steps.'

I had no idea what he was talking about, really. I mean, I got the theory, but there was a big-ass step between sugar and a tasty silver-wrapped treat. I thought about a lot of things, but mostly I thought about the power still flowing out of David into me, sustaining me. I needed to learn how to break that life support. *Had to*. Both our lives depended on it. I reached out for the sugar, took a pinch, and contemplated the white granules as they glistened against my palm. Hmmm. Chemistry. I'd always been good at chemistry. It was no more than floating up into Oversight, then driving down through the atomic structure until you were at the most basic levels and rearranging things.

OK, it sounded simpler than it really was, but doesn't everything? I took a deep breath, closed my eyes, and focused on the chemical structure. Crystals first, until the edges were clear and sharp in my mind. Then down a level to the thickly nested lattices that made up the crystals. Then into the interstitial spaces that made up the layers...

I was reaching out for the glittering, blue-white beauty of the sugar's basic blocks when I felt something tear across my mind like a set of white-hot claws. I yelped, grabbed for my head, and felt myself caught. Impaled on something that felt like a knife through my chest.

We weren't starting with sugar into chocolate after all, it seemed, because Patrick just sat there looking benign and friendly and interested while I screamed and fell to the floor. On the aetheric level, his Ifrit was kneeling on top of me, ripping and tearing at me. I felt the swirling coloured layers of my aetheric form go dark with shock, and struggled to break free, but it was on me, crushing me, and there was no way I could get free. I screamed, both in sound and the aetheric plane. Screamed David's name. Reached for that thick, life-giving stream of silver that pointed the way to where he'd gone, but I couldn't find him, couldn't see him, couldn't see anything for the agony that rippled over me in waves.

The thing on top of me was laughing soundlessly. It reached for the silver cord that bound me to David, and to life, and it took hold of it in black-shadow claws...

I lashed out. I didn't know how to fight like a Djinn, so I fought like a Warden, reaching for power from the aetheric, drawing it up through myself like a spring through a well – hot, pulsing power, blood in invisible veins. I put my hands flat against the thing's chest and screamed as I slammed power into it, through it, out the back of it in a splash of fury so hot I wondered why I didn't burn with it.

The thing howled, slashed at the umbilical, and I pulled more power, spending it recklessly to keep the Ifrit from getting a good grip.

'Help me!' I screamed at Patrick, who was watching with great, bright-eyed interest. 'You bastard!'

'Sugar into chocolate,' he said smugly. 'Trans-mutation. You know this one.'

And somehow, somewhere, I did know. I grabbed hold of that power I'd been slinging so violently and focused it to laser-beam intensity, and allowed my Djinn senses to come back online again. Instantly, the aetheric bloomed into shades and shapes and dimensions, too much, too bright, too confusing, but in the centre of the spotlight was the Ifrit. No nicely concealing shadows this time, just ugly angular darkness, all sharp teeth and overdriven muscles. Not a demon, which I'd fought before (and died in the process). An Ifrit was to a demon what a housecat is to a lion – but to a mouse like me, more than enough to do the job.

'Back off!' I snarled at it. It smirked and whirled away in a blur too fast to follow. Circled around behind me. Ripped at me before I could focus the energy properly. 'Patrick! Call it off!'

'Now why would I do that?' he asked mildly, and ate another piece of chocolate. 'You can't expect others to defend you, Joanne. It's the first responsibility of any Djinn. Preserve your life. Then preserve your freedom.'

I didn't have the energy to spare for a reply. I was looking for a vulnerability, and trying to keep its teeth and claws away from *my* vulnerability – that silver cord stretching off to the horizon. So fragile, my God, no wonder Jonathan was afraid of leaving David tethered to me – David was vulnerable, too, through me…

Behind the coal black skin and shifting aura like a rainbow oil slick, there was something even darker inside the Ifrit, but soft. Fragile.

On the aetheric, I extended my hand and felt metal claws slide free. They were bright and sharp as starlight, translucent as crystal.

I slapped aside the Ifrit's tearing attack and

plunged those knifelike claws home into its body, not to rip or savage, but to deliver something else.

Light.

Darkness into light.

One thing into another.

Transmutation.

The Ifrit turned pale, translucent, insubstantial, and for a second I heard its cry of joy echo through the aetheric, high and beautiful and strange, and then – *pop* – it was gone.

And I was lying on the floor of Patrick's ugly, overdone living room, staring up at a ceiling painted with pornographic renderings in the style of the Sistine Chapel. My Djinn senses were still locked on full, and every damn thing in the place had a history, sweaty and heavy in my head. I wanted to laugh, but I was too tired.

Patrick looked no more like Santa Claus than I did, when I examined him with those senses. No, he was big, tough, cold, and more than a little puzzled.

'Interesting,' he said, and took up another palmful of sugar. This time he made an Andes mint, complete with wrapper. He offered it to me. 'How did you know to do that?'

'Transmutation,' I said, still lying flat on the over-coloured carpet. I lifted my hands and looked at them, flexed a muscle that existed only in the aetheric. Silver-tipped claws, as delicate as frost, slid from my fingertips. 'You said she was hungry. I fed her.'

'Yes,' he agreed softly, with a doubting undertone of wonder. 'So you did.'

I took the mint, unwrapped it, and let it dissolve into a sweet edge of mint in my mouth. Taste was different now. Brighter. Sharper. The shiny green paper of the wrapper had a texture to it like nothing I'd ever felt before.

'So,' he said as I savoured the taste. 'Round Two?'

I'd just almost died, and for some reason I couldn't stop a giggle that worked its way all the way up from my guts.

'Sure,' I said in between helpless bursts of laughter. 'Bring it on.'

Round Two was a disaster. I got my ass kicked. Painfully. This time I ended up lying full length on the banana yellow couch, sobbing for breath, too exhausted to even begin to count the ways I hurt.

Patrick bustled around providing fresh drinks. Unless he wanted to use mine as a topical ninety proof antiseptic, I wasn't interested.

'Now,' he said briskly, and sat back in the red velvet chair. It was shaped like a platform shoe. Looked like something out of JC Penney's Nightmare Collection. 'Let's talk about what you did wrong. Ifrits are an expression of energy, just as we are, and therefore your first instinct was correct, you must appease them, not fight them, until you

have enough power to—' He stopped the lecture to
frown at me.

'You're bleeding all over my couch.'

I groaned. 'Excuse the hell out of me.'

'For heaven's sake, child, just fix it.'

I looked at him blankly. He reached over, took
my wrist, and smoothed a finger gently over one of
the gaping cuts. It zipped shut, faded, and
disappeared.

Blood along with it.

'There,' he said. 'You do the rest.'

Not, of course, as simple as it sounded. I managed,
knitting back flesh and muscle, blood vessels and
nerves. The outfit repairs were easy, by comparison.

I finally managed to sit up, kick off the shoes,
and put my bare feet up on the tacky chrome and
glass coffee table.

'Better,' Patrick murmured. 'Now. Ifrits. They
can be formed two ways. One is a human failing to
make the transition to life as a Djinn – which you
are in grave danger of doing, my dear. They are also
what's left of Djinn when we – well, I suppose the
word is *die*.'

I froze in the act of wiggling my toes. 'I thought
Djinn couldn't die.'

'True, in much the same way that energy is never
lost. But we can be transmuted, like anything else.
Humans never die either, in the strictest sense of the
word; they're transmuted into base materials.
Recycled.'

Ashes to ashes, I thought. Great. Nobody had bothered to mention this in the recruitment brochure.

'If a Djinn is injured badly enough, his or her energy can be broken apart, in which case an Ifrit is formed – they only want to eat, devour other Djinn, and recover their lost energy.' Patrick shrugged. 'If they devour enough, theoretically they could become Djinn again, but nobody is inclined to make that sacrifice, I'm afraid.'

'How often—'

'—do Djinn die? Not often. I can only remember it happening three times in the last, oh, four hundred years.' Patrick's sparkling blue eyes stared off into the distance. 'And truthfully, I don't lose any sleep knowing two of those particular Djinn are gone. Not the best of people.'

'Not people,' I corrected, and got another shrug.

'Potato, potahto. You need to get over your human limits, my sweet.' He was one to talk. Busy checking out the line of my leg all the way up to the leather skirt.

'How long do I have to do this?'

'What?'

'Fight your Ifrit?'

He smiled, tinkled ice in a tumbler full of gold liquor that hadn't been in his hand two seconds ago, and those ocean-deep eyes looked terminally amused. 'Is that what you've been doing?'

I let my head drop back against the yellow

leather of the couch and stared at the pornographic Michelangelo ceiling. In this version, God was a very naughty fellow. 'God,' I said to Him. 'Why did You have to make me a Djinn? You couldn't just make me a stinkbug instead? I'd have been happy as a stinkbug.'

Patrick sighed. 'I've been teaching you a great many things, and you're too smart not to know it. Using your senses effectively, thinking like a Djinn, drawing power from the world around you, knowing your form and your energies on an instinctual level. The Ifrit is a means to an end. You didn't hurt her any more than she actually hurt you.'

In which case, the Ifrit was feeling pretty beat to hell, too. That was nice.

Patrick took a deep gulp of his whisky – if that's what it was – and said, 'Now I think it's time for something a little different.'

'Yeah?' I was no longer giving him the benefit of the doubt. 'Is it going to hurt?'

'Unquestionably.'

'Do I get chocolate when it's over?'

'Perhaps.' His round Santa face expressed his delight. 'Let's take a trip.'

'I'd like to rest first, if you don't—'

He did, apparently, because *whoosh*, I was no longer on the couch, I was being dragged up into the aetheric at a rate equalled only by spacecraft leaving orbit. I yelped – incorporeally – and grabbed a tighter hold of Patrick's essence as we shot up, up, watching his building miniaturise, then New York City shrink into a colourful little candyland, then the world curve off into a beautiful blue-green marble below us. Space was a vast black presence around us, cold and crushing, shot through with the icy sheen of stars. We were hanging at the very edge of where we could go, where the bonds of earth were weakest. Escape velocity.

Do you know what happens if Wardens go farther? Patrick asked. I almost forgot to answer. The world was so beautiful, edged in blues and greens, reds and golds, sparkling with power and life energy. She was magnificent. Alive. Sentient. I could sense her from here, a vast and slow consciousness that was only now beginning to wonder whether the presence of human beings was a Bad Thing. The storms, earthquakes, fires that had plagued human society in ever-growing ferocity since the Stone Age, those were nothing more than the earth shifting in her sleep, waving away a buzzing fly without ever really coming awake. Trembles of the skin. Involuntary sneezes to expel the intruders.

And still, they required every ounce of strength the Wardens Association possessed to keep the human race alive and kicking – and unaware of the danger.

Do you know what happens if Wardens go

farther? Patrick asked again. I scrambled to remember. It wasn't a Djinn lesson, it was a human one, specific to the Wardens. I'd learnt it in class, way back when, on a day when the sky muttered grey and gave Princeton one of those nice spring showers that humans think is the normal course of business for weather. It wasn't, of course. Spring showers are manufactured. Some guy colliding two fronts, carefully controlling the reactions to get just the right mix of wind, rain, and temperature.

We die, I said. In general, human beings could strap on a spacesuit and ride rockets to the stars. Wardens were too tightly bound to the planet. The farther we got from the nurturing heartbeat of our world, the weaker we became. It worked that way on the aetheric plane, too. This was the outer limit of our survival.

You are no longer a Warden, my little blossom.

He yanked me on, past the point of no return, out into the cold black blanket of space.

And I didn't die.

We floated in the sharp emptiness, part of a darkness so profound it was like death, and below the earth pulsed and whispered and murmured in its sleep. All that life, so bright. The stars were hard enough to cut.

Now you know what it's like, Patrick said.

I had no words to describe it, but I tried to put some context around it. *How far can I go?*

As far as you care to. But be careful. Falling

down is not quite as simple as jumping up, you'll find.

It was still a test. *What's the catch?*

Nothing much. Get yourself back where you started.

And he was gone. Just like that. *Blip.* I was alone, floating in a void so empty that not even satellites raced by. The moon was a cold, lonely dot of white just rounding the far side of the planet. The sun's rays were so piercingly bright and intense that I felt them vibrate inside me even in my insubstantial state. In human form they'd fry me like an egg.

Get back? How the hell was I supposed to get back? I wasn't even sure how to move. There was nothing to push against, no forces to work with, nothing but emptiness...

...and the light of the sun, hot and fierce. It flowed like molten gold in the aetheric.

Could I use the sun? Use fire itself to move me?

I reached out, spread myself thin as a whisper, and dropped down into the real world just enough to give myself weight. Still invisible, to the naked eye, but able to trap that energy.

It moved me. Just a little.

It also hurt like that damn Ifrit had gotten hold of me again.

I summoned up my courage and sank further down, one careful level at a time. The more sun I captured, the more I was able to propel myself; the more sun I captured, the more I burnt.

I finally let go of the pain and opened myself to it, and the force of fire hit me like wind in a sail, and I flew. Agony turned white-hot, burnt itself out, became something else. *I* became something else.

I hurtled through the thickening fog of the earth's atmosphere, streaking like a falling star, trailing fire.

I fell back into human form, settled myself like a feather down on lime green spike heels, facing Patrick, and put my hands on my hips.

'Well?' I asked.

He looked down at the carpet. It had melted into a circle about four feet across.

Noxious chemical stew. He fixed it.

'Not bad,' he said, and handed me a cold scotch on the rocks. 'Not bad at all, little one.' The ice instantly melted in the glass from the heat of my skin. The scotch boiled.

I took one step, felt my knees give way, and collapsed face down on the yellow sofa.

And slept.

And this is what I dreamt.

A cold stone room, softened here and there by rough-woven rugs, a few grace notes like a silver candlestick and a red wool blanket thrown over the bed. By the standards of its time, a comfortable enough home.

Under the red wool blanket, a man lay dying.

He was skeletally thin, faded, his blue eyes almost colourless now in the flicker of candlelight. I floated in the corner and watched him. I felt I should know him, but his face was just a skull with skin, like an Auschwitz survivor. He still had a few tufts of thin blond hair spilling out over the hard bundle of cloth that served as his pillow.

There was a woman sitting at his side. She was beautiful, so beautiful, but it wasn't really her face that made her that way. She was actually almost plain – an unremarkable evenness to her features – but the love that spilt out of her was so intense, the grace of her body so informing, that she couldn't be anything else but lovely. She was wearing a long white robe, something that looked vaguely angelic and glowed like satin in the wavering light.

The man on the bed made a tortured sound. His claw-like hand reached out to her, and she captured it in both of hers. Bent her head. I saw a crystal rain of tears falling, but when she looked up again she was at peace.

'Forgive me,' she said, and bent over to press her lips to his parchment-pale forehead.

Someone else was in the room now, walking right out of the walls. Someone I knew. *David*. But not the David I knew now… This one was wearing a medieval cotte and woollen hose, all in shades of rust and russet, and his hair was worn long.

He didn't sense me. His attention stayed on the woman in the chair.

'Sara,' he said. She didn't turn to look at him.

'Sara, it's time to go.'

'No.' Her voice was soft, uninflected, but I could tell there was no moving her. 'I will not let him be lost like this. I can't.'

'There's no choice,' David whispered. 'Please, Sara. Come with me now. Jonathan's waiting.'

'Will Jonathan give me peace?' she asked. 'Will he give me love?'

'Yes.'

'Not like this.' She reached out to ease a strand of pale hair back from the dying man's face. 'Never like this, and David, I cannot bear to lose it.'

'You can't keep it. Humans die. It's the law.'

She looked away from him, and I had the strange, creepy impression she was looking somewhere else.

At *me*. But that wasn't possible, because I knew I wasn't here, really. Not in this time. Not in this place.

Sara's eyes were the colour of amethysts, a beautiful, peaceful colour. She stared at the corner where I floated, and then she smiled.

'The law of my heart is different,' she said, and let go of the man's hand. She stood up, and the white gown fell away, sliding to the floor in a puddle of cloth; under it her skin glowed a soft, perfect ivory. No sculptor had ever captured a form like that, so perfect, so graceful.

'Don't,' David said, and took a step toward her. I know he could have stopped her, but something –

maybe just the heartbreaking longing in her eyes –
made him hesitate.

She folded back the sheets and climbed into the
narrow bed. The dying man seemed to see her, and
those pale eyes widened; the word he shaped might
have been *No*...and then she wrapped her arms
around him. Her pale, white hair flowed over the
two of them like a cloak, wrapping them together.

'No, Sara,' David whispered. It sounded like a
goodbye.

There was a flare of light on the bed, something
so bright it was like the heart of a bonfire, and in it
I heard screams. Terrible, wrenching screams. They
were *dying*, both of them, dying horribly.

David didn't move. Maybe he couldn't. I wanted
to, but it was still a dream, only a dream for me,
and I just floated, waiting, as the fire burnt and the
screams faded, until the light faded, too.

Two bodies, lying senseless on the bed.

One of them opened its mouth to scream, but
nothing came out. Dry, voiceless, horror-stricken.
He had turquoise blue eyes now, and the hair that
had been thin and fragile was reborn in a white-
gold flame around his head.

Restored to life, health, as she must have known
him.

Sara lay unmoving beside him, amethyst eyes still
open. He reached out to touch her face...

...and that ivory skin cracked, turned to powder,
and began to flake away.

A sloughing of skin, for what was underneath.

The soft black shadow of an Ifrit rose out of the pale ruin of the Djinn known as Sara, and the man reached out to it, but it flinched away. Hissing.

He filled his hands with dust and looked at David with tears streaming down his face. No words for it.

No help for it.

David said, in a voice gone rough and strange with grief, 'I pray you are worth this gift, Patrick.'

This time, Patrick found his voice.

He screamed.

I woke up the next day to the smell of bacon and orange juice, and fresh-ground coffee. There was still a bowl of sugar sitting on the coffee table next to me.

I felt hungover from the dream…memory? …nightmare?…and looking around me, I kept seeing that spare stone room, that skull-thin face breathing its last, the unearthly beauty and grace turned to something ugly and twisted.

He'd kept her with him all this time – or she'd haunted him. Impossible to tell how the feelings ran without asking, and I doubted Patrick would have anything revealing to say. He'd left that devastated, screaming moment behind centuries ago. The Patrick of today was cold, savvy, and controlled.

And yet, the sliding, ever-present shadow of the Ifrit who'd been Sara had another story to tell, didn't it? A story of love, longing, honour, sacrifice, tragedy? Did she still love him so much? Rahel said that Ifrit survived by eating other Djinn. And yet Sara remained here, and hadn't done Patrick too much damage.

I refused to think too long about *that* relationship, especially before food.

Patrick had been kind enough to take off my shoes and put a tacky leopard-spotted cotton throw rug over me. I kept it draped over my shoulders and shuffled barefoot toward the kitchen; I was seriously thinking about changing my clothes to something that would be easier to fight in, since Patrick's coaching style evidently owed a lot to the world of professional wrestling. Maybe Spandex and a cute little domino mask. They could call me The Nutcracker.

Breakfast was sitting on the table, perfectly displayed like a cereal commercial. *Serving suggestion.* There were even fresh daisies in a vase in the centre of the table. Of course, the kitschy Elvis plates and Hello Kitty mugs weren't quite what *Better Homes and Gardens* had in mind, but still, he'd made an effort.

'Patrick?'

No answer. I sat myself down and took a bite of bacon and eggs. They were wonderfully fresh, warm, just right. The bacon was crisp without being burnt.

The orange juice was pulpy and tart. Coffee – in

the Hello Kitty mug – was as black as sin and twice as sweet.

The condemned woman ate a hearty breakfast.

I was just polishing off the last bite of English muffin when I felt the unmistakable gust of power that accompanies major mojo being worked, and Patrick walked in, dressed in an utterly unmentionable bathrobe. I was pretty sure that Disney wouldn't have approved of what their cartoon characters were doing on that dark blue satin background.

On the other hand, I was really glad he had on the bathrobe.

He walked over to the table, took a seat, unfolded a morning paper, and peered at me over the tops of his glasses. 'Sleep well?'

'Fine line between unconscious and resting,' I said. 'I think it was on the wrong side of unconscious.'

'Ah.' He rattled the paper. 'Have you seen the headlines?'

He turned the page to face me.

There was a picture of storm surge on the Florida coastline wiping out houses wholesale. The headline read STORM OF THE NEW CENTURY? I sucked in my breath hard, then let it out slowly.

'My doing?' I asked.

He gave me an impish smile. 'Hardly.' He rustled the paper back around again. 'As usual, your friends in the Weather Wardens seem to have everything turned around back asswards. How is it you have all that power and still manage to let thousands die every year from these storms?'

I wasn't about to get drawn into the traditional branch-of-service argument that almost always erupted between Weather Wardens, Fire Wardens, and Earth Wardens. Patrick had once been a Fire Warden, I remembered. I took a thoughtful bite of bacon. 'Um, same way Team Smokey Bear let forest fires eat up half of California last year? That was special.'

He grunted agreement. 'Do you think that with a Djinn at your command you could have done better?'

'Sure.' I shrugged and added a little more pepper to my last bite of eggs. 'More power. More control.'

'Control comes from Djinn?'

I had to think about that one. 'Um, no. Control comes from...the Warden. Power comes from the Djinn.'

'Actually, you're wrong on both answers. Control and power both come from the Warden. The only thing that a Djinn brings is potential.' He took a sip of coffee, added cream, and stirred. 'That's all we are, you know. Potential energy. Humans are kinetic. They create action and reaction. We are just the medium through which they move.'

Which sounded way Zen to me. 'I have no idea what you just said.'

'I know.' He gave me a tiny little quirk of his

eyebrows, reached into the pocket of his bathrobe, and brought out a tiny little bottle, about the size of a perfume sample, complete with a plastic capper on the end. He toyed with it between his fingers, tapped it on the table, and thumbed the cap off. I half expected a fellow Djinn to pop out of it.

None did.

'I'd like to explain something to you,' he said. 'It may not make much sense to you now, but I think it will later.'

I was feeling generous, what with a nice comforting load of cholesterol and fat making a home in my system...which reminded me, what exactly happened to food, inside a Djinn body? Was it the usual system, or something totally different? Maybe it just vanished into energy, no chemical breakdown necessary. Huh. Good question.

'Shoot,' I said, and took in a mouthful of Florida sunshine in the form of orange juice that tasted fresh squeezed. Energy into fruit into energy. I loved physics.

'I'm not a bad person,' he said. Not looking at me now, just studying the small perfume vial in his thick, perfectly manicured fingers. 'Tragically selfish as a man, but I suppose that's far from unusual. I lived a good life. And I loved one woman more than life itself. More than my own honour.'

I remembered the dream. 'Sara,' I said. I caught a quick flash of ocean-rich eyes, quickly turned away again.

'She was...astonishing. There are Warden laws, you know, that forbid Djinn from serving their masters...in that way.' For a guy with a living room that would have made Bob Guccione blanch, he was charmingly indirect when it came to words. 'And an honourable master should never require it. But we – it wasn't a command, or obedience. It was...' He shook his head. 'It was a long time ago.'

I sensed the cold shadow in the corner of the kitchen. Yes, there she was, the blackened ghost of Sara, the Ifrit that roamed eternity looking for a way to heal its damage. It wasn't moving. I could feel its attention fixed on Patrick, and remembered the dream – Sara's intense, powerful love.

'You loved her,' I said. 'She loved you.'

'It's why the laws exist. So that it won't happen again.' Patrick shook his head and peered up at me again, eyes pellucid and untroubled behind the half-glasses. 'I want her back, you see. She's half my soul. I want Sara to live.'

He was trying to tell me something, I just couldn't figure out what it was. But the orange juice was curdling in my stomach. 'Patrick...'

'I don't think you're going to make it,' he said, almost kindly. 'I wish there was a way I could help you, Joanne, but the truth is that like me, you should have died as a human. There's no way for him to save you except the way Sara saved me, and the cost is too high.'

I felt myself frowning. 'Hey, nice pep talk. Aren't

you supposed to teach me how to get through this? Preferably alive?'

'Yes. I know.' The perfume vial clinked as he put it down on the table between us. I watched it roll unevenly back and forth. It fetched up against my Hello Kitty mug with a musical little chime. 'I wish I had some magic answer. Truth is, the only answer I know is going to hurt you. Maybe kill you. Are you prepared for that?'

I sucked in a deep breath. 'Probably not, but what choice do I have?'

'Too true. Well then. On with the show. A friend of yours is here to see you.'

'I don't have any friends.' Depressing, but it had the iron ring of truth.

'Look behind you.' I put my fork down and swivelled in the wooden kitchen chair, thinking, *Crap, here we go with the fighting again*, but I was dead wrong.

It was Lewis Levander Orwell, who was pretty much the last person I'd expected to see. He looked a lot more casual now than he'd been at my funeral, dressed in faded jeans the colour of a storm-ready sky, a loose untucked yellow shirt, and that trademark ironic half-smile that felt as familiar to me as a hug. Funny, because although our relationship had always been intense, it had never been what you might call close, in terms of frequency of sharing personal space. He still never really left my mind for long, and never had.

'Hey,' he said. His low, slightly rough voice had a gentleness to it that I hadn't heard before. 'How are you?'

I stood up and walked into his embrace. A full-body hug, lots of male upper body strength carefully controlled. He smelt of leather and wood smoke, and I wondered if he'd been camping somewhere. Lewis is the outdoorsy type. His hiking boots certainly had the chapped, bunged-up look of having tramped through half the real estate of the world.

I'm not a short woman, and he still had some height on me. Lean, tall, with gorgeous dark-cinnamon eyes...yeah, he could make women's hearts skip and dance, if they came close enough to actually *notice* him. Lewis tended to camouflage himself. Always had. Probably a good thing, considering the kind of power he wielded.

I remembered he'd asked me something. 'Mmmm. I'm doing good, for a dead chick.'

He kissed the top of my head and didn't let me go. I was OK with that. I had the total hots for David, was more than eighty per cent of the way to total head-over-heels in love, but I could still enjoy a strong man pressed against me, yes lawdy.

'You scared me,' he said. 'I didn't expect you to drop off the edge of the planet like that. Don't do it again.'

He loosened his grip and stepped away, and I felt noticeably colder outside and warmer in. Which maybe made me fickle, and more than maybe a complete slut. But I was prepared to accept that.

'You were supposed to come find me,' he said. He had a small frown engraved between his brows, and I noticed that he had acquired some fine lines at the corners of his eyes. He had one of those faces that lines made look distinguished, not run-down.

'Yeah, sorry...got busy.' I flipped a hand around to indicate Patrick's incredibly tasteless pad. 'Um, Djinn stuff. You know.'

'Not really, but I'll take your word for it.' His gaze moved to Patrick, and they exchanged guy nods, the ones that indicated acquaintance but no actual fondness, because that would be less than manly. 'Thanks for letting me talk to her.'

Patrick shrugged, which made the things that Mickey and Minnie – and Mickey and Pluto – were doing on the fabric look even more unmentionable. 'No problem. As it happens, it fits with what I'm trying to teach her.'

'Which is?' Lewis wanted to know.

'Survival.'

Nice to know that it was possible to surprise Lewis, once in a while, although I wished it could be for a less urgent and personal cause; he looked as blank as if somebody had taken an eraser to his face. 'Survival? Jo, anything wrong?'

I fielded that one, since it was an easy ground ball. 'You could say.' I pulled out the third chair at the table for him; he folded himself down, long legs bumping into obstructions that hadn't bothered me, and looked at my coffee cup with such pitiful longing that I picked it up and started for the steaming pot.

'Ah!' Patrick wasn't looking at me, but he held up a finger like some offended schoolmaster. 'Break that habit.'

Right, I'd been through this painful lecture before. Stop being human. Start acting like a Djinn. I stared down at the coffee cup, dived down into the structure and felt it from the inside out, the cool heavy reality of the ceramic, the earth-rich scent of ground beans and water. I couldn't remember if Lewis liked cream, so I subtracted that from the equation, held out my left hand, and materialised a steaming cup of black Java in it.

And felt damn proud of myself, too. You betcha.

Lewis was even more impressed. He didn't say anything, but by damn he looked respectful as he took the mug, lifted it to his lips, and sipped.

And it was a bad time to wonder if I'd fucked up the recipe and created something lethal, but then he was an Earth Warden, he'd be able to tell anyway, and fix it if I had. The perfect guinea pig.

'It's good,' he said, and took another, longer sip. 'Colombian?'

'Guatemalan Antigua,' Patrick answered. 'If she did it right.'

He held up his cup for a refill. I did it without

moving a muscle. Same routine – sip, surprise, cautious approval.

Lewis put the coffee aside and didn't let himself get distracted by the fine imitation of a barista I was doing. 'You said something was wrong.'

No sense in beating around the bush, not with him; I laid it out just the way it had been spelt out for me. David's power constantly bleeding off into me, David getting weaker, me the sucking leech that was going to kill him. Yeah, what a happy story it was, just the kind to make the heart warm and cosy. Lewis's dark eyes got darker as it went along, and even though he always had a kind of inner stillness, he went statue-like and stayed that way. Even after I'd finished.

I finally said, into the ringing and too-loud silence, 'So. You wanted…?'

He looked away. Patrick had put the little glass bottle back on the table, unstoppered; Lewis picked it up and rubbed it thoughtfully between his thumb and forefinger. I wondered if he was thinking about food. I could try whipping him up a nice bagel or something, but I wasn't sure that my culinary skills as a Djinn would be any better than they had in my normal walking-around-as-human days, in which I'd been commonly known as the Lucrezia Borgia of spaghetti sauce.

'I wanted to ask you a favour,' he finally said. 'But given what you've just told me, I'm not sure it's such a good idea right now.'

Patrick glanced over the top of the paper at both of us. 'I'm pretty sure it is.'

'Well, no offence, but you're not the one who'll end up with the nightmares if it turns out to be a *rotten* idea.' Lewis wasn't usually so snappish, in my experience. He was clearly rattled. 'No. Forget it. It's OK. You have enough to worry about already.'

'Wait a minute, you haven't even told me anything yet!' I said. Why do guys always try to make the decision before they even state the problem? 'Come on, Lewis, spill it. What do you need?'

He was still rolling the bottle around in his fingers, focused on it with such precision that I wondered if he was about to try to Copperfield it out of existence.

Hey, I wouldn't put it past him. Glass was a pure, if non-organic, manifestation of earth. He could reconstitute it into a pile of sand, if he wanted. How many degrees of heat did it take to melt sand into glass? I'd slept through most of my basic Earth Sciences classes, since it had all been about the weather for me. I remembered something about trillions of dust particles being used to make a single drinking glass, but apart from the fact that the instructor in the class had been a skinny, obnoxious woman with tortoise-shell glasses and the fashion sense of a lamp shade...

'There's something up there,' Lewis said. 'In the

aetheric. I think it's a rip into the Void.'

'Come again?'

'The Void.' He finally lifted his gaze and met mine. 'The place where demons come from. Where they reach through to leave the Mark.'

Oh yeah, I know all about the Mark. Had one, didn't enjoy it nearly as much as you'd think. Something about demons trying to claw their way out from inside me, incubating like baby spiders in the helpless stunned body of an insect...ugh. Not a pleasant memory. The thought of a repeat engagement filled me with a sharp-edged sense of anxiety. 'There's a demon trying to get through?'

'Not at the moment.' Lewis let the bottle roll out of his fingers onto the tabletop, and prodded it gently around in a circle. 'Doesn't mean one won't. We need to shut the door and seal it.'

'And when you say *we*, that's a royal I'm-the-biggest-bad-ass-Warden-there-is-and-I-don't-need-any-help sort of *we*, right?' Because I really didn't much like where this conversational trail of bread-crumbs was leading. There was a witch at the end of it, and an oven, and a really unpleasant fairy tale.

'I mean that I can't do it alone,' he said. He sucked in a deep breath and came out with it. 'I need a Djinn.'

'Hey, fine, just pull one out of backstock and fire it up there, buddy.'

'I freed them. All the ones I had.' He shrugged.

'Seemed like a good idea at the time. I agree with David about the slavery issue, and besides, I wasn't planning on needing one any time soon.'

'And yet here you are.'

'Yes.' He stopped playing with the bottle, folded his hands together, and just looked at me.

'Oh, no, don't even,' I said. 'I'm nowhere near ready for that kind of thing. Ask Patrick.'

'I did.'

I shot a hot, disbelieving, wide-eyed look at my so-called mentor in his porn Disney get-up. He'd manifested some kind of breakfast while I wasn't looking, but it didn't look anything like a traditional bacon-and-eggs kind of thing; some kind of lumpy-looking yogurt stuff, thin little flaps of something that looked like unfolded blintzes, and a weirdly coloured fruit mishmash. Whatever country it was from wasn't anyplace I ever wanted to visit, or at least eat breakfast in.

'Patrick?' I demanded.

He took a bite of fruit surprise with no evidence of discomfort. 'Joanne?' He put an entire argument into my name, and I lost. He turned his attention back to Lewis. 'She's made progress, but she needs to understand the flows of power. Over time, she could learn, but she doesn't have time. If she's going to make it through this, she has to have a jump start. Such as the one you propose.'

'Hey, pardon me, but nobody's jumping me, OK?' I sucked in a couple of deep cleansing breaths, and tried to be reasonable. 'Just to be clear, you want me to agree to be your Djinn? Your slave?'

Lewis had the grace to look appalled at the idea. 'No! Employee. And only for a short time, maybe an hour or so. When the job's done, I smash the bottle, you're free again.'

'And even if I believe you, what makes you think I can do this thing you want done? 'Cause I'm not exactly the most competent Djinn on the block, in case you haven't heard. In fact, most of these guys barely consider me half of one.'

Patrick grunted and shovelled in pale grey yogurt with lime green chunks floating in it. 'Less than half,' he said. 'I'm afraid that to them, you're a parasite. Better off dead.'

'Yeah, see? Parasite. I'm a parasite. You need somebody reliable. Like David.'

Lewis's face had become a still life. How anybody could sit that quietly… 'I can't find David. Rahel turned me down. Patrick recommended you.'

'And that's your entire list? What about the three you freed?' Because I was thinking hey, talk about owing favours…but his tense expression didn't relax. I wasn't breaking any new ground.

'They're gone,' he said. 'No longer on this plane of existence.'

I tossed that one to Patrick for an explanation. He gave another insouciant shrug. 'They don't want to be imprisoned again. You can understand their point of view. I myself am not willing to risk it, either. And while I trust that Lewis wouldn't even consider it unless it was an emergency, I'm afraid that an emergency to the Wardens doesn't necessarily constitute an emergency to *me*. There are plenty of Wardens equipped with Djinn. Let one of them handle it.'

Lewis's chin set in that stubborn line. A muscle flickered in his jaw. 'They can't see it. I think the only ones who can are the Djinn and humans with all three forms of Warden powers.'

'Meaning, only you.'

Lewis nodded.

Patrick slurped through another spoonful of slimy crap. 'My, doesn't that just make you indispensable, my friend? Fate of the world, depending on you? Whatever did we do before you came along?'

And the award for most cutting sarcasm goes to... Even I flinched. Lewis, not accustomed to having people accuse him of megalomania, just blinked and looked a little lost. 'I'm just giving you the facts.'

'The fact is that you *want* it to be you.' Patrick levelled a spoon at Lewis like a nun with a ruler, ready to slap hands. 'You need to be the hero, boy. A common human failing.'

Lewis opened his mouth, shut it with a snap, and pushed his chair back. 'Fine. Sorry to have bothered you. I'll just see myself out then. Oh, and I love what you've done with the place, Patrick. Kind of a whole Christopher-Lowell-goes-over-to-the-dark-side thing.'

Another shovelful of crap into Patrick's mouth, this time the weird otherworldly-looking flat blintzes. 'Oh, don't be so sensitive. I didn't say you were necessarily wrong. Occasionally you *should* be the hero. I'm just saying that it's not a good habit to acquire. No long-term prospects. Cowards live longer.'

Lewis, already standing, wavered indecisively between staying and going. I put my coffee down and stood up, too. 'I understand what you're trying to do,' I said. 'I just don't think I'm ready.'

'Yeah. I get it. Thanks anyway.'

He turned to go. I grabbed him by the arm. 'I didn't say no. Convince me.'

'Of what?'

'Why I'm ready.'

He moved closer, or maybe it just felt that way; he had that kind of aura. Once it grabbed hold, it sucked you in. I felt weightless, drawn in by the intensity of his power and conviction.

'It doesn't matter if you're ready,' he said. 'Nothing ever stops you, Jo. Nothing ever has. I need you because you're the only person I've ever known who's completely incapable of losing a fight.'

I felt a blush burn hot up through me – not a human blush, not really, this was more happening on the aetheric level than travelling through capillaries – and I said, with more humility than I probably ever had in my life, 'Yeah, well, you don't know very many people, Lewis. Your communication skills kind of suck.'

He gave me a long, slow smile. 'You didn't always think so.'

Which led me to memories that were neither situation-appropriate nor really germane, but were damn nice to recall. Storm energy flaring all around us, two bodies naked and moving in that sweet, hot rhythm, lubricated by sweat and lust and the awesome power of the moment...

Not a bad way to lose your virginity, all things considered.

'So,' he said, and raised his eyebrows. There was that cute little line between his eyebrows again, the one I wanted to smooth away with my thumb. 'In or out, Jo?'

Patrick, still sitting at the table, rustled his paper as he turned pages to check out the funnies. 'She's in.'

Lewis didn't glance at him. 'Is she?'

I reached out and scooped the perfume vial off the table. I held it out and dropped it into his open palm, then folded his fingers closed over it. 'Guess so.'

There was a surprising lack of ceremony to the whole thing. First we waited for Patrick to finish his breakfast, which looked more revolting by the moment, and then for him to shuffle off to another room with his paper and unmentionable bathrobe. Lewis and I played *my-God-how-tacky-is-that?* with Patrick's collection of objets d'crap, finally coming to the conclusion that only a going-out-of-business sale at a whorehouse could really explain a lot of it. When my own personal Obi-Wannabe reappeared, he looked sober and dressed for action in khaki slacks, a black silk shirt, and around his neck some kind of silvery chain that had a bit of the disco period to it.

Lewis excused himself. I watched him go, then turned my attention back to Patrick.

'Does this have the Jonathan seal of approval?' I asked. It was kind of a joke. And kind of not. Patrick shot me a nakedly assessing look.

'Jonathan doesn't concern himself with the details of the manufacturing process,' he said. His lips twitched into a strange little smile. 'Not anymore. Although he once was – how would you say it? – a great deal more hands-on in his management style.'

I settled down on the banana couch and drew my legs up more comfortably, hugging the tacky leopard throw close around my shoulders. There was a chill in the air – or, more likely, in me. 'You know, nobody's been overly forthcoming about the guy. What's his deal?'

'Jonathan?' Patrick's thick white eyebrows climbed heavenward. 'You realise you're asking a foolish question?'

'An obvious no.'

The eyebrows compressed again, this time into a frown. 'You can know the history of anything and anyone you wish, Joanne. All it takes is a bit of concentration. You should know this.' He looked woefully disappointed in me. 'You tell *me* about Jonathan.'

He reached out and touched me with one blunt finger, right in the centre of my forehead.

It was like being hit by a cement truck at eighty miles an hour, head on.

My head exploded into colour, light, chaos, pain, heat, cold, fury. I gasped and struggled to hang on to something, flailed around, found a memory. I grabbed it and held to it with iron strength.

Jonathan, handing me the cold, sweating beer bottle.

Jonathan's eyes, dark and endless as space, meeting mine for the first time.

There. Patrick's silent whisper in my head. *Go there.*

He shoved me, hard, from behind, and I tumbled out of control into chaos.

When I got my footing again – whatever footing consisted of, in this place – I was standing on a raw piece of rock, dizzyingly high up, and an ice-sharp wind blew through me. It caught my long black hair and snapped it back like a battle flag. I was different, here. Snow-pale, dressed in filmy black robes that rose on the wind like a cloud.

I faltered when I realised that I was inches from the drop, that gravity was singing to me like a siren. I dropped down into a crouch and put both hands on the cold stone. Lightning flashed in a hot pastel curtain overhead, and far down below, far down in the mud, men were dying.

I could feel that. Feel every wound, hear every scream, taste every drop of blood being shed.

'And it came to pass, when he had made an end of speaking unto Saul, that the soul of Jonathan was knit with the soul of David, and Jonathan loved him as his own soul,' Patrick whispered. He was next to me, solid and flaring white-hot. Beside him, behind him, a black ice-edged shadow. 'Although this is not that Jonathan, or that David, the verse is still true. If you want to know about Jonathan, you will know it here.'

Here. That was the Ifrit's silent whisper. I looked down, trembling, wanting desperately to go because there was so much death here, so much pain.

So many dying.

There was one who shone. Glittered with power. *Warden.* He was tall, spare, moving with grace and speed as he turned and fought against the ones coming at him. The lightning kept calling to him, but he wouldn't answer. The *Earth* was calling to him, her voice like thunder, like rivers flowing, like the slow rising cry of mountains.

He wouldn't answer her.

'Oh God,' I whispered. 'He's like Lewis.'

No, he was *more* than Lewis. The world itself was wrapped around him, through him, like a lover holding him. Not just a man who controlled the elements, but was loved by them.

Fiercely defended.

Rain sheeted down, silver as tears.

He was rejecting her love, there on the battlefield. He was fighting as a man, not a Warden. Sword in his hand, solid blows of metal on metal, his leather and metal armour taking cut after cut. Blood...

I felt it coming. The world around me felt it coming.

A lunge. A spear angling up, punching past hardened leather and too-soft bronze, ripping...

I cried out. It didn't matter, the whole world was crying out, the Mother crying out for her dying child, and even though I was at the mountain's peak, looking down on a struggle of ants, I could *see* Jonathan, see him struggling to pull the spear out of his chest with both hands, face fierce and bloody with determination.

No no no...

Lightning hit him, burnt the spear to ash, melted metal.

Transforming him in a crucible of pure fire. That wasn't just lightning, not just energy and plasma and science. That was something else.

Pure, implacable *magic*.

Someone else on the battlefield crying out, too, crawling through thick bloody mud, a man, just a man – dying already, with a dagger buried in his chest.

Crawling into the fires of life in a useless attempt to save his friend.

There was a feeling of an indrawn breath.

Every creature left in that valley died – sucked instantly dry of life, of breath, of soul. Gone. Empty bodies fell as one, thousands of them, gone. It spread in a ripple of falling corpses and armour in concentric circles from the place that lightning still danced and raged.

It kept spreading. Farther. Shepherds and sheep dying on hills miles away. A village, twenty miles farther. A city of thousands falling limp.

'Stop!' I screamed. But it wasn't going to stop. The raving grief of the world was pouring out, like blood from a heart wound, and it was going to take everything in its madness.

Patrick's hand pressed my shoulder, hard. I heard his deep intake of breath...

...and saw one man drag another out of the white flare of lightning, far below.

Whole. Unharmed.

No longer men at all.

Djinn.

'"And Jonathan told him, and said, I did but taste a little honey with the end of the rod that was in mine hand, and, lo, I must die,"' Patrick said softly. 'Now you know what it takes to make a Djinn, little bird. The wrath of the world.'

My attention was riveted on the two Djinn below. One was holding the other, staring numbly at the death around them.

Jonathan's eyes were still dark, dark as space. Dark as the day that had birthed him.

David's eyes were as copper as the dagger that had killed him.

He held Jonathan in his arms and wept in the rain, and I knew he was weeping for joy, for sorrow, for guilt because he hadn't pulled his friend out of that fire soon enough to stop all this death.

'You wanted to know about Jonathan,' Patrick continued. 'No one ever wakened the Mother before him. Pray no one ever does again.'

He touched me between the eyes, and took it all away.

It hadn't been more than a minute. I huddled there on the couch feeling cold in a rain that didn't exist, tingling from the memory of unbelievable power, and clutched the leopard throw in a death grip around my shoulders. Patrick still stood looking down at me, utterly unaffected by what I'd seen.

'How many?' I whispered. His eyebrows twitched. 'How many died?'

'That day?' He shrugged. 'Enough to create Jonathan. Enough left over to create David as well. We're born of death, didn't you know that? But so are humans. So is everything. Don't let it get you down, sunshine.'

I just sat and shivered.

Lewis emerged from the back, hesitated over the sight of me all cold and shaken, and gave Patrick a look. Patrick shrugged again. 'Jo? You OK?'

'Sure.' I closed my eyes and willed it all away. 'Why the hell wouldn't I be?'

Lewis took an uncomfortable perch on the shoe chair. Patrick himself picked a plastic thing in the shape of a hand, wished some kind of alcoholic beverage into his hand, and waited for the show with the genial half-interest of a golf fan at a tennis match.

'Go ahead,' he said. Lewis and I looked at each other. Lewis rolled the bottle between his fingers again, testing it for durability, apparently. 'Just do it. It's not that hard.'

I wasn't sure I could do this. I wasn't sure anymore I wanted to do it. *God*, if it took that much power to create a true Djinn, how was this going to help me? How could it help anyone? I squeezed my eyes tight shut again, fighting back tears.

Someone took my hand. Large, blunt, warm fingers. I looked into Patrick's sea blue, tranquil eyes.

'Do you want to die?' he asked me, very softly. 'If you do, stop now, Joanne. Stop before you suffer any longer.'

I thought about David, running through the rain and mud, bleeding out his life, reaching out for something greater than himself. Stopping the greatest power in the world – *of* the world – from consuming life.

That was my heritage.

That was what had given *me* life.

Seemed pretty damn cowardly to give it up without a fight.

'No,' I said. 'I'm fine. I'm good. Back off, Santa.' Patrick smiled and resumed his seat.

Lewis took a deep breath, opened his palm and balanced the open bottle there. 'OK. Ready?'

'No. Just get it over with.'

'Be thou bound to my service,' he said. I was expecting something portentous in his tone, but this was an off-the-cuff style, so portent-free he could have been ordering pizza. I didn't feel any different. I made a little *come on* gesture with my hand. 'Be thou bound to my service.'

Patrick leant forward on the arm – thumb? – of the plastic chair, and I wondered how it would feel to sit in a chair that was shaped like a hand. Like having your ass grabbed by a giant, maybe.

'Be thou bound to my service,' Lewis finished, and something changed.

It wasn't immediately evident to me what it was. I mean, yes, I *knew*, but it started at some cellular level and worked its way up. Fast. I felt odd, then I felt weird, then I felt out-and-out funky.

And then I came apart in a silent explosion, mist swirling, and somehow I could still see, but not with human eyes, and not in the human wavelength...not on the aetheric level, but definitely accessing some of that plane to do what I was doing.

And then the wave crested, and I felt myself being turned inside out, torn apart, remade...reborn.

Into myself. Only...different. Better. Faster. Stronger.

Dissolving.

'Hey!' I yelped, but by that time my body had given up the flesh. I was a thin grey mist, moving faster, being sucked in by a gravitational force so huge I might as well have been a dust speck moving toward a black hole.

Which was the little perfume bottle in Lewis's hand. I plunged into that tiny, tight container, squeezed like Concentrate of Djinn, and no matter how hard I tried to leak back out again, it wasn't happening.

Shock was being replaced by an all-over warm feeling of fury. Man, I didn't like this. I *so* didn't like this.

Lewis said, after what seemed like half a millennia, 'Come out, Jo.'

And the negative pressure holding me in the bottle eased. Bam, just like that. I blew out of there fast, swirled around him like a cloud of angry bees, and folded myself back down into flesh again.

It took some concentration, but this time I managed to do it pretty fast – just a fraction of a second between skin and clothes. Kind of like one of those tip-the-pen-the-clothes-come-off sort of things. Lewis looked a little surprised, and then he looked a little smirky, and then a second later he remembered he was a gentleman and pretended he hadn't seen a thing.

'You OK?' he asked. I looked down at myself and was relieved to find I was still pretty much the same person, only I'd acquired a more down-home wardrobe of blue jeans, sturdy shoes and a denim shirt. Work Djinn. I was ready to fetch and haul out on the construction site.

'I'm good,' I said absently. I was busy trying to reset the outfit to something less – literally – blue collar, but unfortunately that now seemed to be outside of my control. Lewis's doing, whether he knew it or not. Great. At least I knew what turned him on, now. Sturdy women in sensible shoes.

'You OK?'

'You just asked me that.' I looked up at him, puzzled.

He gave me a little tilted half-smile. 'Exactly. You OK?'

Oh. Rule of three. I felt the compulsion kick in, and heard my mouth say, 'Hell no, you idiot, I'm not all right! I died less than a week ago, David's being held prisoner by some bad-ass Djinn with delusions of godhood, and I just got my butt stuffed into a bottle! By you! *With crappy clothes!*'

He heaved a big sigh of relief. 'You're OK.'

'Sure. Fine. Whatever. Let's do this thing.' I was more than a little unnerved, because I damn sure hadn't meant to say any of that. Well, OK, maybe the part about crappy clothes, but the rest of it was dealing-with-it stuff. So the compulsion thing actually worked. Interesting. 'Give me an order. Something small.'

'What's the use of that?' Patrick asked. I'd forgotten all about him, but there he was, still sitting on the hand, arms folded, watching me with those crystal blue eyes and bad-Santa leer. He'd seen the same flash-peek-show that Lewis had, he just in no way imagined himself a gentleman. 'If you're going to do it, do something productive. Let her really get her feet wet.'

Lewis considered that for a few seconds, then waved a hand around vaguely at Patrick's porno theatre-circus tent apartment. 'OK. Redecorate this place.'

Patrick came up off the hand like he'd been goosed, but it was too late.

Talk about something *happening*.

Power slammed into me – rich, thick, golden, unstoppable. Lewis's potential. I now had access to everything Lewis had, everything he was, everything he could be. The amount of energy stored in him was unbelievable – enough to destroy cities, level mountains, reshape the face of the earth.

It was more than enough to do a *Trading Spaces* on Patrick's apartment.

I started at one end and swept through it like a colour-coordinating storm. The carpet morphed into a neat champagne beige. The walls turned light cream. The statues disappeared altogether in a swirl of mingled body parts, gone to bad-plaster heaven.

The porn tribute to Michelangelo was replaced by a nice mullioned ceiling, with gold accents. I added a wine red accent wall and replaced a black velvet painting of a pneumatic-breasted naked girl with a Mondrian. I didn't think I'd just stolen an original, but hey, I was new at it.

Furniture. The banana couch turned to dark leather, butter soft, with manly little brass studs on the legs. Lewis's platform shoe chair became a matching armchair.

I made Patrick's plastic hand chair disappear completely, along with the tacky chrome coffee table.

'Stop!' Patrick sounded absolutely horrified. 'What are you *doing*?'

'Public service,' I said, and added a nice brick fireplace with an art-deco brass screen. And a little china vase holding matches next to it. I turned to Lewis. 'Any special requests?'

He was squinty-eyed with glee. Truthfully, so was I. Damn, this was *fun*...unlimited power crackling at my fingertips. I could do anything. *Anything*.

'I think she's got the hang of it,' Lewis said to Patrick.

Patrick walked helplessly in circles, not knowing

which way to stare; every new revelation brought an additional flinch of despair. I fought the urge to spitefully add a copy of *Great Homes* to the new deco-styled cherry wood table because no, that would just be rubbing it in. 'Yes. I think...she might have.'

Lewis retrieved the plastic stopper on the little perfume bottle and dumped both bottle and stopper into the pocket of his blue jeans. 'Are you ready?' he asked me.

I was still on a redecorating high. 'Are you kidding?' I couldn't control the laugh that bubbled up out of me, fierce and hot with delight. 'Show me the problem. Damn, this is good!'

I felt him rise up. Since he was human, he didn't disappear in the real world; his body just stayed there, temporarily vacant. I rose with him, noting with interest the silvery cord that connected him back to his flesh, and emerged into the negative-space glittering fairyland that was the aetheric plane. It got more beautiful every time I visited, I discovered. Maybe my Djinn eyes were still adjusting, but whatever caused it, the colours were stronger this time, the glitter and shimmer and depth of them more intense. Lewis had an aura like milk glass, cool at the moment but far stronger than anything I'd seen on a human before. Not like a Djinn aura, either. Something...unique.

Human voices didn't carry well up here, so he touched me and pointed. I grabbed on to him – he was still solid here, and more or less the same in form – and we began to move across the landscape, heading up and at an angle to the right.

Way up. *Way, way* up. The earth curved away beneath us at the edges, pearl-bright and beautiful, misted in clouds. He kept pulling me. I felt what little resistance there was to aetheric travel – and there had to be some, for reasons of not-so-simple physics – begin to lessen. We were reaching the edges of where it was safe for a Warden to go.

I let go of him and hovered next to him. He lifted his hand again and pointed. This time I could feel the force of will that went with it, the compulsion that would guide me to the destination.

Way the hell out there. Farther than even Patrick had taken me.

Into someplace that, in this reality, wasn't even really space.

I had no choice, I found; I was already moving. I felt Lewis's hand touch me one last time, gently, as I darted away, swimming like a fast, elegant mermaid through that sea of increasingly thin resistance.

I set myself to glide the rest of the way, and before long I saw it. Not so much a presence as an absence; space out here was big and empty and a kind of neutral grey, shot here and there with fleeting speckles of power being transferred from one place to another. I braked myself, spreading thin against the barely felt touch of the sun, and hovered, considering the problem. The Void didn't manifest itself here, on this plane. I'd have to go up to see it.

Up from the aetheric are other levels, but David had already warned me not to go exploring on my own without a guide; David, however, was nowhere to be seen. And I had a compulsion.

Three layers up was the highest possible level of the known universe, at least the highest we could reach. Its most primitive, primal form. The black-and-white template for the sixteen million colours used back on Earth. It was hard to focus on anything for long, because there were no familiar landmarks, nothing that conformed to human sensibilities. Just swirls, drifts, eddies. I couldn't even get a sense of the rhythm of the place, although I was sure it had one. Either the heartbeat was so simple and subtle it defied detection, or so complex and multi-layered I couldn't hope to understand it. Either way, not helpful.

It took me a while, watching, to realise that there was a kind of order to the chaos.

Everything moved in the same direction. It moved in circles, sometimes, but the circles were always counter-clockwise, just like the flow of the wind-fluid-matter stream.

There was one area moving in the other direction. Clockwise. I focused on it, stared hard, and felt a kind of *absence* there, a kind of grey confusion. It didn't want to be found, this thing. It was a trap door into our world, and it was designed to stay hidden. I drifted slowly over to it, moving against the current, and paused at the very edges of the spiral.

It felt like...nothing. In fact, I couldn't even be sure that I'd touched it at all, except visually, where the fog phased into a bluish colour as it came into contact with my presently-not-solid form. Was that good? I couldn't tell. My senses weren't helping me out at all on this one. As far as I could tell, this swirling eddy looked just like all the other swirling eddies, except that this one went right instead of left. Not a lot to go on, really. I would have preferred a nice big sign that said THIS WAY TO THE VOID, but I supposed I'd have to settle for what I could get.

I reached for the hot golden flow of Lewis's power, and began the strange job of closing off the rift. Where I touched the moving pool of energy, I sampled the normal space around it and began replicating it over the tear. It was a little like darning – take good material, stretch it over bad stuff, tack it in place.

It was also *hard*. The stuff kept slipping under my touch, trying to writhe away. Definitely not just some hole in space. This thing was alive, and it didn't like me. I persisted. It resisted. Little by little, I gained on it.

I was almost done when it gave one last, convulsive twist, turned, and jumped right out of the fabric of space and tore into *me*.

If it had been the normal world I'd have stumbled backwards, screamed, and tried to slap the thing off of me; it was definitely, horribly alive. What was worse, I couldn't even really sense it. If I lost sight of it...

I wrapped both hands around it – or what passed for hand-equivalents here – and began to squeeze. All of Lewis's potential flooded into me, concentrated into my grip and gave it world-crushing strength.

I felt the thing give with a hot little *pop*. It dissolved into a rain of silvery light, cold and glittering and totally undetectable as soon as it passed beyond my aura.

I'd seen that stuff before. Where?...with David. On the aetheric level. He'd thought it was odd then.

Now I knew where it had come from.

The rip tore open again and started whirling widdershins again. Oh *man*...that hadn't gone well. As I brushed my hand over the surface I saw that sparkle again, saw the fireflies leaping out, away, into the primal essence of the universe.

This was really, really not good. And now I had ripple effects to deal with from the rip coming open again. That had sent shock waves of power throughout the planes – I'd felt it myself, like a sonic boom in my soul.

I left that plane and took the express down, and I didn't like what I was seeing. Swirling clouds of silver fog on the next level. Hot invisible winds that stank of sulphur on the next.

In the aetheric, power was swirling like dust caught on the leading edge of a storm. I dropped back down next to Lewis, who was busy trying to get control of the thing – not a task for one Warden, no matter how powerful – and I quickly reached out to amplify what he was doing, pulling back waves of charged particles, changing the frequencies of vibrating and propagating wave forms. I started negative cancelling waves to try to flatten out the effects, and felt Lewis's burst of affirmation. *Yes!* We did it together, levelling, smoothing, pouring figurative oil on the literal waters.

I took hold of Lewis and pulled him down to the real-world level again. He thumped back into his body with a little plucked-string sound that was probably audible only on levels a Djinn could hear. I did the hi-I'm-naked-no-I'm-not thing again, wishing Patrick weren't so intensely scoping me out, and realised I had my hand flat against Lewis's chest. Mmm. The crisp, cool feel of his cotton shirt under my skin, the warm tingle of body underneath...

If I thought I'd been flying high after the decorating, I was definitely pulling g-forces now. My whole body was humming and vibrating, like it had just been through the best sex of its life.

'Wow,' I said involuntarily, and then blushed and

dropped my hand and stepped back. 'Um...did we...'

'Afraid not,' Lewis said. Was that a nice flush to his cheeks? Sure looked like it. 'The rip's still there, I can feel it. Now we've got other problems to take care of.'

'The waves?' I wasn't talking about the ocean, but the aetheric; he got the reference.

'There's a pretty severe widespread disturbance, and it's running through all the manifestations. There's stress under the tectonic plates in California. There's a supercell forming out in the Atlantic. There's a forest fire starting in Yellowstone.' That gave me a hot twitch of memory. Yellowstone was very sensitive to powerful forces, and once it got going, even the combined might of the Fire Wardens was only going to slow it down. Having emergencies manifest in three different ways would split the ability of the Wardens to act effectively – the Earth Wardens couldn't get in to help the Fire Wardens contain any blaze; the Weather Wardens couldn't help dump water to slow it down. If each of them had their own separate but equal crisis...

He gave me a very direct look. 'I promised you it would be one favour. Not two.' He took the empty bottle out of his pocket and held it up. 'I'll keep my word.'

'I know.' I did. Lewis wasn't a saint, thank God, but he was definitely a man of ethics and honour.

'I'm releasing you from it. Not only did I not close the rip, I think I might have made it worse. Besides, you need me for this. There's something majorly weird about this.'

He bent his head, an old-fashioned gesture of salute and gratitude. It occurred to me, late and strangely, that he had no alter ego presence in Oversight. Lewis was Lewis, whatever set of eyes I used to look at him. I was used to seeing humans as they thought of themselves – a plain girl as a ravishing beauty, a corporate-type guy as a knight in shining armour. But Lewis didn't have any illusions, or any false fronts. He just *was*.

'Let's get to work,' he said. His voice was husky, low, and full of an emotion he didn't want me to hear.

Lewis took over where he was strongest – manipulating the earth itself, struggling to bleed off energy that was building up to a major break-California-off-into-the-ocean explosion. I went to the sea.

The Atlantic, on its best days, doesn't have the peace of the Pacific – the light is different, out here. The waves seem glassier, more knife-edged, and the sense of something moving under the surface is very strong. I sped along on the aetheric and formed myself back into human flesh, but kept myself hovering about ten feet over the surface of the water, feeling the energy flow. This hadn't changed.

I still had the instincts of a Weather Warden, even if I no longer had the same physical channels.

The ocean was cool and edgy underneath me, muttering in the language of power; there was something unsettled here, but it wasn't the usual evaporative cycle stirring up trouble in the troposphere or mesosphere. No, this was something else. Nothing I could sense, specifically, and that worried me. I traced the cooling and warming cycle. Sunlight on water, evaporating drops to mist...mist rising, cooling as it went...droplets drawing each other into close embrace, forming clouds...clouds growing denser as the drops crowded closer, and energy was released...warm air up, cold air sinking, pressing out the clouds into energy-storing layers.

Nothing unusual here. But there *was* something wrong.

Something in the clouds. Something that shouldn't be there.

It was – what?

I rose up, feeling the mist chill on my skin, sliding like invisible rain...then the drops forming, soaking my denim shirt. I was heavy with dew. The air had the metallic taste of ozone, and it scraped the back of my throat when I pulled in a cool, thick breath.

I saw a tinkle of blue at the corner of my eye.

And then I knew.

Shit!

I flamed out of there, *fast*, blew myself into mist and reformed and hoped I hadn't taken in too much of it, and then I bugged out of there, arrowing for Lewis at top speed.

I almost ran into Patrick, who was still ambling around his house, staring morosely at the politically correct ceiling; I didn't stop to apologise, just misted right through him and braked myself out into human form. *Way* better this time. Apparently, panic greatly enhanced my organisational skills.

'It's the sparkly stuff!' I yelled. Lewis wasn't there, at least he wasn't in spirit; he was out of his body again, up in the aetheric. I shot up a level, followed the thread, found him doing whatever it is Earth Wardens do to control earthquakes. Not that I'm not sympathetic to the damage a big shake can cause, but once I spotted him I tackled him like a noseguard, snapped him right out of the aetheric and down into himself with a thud.

He staggered, braced himself with a hand on the back of the leather couch, and smacked the other onto his forehead. Owww. I'm guessing that I'd hurt him.

'What?' he yelled at me.

'It's the goddamn blue stuff! Fairy dust! Sparklies!' I repeated, louder than him. 'Listen, when I tried to seal this thing, it sent out this puff of – coldlight. Looks like glitter. I didn't think it was anything, really. But it's *here*!'

'What?' He was still dazed. I'd given him a hell of a shot.

'It's here in the clouds. And this crap is *weird*,

Lewis. I can't really feel it, I can only see it when I touch it. It has a kind of – sparkle.'

'Sparkle?' His eyes had taken on a hard, opaque shine. 'You slammed me out of there and disrupted me for a *sparkle*? Tell me you're kidding—'

'Listen!' I yelled over him. '*It's everywhere! It's in everything!* It shouldn't *be* here!'

He was starting to get it. The opacity was fading out of his eyes, being replaced by a clear, deep look of alarm.

'I don't know what the hell it's doing, or how the hell to stop it. Tell me you know.'

His mouth opened, but there wasn't an answer forthcoming. In fact, he looked downright speechless.

'Oh hell,' I supplied for both of us. 'I'm glad you're the boss, because as far as I can tell, we're totally fucked.'

Next stop: panic city. Everybody out for the apocalypse.

Big problem. There was nothing wrong with the weather patterns over the Atlantic, anyone with an ounce of Weather sense could tell. And yet, the supercell shouldn't have been there, according to physics. It made absolutely no sense. If I'd still been in the Wardens, I knew there would have been conference calls in progress, with people eyeing this thing from different sides and trying to figure out what the hell was going on. I wondered if they could see the sparklies, and I thought they probably couldn't. Whatever the stuff was, it barely radiated in a wavelength Djinn could see, much less humans. No, I was pretty sure that they wouldn't be able to figure it out.

Which left me, and Lewis, and maybe Patrick. And any other Djinn we could convince to take a look.

'Clearly,' I said, as Lewis and Patrick and I compared notes, 'this stuff's not natural to our planes of existence. Can you see it?'

I'd directed the question to Lewis, and he indicated a no. 'Everything looks normal up on the aetheric.'

'Yeah. That's what bugs me. Because it doesn't look at all normal to me.' I couldn't sit still; I got up and paced, wished I had on something besides blue denim and work boots, because this was a situation that screamed for bitchen black leather and tight boots. *These boots are made for walkin'*... 'The stuff's like evil pollen. Who knew it could sift through three planes of existence and end up here so fast?'

'Unless it's been coming through the rift for a while,' Lewis said. 'That's possible. The fact that you just now saw it might have nothing to do with it, really. If it's something subtle and largely undetectable, we could have a problem that's been slowly getting worse.'

'It's not pollen,' Patrick said. He was in the far corner of the living room now, straightening a

Monet landscape under the recessed lights. 'From your description, it's more like radiation. You said that David tried to seal some in an energy bubble?'

'Yeah. Didn't work.'

'That's very interesting,' Patrick said, and stepped back to admire the Monet from a distance. 'That means that the normal aetheric barriers can't stop it, because they're all energy-based. This...coldlight, for lack of a better word...seems very dangerous indeed.'

Lewis looked up from his contemplation of the carpet. 'We don't even know that it *is* dangerous.'

'It issues from a hole into the Void where demons lie,' Patrick pointed out. 'It's rare that something of that pedigree turns out to be happy fairy dust.'

'Not that I doubt you, but are you sure it's not just that you're not used to your new senses yet?' Lewis asked me. Which was, actually, not a stupid question at all.

'I don't know,' I said, with a great deal less arrogance and a great deal more honesty than I usually had. 'Ask him, he's got a few centuries on me.'

Patrick was rambling the apartment again, looking lost and morose; he was milking it, of course. Not like he couldn't have fixed everything back the way it was, if he'd wanted. Maybe he was adjusting to it. 'What?' he asked, although I knew he'd been listening to every word. We'd been a lot more interesting than the stacked bowl of Chinese ornamental balls on the coffee table. 'Bother. I can't give an opinion until I've had a look.'

'Then come on.' I held out my hand. He ignored that, put his arm around me, and copped a feel. Which, thankfully, was a little insulated by the sensible denim that Lewis had chosen for me to wear. I moved his hand without more than a sidelong look, and up and away we went.

Well, Patrick said, in the way Djinn have of communicating up there in the aetheric, *that's different*.

We hung there for a while, watching the storm rotating and building while the fragile milk-glass bursts of power came from all sides, like flashbulbs going off around a celebrity. Wardens at work. They looked weirdly anaemic to me, now, but I could feel the hot blue pulse of other Djinn focusing and defining that force, putting it to precision work.

The only trouble was that there was nothing to fix here – nothing that *could* be fixed. The storm was slowly building. I'd already tried all the traditional stuff – disrupting the convection engine that was feeding the process; adding cooling layers underneath to isolate the updrafts; bringing in strong dry winds to shred the structure of the thing.

Nothing worked. And the Wardens who were trying it now were clearly singing from the same choir book, so we were going to be well into the second verse soon which would be, in the immortal words of Herman's Hermits, the same as the first.

Look, I said to Patrick, braced for it, and trailed a very small part of myself through the mist.

A blue, sparkling pocket galaxy flared where I touched. I shook myself – how was it possible for my flesh to creep when I didn't even have a body? – and watched the shining stuff float free like a festive, toxic cloud. Patrick's low, pulsing aura backed hastily away from it.

What the hell is it? I asked him. I got a hot orange pulse of alarm in response. *OK, were there actual words with that?*

Not ones I'd care to repeat in English, he sent back. *I suppose the nearest equivalent would be, I haven't the vaguest fucking idea. Nor do I have any desire to. And I'm leaving before I have a much closer acquaintance with it. I suggest you get your ass out of here as well. Now.*

He vanished instantly. Talk about bugging out – he wasted no time at all. I'd never seen a Djinn have a panic attack, but that looked like one to me. And hell, I was kind of having one myself. Not feeling especially fine about my part in all this.

I bugged out right on his tail, and followed the contrail back home. We touched down into the newly renovated apartment at the same time, and this time I managed the reconstitution without any R rating. Once I thought of it as math – higher math, but still math – all I had to do was expand the equation of me to include the outfit. Better still, it was simple to vary it. Change a variable, here and there, and you get something suitable for wearing to a star-spangled party. Or a bag lady convention.

The one thing I could *not* seem to get right – still – was hair. Well, I'd never been a wizard at it in my mortal life, either. Maybe I was just destined to be curly.

Patrick wasn't thinking about my hair; he was thinking about what he'd seen and backed hastily away from. He pointed a shaking finger at me, couldn't think of anything to say, and swung around on Lewis, who had arrested a restless pacing to stare at the two of us.

'You!' Patrick snapped. 'If you'd just left well enough alone...'

Lewis made no reply. He just resumed pacing.

'How did this get to be Lewis's fault?' I blurted, and then wished I hadn't. I mean, obviously, it got to be his fault because he'd ordered me to meddle. Dammit. 'Cancel that. What I meant was, what do we do now?'

'Yell for help. Loudly. Repeatedly.' Patrick walked over to the telephone a – tasteful cream-coloured unobtrusive one, to replace the Harley-Davidson model he'd been using before – and started dialling. 'And then take a very long vacation, some-place else.'

Which I didn't think would do a damn bit of good, because if this stuff had seeped down this far, it had probably contaminated the higher levels, too. Unless he meant Aruba, which was probably not glitter-free either, but still very nice this time of year.

'I'll tell the Wardens,' Lewis said. 'But I'd like to do it in person. Jo—'

'Who are you calling?' I asked Patrick, since Lewis hadn't phrased it in the form of an order and was probably too polite to do it for at least another five minutes. Patrick finished dialling a number that was too long to be to any country on Earth. He didn't speak, just hung up the phone. I understood instinctively what he'd been doing – not dialling a phone, in any real way, but using the metaphorical human device to send a message through the aetheric, a kind of sympathetic magic. I even knew who he was calling. 'Oh, God, you're calling Jonathan.'

'Who won't show his face,' Patrick said, with a bitter-lemon twist of his lips that made me wonder just how comfortable *that* relationship was. 'He doesn't leave his house.'

'Why?'

'Because it doesn't exist on any of the planes. It's a kind of…' Patrick paused for thought. 'Bubble, I suppose you'd say. It's for all of our protection. If Jonathan was ever claimed, the consequences… Let's say they wouldn't be good. Not good at all.'

So maybe Jonathan's plush little refuge wasn't by his choice. Which made me wonder just who really was in charge, among my new friends and family. Politics. Still hate 'em. Djinn politics just made my head hurt worse than human ones.

Ten seconds or less later, I felt a kind of shift in the room, like some balance of energy had tipped. It was subtle, but it made me wonder...

...and then Rahel walked out of the master bedroom, examining her talons with a critical, casual grace. She looked up, acknowledged Patrick with a fast, white glint of teeth in her dark-skinned face, and then slowly took stock of the room.

'Love the makeover,' she said. 'Since I doubt you grew any taste since last I saw you, I imagine Sistah Snow was behind it. Yes?'

Her smile faded fast when we started talking. A quick trip to the aetheric to show her the contamination, and back down to reality to see Rahel's completely unnerving frown. Her eyes were glowing, hot and gold, and she just looked, well, *strong*. Strong enough to dissolve me into a sticky pool on the carpet just with the force of that stare.

'I'm sorry,' I said. It was totally inadequate.

She didn't blink. 'Not your fault,' she said, which was not at all what I expected to hear. 'This is something I have never seen, either. I would have done the same, if I had been given the same order. With perhaps exactly the same result.'

'So what do we do?' Lewis asked.

A short, pregnant silence. Her stare didn't seem quite so menacing, but it was still as intense as a laser.

'I think,' she said slowly, and transferred the gaze to Lewis, 'that perhaps I should consult with

Jonathan and find a way to make this right. You stay here. The fewer who travel the aetheric, the better, until we know what the consequences might be.'

'I'll go,' I said.

Rahel looked at me sharply, and unpleasant recognition dawned in cat-bright eyes. 'Ah,' she said. 'I did not see it at first, because it changed you very little. But still you're claimed, aren't you? And chained.'

'It's not so bad,' I said. 'All the build-up, I was expecting something a lot worse.'

'A good master makes a good servant.' She leant on the word *servant* with a heavy weight of disdain. 'I don't think this is at all wise. Lewis, you should know better.'

'I wouldn't have claimed her if you'd given me a choice.'

Ouch, the look that swept between them was like two master fencers, lunge and parry and riposte faster than thought. Lewis certainly felt comfortable around Djinn. I wondered when familiarity had happened to breed that particular contempt.

'I am *not* your slave,' Rahel said.

'Apparently, you don't believe in working for a living, either.'

'*Sssst!*' It was less a sound than a burst of electricity from her, snapping like a whip. It didn't touch Lewis. I don't think he even flinched. 'Djinn did not make this portal, did not create this *pollution* you speak of. Humans meddled in things they didn't understand, and this is the result. Chaos.'

'Djinn being perfect.'

'More perfect than...'

'Excuse me,' I said loudly, 'can we please focus on the problem? Because I for one don't really feel this is getting us anywhere.'

Rahel looked murderous. Junior half-Djinn were not supposed to get uppity, apparently.

'Where's David?' I asked.

She favoured me with something that looked dangerously close to a sneer.

'Running to your saviour?' she asked, sweet as a batch of overcooked fudge. 'Jonathan has a use for him. You're to learn to fly for yourself, little bird.'

'Fine. Then let's go see Jonathan,' I said.

She stopped me with an outstretched hand. Did the fingernails look longer and sharper? Yeah. Definitely. 'Slaves do not go there.'

'Excuse me?'

She flicked her eyes toward Lewis. 'Nor do humans. I will go. *Not* you.'

'She's *not* a slave,' Lewis said, and stepped into Rahel's space. He was taller, broader, but I couldn't be sure he was stronger. In fact, the chances of him even holding his own against her were thin. 'She's an ally. I don't suppose you get the concept.'

'An ally who accepts any order you choose to

issue, no matter how degrading? Who has no choice but to comply?' Rahel swept me with a hard look. 'Do not fool yourself, little Snow. A slave with a kind master is still a slave.' The look ripped Lewis, too. 'And a slave's master has no honour.'

'Maybe I'm crazy, but I have the strong feeling that if we don't get this straightened out, it may not matter whether I'm free or not. Everybody gets the same crappy deal.'

'Likely you're correct.' She quirked her head to the side, an alien-looking catlike movement that made me jump a little. 'And yet I will not take you.'

Fine. I plopped down on the comfortable brown leather sofa and put my work-booted feet up on the coffee table. 'I'll just sit and watch the world get eaten, then. Hey, be sure to call me if the apocalypse comes. I need to get some 400-speed film, make sure I get good pictures.'

She gave me a snarl, and vanished. *Whoosh*. There was a breeze – displacement of air – and I transferred my stare to Patrick. He looked blank and angelic. Put a red suit on him, and he could be handing out candy in a mall and asking kids what they wanted Santa to bring them.

'You're not going?' I asked.

He cleared his throat. 'Let's say that I'm not welcome in those particular circles.'

'Because of the way you were made Djinn?'

'Among other things.' He shrugged. 'I've learnt to live with disappointment.' He stretched out his arms and manifested a light camel-coloured coat, something appropriate for a spring day. 'I have not, however, learnt to live with this…redecorating. I believe I'll go for a walk. Call me if the world ends, there's a dear.'

He blipped out. I stared at the spot where he'd been, frowning and wishing I still lived in a world where people used doors.

Lewis ambled around and settled down next to me.

'So,' he said.

'So,' I agreed. 'Son of a bitch.'

'Who, me?'

'The situation.'

'Ah.' He rubbed his hands lightly together. 'Guess I'd better get back to work. I've got the pressure mostly relieved in the plates around the San Andreas, but I need to get a team of Earth Wardens on it. And the Fire Wardens need the tip-off about the Yellowstone fire, too.'

He glanced over at me, eyebrows up.

'What?' I asked.

'That was a codependent way of asking you to do it for me.'

'You want me to run your *errands*? Bite me, Lewis.' After Rahel's rather rabble-rousing speeches about slavery, I wasn't feeling any too subservient. 'How'd the rip form in the first place?'

'I don't know,' Lewis said. 'Like Rahel said, this is new. I've never heard of this stuff coming through before. It's almost always a demon, reaching through to put the Mark on a human; once the Mark matures, they can make the crossing to the human plane directly, without going through the aetheric levels. Safer for them. But this stuff...'

'Maybe it can be destroyed.'

'We don't even know what it does.'

'Yeah, but even so I think we'd better work from Patrick's theory: nothing good ever comes out of the Void...'

I stopped, hesitated. There was something...

'Jo?' He was staring at me, wide-eyed. I wondered how bright my eyes had just flared.

'Stay here,' I said, and got up to take a look around.

The first thing I spotted after passing into the kitchen was the almost-there shadow of Patrick's Ifrit, hiding in the gloom behind. Watching me. That predatory interest made the hair stand up on my neck.

'Hey,' I said to it, and took a step closer. She shrank farther into shadow – not aggressive today, certainly not the ripping, shrieking fiend that Patrick had set on me just yesterday in training sessions. 'Don't be afraid. I'm not going to hurt you.'

'It's not you I'm afraid of,' it said. 'Don't blame him for this. He doesn't understand.'

'Understand what?'

'It will kill all of you.'

For some reason, I didn't have any doubt about what it was. 'You can see it? This light? You know, the glitter?' She nodded, or at least I thought she did. 'Do you know what it is?'

'Yes.' A bare, sighing breath. I felt myself tense up. 'Knowing will not help you.'

'Why?'

'It does not help me.'

Great, Ifrit were just as evasive as Djinn when it came to the important stuff. 'Look, just tell me, if you know. What is this stuff? How do we stop it?'

'It is life,' she whispered. 'It is love. It is death.'

Point taken – Ifrit were *more* evasive. 'How about in more, you know, technical terms…?'

She seemed to be trying to tell me, struggling to describe something that she didn't have a language to cover. 'It has happened before.'

'But Rahel said…'

'She was not told.'

'Sara…'

'*Do not say my name!*' It was a cry of mortal pain. 'You don't understand. Love consumes. Love *must* consume.'

I heard Lewis say something from the other room, his voice rising into a question.

'Lewis?' I called.

The Ifrit said, 'He is a man. Men are weak. They don't always see…' Was she talking about Lewis?

Patrick? I had no idea, but she wasn't making any sense that existed in my reality. Ifrits were crazy, I knew that much already. 'You must choose. I could not.'

'OK,' I said, and held up my hands in surrender. 'I'll choose. No problem. Ah...Lewis?'

I backed away – not quite confident enough to give her my undefended back – and came out into the living room again.

Patrick was back, and he'd brought friends. Two of them, to be precise. He was in the process of taking his coat off and hanging it on a tacky-looking gold rack – had I put that there? Ack! – while the other two looked around, evidently checking out my interior decorating skills. I didn't know the kid – sixteen, seventeen at most – who stood looking pale and mutinous and typically disaffected; he pushed hands into his pants pockets and slumped in a don't-notice-me attitude. He needed a haircut, but that was probably just the generation gap talking.

The woman had her back to me, but those curves looked familiar.

'Patrick?' I asked. His too-blue eyes flashed to me, and then away. He looked uncomfortably guilty. 'What's up?'

Lewis was up off the couch, now, too, clearly wary. He didn't like drop-in visitors any more than I did, especially not right now, when things were so...weird.

'I'm sorry,' Patrick said. 'You see, I had a pre-existing commitment.'

'Sorry...?'

'A business partner,' he said, and indicated the woman, who was still studying the Mondrian with her back to me. 'We have something of a barter arrangement. I owe her something.'

She turned, finally, and it took me a few seconds before the memory ball dropped. Yvette Prentiss, from my funeral. She was out of uniform – no lace dress – but skin-tight jeans with lace insets on the sides and the tight lace shirt, no bra in evidence, made a definite fashion statement. The statement said, *Hi, I'm a total slut, climb aboard and ride me like a rented pony.* Bear in mind, this is coming from a girl with a finely honed appreciation for trashy outfits. I once spent two hundred bucks on a pair of thigh-high patent leather boots, just to say I owned them. But there are limits.

Her eyes widened, and kept on widening. On her, that looked sexy. Her pouty, collagen-enhanced lips parted. 'Oh,' she whispered, low in her throat. 'I know you.'

'Yvette?' Lewis had stepped into the conversational gap. He took a couple of steps closer, and extended his hand. 'We met at the—'

'Memorial service,' she supplied, looking past him at me. 'For her.'

Lewis turned and looked, too, as if he'd forgotten all about that. 'Well...yes. She's—'

'—Djinn.' How sweet, they were finishing each other's sentences. Lewis still had hold of her hand. I didn't care for that at all, but I could see from the warm, oh-so-sexy smile she favoured him with that she liked it just fine. 'Thank you, Patrick. But you know she's not exactly what I was looking for.'

Patrick cleared his throat uncomfortably. 'Yes. Well, another small problem...she's already been claimed.'

Yvette's smile died a fast, ugly death. Her prettiness had a hard edge to it, I found, like a razor blade under velvet. 'This isn't what we agreed.'

'I know.' He helplessly indicated Lewis. 'There were...considerations.'

Her green eyes locked onto Lewis's face and held there. The smile came back, but I didn't trust it. I couldn't tell from Lewis's bemused expression if he was even paying attention to anything but the generously revealed swell of her chest.

'Of course,' she said. 'Well, I'm flattered to meet you again...sorry, I didn't catch your name...?'

'Call me Lewis,' he said. She was pretty much the last person I'd pick to know who he was, but I could tell he didn't feel the same way. 'You were looking for a Djinn?'

'Well, yes.' She looked sad-clown distressed, but not enough that it made her look less than stunningly attractive. 'I'm afraid mine – well, a friend of mine needed his services. I'm currently without support. I was hoping to persuade your friend to work for me. Temporarily. It's important.'

Lot of that going around. I folded my arms and tried to look threatening. Neither of them paid the least bit of attention. Patrick wouldn't meet my gaze, either. The kid was roaming the room, checking out the stuff. He looked back over at Yvette, who nodded slightly, and went back to messing with movables, picking them up and putting them down. Checking for price tags? Jeez.

'I'm afraid she's booked up,' he said. 'But maybe there's something I can do for you.'

Her eyes raked him up and down. Blatantly. 'I'm sure that's perfectly true.' She giggled.

He laughed. I hadn't heard Lewis laugh in – well, I don't think I'd *ever* heard him laugh. Not a yuk-it-up kind of guy, generally. His humour was quiet, his sexuality – well, until now, I would have thought it was kind of subdued.

'Nothing I can do to change your mind?' she asked, and looked up at him from under thick lashes. Moved closer. 'You look like you'd drive a hard…bargain.'

I rolled my eyes, thought about picking up the phone. *Hello, Central Casting? Are you missing your Seducto-Bitch stereotype?* Surely he could see it was an act.

'I've been known to…bargain,' he said, and smiled at her. Was that a leer? Was he actually *flirting* with Miss Artificial Intelligence of 2003? 'Maybe later we could—'

She arched against him like he was a pole and she was the stripper. 'How about a little negotiating session now?'

This time, I did find my voice. 'Ah, excuse me?'

She put her hands in his pockets, pulling him groin to groin for a vertical lap dance. He was trying to step away, but not really putting any effort into it. More of the token I'm-a-nice-guy-but-I-can-be-persuaded sort of resistance. I knew, because I'd done the female version of it often enough. And hey, once with Lewis.

David hadn't liked her. Not at all. And I was more than willing to go with David's instincts, especially when mine were screaming bloody murder.

'Not now,' Lewis said absently to me. Which was not *quite* an order, but had the definite aroma of one. And I didn't like that *at all.*

'Hey!' This time I put some lung power into it. 'Lewis! Use the big brain. What the hell does she want? And if you think that for one minute I'm going to work for this cut-rate road show temptress...'

Her hand came out of Lewis's pocket.

She was holding the small perfume vial in her hand, and a small plastic stopper. *My* bottle. I felt a lurch, as if gravity was shifting, and felt a sickening sense of despair close over me. Oh God...

Lewis pulled free and shoved her back. His eyes went wide. He reached out for the perfume bottle, grabbed hold of her wrist…

…and the kid, who'd been examining a heavy glass bowl, lunged forward and hit him in the head with it. Lewis staggered and went to his hands and knees. The kid – tall, gawky, pale, his knuckles white around the edges of the leaded glass – raised it for another blow.

'Stop!' I yelled, and reached out to give him the most powerful whammy that I still had at my command.

'No, *you* stop. Right there.' Yvette's cool, southern-smoothed voice. I jerked to a halt. Utterly, completely out of control. No, *in her control*. She was holding my bottle, and that meant she was holding me, too. Body and soul.

'Now, is that really necessary?' Patrick asked weakly, and waved at the boy and Lewis. 'You have what you want. There's no need for all this violence—'

'Shut up, Patrick,' Yvette snapped. Patrick winced and turned away, shoulders hunched. He raised his hands in surrender.

Lewis was still trying to get to her, crawling slowly now, blood dripping out of his hairline to spatter the flesh-pale carpet. His voice was weak and deep in his throat. 'Jo, *go*, get out—'

'You. Do not move,' Yvette said, precisely. Nailing me in place as the boy with the glass bowl advanced again, skittishly, aiming for another swing at Lewis's head. 'Kevin. Do it.'

'No!' She hadn't made me stop talking, just moving. I screamed it as the boy lifted the heavy bowl. I reached desperately for power...

But Lewis got there first.

The bowl shattered into sharp-edged, spinning pieces in the kid's hands. He cursed and dropped it, shaking cuts; more blood flew out at velocity to spray the walls.

He kicked Lewis in the head, taking his anger out on the nearest and most helpless target. Lewis went down. Stayed down. I couldn't see him from where I was, pinned in place by Yvette's merciless command.

Patrick rounded on them, shouting, 'That's enough! No more!'

The boy stopped, panting. His face was corpse-pale, shining with sweat.

'You planning on getting righteous on me now?' Yvette asked. If she was perturbed that Patrick had just ordered her teen psycho around, she didn't let it show. 'Where are you planning to get your next meal for your beloved Sara? You going to ask *him* for it?'

'Just – stop.' Patrick swallowed hard, fists clenched. 'Not in my house. I'll not allow this.'

'But you'd allow *this*.' Yvette pulled a frosted-glass bottle from a purse she'd dropped in the corner. Rattled it suggestively. Popped the rubber cap on the top.

A Djinn formed. A man, gorgeous, a study in

gold and bronze. He looked utterly delicious, except for the stark terror in his eyes. He started to back away, but she froze him in place with a whispered command, and walked all around him, trailing her fingers over his gleaming skin.

I remembered something David had said. *They had appetites in common.* Well, I knew Bad Bob Biringanine's appetites well enough to be sickened by that.

Patrick went sickly pale and protested, 'Don't—' but it was too late.

The black shadow of the Ifrit slid around the kitchen door, flowed over carpet.

'I see she's hungry,' Yvette said, and moved out of the way. 'Want to lecture me about morality now, Patrick?'

He hung his head.

The Ifrit leapt like a hunting cat. Ripped into the Djinn with flashing claws, digging deep. The Djinn's mouth was open, but no sound was coming out. He wasn't fighting. He was just...dying. Dying horribly. Disintegrating into wisps of blood-red, pain-heavy mist.

She sucked him in through that black gaping maw of a mouth and swallowed him whole. Nothing left. Not even a scream. I was frozen by Yvette's command, but I wouldn't have had the courage to run even if I were free. There was something so predatory, so cold in the air...

The Ifrit turned her non-face toward me, sniffing,

and I went utterly cold. To stand here and be devoured without a fight was the worst fate I could imagine.

But then she changed. Frosted black skin going pale, smooth, glorious. A glowing waterfall of white hair. Her eyes were the last thing to change, flickering from dead black to a deep dark amethyst.

Sara, as I'd seen her in the dream. She stretched out her arms mutely to Patrick, and collapsed. He rushed to her, picked her up and cradled her in his embrace, lips pressed to the soft waves of her hair.

He was whispering something to her, over and over. *I'm sorry, I'm sorry, I'm sorry.* When he looked up at me, the misery in his eyes hit like a blow. 'It's the only way,' he said. 'She has to eat...'

And she ate other Djinn. I couldn't imagine how lucky I'd been the other night, when he'd put me in a cage match with her, or even when I'd been chatting with her in the kitchen. What had she said in the kitchen? *Don't blame him.* She'd known what he was going to do. They'd done it before.

Yvette's cool green eyes were all over me like sticky hands. She'd forgotten all about Lewis, unconscious on the floor. 'You're like Patrick, then. Human, changed by a Djinn.'

I don't think I'd ever been so ashamed of my origins. I gave her a burning glare back. 'So what does Patrick do for you, to get your cast-offs?

Besides pimp out whoever he can get his hands on?'

She had the sweetest, most revolting smile. 'Why, I don't think the business details of our arrangement are going to be your concern, pretty girl. No, I think you'd just better concentrate on making my son Kevin *very* happy.'

Yvette tossed the kid the bottle. He almost fumbled it. I had that one second to move while the bottle was out of her control and passing into his; I used it to race to Lewis's side and pour what healing energy I had into him.

He was hurt. Badly. I couldn't do enough, wasn't *good* enough.

'What are you doing?' Patrick protested, clearly thrown – not talking to me, but to Yvette.

She rounded on him with clenched fists. 'Getting rid of the trash. You think I wanted *her*? *You* told me you had a way to get to David.'

'I do!' He nodded at me. 'He'll come for her. As soon as he knows you have her, he'll come running.'

'He'd better,' she said, and gave him a full smile, with teeth. 'If he doesn't, there's no place you can hide from me. You know that.' She shot a look at me, and I was struck by the sheer callous indifference in her eyes. 'Put your toy away, Kevin. I want to go home.'

The kid clutching the bottle pointed at me and said, 'You. In the bottle. Now.'

I had no choice, none at all. I felt myself breaking apart, looked up to see Yvette watching me with dreaming sea green eyes. 'Don't you worry, sweetie,' she said as I was sucked away into grey oblivion. 'I'm sure we'll think of something interesting to do with you.'

You wouldn't think you could dream in oblivion, but well, there you go. I dreamt I was a child again. Very small, too small to understand the world around me – a toddler, teetering around on stubby uncertain legs and grabbing for anything pretty, shiny, interesting, dangerous.

I dreamt of being held in someone's arms, maybe my mother's, with my head pillowed on her shoulder. I remembered rain, falling like perfect diamonds from the soft grey sky. I remembered wind licking cool over my skin. I remembered thunder vibrating through me like the voice of God.

Dreams and memories are so very close to the same thing.

In the dream, in the memory, I fell down on the cool, damp grass and wailed in fright, and there was somebody there, gathering me up, holding me, stroking away the pain and fear and tears.

Shhhh. It was my mother's voice, warm and blurred the way things are in dreams. *They'll hear you.* I was too young to talk, but somehow I was talking anyway. *Who?*

Her hands smoothed my hair in gentle, careful strokes. *You know.*

I did. I cuddled in closer to her warmth. Overhead, the clouds muttered to each other in a language I could almost understand, and I reached out to them and felt them draw closer, all soft edges and cold alien intensity.

They wanted me. I wanted them. In my simple child logic, I thought that meant there was no danger; anything that was interested in me had to be my friend, didn't it?

I didn't understand that interest could also be hunger. That there were parts of me that were tender and juicy and oh so delicious, and that the world was full of predators who wanted to scoop out those tasty titbits. No, I didn't understand that.

But my mother did. *Be careful*, she whispered in my ear. *Something's coming. You need to be ready, sweetheart. You need to understand how to see behind the smiles.*

What's behind the smiles? I asked her, in my little-child voice. She showed me teeth. Long, sharp, needle-thin teeth, the better to eat you with, my dear.

Don't trust anyone, she hissed. And then she let go, and I fell up into the clouds, and felt myself being stripped raw, pulled apart, burnt, broken, destroyed.

See, it was just a dream. Or a memory. Or a nightmare.

Except the parts that actually happened.

Chapter Two

The next thing I knew was a rush of cool, sweet air. I convulsively wanted to breathe but I had no lungs, and no body to hold them. Still, part of me knew what to do. I followed the breeze up, out, into the light.

I came out of the perfume vial, which lay on its side on a Cheetos-dusted coffee table, right next to a much-creased and sticky edition of the *Sports Illustrated* swimsuit issue. I ghosted up slowly. It felt like I was drugged stupid, unable to will myself to do anything but wait, drifting, for meaning.

Shit. This was *so* not working out for the best.

'Uhhhh…'

An uncertain human voice. Soft and hesitant as it was, it still echoed through me like a church bell. Something in me went completely still, waiting. I was focused like a predator waiting to pounce.

This felt nothing at all like what had happened

between me and Lewis. Nothing at all. It was perfectly horrible.

'Anybody there?' the voice asked. He sounded scared shitless. *Good*. Welcome to the club, jerk.

'Yes,' I said – not that I meant to say anything, I just was compelled to respond. My voice sounded odd, because it was coming from the very thin air I was at the moment. I filed that away for later investigation, when and if I got be scientific about such things. 'I'm here.'

Oh, God, it was the little bastard who'd beaten Lewis. *Lewis...* God, I'd left him there. How much would he remember? Was he even still alive? *Patrick, you bastard*. I'd make damn sure somebody paid for this.

Seen close, Psycho Boy didn't look nearly as threatening: a gawky, acne-pocked teenager, all long legs and stick-thin arms, wearing a Metallica T-shirt that had seen too many mosh pits. This pimply kid – she'd called him Kevin, oh God, was I supposed to call him *Master*? – sat on the edge of an unmade bed and tried to look everywhere at once, eyes darting like crazy but paying particular attention to the corners of the room. He had a lot to look at, and none of it was pretty. The place was like a Dumpster right before pick-up day, piled with trash, discarded pizza boxes, old cartons smeared with dried Chinese food. A pile of filthy underwear mouldered near the bed. A pin-up of a collagen-enhanced, silicone-implanted beauty in a metal bra and thong was pinned crookedly on the ceiling, for maximum viewing in the lying-down position.

Oh, I could already tell this was *not* going to be pretty. *Lewis. God, what happened to Lewis?*

Kevin shifted nervously on the bed, which creaked like old joints. 'Um...I command you to appear!' He tried to sound like some medieval wizard, but he came off like a self-conscious bad actor, and blotched bright red over his cheeks and forehead.

And even so, I responded instantly. My body built itself far quicker and better than it had before, all layers simultaneously, and I felt a certain weird cock-eyed pride in that, until I looked down at myself.

Oh God.

You already know, right? Of course you do. High-heeled pumps of the come-fuck-me variety. Thigh-high hose fastened with garters. Lacy thong panties under a tiny little black frilly skirt with a white apron. Black corset top, and believe me, I was now filling it. Generously.

I shuddered, looked up and found my reflection staring back at me in the mirror.

Pale skin, fire engine red pouty lips, eyes of an unsettlingly bright shade of silver. I looked like the porn version of Magenta from *Rocky Horror*.

Kevin looked shocked. Genuinely shocked. Not as much as I felt, though. When I found David again, I was going to ask some *very* tough questions about the rules of this particular nasty game.

'Mom!' Kevin yelled, and then went pallid as he instantly thought better of that course of action. He dashed to the closed door of the room – decorated with more soft-porn posters – and clicked over two deadbolt locks in fast succession to lock her out. 'Uh, never mind, sorry, mistake!'

He turned to face me, back firmly against the door, and I stared at him. Couldn't say anything, really. Couldn't do anything except seethe and wonder what in the hell was happening. She said she wanted David. David had been afraid of that, back at the funeral, I'd sensed it all over him.

Now she had me. Could I warn him away?

I reached for that warm silvery umbilical that stretched into the aetheric, and was relieved to find it still intact. David was still alive, at least, wherever he was and whatever Jonathan had him doing. I tried to send a whisper along the line, but it hit something, some kind of barrier, and died.

When I blinked, I saw a blue coldlight sparkle whirling around me. *Oh God*. It was not only still there, it was getting worse.

'Who are you?' Kevin asked me, drawing me back to the world. I didn't feel any compulsion to answer, so I didn't. I just stared at him. The silver eyes had to be unnerving – hell, they'd unnerved me in the mirror – so I kept them straight and level, boring a hole into him. He got nervously, self-consciously strident. 'Hey. I asked you a question! You have to answer.'

No, I didn't. This kid clearly didn't have the rule book memorised, because he'd forgotten all about the Rule of Three, which even *I* had known before meeting my first Djinn. Ask three times, they answer. Anything they tell you before then, forget it.

We are consummate, conscienceless liars. And from the pure cold fury boiling inside of me, I was starting to think we had an extra helping of psychopath to go along with it.

The cold stare was getting to him, all right. I could see it in the nervous tic developing around his left eye, and the quick movements of his hands as he tried to figure out the best way to lounge and look cool under pressure. He finally settled for slouching with his hands in his pockets and going for a half-lidded, defiant stare back at me.

'Nice outfit,' he said. I didn't smile. The little bastard had done this to me, whether he knew it or not; I had a new appreciation for how little I'd changed when Lewis had claimed me. Obviously, what Lewis wanted and what he saw in me were almost the same things – in retrospect, one hell of a compliment. Kevin wanted a living blow-up doll, apparently. The implications of that were not especially comforting.

He looked pouty when I didn't respond. 'Fine, be that way, I don't give a crap.'

He did, of course. It only took about another thirty seconds to wait him out. I felt like a participant in Short Attention Span Theatre.

'Well?' he snapped, and pushed away from the door. Not much, just a couple of inches, but I still didn't like it. Better if I could keep him cowed and thoroughly unnerved, but unfortunately the shock was starting to leave him, and now his voice was taking on an unpleasant whiny overtone. 'Don't just stand there like some dumb slut, *do* something!'

'What would you like me to do?' I asked. I meant it to be sarcastic, but it came out in a sultry, smoky, seductive purr. Gee, wonderful. I had the 1-900 voice to go with the yard sale Frederick's of Hollywood outfit.

Well, one good thing about the voice, it derailed him completely. He was too hornily captivated to realise that he actually *could* order me to do things. So far.

This was going to take some real juggling skill. Best thing to do was to take the initiative, and since I didn't feel anything stopping me, I took a step toward him. I made sure my new stance had that Xena Warrior Princess bad-ass cachet to it.

'What's *your* name?' I asked him. He backed up again, lips parted, brown eyes wide and riveted behind the glasses.

'Kevin – Kevin. Kevin Prentiss.' He cleared his throat and tried to make it go deeper than its current punk-kid range. 'What's yours?'

'What do you want it to be?' Because I wasn't going to have this horny little bastard calling me by my real name. And the twenty questions was a way to waste time.

'Um…Honey?'

I lost my sense of humour. 'You're kidding.'

'No.'

'Really.'

He hadn't expected resistance. 'Um, no?'

'OK, let me put it this way: You'd *better* be kidding.'

He blinked. 'You're arguing with me?'

'Of course not,' I purred. I really did. I wasn't trying to purr, it was just the way things were going today. Apparently, my new voice had a built-in seduction filter. 'Why would I argue with you?' Always answer a question with a question.

'I don't know, but you shouldn't be arguing with me, you should be—'

'What?' I interrupted, and crossed my arms. It was, not coincidentally, in the classic *I Dream of Jeannie* pose. Maybe I could change his subconscious wish. Even frothy pink and orange gauze and a blonde horsetail through an organ-grinder-monkey hat would be preferable to slinking around in this outfit.

He licked his lips, watching me. Uh-oh. Not having the desired effect. 'You should be obeying me. Like, when I say do something, you should—'

'You haven't told me to do anything yet,' I pointed out.

'Well, I would if you'd just—'

'Take your time.'

'Let me—'

'Really. Take your time. Think about it. Because you've only got three wishes.'

Which was bullshit, but I figured if he didn't understand the Rule of Three, he probably got his entire Djinn education from Saturday morning cartoons anyway. Man, I *really* wished I had control of my appearance. Even aside from the currently occurring fashion disaster concerns, it would have been great to do that whole Arabian Nights shtick, half-misted. Plus, no teenage boy is going to assume he can screw a girl with mist for legs.

'Just...three?' He sounded breathless. Oh boy. Tell me he hadn't worked these out in advance.

It was too late to switch it to one wish. Damn.

He opened his mouth to blurt out something that I just knew was going to involve hot oil and rubber sheets, so I jumped in with, 'You really ought to think about it first. It's like making a deal with the devil. There's always some loophole that ends up turning things sour. Like, you say that you want a million dollars. I give you a million dollar life insurance policy and kill you. See?'

He stopped, mouth still open far enough that I could see some cavities forming on his back molars.

Then he got a sly, shallow look in those brown eyes, and closed his mouth and smiled.

'You're trying to stall,' he said. 'You're afraid of me.'

Well, yeah. I'd already seen the dark side of Kevin, as he kicked Lewis in the face with every evidence of sociopathic glee. 'Am not.'

'Are too.'

'Not.'

'Too.'

We both jumped at a sudden rattle of the door-knob. It jiggled back and forth briskly, three times, and went still. An annoyed female voice said, 'Kevin? What are you up to in there?'

'Nothing!' His voice went into the boy's choir range and cracked. 'Mom, a little privacy?'

It took me a minute, but I placed the voice with the wish-I-could-forget-it memory of Yvette Prentiss dry-humping Lewis just before all of the trouble began. Mom? Well, she'd certainly got started early, if she was old enough to have a son Kevin's age; she didn't look a minute over thirty. Sure, flawless make-up, Botox and lots of spa treatments could work wonders, but not *that* many.

I suspected she was the trophy stepmother, stuck with the unattractively teenaged son-by-marriage. The father was obviously out of the picture, no doubt dead, and the kid was one of those ugly iron candelabras you get as a Christmas present and don't dare give away because, well, what would people think? Yvette sure hadn't been dragging the anchor that was Kevin around at my funeral. Would have spoilt her perfect image, not to mention hashed her chances for scoring another bad, rich daddy.

Or maybe I was doing her a disservice. Maybe she'd been knocked up at age thirteen, courageously endured the pregnancy, overcome daunting odds to be a good mother to her obnoxious-going-on-creep of a kid. Maybe she was just looking out for the two of them the best way she knew how, using the natural advantages she'd been given.

Uh-huh. And I was Mother Teresa in a Magenta outfit. Riiiiiight. She'd used the kid to commit assault, at the very least. Homicide was certainly still a possibility. *God, Lewis...*

The doorknob rattled again. Loudly. Longly.

'Open up!' Yvette snapped. She didn't sound like a courageous Madonna figure. She sounded like a bitch with a bad attitude. 'Right now, Kevin, or I swear...!'

'Um, OK, OK, coming...' Kevin threw me a *help me!* look. I just stared back. He changed his tone to a scared, tense whisper. 'Back in the bottle?'

I didn't feel compelled. I just raised my eyebrows and cocked my head to stare harder. His anxiety level shot up another ten levels, and the whisper got even thinner. '*Please?* Back in the bottle?'

Yvette hit the door. Hard. It rattled on its hinges.

'You're killing me here, *please*! Get back in the bottle!'

Whoops. Command mode. I felt myself instantly dissolving into mist, felt that toilet-bowl swirl of the bottle dragging me in, and braced myself for the pain I knew was coming.

Yep, being squeezed like a baby in a birth canal was not my idea of fun, but there I went into the bottle, and I felt the world tilt as Kevin grabbed it up. Seen close through the glass, his fingers were huge and grimy and definitely nothing I ever wanted to have pawing my skin, substantial or insubstantial.

And then he twisted the stopper home.

Lights out.

I dreamt again. I guess that was what Djinn did in bottles…dreamt. Sure as hell wasn't anything else to do. To make matters even more strange, this one wasn't even my dream.

It was David's.

He was pacing restlessly in a strange square glass room I didn't recognise, coat swirling like smoke around him from the violence of his turns. His hands were clenched behind his back, and his whole body vibrated with tension. As I watched, his legs began to blur and become mist; he hissed out something in a language I didn't know and exerted a pulse of will that I could feel even in my drifting, dreaming state.

His legs went solid again.

He threw himself violently against the glass,

pressing hard, so hard I felt the effort like a distant earthquake. Outside of the glass, there was a giant-sized world, distorted into warped shapes and weird colours. People moving around out there, giant blobs of colour and form. One of them caught my attention – neon yellow outfit. Rahel?

David was inside a bottle. Unlike me, he wasn't sealed in, but for some reason he couldn't get out, either.

Where David was pushing, the thick glass vibrated. I felt the energy building in waves as the thick surface began to whipsaw violently, rippling. David pushed harder. The glass bowed out in a bubble, went from clear to milk white, distorted…

David collapsed to his knees. The glass snapped back into shape with a ringing, singing *pop* of energy. Clear and perfect.

'Let me go,' he said hoarsely. He was exhausted. Reflected light glittered on his copper-brushed hair, pale gold skin, bright-penny eyes. 'Please, let me go to her. You don't know what you're doing.'

No sense of arrival, but suddenly Jonathan was sitting in the far corner. He was still dressed in casual human-normal clothes, but there was nothing normal or human about the power behind his eyes, or the cell-deep weariness. He looked infinitely worse than last I'd seen him.

David climbed back to his feet and turned to face him. 'I have to go, Jonathan, *now*.'

'You're not going anywhere,' Jonathan said. His

voice was thin, tired, and hoarse. 'This is the only safe place right now. Going out there is useless. And you know I'm right, so don't give me that look.'

David's eyebrows knitted together in an angry line. 'What look?'

'That look. The you-don't-understand look. Hell, I understand, I've been in love, too. But the survival of the Free Djinn comes first, it has to. We're talking about losing *everything*. You want to end up dead, or worse?'

'Of course not.'

'Then quit fucking around and try to understand that everything doesn't revolve around your heart-aches.'

David took a step forward, fists clenched and face tense. 'Oh, I understand, believe me. I've played chess with you too many times not to. But I'm not going to let you use her as a sacrifice pawn, Jonathan. Something's happened to her. She's been taken.'

'I know.' Jonathan propped his head against the glass wall with no evidence of comfort. 'Patrick arranged it. Look, I know you don't approve, but she needed to learn the ropes. It was the best thing.'

'Fuck!' David kicked the wall hard enough to draw a humming sound out of the hard surface. 'You incredible bastard. You arrogant son of a—'

'—bitch,' Jonathan supplied, and closed his eyes. 'You've called me that before, you know. And trust me, in this particular case, flattery will *not* get you a free pass out of here. She needs this if you want her to survive. Don't be stupid. She's perfectly safe with Lewis…magically speaking, anyway.'

'Stupid?' David repeated, and turned slowly to face him. Oh God. The look on his face… He lunged across the space, braced himself on stiff arms, face-to-face with Jonathan. 'You think it's *Lewis* that has her?'

Jonathan's eyes flashed open. Just a second of doubt in those old, tired, very powerful eyes. He didn't answer.

'It's *Yvette*,' David whispered. 'Don't you understand? I don't know how, but she's got Joanne. You know what she'll do.'

Jonathan might have flinched – barely – but whatever impulse he had toward concern shut down fast. 'Better her than you.'

David pulled back a fist, cocked it, looked ready to slam it straight into Jonathan's face.

He still didn't flinch. Didn't blink. David backed away, sank down in a crouch against the wall a few feet away, and buried his face in both hands for a few seconds.

'Does it ever occur to you that maybe she might be as important as I am? As you are?' he asked.

Jonathan cocked both eyebrows toward sarcasm. 'Frankly? No. Never occurred to me. And wait…no, not occurring to me now.'

'Let me go. Yvette wants *me*,' David said. 'Don't pretend you don't know that. She always has. She tried to talk Bad Bob into it half a dozen times. Give her an opening, she'll jump at the chance. I know how to manipulate her. I can be free in a matter of hours and bring Joanne with me.'

Jonathan puffed his breath out impatiently. 'And your point is…?'

'I can do this. Joanne has no idea what she's up against. I do.'

A half-second of hesitation, which was probably more than the idea deserved, and then Jonathan said, quietly, 'No. You're staying here. Believe me, you'll thank me later.'

'Will I?' David was doing something odd. He stood up, shrugged out of his olive drab coat and let it slide to the floor, then unbuttoned his white-and-blue shirt with jerky, nervous motions. He added it to the pile. Stripped off the soft grey T-shirt next, revealing gold-burnished skin. While I enjoyed the view, I wondered what the hell he was doing. 'You've never been claimed, Jonathan. Never, in your entire history. You have no idea what it's like.'

'I know what it's like,' Jonathan said, in a tone that meant it was an old, boring argument. He was watching David with a frown that was getting deeper by the minute. 'And what the hell are you doing?'

'It's rape,' David continued. He unbuttoned his blue jeans, unzipped, slipped them down. 'Having your will taken away from you, forced to do whatever they want you to do. Not even owning yourself. No matter how pure the intentions, how kind the master, how much good comes out of it, it's still *rape*. Don't you get that? You gave her to Patrick. Patrick gave her to Lewis, and maybe she submitted to that, but *this*...no. You have no idea. And I'm not leaving her in Yvette's hands, not alone.'

No answer this time. Jonathan continued to stare up, no change in his expression. He might have been thinking about the merits of Guinness over Sam Adams, for all I knew. Or the secrets of the universe.

David stripped off underwear, dropped them on the pile, and turned back to the glass. Spread his arms wide. Naked, he gave off a halo like polished gold. I felt him drawing in energy, felt the gigantic swirl of power on the aetheric level. He extended his hand out to the glass on the window and touched it, pressed his palm flat against it.

'Are you going to let me go?' he asked.

'No, because you have no plan beyond throwing yourself blindly on the grenade and hoping somebody will mop up the mess.' Jonathan didn't sound in the least worried. 'Put something on before you catch a cold.'

David went very still, and I felt the lancing burn of power flash out of him. Straight into the glass, fine as a laser. It slammed into the barrier, bowed it outward, turned it opaque as milk, kept pushing.

'Never gonna happen, Davy,' Jonathan said.

'Trust me. You're bleeding off so much power to keep that girl alive that you couldn't shatter a soap bubble right now. And hey, you want my opinion, I think the girl's pretty tough. Maybe she'll surprise you. Maybe the last thing she needs is for you to come galloping to the rescue, that ever occur to you?'

I felt David pulling hard on the umbilical that still bound us together, trying to access whatever power I had stored, but it was like a trickling stream trying to fill up a huge dry riverbed. God, was he really *that* drained? *That* weak?

Jonathan continued to stare, lips pressed tight, eyes dark with knowledge. 'You're going to kill yourself. Stop it.'

'No.' David was weak, draining fast, but he was still pouring everything he had into the effort to break the prison. '*You* stop holding me here.'

'Put your goddamn clothes back on, David. What kind of a point are you trying to make? That you're leaving all of this behind for her? Being reborn? I got it, already! Symbolism 'R' Us!'

No answer. David was fiercely focused now, hands trembling. I could feel the intensity of his commitment. He wasn't going to stop.

Jonathan must have known it too. It was in his raw plea. '*David!*'

The clothes lying on the ground ignited into white-hot flame. David was glowing like a gas flame, using himself ruthlessly. Destroying himself.

'Let...me...GO!' It was a deep-in-the-throat growl, furious and enraged. The glass was bubbling with the force of the attack.

Jonathan had gone sallow-pale under his tan. I could sense how deep this went between them, how much trust was being ripped apart in this moment.

How much love was being destroyed.

'Fine,' he finally whispered. 'Go. Kill yourself, dammit.'

The glass exploded like a bomb. David misted and was gone before the first glittering shards fell.

Jonathan, left behind, closed his eyes and sank down against one wall of the prison – the refuge? – and braced his forehead against his hands.

The bottle sealed itself without a sound, walling him in.

The dream faded into a grey, sick, constant light, sparked with cold blue flashes.

Don't, I murmured in my sleep. *Don't do this for me.*

But I knew him better.

The next time I got poured out of the bottle, things were different. For one thing, I was in another room – clean, this one, scrupulously Martha Stewarted, from the stacked pyramid of oranges in a low green tray to the matching rug and throw pillows. The place was so coordinated it could have joined the Ballet Russe. I felt claustrophobic. Patrick's digs had been louche and tacky, but at least they'd been bursting with energy.

There was only one word for this room. Soulless. When I put on flesh, I was standing on champagne-pale carpet in my spike-heeled pumps, looking like a hooker at a Suzy Homemaker convention. The expression on Yvette Prentiss's face was almost worth the incredible embarrassment of the outfit.

'Kevin!' Yvette said sharply. She was sitting on a vanilla cream satin-striped sofa, looking gorgeously, deliberately casual, much like the room. Nothing casual about it – you don't get that artless elegance by just tossing on some jeans and touching up the lipstick. Hours of prep had been involved.

Kevin, on the other hand, looked like he'd just been rousted out of bed. Wrinkled, unkempt, wearing a faded-out grey T-shirt with a tear in the sleeve and a pair of jeans so wide-legged they flared like gauchos. Naturally, the jeans were about three sizes too big, so they could ride fashionably low on his hips and display at least two inches of not-very-clean BVDs. I didn't think his hair had ever been visited by either the Comb or Shampoo Fairy.

He had a three-second delay to her angry snap, probably because he was still in awe of the Magenta outfit he'd managed to stick me with. 'Um, what?'

'Did you open the bottle before?'

'No!' Patently a lie. He was terrible at it. 'I might've, ah, peeked. Just a little.'

She just gave him a scorching look of disgust,

stood up and came to walk around me. I waited for her to kick the tyres and ask how much mileage was on me. Oh, I so wanted to tell her to kiss my French-maid-costumed ass, but naturally, I couldn't. I couldn't do anything but stand there, simmering. *What did you do with Lewis, you incredible bitch?*

'Get rid of that,' she said to Kevin.

'What?'

'The outfit. Obviously.'

'Oh.' Kevin seized the opportunity. 'Take off your clothes,' he said to me. It was a direct, unequivocal order. I thought fast, and removed the apron with a flicker of consciousness. He waited, in vain, for me to do the rest. 'All your clothes,' he amended. Crap. I shut my eyes and did it, shedding stockings, shoes, skirt, corset, thong – everything. Standing in bare feet on carpet, feeling air conditioning breathe its way across my skin.

Yvette groaned. 'Oh, for heaven's sake, put her in something decent. Conduct your perversions on your own time.'

Never thought I'd be grateful to her, but I opened my eyes and stared at Kevin again, waiting for the order. He was too busy drooling. Yvette reached over and smacked him on the back of the head, hard, and he winced and ducked and said, 'OK! Put something on. Something, you know, nice.'

I went for a severe black pantsuit in peachskin, a form-hugging pale silver shirt, and some discreet low-heeled Stuart Weitzman shoes, with tassels. I reached in the vest pocket of the jacket and fished out a nice pair of Ray Ban sunglasses to finish it off.

'Better,' Yvette approved. 'You have good taste.'

'Thank you,' I said. Pretty much meaning *fuck you*, but without the actual words.

'What's your name?'

Since she wasn't my master, and it wasn't a Rule-of-Three question anyway, there was no reason for me to tell the truth. 'Lilith,' I said. Sounded exotic and faintly evil. *Hi, I'm Lilith, I'll be your evil servant today*. Yeah, I liked it.

'Lilith,' she repeated. She did the walking-around thing again, checking me out. 'You'll do.'

'For what, exactly?' I asked. She looked shocked. Apparently, Djinn were not quite so aggressive in her experience. 'Who are you?'

She wasn't going to answer questions from the help. She glared at Kevin, evidently blaming him for my bad attitude, and said, 'You understand what to do?'

'Yeah,' he said, and looked as resentful as I felt. 'I get it.'

'Don't screw it up.'

'I won't.'

'You know how important this is.' God, she was picking at him like a scab. She'd probably say that she was just reinforcing the point, but I saw the light in her eyes. She just plain enjoyed making him squirm. It was an uncomfortable sort of fascination.

Kevin, of course, got defensive. 'I got it, already! Jeez, Mom! Take a pill!' I almost felt sorry for the kid. Messy, hormonally overloaded, unattractive, burdened with a stepmom from hell…

And then I remembered him checking me out like some fifty-year-old drunk in a strip club, and the impulse toward sympathy went away.

'OK.' Kevin took a deep breath, clenched his fists, and said, 'Yo. I want you to do something.'

I was unimpressed by the build-up.

'I want you to cause a really big fire in—' He shot a look at Mom, who was staring at him like a harpy ready to pounce. '—in a town called Seacasket, Maine.'

What the hell…? Didn't matter. I could already feel the circuits kicking in, the Djinn hardwiring powering up. 'Yeah, sure, OK.' I was already figuring all the ways I could stretch that one. A really big, pretty, contained fire that didn't burn anything. Spectacular, not dangerous.

Yvette made a frustrated sound in the back of her throat that sounded like a purr, and addressed herself directly to him. 'The whole town. Destroy everything and everyone in it.'

'Uh, yeah. What she said,' he said to me. He didn't sound enthusiastic. 'Big fire. Destroy the town and everybody in it. Now. Uh, and you can do that misty thing to get there.'

The part of me that couldn't be controlled was already reaching out for power, tapping into Kevin's potential, drawing it down into me in a rich blood-tide flood. God, it was so *strong*... I'd thought it was just Lewis that had this much power, but to find it in someone like *Kevin*...it was incredible. Immeasurable.

And I was about to use it to roast an entire town alive. *Oh God, no.*

'Go,' Kevin said, and waved his hand around awkwardly. 'Do what I told you.'

To my utter horror, I found I couldn't stop myself. I was already misting out. Kevin, the Martha-Stewart-perfect room, Yvette...all fading into nothing.

He hadn't told me to travel the aetheric, so I stayed in mist form, moving as slowly as real-world physics would allow. I was a hot storm rolling through clouds and sky, burning with purpose, out of control, and lives were going to be lost when I arrived, no question about it.

I had to think of a way to stop this. *How?* I wasn't in control of it, not at all. It was controlling me, I was just the conduit through which the power would flow. Fine, if I was a circuit, maybe there was a way to insulate myself. Muffle the damage I was going to do. How? *Think, dammit!* All that training in weather, and none of it was any help at all now...

Or was it?

I reached out and grabbed a spangled net of storm energy from the sea and dragged it behind me like a train on a wedding dress as I arrowed past, heading for Seacasket, Maine.

I knew, without having to ask why, that there were 1,372 people in Seacasket. Not to mention pets, farm animals, birds, insects, plants, all the things that made up the ecosphere, that made life possible and desirable.

I had to find a way to save them.

It felt like a long time, but it could have only been a few hours at most between leaving the Prentiss house and landing at the corner of Davis and Cunningham, right next to a sign that said SEACASKET CHAMBER OF COMMERCE WELCOMES YOU, decorated with the seal of the Rotary Club and logos for Hardee's and McDonald's. A smaller sign below read HOME OF THE CRIMSON PIRATES, STATE CHAMPIONS LADIES BASKETBALL 1998.

Seacasket, for all its rural sensibility, had a Starbucks directly across the street from me. There were five or six people in there, sitting at tiny uncomfortable tables sipping mochas or cappuccinos or half-caff skim deluxe grande lattes. There were a couple of kids running down the sidewalk chasing a runaway beagle puppy, and a few cars driving by, people talking, laughing, oblivious to the death I was bringing with me.

No. No no no no.

I tried. I tried with all my might to stop it, but my hands went out, and the power that I'd sucked out of Kevin, that rich textured power that filled me to bursting, it shot up into a hot dome over the town.

No!

I couldn't stop it, but I could try to mitigate it. At the same time as that compulsive part of me started authoring destruction, the other part of me – the part that was still partially free, at least – started desperately weaving together the wind. Not enough time for this, not nearly enough; weatherworking required subtlety, delicacy, like neurosurgery. This was more like a battlefield amputation, with the patient alive and screaming. I increased the density of the air, heated it faster than a microwave oven, created a corresponding cold front and slammed the two together.

Instant chaos. Overhead, beyond the hot fury of fire that was gathering over the town, I saw clouds exploding in blue and black mushrooms. Silent, but incredibly powerful. I watched it in Oversight as the cotton white anvil cloud boiled up, and up, and up, hot air struggling to climb over cold, water molecules slamming together in so much violence that the energy generated exploded outward in waves. The collisions sparked even more motion, forced expansion against the unmoving wall of the low pressure system.

Go, go, go! I was begging it to move faster, even though it was the fastest I'd ever built anything like this – fifteen seconds, from clear sky to first pale pink flash of lightning.

I wasn't looking for rain, though. Rain wouldn't even begin to derail the firestorm I was about to unleash on this place. It would instantly evaporate into steam, and for all I knew, kill even more people. The kind of power I was carrying wasn't something that could be put out with a fire hose, anyway.

The kids on the street stopped, looking up, open-mouthed with amazement. The dog started yapping.

Thunder boomed like cannon. It rattled glass in windows. Two car alarms shrieked in fright, and I felt the pressure of bad weather building, hot and still and green. *Yes.*

I couldn't hold the fire. It was coming down, an acid rain of napalm from the sky. It hit the tallest building in sight – a bank, maybe – and draped it in orange-red streamers that exploded white-hot when it found something to feed on. Seven floors above the street, hell had descended. I could feel people screaming, feel the pulse of their terror, and I *couldn't stop it.*

Fire crawled lazily over the building, dripping in hot strings from windows. Burning the place from the outside in, from the top down. *Get out. Get the hell out, now!* Because that place would be an inferno in minutes. Could I do something else, *anything*?

I looked down at myself and saw that I was surrounded by a thick, sparkling layer of blue.

Coldlight, moving over me like a crawling blanket. Oh God. What in the hell was it doing to me? I couldn't *feel* it. Couldn't feel it at all.

I stared blindly up into the storm, willing it, begging it to do what I needed it to do.

And something answered. It was raw and primitive and barely more than an instinct, Mother Nature twitching in a nightmare. The blast of energy broke over me like a drowning wave, and I went to my knees, still staring up at the arching, strangely beautiful firefall that was going to destroy this place.

And then the tornado formed above it.

It started small, an indrawn breath of the storm, a tentative wisp of vapour like a tongue tasting the air. I fed it energy. *Come on, baby. Live. Work for me.* It pulled in strength, drove down in a black twisting rope toward the tasty, tempting energy buffet that was the firedome.

It connected, swelled, and took on a roaring, freight-train stability.

Nothing can resist that force when it gets going. Especially not fire, which is nothing but energy given plasmatic form; it's just food for the process. A stream of fire broke free of the dome and spiralled up inside the tornado like a gas flame into a lantern.

The result was unholy. Beautiful, terrifying, like nothing that most human beings had ever seen or would ever want to...a storm shot through with crawling, vivid orange as the fire struggled to keep its cohesion. The tornado sucked up the thick, clinging plasma like Jell-O through a straw.

The firedome broke apart. Individual napalm-hot streams fell like ribbons on the town, but the majority of it was drawn into the tornado and spewed out in a fading glow above the anvil cloud, where the thin atmosphere of the mesosphere starved it of fuel. The rapid cooling would help feed the engine of the tornado, as air sank and was drawn back into the express-elevator rush of the spiral.

The compulsive part of me was still trying to fulfil my master's command, which meant I kept forming fire up there in the sky, trying to put the dome back together. The tornado kept vacuuming it safely away. It occurred to me with a cold shock to wonder how long the compulsion would make me do this. I could feel my fuel tanks edging down toward empty. The energy output was enormous, and I couldn't even draw strength from the sun, because I'd created an instant overcast.

Maybe I could draw power from the fire itself, sort of a cannibalistic loop? No – when I tried to grab hold and suck it back into me, I couldn't find a grip. It thrashed away from me like a writhing snake.

I couldn't keep this up forever. The storm was running on its own now, but I needed to keep control of it. Unchecked, the tornado could do as much damage as the fire, and that really *would* be my fault, in a whole new ugly way. The winds in the tornado wall were reaching speeds of about 250 miles per hour, a solidly terrifying F4. That wasn't my doing, of course. Truth is, once you get the forces of nature going, they don't need a lot of tender loving care. I had to conserve my strength to try to *stop* things, not keep them going.

Somebody was tugging at my black peachskin coat, trying to get my attention. I tumbled out of Oversight and felt my body starting to mist; I pulled myself together and turned to look over my shoulder.

Two kids and a dog. All equally scared. The little girl, red-faced, was crying big crystal tears and clinging to her brother; he was all of ten, struggling to be brave and hold on to both little sister and a wiggling, whining beagle.

'Lady?' he asked. His voice was high and trembling, pure as the tones of an angel. 'Help?'

He was so damn polite about it, with death whirling a couple of hundred feet overhead, with the bank burning like a bonfire three blocks away. People in the Starbucks across the street were screaming and cowering behind the counter with the baristas.

I put my arms around the three of them and pulled them close, sheltered them with my body as the fire overhead fought the suction of the wind to come down like a burning blanket.

The compulsion wasn't going to stop. It would go on until I couldn't keep control of the tornado. I'd created twice the disaster instead of averting the one. The fire would come, and then the tornado would kill whatever survived.

The hair prickled on the back of my neck.

Something big...a white surge of power sweeping through, clearing out the fire, breaking the processes I'd set up inside the storm. It rolled like a glittering razor-edged sea.

It tasted familiar. No, it *was* as familiar as the power humming inside my own body because it was the same damn thing.

It was David.

I raised my head slowly as the silence fell, that hot green silence like the one before the tornado's freight-train rush...the fire at the bank building flared once, blue-white, and vanished into a hiss of smoke. The streamers of flame winked out.

David was standing across the street in front of the Starbucks, copper-brushed hair catching light like silk. He was in his travelling clothes – blue shirt, blue jeans, olive drab wool coat that belled with the wind.

He looked so tired. So horribly tired. And there were crawling blue sparks all over him, too. Glittering in a barely visible umbilical between us.

'Joanne,' he whispered. I felt his voice, even from so far away, like breath on my skin.

I didn't say anything out loud – couldn't – but I

felt the compulsion rising up again, felt the fire sucking energy and pouring it into a manifestation that glittered and grew above my head. A snowball on fire. A boulder. A sun. The light from it was so bright it bleached the town to grey-white shadow.

Stop me, I begged him. I knew he could hear me, vibrating through the connection between us. *Kill me if you have to. Cut the cord.*

He looked up, at the growing ball of destruction flaming in the sky, and then back at me. I didn't have to tell him I couldn't stop. He knew. He understood.

I looked at him in Oversight and saw him outlined in pale, shimmering orange, a colour that felt like suffering, weakness, approaching death. When I extended my hand toward him, I could see the same colour drifting around me.

This was killing both of us. I was draining my master Kevin at the same time, *three* of us going down...

Stop me, I said again. The silver rope binding us together was pale now, pulsing in time with our shared heartbeats. *God, David, please, I don't know how...*

I know, he said. *She just wanted to get my attention.*

I didn't see him move, but he was suddenly there, tackling me violently backwards to the ground, away from the children and the wildly yapping beagle. Overhead, the sun exploded into a white-hot fury, but I didn't see, couldn't see, because we were falling through the ground and into the aetheric, racing back along the invisible path I'd taken to get here. *No!* I battered at him, tried to get free, tried to warn him that he was killing us both. He didn't respond. Faster. Faster. The whole thing was a blur of lights, colour, motion, whispers, screams...

...and the two of us fell with a hard thump onto the pale champagne carpet of Yvette Prentiss's living room. Before I could even register where we were, David was already rolling away, reaching for the open perfume vial that lay on the table, but before he could reach it Kevin's grubby hand snatched it up.

I felt the fury in David at the sight of her smug smile. He was going to rip her apart. There was no softness in him now, no consideration, no humanity. He was nothing but fire, ready to burn.

And then he shuddered, staggered, and collapsed to his knees. I could already feel it happening inside of him. Death. Coming fast. He'd poured so much out in stopping me that he had nothing left, nothing to draw on but me and he was refusing to do that...

I could feel it in myself, too. I turned and screamed at Kevin, '*Order me to heal him! Now!*'

I had no idea I could produce a voice like that, so utterly sure of obedience. Kevin instantly complied. 'Heal him.'

'No!' Yvette shrieked, but it was too late, and I

was already pulling on Kevin's store to replenish the failing energy levels in myself. David collapsed over on his back, fading into mist and reforming with every breath, and I poured life back into him with everything I had.

Close. So very close.

David groaned and rolled over to hands and knees, then managed to get to his feet. Swayed like a three-day drunk. His eyes flared bright orange, and he looked straight at Yvette Prentiss.

And then he lunged for her.

'Don't let him hurt my mother! Hold him still!' Kevin yelled. Direct command, no equivocation. I had no choice.

I turned, grabbed David and held on as he tried to throw me off. I wasn't stronger than he was, not normally, but with Kevin's power pouring into me there was no stopping me. And he was weak, and tired, and hurting.

I pinned him against the wall of her house, rested my head against his and whispered, 'I'm sorry, I'm so sorry, David.' I felt the hand trying to shove me away change to a caress. No words. We didn't need any. 'You shouldn't have done this. Oh God, please, please go, I can't stop you if you go...'

Yvette had another bottle ready. This one was dark blue, oblong, some kind of fancy kitchen bottle built more for display than actual containment, but it had a rubber stopper and it would do the job. She uncorked it and put it on the coffee table next to my tiny open perfume vial.

Where her hand moved, I saw a flicker of blue, falsely cheerful glitter. It had followed us here, too. I could see it shimmering around us, darting like fireflies.

David's eyes met mine. Still flecks of copper swirling in his irises, but he'd never looked so human to me, so precious, so vulnerable.

'I can't go,' he said. His voice was soft, sweet, forgiving.

This was my fault, all my fault, oh God...

He put his hand on my cheek. I turned blindly into the warmth, wanted to cry but no longer knew how.

'Be thou bound to my service.' Yvette's voice was low, seductive, and charged with triumph.

'No matter what happens...' David whispered against my skin.

'Be thou bound to my service.'

'...I love you. Remember that.'

'Be thou bound to my service.'

He kissed me, one last time, our lips meeting and burning, our souls mingling through the touch, and then I felt him torn apart, ripped away.

I felt him die.

I turned and watched the mist stream across the room, coil into the bottle, and watched Yvette slam the cork down in place.

The sense of David's presence vanished instantly. Gone.

I lunged at Yvette, forming steel-hard claws from the fingers of my right hand, and I was halfway to her throat when Kevin screamed, 'Stop!'

I did. Instantly. Fighting with every twitching nerve, but losing against the overwhelming force of his command.

'You can't hurt my mother.' He sounded spooked. 'Or me.'

I felt the claws misting away from my hand. Yvette raised her chin and exposed that fragile, perfect throat to me, and I wanted more than anything to wipe that smug, was-it-good-for-you smirk off her face.

And I couldn't. Son of a bitch!

She said, 'Don't be a fool. You won't be the first Djinn that I've had to teach a lesson.'

I remembered David's near-pathological hatred of her, and felt it burning hot as acid in my stomach, too. Oh, this wasn't going to end well. Not if I had anything at all to say about it.

She turned to her son. Kevin was staring at me, mesmerised. He licked his lips nervously and said, 'Did you really destroy that town?'

I didn't feel compelled to answer – Rule of Three – so I just stared at him with my burning silver eyes. Had I? I hoped to hell not. But I wasn't really sure.

My rescue came from an unexpected source. Yvette said, 'David stopped her. But then, he had good enough reason. Seacasket has something in it he'd kill to protect.' She got up off the sofa and walked around to face me, insinuated sharp-nailed fingers through my hair and arranged it to her liking around my shoulders. 'You're very striking, did you know that? He must feel something incredible for you, to have done that. Believe me, David's long ago learnt the value of self-preservation. The fact that he's so devoted to you is truly amazing.'

I gave her a smile. 'He just wants me for the sex.'

She gave me a smile right back. 'He could get that anywhere.' Her raised eyebrow strongly implied he could get it from her, at better rates, at higher quality. 'I know who you are, you know.'

Of course she did. She'd been at my funeral, stood there looking at the enormous overblown photo of me wreathed by flowers. Her fingernail tapped my cheek, hard enough to sting.

'You killed a friend of mine,' she said. Her voice had dropped down into that throaty, seductive range again. I wondered if she always used that when she talked about killing. 'He was a very special man.'

'Bad Bob? Oh, yeah, I heard he was keeping you in condoms and rent money. Sorry for your loss.' Bad Bob had put a demon down my throat. I had no fond memories.

She slapped me. Well, tried to. I went to vapour and reformed immediately after her hand sailed through the space where I'd been. That was kind of fun. She stumbled into the coffee table from the force of the swing, and for a second the fury in her made her ugly. Uglier than anyone I'd ever seen. *Whoa*. There was the real Yvette Prentiss, the one who hid behind the pretty soft skin and silk-smooth hair and mouth-watering figure.

It was gone so fast I couldn't be absolutely sure I'd even seen it, until I looked over at Kevin. The fear in his eyes told me everything.

'Bob Biringanine was a *visionary*!' she snapped at me. 'You're an ant crawling on the corpse of greatness. Kevin! Tell her not to do that again!'

'Do what?' he asked. She rounded on him, and I saw the flinch from ten feet away. 'Tell her, uh, not to do that vanishing thing?'

'Yes.' She hissed it, like an angry snake. He swallowed twice, rapidly, and looked over at me.

'Uh, don't do that vanishing thing anymore. Making yourself all misty. Unless I tell you to.' He didn't look back at Yvette, stared at the carpet and his ragged tennis shoes instead. 'Can I go now?'

She continued to stare at him, and I didn't like the light in her eyes. Not good. Definitely not good.

'Yes.' She flipped him the perfume vial. He nearly fumbled it, and I felt the Djinn circuitry heating up with anticipation. Of course! Any chance there was that he might drop it... I couldn't do much, but I could nudge it along once it was out of his hands, make sure it hit the sharp edge of the coffee table with enough force to smash it into oblivion...

He held on to it. Damn.

Yvette nodded toward me. 'Take her with you.'

'Yeah, OK. You. Come with me.'

I didn't want to go. I wanted to stay here, guarding that blue bottle that held all that remained of David, but I couldn't disobey a direct order. Kevin walked out of the living room, and I had to follow him.

The last sight I had was her sitting down on the sofa again, picking up the blue stoppered bottle and holding it between her hands.

The expression on her face – avid, delighted, anticipatory – made me go arctic cold inside.

Kevin walked through a door that read KEVIN'S ROOM DO NOT ENTER OR ELSE! It was decorated with skull-and-crossbones decals, pentagrams, line drawings of naked girls grabbing their ankles.

Ah. Home rancid home. He shut the door behind me, stared at me for a couple of seconds, and put the perfume vial down in a nasty-looking ashtray filled with candy wrappers and what strongly resembled the butt ends of a few joints. I looked around. Kevin's room wasn't any more attractive on second viewing than on first. There was no place to sit, other than the dingy rumpled bed, and I was *not* going there.

Kevin flung himself down full length, staring up at the pin-up on the ceiling. Hands behind his head. 'Did you really almost kill those people?'

'Did you want me to?' I countered, and crossed my arms. He shrugged, as much of a shrug as he could manage lying down.

'Probably would have been kind of a mercy, living in a Podunk town like that and all.'

'Why Seacasket?' I asked. He continued to stare up at the centrefold, who pouted and simpered in a frozen second of humiliation. 'Something special about that town?'

'Something about it being important to him. You know. *David*.' He gave the name a contemptuous twist of his lips. 'She's had a hard-on for him for years. Tried to get him before, but Bad Bob wouldn't let her have him for more than a couple of hours. Said she might break him.'

Too much information...I tried not to think about what it meant. 'What now?' I asked.

Another horizontally muted shrug. 'Don't know. Not like she tells me shit.' Definitely more than a little resentment there. This kid was turning out to be interesting. Maybe there was a way to use him...

I stopped the thought train with a squeal of brakes when he suddenly shifted his gaze to stare directly at me. 'I like the other outfit better.'

Crap. I tried not to let him see how much that alarmed me. 'Which one?'

'The one you had on before. With the, you know—' He mimed breasts. 'And the stockings. The one with the apron.'

He still hadn't told me to put it on. 'Wouldn't you like something a little classier?' Dumb question. I was surrounded by glossy photos of women wearing stupid smiles and strips of cloth no bigger than Band-Aids. *Classy* didn't enter into it.

His dark eyes went hard. 'I don't give a shit if you like it or not. Just put it on.'

Well, that was direct. I had no room to manoeuvre. The peachskin pantsuit vanished, replaced with the Frederick's of Hollywood French Maid Nightmare.

Truthfully, I kind of liked the shoes, in a trashy, over-the-top kind of way, and I might not have minded putting the thing on to see the look in David's eyes, but to see it in this kid's...worthy of a shudder. Or two.

The corset top definitely lifted and didn't separate. I looked down at my bulging décolletage and saw I'd been given something new. A classy-looking upside-down pentagram tattoo, just over my left breast.

Unsettlingly close to where there'd once been the black stain of a Demon Mark.

I looked up. Kevin was sitting up in bed, watching me. He licked his lips and said, 'Turn around.'

I did. All the way, back to face him.

'I thought you said I only had three wishes?'

I kept quiet. He wasn't stupid. He knew I'd lied.

'You got any idea what my mom's doing out there your friend? He is your friend, right?' Kevin studied me with too-intelligent eyes, looking for sore spots. 'More than a friend? You fucking him?'

'You're way too young to ask that question,' I said primly. The Julie Andrews tone didn't go with the blow-up doll outfit.

'You'll tell me. You have to.'

'Why do you want to know?' I asked. Which threw him, a bit. 'And anyway, how do you know how many wishes you get? Maybe it's ten. Maybe it's twenty. Maybe the next one is your last, and then I get to rip you into little screaming shreds. Care to try your luck?'

I smiled when I said it. Friendly. Warm. Inviting. He pressed himself back against the headboard, where Miss July of 2003 was squashing her bare breasts together for his inspection.

'What's the use of having you if I can't do anything with you?' he asked. Petulant little jerk. 'I mean, maybe I'll just do it anyway. Wish for what I want most.'

'And what's that?'

He hadn't really thought about it. I hoped he wasn't going to pop off with something stupid, like world peace, but I needn't have worried; Kevin would never think about anyone or anything larger than the confines of his little self-centred universe. He finally came out with, 'I want never to have to work for a living.'

I blinked slowly, thinking that over. Teenage thought processes were so different from adults... An adult would have asked for truckloads of cash, under the assumption that truckloads of money meant no more work. Which wasn't unreasonable, as assumptions go. But Kevin had asked for something completely different.

'So, hypothetically, if you asked for that, you wouldn't be disappointed if I made you a quadriplegic breathing through a tube?' His turn to blink. His mouth opened, produced silence, and closed again. 'I mean, you wouldn't ever have to work for a living, would you? Or I could just kill you. You'd never have to work for a living that way, either. Or, let's see, I could kill everyone else in the world. Never have to work for a living that way, either. Or I could turn you into a big slobbering dog that your mom can feed every day—'

'Stop it!' He looked appalled. 'You're making it all—'

'—complicated?' I finished. 'It is. You want a Djinn, you got one. But we're not fuck-toys, Kevin. We're older than you—' Even me. '—we're smarter than you, and we have absolutely no problem in finding the wrong interpretations of every single wish you are stupid enough to utter in our presence. We're *dangerous*. Get that through your head. You can dress me up like a doll if you want to, but you'll never control me. I'm going to control *you*. So the best thing you can do is take that bottle and smash it, right now, before I get the opportunity to really hurt you. Because I will, Kevin. I'll hurt you so bad it'll make your mom at her worst look like Mary Poppins.'

I had him. I *so* had him. It was all I could do not to gloat. He looked about to vomit with fright.

And then he calmed down, swallowed, and said, 'I know what I want. It's what you want, too. I want you to kill my mother.'

Not that I couldn't understand it, but I felt like it was one of those cartoon moments, the one where you have to smack the side of your head to make sure there's nothing stuck in your ear. I stood there in my ridiculously sexy French Maid outfit and said, 'Excuse me?'

'Yvette,' he clarified hastily. 'My real mom's already dead. My dad, too. I guess what I mean is that I want you to kill my stepmom. Yvette Prentiss.'

I wanted to grin and say, 'Done!' and rush out there and put the big Djinn smackdown on her, but truth is I wasn't all that eager to be killing anybody. Not even a top-rated bitch like Yvette. I was all too aware of how much power there was, flowing from Kevin to me, and how awesomely easy it was to use it. The compulsion was clicking in, but not strongly; there were, I sensed, still grey areas to exploit. I went for them. 'There are all kinds of meanings to *kill*, you know…'

'Dead,' he said. 'Kill her dead. Slowly. Make her suffer.'

He was getting into it now. Which was not my intention. 'OK, let's just…calm down.' Because the compulsion was getting stronger, the power flow cresting like the tide. 'I will. I swear. But let's talk about it first.' Because, luckily, he hadn't specified *now*, the way he had when he'd sent me to Seacasket to commit arson and homicide. 'Why?'

He gave me a dark look. 'What do you care?'

I didn't, really. I was too busy thinking about Yvette putting her hands all over the bottle that held David trapped, seducing Lewis so that innocent little Kevin could sneak up and hit him from behind. 'Yeah, well, what do *you* care? I'm just curious.'

Long silence. He flopped back down on the bed, sounding depressed. 'She's a bitch.'

'You're going to run into them. Get used to it. In fact, pretty much all of us can be bitchy from time to time. Goes with the double-X chromosomes.' Just like Kevin was never going to win any Y-chromosome personality contests, either. 'You can't go around having me snuff out every life that annoys you.'

'Why not?'

Ah, great, a sociopath in training. Again, not the conversational path I was eager to follow. 'What's she done to you, other than be a bitchy stepmom?'

He stared up at the pouting centrefold over his bed, put his hands under his head, and said, 'She makes me do things.'

I had a bad feeling. 'Like?' I was really, really hoping he'd say *clean up the room, take out the trash*…but one look around convinced me that couldn't be true.

He sat up, grabbed the first thing that came to hand a – CD player – and threw it across the room hard enough to smash it to bits against the far wall. 'What the fuck do you think I mean, say my prayers? Brush my teeth?' His flare of rage was sudden, violent, and totally untelegraphed. I had no reason to be afraid, but if I'd still been human I'd have felt utterly exposed. 'She *makes me do things*, you stupid bimbo! Bad things!' He was blazing in Oversight, white-hot, as if some door had opened into hell. 'I want it to *stop*!'

Oh, God. Not what I'd expected, not at all. Nor what I was even vaguely equipped to handle. I pitched my voice low. 'Kevin, you can make that stop without killing her.'

'You don't know shit about it.' Tears quivered in his eyes, jewelled his long, lush eyelashes. 'God, you don't *understand*… I can't even tell you…'

'I know this. You have the power to make her stop, Kevin.' I edged over slowly, walking around the piles of wrinkled filthy clothes and discarded trash, to perch on the edge of the bed next to him. 'You're going to be a Warden. You have the power to control things around you. I don't know if it's weather, or fire, or earth—'

'Fire,' he said, and shut his eyes. 'It's fire.' Which explained the fury of the power that poured into me from him – it had the quality of fire to it. Out of nowhere, I remembered Rahel once telling me, *Fire burns the hand it serves*. Kevin was unstable, volatile, and he had way too much power at his disposal. I couldn't believe the Wardens hadn't already spotted him and started the process to neutralise or control him. If ever there was a reason for neutering someone, taking away their power...

'I burnt the house down. That's how my dad died.'

I didn't want to believe it, but I could sense the truth of it in him. God, such a burden for a sixteen-year-old boy. His father's death, the crushing load of a developing talent of this magnitude, and if he was telling me the truth, some kind of sexual abuse...no wonder he was screwed up.

I wasn't qualified for this. I wasn't sure anybody was.

Kevin kept talking over my silence. 'Bad Bob told me they'd come for me, take me away, but he said he'd protect me.' Yet another public service from Bad Bob Biringanine. Probably as a favour to Yvette, which meant he was banging Mrs Prentiss before the late Mr Prentiss had gone to smoke inhalation heaven. 'Guess he won't protect me now.'

Since I killed him. Right. I studied the frilly lace on my tiny, entirely useless apron. Prodded it with a fingernail, which was painted in hooker red. 'So now you have me to protect you. Is that the general theory?'

'Sure. Nobody's going to come after me if I have

a kick-ass Djinn.' He favoured me with a look. I didn't have the heart to break it to him that if the Wardens found out some underage, untrained kid with a penchant for firestarting had a Djinn, they'd trash the continent looking for him. 'You got me distracted. I said I want you to kill my mother.'

'And I think you should think about that a while.'

He rolled up on one elbow to stare at me. 'Oh, I have. I've thought about it for years. I lay awake at night thinking about it. So you just go—'

'I should find out what she's doing,' I blurted out. 'You want me to kill her – what makes you think that she's not ordering her new Djinn to do the same thing to you? I mean, that's why she wanted you, right? To get me? And through me, to get him?'

He was listening. Not talking, but I could feel him hanging on every word.

'Wouldn't you like to know what she's doing? I could find out. It wouldn't be that hard. She'd never even know I was looking.'

No teenager could resist an opening like that. And a kid who'd been deprived of control his whole life… I was faintly ashamed of myself for feeding his paranoia, but not enough to stop myself.

Kevin wavered, frowned, and said, 'You can do that?'

'If you order me to. I can be invisible. I can go anywhere for you.' And do anything, but it was best not to bring that up. I looked at him from under my eyelashes, pitched my voice low, and said, 'It would be easier if I didn't look quite so...unique. May I change my clothes?'

He sighed and flopped back in a boneless heap of surrender. 'Whatever.'

I put the peachskin suit back on again, covered my eyes with sunglasses, and stood up. 'So I can go?' I asked.

'Whatever.' He sounded hurt, and stubbornly put-upon. 'Just come back. Tell me what she's doing.' He snorted. 'Like I don't already know. She's playing with her new toy.'

I paused, stricken, with one hand on the doorknob. I couldn't get the images out of my head. Kevin threw an arm over his eyes. 'I'm gonna sleep,' he said, grunted, and turned over with his back to me. 'I'll call you when I want you.'

I escaped out into the hall, found my way back to the living room. Yvette was nowhere in sight. Neither was the blue bottle. *Playing with her new toy...* God, no. I had no idea what he meant, but it definitely didn't sound good.

When I moved, I saw a definite fairy-dust after-glow. The coldlight infestation was growing in the real world, just like the aetheric. Of course, so far it didn't seem to be doing anything inimical to me – just decorative. David didn't seem to be suffering ill effects, either.

But then there was the storm, out in the Atlantic,

powering up like some unstoppable juggernaut. It was still there, still growing, and it had to be the coldlight at the heart of it, didn't it? Nothing else made sense.

One problem at a time. This second's had to be Yvette, and getting David out of her well-manicured clutches.

First I had to make sure I couldn't be noticed. I remembered the buzzing sensation that Rahel had used to conceal me at the Empire State Building…a certain frequency, a kind of invisible hum…

I felt it come into tune. When I opened my eyes again I could see a slight blur around me, like shimmer from hot pavement. Couldn't be sure I had it right, but there was no test like the present.

I checked the kitchen. It was clean, modern, neatly organised. Even the salt and pepper shakers were in their places. I opened the refrigerator, just out of curiosity, and found regimental model-home organisation. All the labels were turned outward. Vegetables in the lettuce crisper wouldn't have dared to be less than perky.

Creepy.

The one interesting thing about it was that she had a secret stock of mint chocolate chip ice cream stuffed in the back of the freezer. Premium stuff, not the skim low-fat artificial sweetener crap. I took the carton out and weighed it. Half-empty. It wasn't Kevin's. He wouldn't have cared whether or not anybody saw it, and I suspected the kid had never left an ice cream carton half-empty in his life.

I put everything back and proceeded down the hallway. An extra bedroom turned out to be an office. Everything was in files and folders, neat as an office supply store. No photos. In fact, she had no photos anywhere in the house that I'd seen. The art was all generic, carefully chosen to make absolutely no impression on anybody. I left the office. Three doors left – one was a bathroom, and as much as I'd hated Patrick's trashy Wal-Mart happy faces in his loo, this one was worse. Ducks. Why did it have to be ducks?

The room it opened into was the master bedroom. I admit it, I was scared to go, but I couldn't mist; Kevin had specifically forbidden me to do it. I eased the door open slowly, one inch at a time, alert for giveaway creaks.

I needn't have bothered. She wasn't in there. The bedroom was clean and soulless as a hotel room. Didn't look like a place to let loose unrestrained passion, or any passion at all, come to think of it.

That left the last room. I took hold of the doorknob and felt *something*. A kind of vibration, a warning...

I eased open the door and stepped inside.

The room had started life as a converted garage, then been gentrified with faux wood panelling and plush carpeting. Nothing much in it, but there was an aura to this place like nothing I'd ever felt before. Inanimate objects soak up energy, and that energy becomes visible in Oversight. The place looked dead normal, down here in the real world, but when I blinked and shifted into Oversight the real story came out. Red, rancid glows from the walls. Rotting greens. Pus-dull yellows. This place had seen suffering, and horror. It reminded me of Luminol, the stuff the police use to bring out old bloodstains...the ghost of evil, shining out of the darkness. Pain never dies completely, and this room was suffering.

David stood in the centre of it, motionless, blank as a snowfield. He still retained his dark-copper hair, but it was shorter now, revealing the hard lines of his cheekbones, the strength of his face. The round glasses were gone. His eyes had gone dark. Very, very dark.

He was wearing black leather – pants, jacket, all of it looking butter soft and more than a little sexy. More than a little dangerous, too. Frightening. I wondered if she hadn't actually expressed something essentially true about him that I'd never really quite grasped before...because David now looked like a predator.

Yvette walked a slow circle around him. There was something feline about the way she moved, both in the graceful sway of it and the predatory fascination.

Over the pulsing, thread-thin silver cord, I whispered his name. The dark eyes shifted and focused on me. I'd moved out of the doorway into a corner, shutting the door behind me; Yvette glanced toward me but saw nothing. David continued to stare.

Get out, he whispered to me over the silvery thread connecting us. I felt the warmth wrapping around me like an embrace. *Please. You can't help me.*

I'm not going anywhere. An echo of the pledge he'd made to me. I said it even though I was terrified to watch this, terrified that I couldn't do anything to help.

Yvette was holding the bottle in one hand, swinging it carelessly. Taunting him. Even if she dropped it, the carpet would break the fall; she'd have to throw it hard at the wall to even crack it. Still. If I could catch it on the upswing, it was possible I could help that along...

She froze in mid-step. Her head snapped around, searching corners. She'd sensed something. How? I was sure I'd done it right...

'David?' she asked in that sweet, purring voice. 'Someone here?' No answer. She understood why, unlike Kevin, and kept going without a pause. 'Someone here? Someone here?'

I felt the compulsion click in, even across the room. David said, 'Yes.'

'Show me where.'

He pointed. Right back at her. Yvette smiled. 'Clever boy. Are we going to play these same tired games again? I thought you knew by now that I don't tolerate that kind of thing.'

He lowered his hand to his side. She leant forward and kissed him. Long, hard, hot. The same sultry, meaningless dance she'd done at Patrick's apartment, with Lewis. She was professional at it, I had to give her that much. 'I still think there's somebody here,' she said when she pulled back for air. David remained still, blank-faced, unresponsive as a store mannequin. 'Maybe that little silver-eyed friend of yours? Well. I've never minded an audience, I have to say, and you always seemed to perform better in front of one.'

Bitch.

There had to be something I could do.

She unzipped the black leather jacket, slowly, sliding her hands inside on the warm gold skin. I gritted my teeth. *You can't hurt my mother.* Kevin had given me that command. Since he hadn't been specific enough about his command to kill her, the two orders were floating around in limbo, the first one still applying. I wanted to wrap my hand around her throat and squeeze until she came apart, but I wasn't sure I should even try it. And trying and failing would be far worse, just now.

'Take that off,' she told him. He stripped off the jacket and let it fall in a glistening heap to the floor.

'You know what I want, David. What I always want.'

Oh, I had a pretty good idea, too. Or thought I did.

He proved me wrong.

I watched, sickened, as he reached out for her...

...grabbed her by the hair, and slammed her face down on the carpet.

Still no change in him. Controlled, calm, utterly emotionless.

Oh *God*.

He rolled her over, and the flushed, breathless excitement on her face said it all. No wonder this place reeked of sickness. Yvette was one *very* sick lady.

I dropped the concealment. She spotted me instantly over David's shoulder as I walked slowly forward, and the insane glee in her eyes was almost as nauseating as what she was about to force David to do. I remembered the dream, David's desperate attempt to make Jonathan understand. *It's rape.*

'I thought you were there,' she said. 'Excellent. Maybe I'll have you join us.'

'David,' I said calmly. 'Would you like for me to do something about this?'

He couldn't speak, of course. Couldn't do anything. He was fixed on her, and I thought I read utter despair in those dark, alien eyes.

'What do you imagine you can do?' Yvette asked me, sugar sweet, looking ravishingly beautiful spread out on the floor. So very pretty. So very twisted. 'Other than admire his technique.'

I crossed my arms and maintained my cool. 'Well, I could do what your son suggested and kill you. What do you think?'

She froze, staring up at me, and her face was for a few seconds comically surprised. 'You're lying.'

'Well, yes, we Djinn do that. Believe me or not.' I shrugged to show the depth of my not-caring. 'Suit yourself.'

I looked at David, who was still frozen, waiting for her command. Leashed, but far from tame. She got up, still watching me, and put her hand on his shoulder to bring him up with her. Slid it in a proprietary way along the warm glory of his skin, up his neck, over a well-shaped ear, to dig her fingers luxuriously into his hair. No protest from him, and no flinch. I knew he had more latitude than that – didn't he? – but he wasn't refusing anything from her. Maybe she'd already given that command before I came on the scene. Or maybe he was drawing her in, making her careless.

I hoped.

'Did he used to be yours?' she asked me, and made the hand into a fist, jerking his head sideways toward her. Still no change of expression from him. I tried to listen, to see if he was sending me any whispers along the shared bond between us, but all I heard was silence. He'd gone deep, and far away from me. What was left might be something I didn't know and couldn't count on.

'I don't own people,' I said. God, I sounded self-righteous. I decided that was OK, because I felt pretty self-righteous, too. 'We freed the slaves in this country, or did you flunk history along with your sanity test?'

She turned and looked at David, pulled his head closer to hers and whispered something in his ear, then turned back to me, cheek pressed against his.

They both smiled. I felt a cold streak form along my spine, felt goosebumps rising under it, because those smiles were soulless, and dead, and dreaming of something awful. I remembered David smiling at me, the day I'd met him on the road after I'd spun the car out in a cloud of dust. I remembered the sharp, intelligent wit in those beautiful eyes. I remembered his skin, waking and shivering at my touch.

She couldn't own any of that. What she did own was a shell. Skin. A ghost.

I kept telling myself that, but I couldn't stop the sick, awful horror of this from threatening to choke me. Her hands were still moving on David. I wanted to rip them off at the wrists.

'My little Kevin finally grew some balls? You're bluffing, sweetie pie. He couldn't.'

I looked around the room. 'He's been in here, hasn't he?' No answer. Yvette sat up. Her blouse had popped a couple of buttons, but the view didn't impress me. 'You and little Kevin, playing games. How heart-warming. And you think he wouldn't want you dead? Honey, I just met you and I *so* want you dead.'

'So you come here and warn me?' She was regaining her composure. 'Not likely.'

'I'm not all that eager to be Kevin's little love slave, either,' I said. Everything I was saying had the ring of truth, because, well, it was. 'I'm here to offer you a deal.'

She blinked. Deals were made from positions of power. We both knew I didn't have any. 'Don't be ridiculous. You were entertaining for a few seconds, but you're getting boring. I hurt things that bore me.'

When I smiled, I borrowed a trick from Rahel. Shark teeth. The flinch was well worth the discomfort. 'There's something you want more than David,' I said. I was guessing, of course, but with someone like her there was always something else. Toys got old the instant she had them in her hands, and besides, she'd had David before. No thrill of corruption there. 'I can give it to you.'

She actually froze for a few seconds, considering me, and I saw the hot light of greed flicker in those green eyes. 'And what exactly would that be?'

I shrugged. 'You know well enough.' Ah, the Djinn talent for misdirection. Still serving me well, thank God. 'If you want to waste me on a fool like your stepson, that's your right. But think how much more you could accomplish, if you had *me*.'

She didn't know. To her mind, I was already assuming legendary powers and proportions...a human reborn as a Djinn. She couldn't have any idea of how much of a handicap that was. In fact, she probably thought that was what I was offering her. Life as a Djinn.

Over my dead body. Spirit. Whatever.

'Not very loyal to him, are you?' she asked. 'Why should I think you'd be any more loyal to me?'

I shrugged. 'The kid's weak. You know that.' So was she, in a totally different way. Weak and greedy and sick. 'You want to use David as some kind of cheap toy, that's your prerogative. I just thought you should expand your horizons a little. The world's a little wider than your bedroom.'

'You think I'm not ambitious?'

I didn't have to fake the cynical smile. People like her were always ambitious.

'You made a mistake,' I said. 'You could have had Lewis on your side. Now you've made a bad enemy. You're going to need help to stay alive once he gets back on his feet.'

'Lewis?' she asked blankly, and let go of David. She'd completely forgotten about him.

'Lewis Levander Orwell? Yeah. That guy. The one you were rubbing like a magic charm to get your hands on *me*. You traded down, honey. Having Lewis would have been quite a feather in your cap. Talk about advancement... Only now, of course, you're just the bimbo who bashed his head in, not the one who brought him back to the Wardens.'

That shook her. She'd had victory in her hands and walked away, and that had to hurt.

'You're a lying, treacherous bitch,' she said, low in her throat, and wrapped her hand around David's bare arm. 'You really think you're going to make a *deal* with me? I don't deal with the likes of you. *Ever*. You serve me, or you suffer. Your choice.'

Kevin's instructions to kill her were starting to look really, really tempting. Maybe if I just hurt her a lot...no, I'd seen the look on her face as David threw her down to the floor. She'd probably think it was foreplay.

'Serve me or suffer.'

'Already got a boss,' I said, and spread my hands. 'Such as he is.'

She didn't like being denied. 'Take her,' she said, and released her hold on David.

He lunged for me, and God, he was *strong*. I yelped and tried to break free but his hands were crushing my arms, holding me still, shoving me back against that wall that, in Oversight, still dripped psychic blood. I wanted to mist away, but Kevin's command earlier effectively prevented that. Trapped. Blue sparks zipped and swirled around me, thicker now, thick as a bag of glitter dropped from the ceiling. I blinked to clear my eyes. The things were swarming over David, too, clustering on his skin.

'*David!*' I whispered. Nothing sparked in the dark, dead eyes. I wondered what she'd told him to do to me. Wondered if it was anything I'd be able to stop. The things that had happened in this room…they crowded like phantoms, brushing at the edges of awareness, given strength by my fear and David's aggression. I could almost see some of them, and just the hints made me feel weak and ill. What had David told me? She and Bad Bob had tastes in common.

Like Kevin, he'd been made to do things, probably here in this room. Things I couldn't begin to understand, even with the ugly hints I'd already been given.

He twisted sharply at my arm, and I felt bone shatter with a dull cracking sound. Pain screamed through me, and in the next second it took on another horrible dimension as more bones in my body began to break. David's doing. Destroying my physical form.

Instinct made me rebuild, but I couldn't do it fast enough. His power ripped at me like a wild thing, shredding muscle, pulverising bone, exploding vital organs.

I couldn't even scream. My mouth opened, but all that came out of it was a hot bitter trickle of blood. I collapsed against him. Something in me kept struggling to reassert the template of my natural form, but he was stronger at this, better. He knew exactly how to hurt me.

He eased me down to the carpet. I lay struggling to move, feeling life energy leaking out of my broken body, and begged him silently to *stop*.

Yvette had moved closer. She leant over him now,

staring down at me, a blank-faced goddess with unclean eyes. 'You know what I want,' she told him, and caressed his hair again, running the short auburn strands through her fingers. Petting him, the way she'd pet a particularly glorious and dangerous animal. 'Make it last.'

He reached for my throat.

I felt another will impose itself over mine.

Right on cue, I vanished.

I collapsed in a heap, blind with shock and pain, and knew I was somewhere else. Where?

Ground-in, Day-Glo orange spots in the rug just inches from my face, and a few more feet away, a grease-stained pizza box with its top partly open. A fat brown-shelled roach was scuttling along the top of it. It stopped to waggle its antennae inquiringly, then decided I was no threat to its conquest.

I couldn't breathe. My lungs had been ruptured. My body – human, not human, whatever it was was – shutting down. That wouldn't kill me, I sensed, but it would trap me inside of a dead shell. Not the way I wanted to escape, especially since it meant I wouldn't be going anywhere.

'Yo!' Kevin's pimply, pallid face appeared in my field of vision, pointed at a weird horizontal angle. He was bending over, staring at me. He waved a hand in front of my eyes, snapped his black-fingernailed, blunt-cut fingers. 'You OK?'

I couldn't answer. I slowly blinked my eyes,

which was about all that my body was capable of doing for me at the moment.

'Oh,' he said, and straightened up. He prodded me with the toe of a particularly crappy-looking sneaker. This close, the smell of his feet was rancid, like mould-ridden buttermilk. 'She got to you, huh? Yeah. Thought so. So, can you fix yourself?'

I blinked again. If ever I needed the kid to catch a clue...

'You can't, can you? You need me for that.' He crouched down, staring down at me. 'You *need* me. How about that? Not so high and mighty now, are we?' A thick finger prodded at my flaccid arm, and broken bones grated together. 'What if I just leave you here, huh? What's your game plan then, bitch? Lay there and bleed on me? Some fucking guardian you are.'

He sounded surly, but there was a tremor deep down. He was scared, all right. Not of me. He knew what she was capable of, and he wanted a friend. Protection. *Something*.

I tried to move my lips, but it was useless. I couldn't even blink anymore. My eyes were fixed and staring. I heard my heart murmur one last, regretful beat, and then the blood in my veins slowed and stopped.

Death was anticlimactic, as a Djinn. I kept waiting for something, anything. I still had senses – I could hear the rustle of Kevin's baggy jeans as he paced back and forth, could smell the unwashed aroma that eddied off of him through the room. Under the bed, the cockroach emerged from the pizza box with a couple of its friends, paused, and tried to figure me out. I must not have looked tasty. They went the other way.

Kevin's bedroom door suddenly blew open. Locks tore off of the frame and hit the far wall with enough force to put holes in the Sheetrock. I didn't have a good view, but I heard Kevin's pacing stop and stagger backward. He stumbled right into me, lost his balance, and fell. I felt him roll across me, hot and sweaty and tense with panic.

The swirl of power that went through the room was unmistakable.

David was here.

Kevin grabbed my limp, broken hand and yelled, 'Fix yourself, dammit! Stop him! Don't let him hurt me!'

Game on.

I felt my body instantly begin to heal, drinking in power from him to rebuild itself, and before I was anywhere near better I rolled away from him, away from his grip, and came fluidly to my feet to stand between him and David. Blue sparkles flashed all over me with false Vegas cheer.

Yvette was with him, of course. Still smiling.

'You left.' She pouted. 'It was just getting interesting. We're going to have *lots* of fun, sweetie, aren't we?' The butter-wouldn't-melt-in-her-mouth tone turned cold and cutting as she focused past me, on her stepson. 'Tell her to submit.'

'Yeah?' His voice wavered, but didn't break. 'Maybe I won't.'

Why the hell had she ever taken a chance and given him a Djinn? No, I knew why…because she thought he was completely under her control, and she knew that having two Djinn under her direct control could be dangerous. Well, arrogance was part of her pathology.

David moved a step closer. I matched him like a mirror image. Kevin's order had me, of course. If David made any aggressive moves at all, I was free to stop him, and to use every ounce of power Kevin possessed to do it.

'News flash,' I said aloud, straight to her. 'Not the submitting type. You want to take me, you can try, but it's going to be one hell of a fight, and believe me, the damage won't be anything you can patch up with base make-up and a couple of Band-Aids. I *will* hurt you.'

'Yeah,' Kevin agreed. 'And I'll let her. No, I'll *order* her to do it.'

Her green eyes flicked to him, and the look on her face… If I'd had any doubt that she'd played her sick little games with him, that put them to rest. The pure, nauseating hatred made me feel filthy to see it.

'You stupid little bastard. I give you a toy, and you try to *threaten* me with it? You're pathetic. David, I want you to—'

'Kevin, I want to take you out of here,' I interrupted her, and looked straight at the kid. 'I'll take you out of here if you want me to.'

He was no fool, even with the obvious social handicaps. He smiled, showing me crappy dental hygiene, and said, 'Yeah. Take me somewhere. Somewhere else.'

It meant leaving David, oh God, I didn't want to do that, but I didn't have a choice. I had to do what I could. Patrick had said it. *First, preserve your life.* I didn't think I could die here, but I'd damn sure wish I could.

I grabbed Kevin, wrapped him in my arms, and pulled on that vast pool of energy stored inside of him to take him…

…back to Patrick's apartment.

Not a smooth ride through the aetheric. I tried to avoid the worst of the blue flares, but it was worse now, burning everywhere. A cheery fairy-dust snowstorm.

Patrick's apartment place was empty. Bloodstains on the carpet, already dried. No sign of Lewis, or Patrick, or Sara. No sign that Rahel had ever returned.

I let Kevin go, shook off another thick moving layer of sparklies, and knelt down to touch the stiff brown-soaked fibres on the floor. Lewis's essence. Through it, I could trace him. Find him…

'What now?' Kevin asked me. He avoided the

bloodstains and went around to the other side of the couch, where he wouldn't have to look at what he'd done. 'She'll come after us, you know. She's not going to let us go. All she has to do is tell him to find us.'

He had the perfume vial in his pocket, stuffed in among a pack of condoms that at this rate he probably would never need. Nothing hard enough for me to shatter the glass against. Pure luck, probably. He wasn't clever enough to protect it on purpose.

I stayed where I was, in a crouch, touching the evidence of his guilt. 'Yeah, well, if you still want me to kill her, I'm up for it.'

'Really?' Hope and dread, all packed into one word. 'Holy shit.'

Lewis, where the hell are you? I really didn't feel well. Maybe it was the cost of David's deconstruction of my body. Dying had to come with a price. I needed Lewis, not just because I was worried, but because as a human he could physically take the bottle away from Kevin and shatter it. Lewis was my only real hope of freedom, unless Kevin made a monumental error. Which was not beyond the realm of possibility, if I stayed alert.

Speaking of being alert...my brain finally caught up with the fact that Kevin wasn't giving me orders, he was *listening* to me. And my clothing had stayed the way I'd chosen.

He wasn't seeing me as a slave just now. He was seeing me as a friend.

'I need some help,' I said aloud. 'Your stepmother's got power, and now that she has David, she can do a lot more. We need to talk to the Wardens. They can help neutralise her without too much of a fight.'

All true, again. I was trying not to lie to him, because I knew it would come back to haunt me later.

The blood told me that Lewis had lain here unconscious for a long time – hours, maybe – before he'd finally come to his senses and left. Things were vague, from then on. He might not have been thinking clearly. Still alive, though. That came through with a clarity that eased a knot deep inside of me. I'd really feared that we'd left him here to die.

'The Wardens would never take my side,' Kevin said. He flopped down on the leather couch, folded his hands on his chest and stared up at the mullioned ceiling that had previously been far too X-rated for a kid his age. 'They'd kill me. The old guy said so.'

'Bad Bob wasn't exactly a paragon of truth and virtue,' I told him. 'He lied to me, too, lots of times. Look, you can trust me, Kevin. I promise that I won't try to hurt you.'

I came around to the other side and sat down on the edge of the couch, looking down at him. He kept staring at the ceiling, but there was a suspiciously bright shine in his eyes.

'I can't go home,' he said. 'She'll kill me now. She really will.'

'I won't let her.'

'Yeah?' A hot, burning flick of those miserable eyes. 'Like you could stop her. At least while she has that *guy* of yours.'

'I'll fight if you will,' I said. 'Come on, Kevin. You told me you wanted her dead. How about just removed? Taken away? Unable to hurt you again? What about that?'

He thought about it, fiddled with the loose riveted button of his jeans, and finally nodded. 'Yeah. OK. Just so long as I never have to see her again.'

I sucked in a deep breath, closed my eyes, and let it out. I propped myself in a chair and dialled a number from memory. As my fingers moved, I saw them picking up blue sparks, and shook them to get the crap off – not that I could feel it, but it creeped me out. I'd seen for myself how the stuff was drawn to the use of power, back in Seacasket – we'd been swarming with sparks.

Paul Giancarlo's rough, Jersey-flavoured voice said, 'Yes?' The tone was sharp and impatient. Maybe he'd been dealing with telemarketers all day.

I opened my mouth, started to speak, and suddenly hesitated. This was a step I hadn't expected to take, and I sensed that it was a big one.

Maybe the kind you couldn't take back later.

Things would never be the same.

'Hello?' He sounded pissed, and two seconds from slamming down a hang-up.

'Paul?' I said. My voice shook a little. 'It's Jo.'

Silence. I couldn't tell what was happening on the other end. Then, very quietly, 'Jesus.'

'No, just Joanne, although I can see how you might make the mistake, coming back from the dead and all.' I sounded too maniacally cheerful. 'It's a long story, and I don't think we have time right now.'

'You're alive?'

'Again, yes, and we don't have time. I need to find Lewis—'

'Lewis?' Paul had recovered fast. His tone was back to crisp and businesslike, at least so far as I could tell. 'Yeah. He came here. Had one hell of a head wound. I tried to get him to let an Earth Warden take a look at him, but no way would he do it. He took off about an hour ago, maybe less.'

'Did he remember what happened?'

'Do you?' Paul countered. 'He said your name, but I figured…you know…'

'Head injury, yeah.' I rubbed numbed fingertips together. 'Things have gotten complicated.'

'More than you with a Demon Mark?'

'Yeah.'

'Fuck me running… OK. How much trouble are you in right now?'

'About all there is.' I closed my eyes, went up briefly into the aetheric, then back down, fast. 'Not just me, though. All of us.'

He grunted. 'I don't have time for coming-back-from-the-dead riddle hour. You got some ghostly warning to deliver, just do it – there's a storm off the Atlantic seaboard that's going nuts—'

'And a fire in Yellowstone, and tectonic pressure in California,' I said. 'I know. And it's worse than you think. Way worse.'

That got a moment of silence. Paul was a pessimist. If it was worse than he thought, it was pretty damn bad, and he knew it.

'Jesus, Jo, what the hell are you into now?' he asked.

'Favour for a favour. You do for me, I'll tell you. You've got a Warden working for you named Yvette Prentiss?'

He made a sour noise. 'Nominally. I've got an all-hands call out right now, and she ain't even picking up the phone. She's fired, soon as I get the time to sign the paper. Not that I shouldn't have fired the crazy bitch years ago, but she had some friends—'

'Yeah, Bad Bob, I know. Listen, I need you to get Miriam and the Power Rangers over to her place. Now. She's broken just about every Warden's code there is, and what's left won't last the night.'

'Look, I don't have a lot of time for disciplinary—'

'She's stolen a Djinn,' I said flatly. 'She's torturing him. *Paul*. She's going to destroy him.'

Silence, again. Long, crackling silence.

'Paul?' I prompted.

'Lewis already asked me for her address. Shit, Jo, I can't do this right now. We've got all hell breaking loose around here. I'm sorry about Yvette, and yeah, we'll take care of her as soon as we can, but right now we've got innocent lives to save, and three fronts to fight on. So it'll just have to wait.' He sounded grim, but determined. 'I'm sorry.'

'Yeah.' I tasted ashes. 'I understand. Thanks.'

'Wait, tell me—'

I hung up on him. Immediately, the phone began to ring. Caller ID, auto call-back, something like that. I let it clamour for attention and sat, thinking hard.

'They're not gonna help,' Kevin said. He was sitting up, draped over the back of the couch, acne-spotted chin propped on thin arms. 'I knew it. Nobody ever helps. Well, fuck her anyway. We can go anywhere, right? Do anything? I don't need her. She can just do whatever.'

Lewis had asked for the address. He knew that Yvette was involved. But he was going over there hurt, disadvantaged, and she had David to use as a weapon...

'We're going back,' I said.

Even from across the room, I saw Kevin's morose expression turn mulish. 'In your dreams.'

'Kevin, we have to go back. It's up to us to stop her—'

'From screwing your boyfriend?' He blew a raspberry and flopped back down on the couch, out of sight. His voice stayed annoyingly stubborn. 'No. Not gonna happen.'

'She'll come after you.'

'No she won't. She's got what she wanted. Me, she's just as happy to be rid of.' Leather creaked as he stretched. 'You know what this place needs? A bitchen big-screen TV. With adult channels.'

Indirect. I ignored it. 'Kevin—'

'I want a big-screen TV. With adult channels.'

I screamed inside with frustration. I could have wasted time optioning him to death – *Standard or widescreen? Brand name? Model number?* – but time was something I no longer had. I just used the power he poured inside of me to find the biggest, most ostentatious TV I could find and transport it to an empty wall in the apartment. Plugged it into main power. Created an invisible satellite hook-up. Materialised a remote control on the coffee table. 'Anything else?'

'DVD.'

I gave him that. I also skipped the intermediate steps and gave him a cutting-edge sound system, big honkin' speakers, a full CD rack based on the most recent Billboard charts, headphones, amplifiers, every movie in the last twenty years (at his age, he wouldn't care about anything else).

'Bitchen,' Kevin said, awestruck. He got up to fiddle with the remote. 'Whoa.'

'Let me go,' I said. He froze, hands still twisting knobs. 'Kevin, please. I'm asking you as a friend. Let me go and do *something*.'

'Friend?' he echoed. There was something lost and little-boy in that word, something fragile. 'I don't even know your real name.'

'Joanne,' I said quietly. 'My name is Joanne.'

'Huh.' He pulled out a CD and examined it. 'I liked Lilith better.'

'Kevin…'

I watched his shoulders hunch together under the threadbare, ripped T-shirt, remembered his step-mother's love of S&M…S, probably, in his case. He'd never had a friend, at least not since Yvette came into his life. Alone. Scared. In pain.

I could bully him into anything I wanted. I would, if I had to, for David. But it would haunt me worse than anything else I'd ever done.

'If you're really my friend, you won't go,' he said. 'You'd stay here. Take care of me.'

How young had he been, the first time she'd hurt him? The quaver I heard in his voice was the cry of a child too small to understand why it was happening. *Bitch*. I ached with the need to do something to her, anything, to even the score. I understood David's black fury now, when he'd seen her at the funeral. He'd had a close, unclean relationship with her for too long not to hate her.

I walked around the couch to where Kevin was

randomly picking up CDs and sliding them back into the rack, hands shaking.

I put my arms around him. For a frozen second it was like embracing a corpse – no response at all – and then I felt his muscles relax and huddle into me, accepting the comfort. He smelt bad, but I didn't have to breathe if I didn't want to. I wondered how much of his slovenly approach to hygiene and housekeeping was designed to keep the perfectly coifed, house-proud Yvette at a distance.

I caressed his oily, lank hair and whispered, 'Kevin, I *am* your friend. And I'll come back to you. Just please, let me save him. You don't want to leave him there. You know what'll happen to him. You've seen it. You've *felt* it. You have the power to save somebody, Kevin. Use it.'

He slipped a hand into the pocket that I knew held my bottle, but he didn't bring it out. It was almost like he was clutching a rabbit's foot...his own personal lucky charm.

'You'll come back?' he asked. 'Promise?'

'I swear.'

I held him for another few seconds, which ended when I felt a palm slide down to my butt. 'Hey! Hands!'

'Sorry,' he mumbled, and moved back. 'Don't – don't let her hurt you. And come back.'

I reached out and kissed him. One chaste, gentle kiss. When I pulled away he was staring at me with wide, stunned eyes.

Never been kissed. Nothing sweet about the sixteen he was living.

I spread my arms, ready to rise into the aetheric.

'Stop!' Kevin cried. I looked at him and saw that he'd taken the perfume vial out of his pocket. His knuckles were white around it. 'Wait. I can't. You're all I have.' A deep, chest-heaving breath, like a sob.

'Kevin, no—'

'Back in the bottle. Sorry.'

I screamed out my frustration, but the grey swirl was already sucking me down, helpless, into oblivion.

I didn't want to dream, because I knew what it would be. Something bad. I'd come to the conclusion that the only things Djinn ever dreamt, trapped in oblivion, were really nightmares.

I hate being right.

In my dream, the Djinn were dying.

Each of the three sentient events out there – the forming earthquake, the strengthening fire in Yellowstone, the storm cell gathering in the Atlantic – had drawn Wardens in response. Of those, the top masters of each area had Djinn to focus and amplify their powers. Perhaps a hundred, all total...

...a hundred victims.

I watched, helpless, as the sparklies saturated in a slow, graceful rain through the aetheric, bathing the Djinn like radiation; the more power each Djinn sourced, the greater the concentration of cold blue rain around them. They knew. They knew it was killing them, and they couldn't prevent it.

Some of the Wardens understood what was happening. They pulled their Djinn back, sealed them in bottles, hoped that the damage could be contained.

The rest pushed blindly ahead, focused on the objectives.

In California, tectonic plates rippled, shifted, slid. Earth Wardens were pushed aside by the forces at work, their weakened Djinn useless. The first shudders began, working deep in the earth.

In Yellowstone, fire flowed unchecked, like a river; it crested a hill and raced down, leaping from treetop to treetop, lapping the trunks in a molten river of flame. Trees cracked and exploded with sounds like gunshots as sap boiled inside. There were no animals running ahead of it; the superheated air had raced ahead, killing everything in its path.

Fire Wardens were struggling to build containments, but it was useless. Their Djinn were failing.

Yellowstone was going to burn. Again.

I couldn't even bear to look at the raging fury that was forming out to sea. *Please. Tell me how I can stop this.*

The combined might of the Wardens couldn't stop it. The idea that I could do anything, anything at all, was sheer lunacy.

I felt a presence with me. Something cool and peaceful.

Next to me sat a tall woman with unearthly beautiful features, hair white as snow, eyes pure amethyst.

Sara, I said. She gave me a sad, gentle smile.

Am I? She looked out at the devastation below. *So much pain, for so little. I wish this would end. I wish I could stop it.*

Can anyone? I asked. Rhetorical question. I rested my chin on raised knees like a little girl, and watched the end of the world in fire and flood and the slow rolling of the earth.

Oh, yes. Sara seemed surprised I didn't know. *Of course. You can.*

I straightened up and met her eyes. Such cool, deep eyes, all the flecks and facets of a jewel. No wonder Patrick loved her. No wonder he'd do anything, no matter how horrible, to ensure her survival.

Me?

She nodded slightly. Tears formed in her eyes, ran down her smooth, perfectly pale cheeks.

Patrick knew, she said. *From the first moment he saw you.*

That I could close the rift?

That you are the rift.

I didn't have time to feel the shock of that, because just then the pain started. Sara winced too, laid her hands over her chest and bent forward. It felt like we were being pulled by a fishhook, right through our bodies…tugged somewhere.

What the hell…

Sara looked up. Her eyes were flat black now, the jewel colour lost, and her hair was twisting and blackening into a burnt and petrified ruin.

It's time to go. Remember. Remember.

And then it was lost, all a grey dream, floating in oblivion.

Pop goes the perfume cork.

I was ready, this time – I came boiling out, took form as soon as I was free of the bottle, was already moving to grab Kevin's T-shirt and back him up against the wall.

'You!' I yelled. 'You treacherous, shallow little—'

He was paler than usual, babbling something that I wasn't listening to, because there were Wardens and Djinn *dying* out there. I'd felt it like the death of a thousand cuts inside that bottle. With every life slipping away there'd been another slice, another piece gone from the world. From *me*.

And there was this *summons*. Dragging at me like an anchor, pulling me apart.

It was still there, throbbing *come home* like a heartbeat inside me.

Kevin was holding my bottle in a death grip. I grabbed his wrist and squeezed. 'Drop it!' I snarled. 'Drop it or I take your hand off.'

'Don't hurt me.' He managed to blurt that out,

and I was trapped, another barrier in the road. Dammit. I let go – no choice – and backed away.

We were still in Patrick's remodelled apartment. The TV was showing something that involved a lot of ships in space blowing up, but the sound was on mute. I spun away from Kevin and stretched out my senses, such as were left, trying to find someone, *anyone* to help, because I absolutely had to go. The summons wasn't something that could be denied. The connection to David was still there – faint, but present – and I felt it twisting and vibrating with stress. *God, what was she doing*...no. David couldn't be my first priority. Not now.

'Sara!' I yelled. 'Sara! Please! I don't understand what to do! Help me!'

The shadow of the Ifrit glided past me, drifting, barely visible. I grabbed for it, but it slipped away.

'Feed,' she whispered.

I couldn't feed her. I had nothing in reserve, and so little coming from David that I was afraid to try to pull more; it might snap the connection altogether, leave him bleeding to death out there.

I turned to Kevin. He was still up against the wall where I'd left him, looking spooked and more than a little angry; I didn't have time for that, or for his adolescent angst, or even for his pain.

There was too much pain, now. His – and mine, and David's – was barely a drop in the bucket.

'Order me,' I snapped.

'To do what?'

'Anything!'

He looked blank for a second, then a sly, oily light came into his eyes. 'Take your clothes off and put on the ones I like. The—' He made the corset gesture.

'Sure. Whatever.' I started stripping, using my hands to slow down the process, as the gate opened to his power. I started siphoning for all I was worth, filling myself with that thick dark-syrup flood, and looked for Sara.

She was hovering like a ghost in the shadow next to the massive television. I locked eyes with the black void where I thought her face should be, and began sending Kevin's power into her. Force-feeding. By the time I'd stripped off my pants I'd already formed the lacy undergarments for the Frederick's outfit, so there was no actual nudity involved, but Kevin was looking just as stunned as if I'd done a Full Monty for him. Good. Stunned would keep him out of my way.

I templated on the French Maid outfit and walked forward, to where the Ifrit had gained dark, smooth substance. *Can you hear me?* I asked her. Somewhere under the shadows, I thought I saw a flash of purple eyes.

I hear. It was barely a whisper, but it was there. And it sounded like the Sara of my dreams.

Can you take me where I'm supposed to go?

Jonathan. Such a wealth of sadness in that single word. *Yes. Can.*

What about Patrick?

She seemed to flinch. *Gone. Seeking.*

I sucked in a deep breath that creaked the corset and strained the engineering of its lacings. *Take me to Jonathan.*

Barrier. The sparklies? No, that wasn't meant to be a barrier. It was far too porous. *Hard to pass.*

We had to. I held up a finger to put her on hold as Kevin walked up behind me.

He put his arms around me and pulled me close, and I nearly gagged when I realised how turned on he was. God, how had I gotten myself into this…

'I want you to—' Tactical error. I hadn't finished dressing yet, which meant I still had access to his power. He couldn't give me simultaneous commands.

'Sleep,' I said, spun around in his arms and used some of the power that was still flowing through me to turn back on him. 'Dream about me.'

For a second I thought it wasn't going to work, but then his eyes rolled back in his head, his mouth fell open, and he dropped like a bag of bricks to the carpet. The bottle stayed in his hand, clenched tight. *Dammit*. If it had rolled free…

I tried working on his fingers, but I couldn't get them to relax. Probably some Djinn rule against it anyway. Couldn't break them, since he'd ordered me not to hurt him. Couldn't kill him – OK, not that I would have, but…

I dragged him feet first over to the leather couch, got him comfortably situated, and tried not to listen to the moaning. Oh, yeah, he was dreaming about me. I hoped I'd remembered to Scotchgard the couch.

'Do it,' I said to Sara.

The Ifrit leapt on me, dug talons deep into my chest, and started to feed. After the first few seconds of agony...

...we were falling through the aetheric. Fast. Balled up together, inseparable, feeding on one another like an ouroboros. Falling like a meteor through the aetheric, up through higher levels, the weirdest sensation of gliding in a direction that wasn't up or down or sideways, here or there. I remembered the weirdness of the journey to Jonathan's house, even in the relatively familiar analogue of the elevator. The Ifrit wasn't even trying to cloak this in familiar terms.

The aetheric was a minefield of disasters in progress. To the east, the furious storm was consuming power at a frightening rate; it was a towering whirlwind of coldlight and pure energy, and the few Wardens still fighting it were flickering, weak, and near to breaking. I didn't sense any other Djinn. The fires in Yellowstone lit up the plane like a supernova – consuming everything in all the realms of our reality, nearly obscured by a shell of the swirling blue sparks. No Wardens at all near that, now. And no Djinn.

We hurtled toward the centre of the inferno. I tried to scream, but the Ifrit was drawing everything out of me, every ounce of power and will, and I was deadweight by the time we hit the fires. The pain was so intense I thought that it was over, I was gone, but then there was a sense of pushing through something viscous and thick, of being squeezed, and then a sudden unexpected release.

We tumbled down, fast, still locked together. She was still feeding off of me.

We slammed down onto something hard and unyielding, and I realised I'd been made flesh again, sans tacky French Maid get-up; I was wearing a long pale robe instead, something soft and cool and with a texture like silk.

It was the mirror image of what the woman kneeling astride me was wearing, only hers was a blinding white where mine was a soft cream.

Sara had regained her form. At least for the moment. She was breathing hard, eyes wide and a little wild, and the dull flush in her cheeks could have been exhilaration or post-traumatic stress. Her claws were still sunk deep into my chest, and I could see the pale steady fire of my lifeforce running up through them, into her.

'Get off!' I managed to say, and batted at her weakly. She pulled the claws out, looking stunned and still maniacally excited, and stood up as I rolled over on my side. Oh *God*. I felt a wave of pure nausea and spat out blue sparks. They were sparkling all over Sara, too, but she didn't seem to feel any ill effects from them. In fact, the sparks were going *into* her, not being rejected.

I'd never felt so frail and sick in my life – human or Djinn. I lay full length on the cool, silky wood floor, struggling to keep myself together, and heard footsteps from the other room.

Ah, perfect. Jonathan. She'd brought me to Jonathan.

He looked down at me with those cool, dark, judging eyes, then bent over and picked me up. Paused when he saw Sara standing there, looking unearthly and beautiful and unhealthily stuffed with energy.

'You,' he said. Not welcoming, not unwelcoming, and not surprised. 'Stay here.'

I liked being held in a man's arms again, feeling the strength against me. It made me feel safe, for the first time in what seemed like an eternity. I tried to pay attention, but it was all just flashes and impressions – a hallway, a glimpse of a kitchen, what looked like photos on the wall, an open darkened doorway. Lights flipped on as he carried me in. The softness of a bed sucked me down.

Jonathan looked down at me, and I was surprised to see something in his eyes that might have been respect. 'You made it,' he said. 'How'd you know where to go?'

'Didn't,' I murmured. 'Ifrit.'

He nodded. 'Yeah, she would.' He took hold of my arm and ran both hands down it, like a coach giving a therapeutic massage; warmth cascaded back into me, silent and luminous. Life, coursing through me.

His hands moved on to my left arm, squeezed in energy. Then my legs, right, then left. The steady warm pressure of his hands lulled me into a half-dream.

Over on my back. Somehow my clothes were gone. Hands on my back, working down the muscles, healing.

'What are you?' I whispered. I felt Jonathan's presence like the sun behind me. His fingers were no longer pressing my skin, then were inside of me, touching deep.

He never answered.

I woke up warm and comfortable, with a soft feather pillow under my head and no memory at all of going to sleep. No dreams, either. The sheets smelt faintly of sandalwood, and they were crisp and cool on my bare skin. The room didn't look familiar. It featured a honey-warm wooden chest of drawers, massively carved, and a couple of paintings of space and the stars that looked vivid enough to be windows into infinity. A bookcase, loaded with hardbacks of all shapes, sizes, and colours. A bedside table with another lamp, currently off.

Lying on the rug next to the side of the bed, like a dog curled up for the night, was an Ifrit. It gleamed black in the shadows, and as I stared down at it, it raised its head and grinned at me with black needle teeth. I felt a wave of horror, a flash of dream come to life. *Sara?*

If it was, what I'd given her hadn't been enough to keep her in Djinn form for long. And I'd given her so much – almost everything I had. The Ifrit put its head back down again, curled its long, vaguely human form into a tighter coil, and relaxed. Guard dog? If so, I had no idea how to call her off. Or even if I should.

'Hello?' I tried a tentative whisper, and slid up to a sitting position in the bed. The Ifrit didn't twitch. I kept an eye on it and cranked the volume up a notch. 'Anybody?'

The bedroom door framed a moving shadow. Light silhouetted a tall male figure, and for a frozen, relieved second I thought *David!*, but then he moved into the warm glow of the table lamp and it was Jonathan. He had his hands thrust into the pockets of his jeans, looking casual in pose but not in body language. His dark eyes were too bright and too focused.

He didn't so much as glance at the Ifrit. I found that interesting. The Ifrit raised its head and sniffed at him, climbed to its feet and stalked around him in a circle.

Jonathan kept watching me, though he reached

over and patted the Ifrit on the head. It flopped down, elegance etched in darkness, and I felt it watching him with something like adoration.

'So?' he asked me. I rubbed one bare arm and found gooseflesh popping up, courtesy of a slight chill in the air, or maybe his presence.

'Well, I'm not coming apart,' I said. 'Gotta be an improvement.'

He nodded. 'Came close, though.'

'I figured.' I cleared my throat. 'Um...how many others made it here?' He just looked at me for a long few seconds, and I asked the question I dreaded. 'Rahel? Did she make it?'

He dropped into a crouch next to the bed. I held the sheet up as a modesty cover, but didn't particularly worry about it if he decided to check the side view. He didn't. Quite. 'No. How much do you know?'

'Not too damn much.'

'OK.' He put his bare hand on my bare shoulder, drawing a fresh shiver out of me, but once again I got the therapeutic touch, nothing personal. 'You're clear. You can get up now.'

He turned his back, not as if he was intent on giving me some kind of personal space, more as if he deeply didn't care whether or not I was naked; I formed clothes as I got up, anyway. Blue denim jeans, work shirt, sturdy boots. They seemed appropriate, here.

'What about David?' I asked.

'You tell me.' His back was still turned; he was pulling things out of the bookcase, restlessly flipping pages. Something to do with his hands. There was so much repressed energy in him, I wondered how he survived here, stuck in this house, unable to leave. He didn't seem to be someone with a peaceful interior life. 'He enjoying himself? Having a good old time with the Widder Prentiss?'

Sarcasm thick enough to spread like manure. I heard the pain underneath, though. And remembered the dream. 'I didn't want him to do that. I would have stopped it if I could have.'

'Yeah, well, not always about what *you* want. Or any of us, for that matter.' He shoved the book back in place with unnecessary violence and turned to face me, arms folded across his chest. Forbidding, that was the word for the expression on his face. Flint-hard eyes. Lips in a straight, unsympathetic line.

Anything I said would sound whiny and self-pitying, so I said nothing. Just looked at him. He finally transferred the stare down to his black Doc Martens. 'I notice you managed to get away. Maybe you'll be of some use. We can always use some good solid cannon fodder.'

'No wonder humans don't become Djinn very often,' I replied. 'What with your incredible recruitment efforts.'

Jonathan's lips twitched. It might have been a

smile, but he didn't let me see it to be sure. 'Yeah, well, you get set in your ways after the first couple of millennia or so. Sorry if we haven't made you feel like one of the boys.'

I elected not to get into the gender-specific arguments. 'Does she still have him?'

'Madame de Sade? Oh yeah.' He rocked back and forth on his heels, arms still folded.

'And...'

He looked up. 'You want details?' The tone could have frozen mercury. 'Should've stuck around. Could've been part of the whole experience. I'm sure he would've *loved* for you to see it.'

Oh, he was so angry...showing none of it in his blank expression, but the raw cutting edges of it came through.

'Rahel is on her way,' he said. 'She went to run an errand for me.'

'But you know how dangerous—'

He held up a cautioning finger. 'Don't. Don't do that. You want to stay on my good side, Jo, let's get something straight. *Never* remind me of the obvious. And *never* assume I didn't notice it.'

He turned and started for the door. I called a question after him. 'How bad is it? Out there in the aetheric?'

'Come with me,' he said, and disappeared down the hall. I followed. 'While you were sleeping, you've missed the party.'

* * *

I was unprepared for a living room full of people. There were at least thirty or forty crowded in. Djinn of every size, shape, description, colour, and dressed in every conceivable style. Some evidently had a whole god complex going; the silks and satins were way over the top, not to mention the jewellery. It made Rahel's traditionally neon colour scheme look positively corporate.

Jonathan carved an easy path through the crowd and stood next to the fireplace, watching the jockeying for position; when he caught sight of me standing at the back, he jerked his head in a *come here* gesture that had nothing to do with concern. More like he wanted to keep his enemies close. I grabbed wall space at his shoulder and tried to look insignificant, which turned out to be difficult, since I was drawing stares and whispers. Jonathan held up his hands for quiet. Instant obedience.

'This is Joanne,' he said, and pointed a thumb in my direction.

A tanned, fit-looking guy in what looked like a hand-tailored suit and iron grey tie looked me over with eyes of a pure, unsettling teal colour. 'She doesn't belong here.'

'Yeah, tell me about it,' Jonathan said, but in a tone that didn't invite anyone to actually try. 'Right. Here's the thing. We're what's left.'

A short, pregnant silence. 'What?' someone in the back ventured, looking around. Adding up numbers.

'So few?'

'So many lost?' An alarmed, high-pitched voice from up front, I didn't see who. 'Impossible!'

'I didn't say they were lost. I know right where they are,' Jonathan said. 'Just can't get to them right now. Most are in their bottles, waiting it out. Some...some got trapped on the aetheric. Some can't hold themselves together anymore because of the – what'd you call it?' He turned to me.

'Coldlight. Sparklies. Fairy dust.'

'Right. That stuff.' He looked back at the audience, face bland and notably free of panic. 'Which is coming out of the rift.'

Grey Suit said, 'Then someone must go up and close the rift.'

If the previous silence had been pregnant, this one was stillborn. They all looked at each other. Jonathan waited. I finally raised my hand, very slowly. 'Um...can I say something?'

He looked over his shoulder at me, did a double take, and half turned my way. 'I don't know, can you?'

Great. A grammar teacher, on top of everything else. 'Sorry. May I?'

'Sure.'

'Lewis sent me to seal the rift. I tried, but it didn't hold.'

Nobody spoke, but a ripple went through the room, like an electric charge rolling between contact points. Polarising. Jonathan broke the silence in a deliberately soft voice. 'You *tried*? Great. Amateur hour. Lewis should have known better. Probably made things a hundred times worse.'

'He tried to get some of *you* to help,' I shot back. 'But I understand you had a gut shortage around here that day.'

Yeah, that wasn't smart, but I was tired and cranky and Jonathan was pissing me off, what with all the sarcasm. The room seemed to shudder with disapproval.

Surprisingly, Jonathan didn't seem to take offence. He swept me from head to toe, giving me a new appraisal.

'That the new you?' he asked.

'Old me,' I said. 'Getting sick of being politically correct.'

'I like it. Now shut up.' He turned back to the assembled Djinn, who were agitated enough that I was surprised we didn't have spontaneous firestarting. 'The ones who are trapped out on the aetheric are in trouble. The ones who can't hold themselves together anymore may be dead. We need to do this fast, do it well, and then make sure the Wardens don't screw it up even worse than they usually do.'

'Which means what, exactly?' Grey Suit again. 'That we clean up after them, as we always do? Let the humans stand responsible for their crimes. Let them clear the aetheric.'

He wasn't much impressed by Jonathan, which I thought was interesting, given the extreme respect the rest of them seemed to accord him. Grey Suit had a pale complexion, sharp hatchet-faced bones, and gave off a sense of ruthless energy. I'd still put my money on Jonathan, if it came to a showdown, but I wouldn't have given generous odds, either.

'Yeah. We'll just hang out here, watching our own people die. That's a hell of a plan, Ashan. Right up there with your best.' He punctuated it with a friendly *I have an idea!* gesture. 'Tell you what. *You* go out and tell them we're going to let them die.'

'More of us die if we go out there,' Ashan said without blinking. He had the no-blinking thing down. 'But then you seem not to worry about that. Since you, of course, never leave the safety of your nest.'

Silence. Most of the Djinn were studying Jonathan. Jonathan stared at Ashan.

'Um...' I tried to make it sound deferential, but I wasn't sure I succeeded. 'Shouldn't we find out who opened the rip in the first place?' Jonathan fixed me with a look dire enough to qualify as neurosurgery without anaesthetic. Naturally, it didn't stop me.

'Well, isn't it a good question? I mean, *somebody* ripped it open. Somebody with a lot of power and not enough conscience. Was it a Djinn?'

'What part of *shut up* was unclear to you?'

I returned the stare, full force. Since last he'd

intimidated me, I'd had the hardcore lesson in How To Be A Djinn, and the whole god-of-your-new-existence routine wasn't going to cut it anymore. 'Answer the question. Was it a Djinn who did it?'

'Oh, we are *so* going to talk about this later,' he said.

'I'll take that as a yes. I'm just going on magical theory, here…' Because unlike the Djinn, I'd actually had class time learning about all of the physics of the stuff, the rules, and the various consequences. '…but it seems to me that whoever ripped it open would have a pretty good idea of how to close it. Since he must have known what he was doing. I mean, the thing was pretty well camouflaged when I got there. Discreet, you know?'

I had him. He blinked.

'Or was that stating the obvious?' I asked, and tilted my head to the side.

Neurosurgery. Without anaesthetic. With a dull butter knife.

'We can't ask the one who opened it,' he said.

'Because?'

The argument had taken on a tennis-match quality. The room full of Djinn was just watching us, shifting from one to the other, eyes avid. Rooting against me, no doubt. I didn't care. There was only one opponent who mattered.

'Because he's not here.' Jonathan's fierce eyes were absolutely fiery. 'Drop it already.'

I might have been slow on the uptake, but I

finally got it. *David*. I know it registered on my face, because I felt it like an earthquake inside. *David opened the rift...*

'Why?' I whispered. 'Why in God's name would he...'

Jonathan gave me a pitying look, like I was the stupidest creature in the universe. Which, at that moment, I supposed I was. 'For love,' he said. 'Why else?'

David had opened the rift when he'd made me a Djinn. *You've broken laws*. Rahel had said that, and I hadn't listened. Jonathan himself had tried to tell me how serious it was, what we'd done.

David had opened the rift, and drawn on something on the other side when he brought me back to life.

It was our fault the Djinn were dying.

Chapter Three

Nobody had much to say, after Jonathan made it clear the tennis match was over and the subject was closed. Neither of us had come right out and said what we were thinking, which was good; I wasn't sure I wanted all of these extremely powerful and extremely arrogant creatures to take offence at me. Especially not Ashan, who looked like he could bore a hole in titanium with a sideways glance. There was already an overload of mumbling and fiercely predatory looks toward me. I wished Rahel would show up; she was at least marginally congenial to me. Even Patrick would be welcome right about now, and not because I wanted to body-slam him into the wall; he'd been through this process before me, and survived it. The world had survived. The Djinn had survived. I needed to find out how, and I was pretty sure I couldn't.

My fault. This is my fault. I couldn't keep it from

running through my head. Why hadn't David told me? Why had he never even let on? Had he even *known*?

Of course he knew. It occurred to me, late and cruelly, that the reason Jonathan had kept him here had been to try to find a way to close the rift without killing him, or me. I'd thought it was a punishment, but it had been Jonathan's way of trying save us both. He and David had been working on a way to stop it.

Oh, *God*. I'd misunderstood so much.

Something changed in the room, a kind of stillness. Jonathan waved people away from the centre space, turned, and glanced at me. Apparently, I was the only one who didn't get it. 'Incoming,' he said.

Rahel materialised in the space left open.

She was covered in roiling blue specks. Djinn shouted and stampeded backwards as the sparks began to fly up and out, looking for other hosts; Jonathan moved forward.

Before he got there, Rahel's yellow eyes went blank, and she collapsed in slow motion down to the rug. She was closest to me; I didn't think, I just reached down for her.

My hands sank into her, wrist deep. Not that she was misted – that would have been better, oh God, far better. No, what I sunk into was flesh the consistency of warm butter, bathed in blood and melting muscle. I hit the relative hardness of bone but it was melting, too, dissolving like wax in the sun.

She was trying to say something to me. Her lips were whispering, anyway. I yanked my hands back, trembling, and stared at the smeared warm mess clinging to my skin. Her open eyes flared from a violent storm-black to a pallid blue, shifting colours like a wildly spinning prism.

'Joanne!' Jonathan snapped. He dropped to his knees next to her, extended one hand over her body, and reached out to me with the other. 'Get your ass back. She's contaminated.'

I could see the energy spilling out of his outstretched hand, golden white and so intense that it seemed to warp space around it. Pure life energy, keyed to the magic of the earth. Healing energy. David had said that Jonathan was the strongest of the Djinn; I hadn't quite believed it, until now. He was doing this even here, cut off from everything… That was the legacy of his birth, his connection to the Mother. Of all the Djinn, he was the only one with power of his own.

And it didn't matter. The damage just kept getting worse – flesh slipping from muscle, muscle dissolving to mush. The soft-focus gleam of bone beneath.

She cried out, once, and I felt her agony vibrating through the aetheric. I forced myself to look at her in Oversight; she was crawling with those blue specks, and they were *alive*, moving, eating.

She was being devoured. But they'd been all over me, all over David, they hadn't hurt us, God, what the hell…

'Stop it,' Ashan said. His voice was raw, colourless. 'It's done. You can't save her.'

Jonathan ignored him, ignored everything. He was focused on Rahel, fiercely intense, and the power flowing out of him just kept increasing. I felt it like a pressure against my skin, saw others shying away from it.

Rahel's skin continued to slough away, revealing soft wet masses of tissue. The skin misted as it fell away. Slowly, layer by layer, the muscle began to peel back as well. Jonathan kept trying, uselessly and furiously, to keep her together.

'Stop,' I said, feeling the words turn in my throat like razors. 'Please. He's right, you're just making it worse. Let go.'

His face was pallid and damp with strain, and his eyes were glittering with frustration, but he released the energy and dropped his hand back to his side. He didn't move, though. I don't even know if he *could* move, by then. I felt the energy flow shut down and watched as Rahel's body melted away into a fetid, oily mist.

Gone.

She was still screaming when she vanished.

'Is she dead?' I blurted. Nobody answered. I don't think they could. I had a cold flash of certainty that it was worse than that, far worse, out there on the aetheric. It was a horrible way to go. No wonder Jonathan had shut Ashan down so hard on the very idea of just letting Djinn stay trapped there. It was unforgivable.

What about David? I closed my eyes and reached for that silver link between us. It was faint and thin, but it was there. Unbroken.

Blue specks crawled up my arms.

'Joanne!' Jonathan's voice again, too loud, ringing inside my head. I blinked away blue sparks to stare up at him. 'Shit. I *told* you to stay back!'

Funny that this didn't hurt. It had hurt Rahel, I'd felt it shaking the fabric of the world, it hurt her so much. I could still feel her agony resonating in waves across the room.

Jonathan reached out for me, but I just stepped away. Instinct, I guess.

Because it didn't hurt.

I opened my eyes again and saw the most amazing thing.

Sparks. Blue swarmed out of the air, onto my skin, and *vanished*. The things that had eaten Rahel couldn't hurt me.

Jonathan stopped, staring at me. I sighed, watched the last of the coldlight sizzle into emptiness, and wondered what had him looking so pale and confused.

'I'm OK,' I said. I thought he was worried about me.

Pallor faded to stretched white on his face and

clenched fists. His eyes looked dark and blind.

'Jonathan?'

'Little trouble here,' he said.

I extended a hand toward him…

…and he lit up like a Christmas tree with crawling blue light. *Oh God!* The other Djinn backed away, viscerally terrified, as he wavered and fell backwards against a wall. Closed his eyes. 'Shit,' he said. 'Guess I'm not immune after all.'

Instinct. I grabbed for him as he started to slide down.

The sparks whirled out, climbed my arms, circled me in a storm of blue. Rahel's grisly dissolution ran red in front of my eyes, and I swore I wasn't going to let that happen, not to *him*, not now…

I sucked the sparks in, laid them thick on my skin, and consciously opened myself to them. I opened my squeezed-shut eyes and watched the light show as the sparkles glittered, peaceful and serene on my skin, then faded out into nothing.

I'm made of this. That was why they couldn't hurt me. I was just taking in more of what had formed me in the first place.

Jonathan sat where he was, watching, too. His dark eyes shifted to meet mine.

'Thanks,' he said.

I nodded. 'Favour for a favour. We need to get David back. *Now.*'

'I know,' he said. He sounded tired. 'You look like hell.'

'Funny, I don't feel...' Oh. Yes I did, actually. There went gravity again, twisting all out of shape. This time, I didn't mistake it for coldlight or anything but what it was: somebody trying to call me. That fishhook sensation pulled at me, painful and undeniable. Not Jonathan, this time. And this wasn't a call to safety, either.

Jonathan held on to me while I fought the pull. I felt his will settle over me like a soft, smothering blanket, and the summoning pull was lost in the weight.

'Tired,' I whispered. He already knew that. He was lifting me again in his arms as all the other Djinn murmured to each other, as Ashan stared at me with those cold blue-green eyes.

Back to the bedroom.

The soft feather pillow.

The frosted-coal shadow of the Ifrit, watching.

I slept.

The next day – if days had any meaning here – dawned just as bright and sunny and peaceful as all days did in Jonathan's little kingdom.

I woke up to find the man himself sitting in a chair watching me. The Ifrit was gone.

'Wow,' I said. 'This is getting familiar.'

'Don't wear it out.'

'The bed or my welcome?'

He ignored what was admittedly a pretty weak comeback. 'So. How you feeling?'

'Fine.'

'Good.' I wasn't sure what he wanted, and I had the impression he wasn't either, really. He got up to walk around the room, long strides that didn't quite rise to the level of pacing. More like a stroll, with purpose. 'About the rift up there.'

'What about it?' All my fight drained away at the bare mention of it. I couldn't help but remember the red, tearing agony of Rahel dissolving into mush, or the hundreds of others who were suffering somewhere out there, where I couldn't see them.

'You think it's your fault,' he said. 'Crap. What happened was David's choice, not yours...and he had no way of knowing this would happen. Hell, even I didn't understand what was going on until too late to do anything about it. Once I did, he wanted to go fix things.'

'But?'

'But by then I knew it was too dangerous, and then he went tearing off after you when you got...' He waved a hand, didn't bother to finish the sentence. 'He's not exactly what you might call big-picture when it comes to personal sacrifice.'

'Neither am I. Neither are you.' He gave me a slight nod to acknowledge the point. 'You should've told me about the rift. Or at least about how badly things were screwed up because I was brought back.'

He shrugged, a simple economical straight-up-and-down movement of his shoulder blades. No particular emotion in it. 'Things screw up all the time. Hey. You gotta love the excitement. Granted, this is a lot more exciting than usual...but you stay alive as long as I have, you learn to take these things in stride. The Djinn have faced worse.'

I stared up at the shadows on the ceiling. 'How much worse?'

'Hard to tell until it's over.'

I pulled in a deep breath. Funny, I didn't need it, but it still seemed to calm me. Some human habits were persistent. 'How's everybody else?'

'Sleeping,' he said, and nodded toward the far wall. 'Lots of guest rooms. We run a topflight refugee camp around here.' He gave me a thin, almost human smile, but it didn't last. 'I never thought I'd like you, but you turned out OK. "Gut shortage." That was pretty good.'

'Yeah, sorry about that. I got carried away.'

'No, you're right. One thing Djinn are scared of, it's death. Their own, not anybody else's. It makes us cowards. Look at me! I've been sitting here in this house for so long I don't even know what it's like out there.'

'I do,' I said. 'You're better off in here.'

'Not for much longer,' he said. He held out his hand, palm up, as if he was offering something to me. I looked at it, puzzled, and felt a sudden stab of alarm as a single cool blue spark ignited in his aura.

'They're coming in. I can't keep them out, I can only slow them down. It's going to be one giant blue snow globe in here soon. And even though I'm resistant to them, I'm not immune.' He stood up, swiped imaginary dust from his pants, and gestured at me. 'So, you gonna take the day off, or are you getting your ass out of bed?'

I had already formed clothes under the sheet – the same denim and boots as before. One nice thing about being a Djinn – dress and bounce out of bed, no rework on the hair or make-up necessary. Although the hair was still displaying that annoying tendency to curl. I straightened it again as I asked, 'What now?'

'You said it. We need David.'

'I'll go.'

'You're in thrall,' he said. 'If your little jerk of a master finds out you're where he can reach you, he'll get you back and dressed like a pin-up fantasy girl in ten seconds flat.'

'Ugh. Don't remind me.'

'Oh, I don't know, the French Maid outfit was a little—' He held up a hand to forestall my protest. 'Never mind. Point is, if you go outside of the barrier he'll be able to get you back.'

'He's probably still asleep.'

'He is.' Jonathan nodded. 'Problem is that he was calling for you in his sleep. And if you go outside this house, you won't be able to resist.'

'I still want to go. If I get taken, so be it. I manipulated the kid once, I can do it again.'

'You'd better hope so. Well, you're not going

alone. This is too important to screw up.' He folded his hands together behind his back, stopped pacing, and faced me in a parade rest posture. 'I'm going with you.'

I managed a weak smile. 'Yay, Team Us?'

'Yeah, well, I could have patches made, but it seems excessive.' We exchanged another long few seconds of eye-locked silence. I was worrying about how many Djinn had already told me that Jonathan never left his house. David had seemed pretty adamant about it. This wasn't any little excursion, and suddenly I didn't think I was ready to be bodyguard to the God of My Existence. Plus, what had he just said? *Resistant, not immune.* I didn't want the responsibility for ending a life with the length and depth of Jonathan's.

Jonathan must have read my mind. 'This is going to be hard, you know. Getting David back. She wants him bad.'

No answer to that except the obvious. 'So do I.' I saw the flash in his eyes, and amended it. 'We.'

His ghost-smile manifested again. 'Then let's go get him.'

The cord binding me to David had shrunk to a thin, barely perceptible thread. Worse, it was *shaking*. I could feel the tension in it. No telling how strong it was, how much strain it could stand, but I had the distinct feeling that it was close to the breaking point.

And my time was almost up, anyway. On so many levels.

'You understand what we have to do,' Jonathan said. 'Travel in the aetheric's too damn dangerous. Just skim the surface, stay as close as you can to the thread. I'll be right behind you.'

We hadn't told anybody else except – at Jonathan's insistence – that creepy grey-suited Ashan. 'You're sure about him?' I'd asked out of the side of my mouth, as the door shut behind him and locked me and Jonathan in what looked like a study. He liked fishing, I gathered. Lots of books on the subject, and some big mounted piscine specimens frozen in mid-thrash on the walls.

'Ashan?' Jonathan finished writing something down, reached in a desk drawer and took out a seal that looked massive and antique. He brought it gently down on the paper. When he took it away, there was a glowing design in the paper, nothing I could read or even vaguely recognise. 'Kind of an asshole, I know, but he's reliable. Anything ever happens to me, he gets the big chair.'

'Not David?'

'Not anymore.' The tone was so colourless I knew there was pain behind it. 'You're good to go?'

'Ready.' I wasn't, really, but there didn't seem to be any really good choices, otherwise. Jonathan put the paper on top of his desk, turned to me and gave me an *after you, Alphonse* gesture.

I took a deep breath and flowed to mist.

In Oversight, the thread stretched out toward the horizon, thin and glittering and still somehow alive. I touched it, wrapped myself around it and started winding around it like a vine snake. Moving fast, but staying in the physical plane. The thread had aetheric properties, which worried me; I couldn't stop to help Jonathan if he got badly infected. I couldn't be sure, but I wasn't seeing any blue sparkle, other than a stray particle here and there. So far the connection looked clean.

The thread travelled through Jonathan's house, straight out through the roaring blaze in the fireplace. I didn't dare phase out completely, but I tried a moderated waveform to travel on, to avoid the fire. If it was a real fire at all. Nothing around here was what it seemed, especially not Jonathan. He didn't feel like a Djinn at all, especially now that we were both in an incorporeal state. He felt...hotter. Stronger. More *present*, somehow.

My waveform skirted perilously close to a place I didn't want to go. I saw blue sparks dancing close, and dropped back down. Jonathan's place was still relatively spark-free, at least so far. I wondered if his defences were good enough to protect all of the Djinn who'd taken refuge in there. He hadn't seemed all that positive in his outlook. *It's going to be one giant blue snow globe in here soon.*

Even as I watched, a single blue spark flared

against my aura, then two more, drifting gently and then falling away. The stuff was getting through, after all, just very very slowly.

I flashed through a barely seen criss-cross of bricks and mortar, winding along the silver thrumming thread as fast as I could. I moved out of the darkness, into what felt like sunlight. I soaked up the wild, undirected energy gratefully; without David's infusions of blood-rich power, I was rapidly getting tired.

I looked behind me on the thread – directed my awareness, actually – and sensed that Jonathan was still with me, whispering his way along with every evidence of perfect ease. Well, well. I wasn't overly surprised. I didn't imagine there was much that Jonathan couldn't do, if he really wanted to. Except that this might be the first time in a long time that he'd left his...sanctuary, and there might be a learning curve for him out here in the real world...

Wham!

It was like hitting the Great Wall of China in a bullet train. I stopped, stunned into silence and nearly into unconsciousness. My mist form spread out into an uncoordinated cloud, then slowly, slowly formed itself back around the thread.

Whoops. Found the barrier. Damn. How had Sara gotten around it, when she'd brought me in at hyperspeed?

And why did the thread go right on through it?

No help for it; I had to get *really* thin. If the thread could pass through, I could slide myself along the thread through the barrier – theoretically. All I had to do was, ah, become the thread, right? Yeah. Be one with the thread.

Another blue fleck touched me and flared like a star. I was out of time. If Jonathan's hideout was being invaded, there couldn't be too many safe places left. I hoped whatever other Wardens were left had sense enough to keep their Djinn safely in their bottles, but the Free Djinn...they had no such protection. Just crawling inside some old Jim Beam container wouldn't do it; it wasn't the bottle that made the difference, it was magic. Without the magic, glass was just glass.

David. I sent it along the thread, because the barrier was holding. I wasn't getting through. No response. I directed my attention backwards. *Jonathan, can you drop this thing long enough for us to get through?*

No, he sent back. *It's the only thing standing between them and what's out there.*

Any hints?

Try harder.

Yeah, that was good. Try harder.

I felt a giant-sized shove in the back, and grabbed on to the thread for dear life as it began to move. Slowly. Pulling through the barrier one torturous, tiny jerk at a time.

I thought it would scrape me right off, that wall

of power. I compressed myself, spread thinner, thinner, almost to nothing.

A sense of being dragged through thick, quick-setting cement. Of intense, murderous pressure.

Pop.

Free. I arrowed along the thread fast, driven by the force of the pull, with the close-following shadow of Jonathan sailing in my wake. The distant sunrise on the horizon grew brighter. Hotter. Closer. I could sense David now, but he felt…different. Muted.

I didn't slow down.

I tumbled back into human form, all arms and legs and curling hair, hit the ground awkwardly and went to hands and knees. I was suddenly grateful for my newly demure clothing choices. What looked awkward in blue jeans would have looked downright kinky in a leather miniskirt and lime green Manolos.

Especially in a grungy city alleyway.

I'd expected to materialise in Yvette's perfectly kept living room, but no such luck – on my hands and knees in garbage, looking up at a grungy guy dressed in geologic layers of oily, tattered clothes, a bottle of Thunderbird halfway to his lips. He stared at me without any real comprehension.

'Hey,' he said.

'Hey.' I climbed up to my feet and wiped crud from my hands. 'How you doing?'

He gestured vaguely with the bottle. As answers went, it was perfectly understandable.

'Yeah, me, too,' I said. 'So. Where am I?'

He blinked at me, then grinned. 'Here.'

A perfectly Zen response. I gave up on the Dalai Lama and looked around for Jonathan. He was standing farther down near the mouth of the alley, staring out; I picked my way around overturned trash cans, piles of crap, and a particularly feral-looking cat with a rat in its jaws.

'I guess you were on target,' Jonathan said, and nodded out at the street. I focused past the swarming cars and ceaseless stream of pedestrians. On the other side of the street rose a stubby-looking tower, part of a complex that I knew all too well.

'The good news is, at least we know where he is.'

We were looking at the bad news.

The UN Building.

It was the World Headquarters of the Wardens Association.

Technically speaking, the UN Building isn't. It's a compound of four interconnected structures – General Assembly, Secretariat, Conference, and Library. I had a nodding acquaintance with the place, which was better than about ninety-five per cent of the other Wardens could claim; I'd been to closed meetings in the Conference building, and the Wardens Association offices in the Secretariat tower. (By New York standards, it wasn't much of a tower, really. Thirty-nine floors. Hardly worth the nomenclature.)

Jonathan and I ate hot dogs from a sidewalk cafe and examined the problem as the sun slipped toward the horizon in smoky, obscured glory. Traffic continued to be heavy, dominated by yellow cabs; the entire block had become a secured no-parking zone, with sharp-eyed security personnel stationed at discreet but effective intervals. None of whom noticed us, of course. All part of that Djinn mystique.

I finally took a break from consuming preservatives to enquire if we had an actual plan in the offing.

Jonathan tossed back the last mouthful of a giant-sized cup of industrial-strength black coffee. He was loving the cuisine, which I guess was a break from home-cooked meals back at Rancho Impenetrable. 'Best I can figure, your pals at the Wardens Association actually got off their asses for once and did the right thing. Rounded up Yvette, confiscated David's bottle – with him in it. Lewis must have gotten caught up in the raid.'

'Not great,' I said.

'Not really.' He took a bite of hot dog. 'You and I can't get into the vault where he's being kept. No Djinn can; we need a human for that, one with access. Problem is there aren't a whole lot of those falling off of trees. And once we're in the building, we're going to be at some pretty serious risk.'

I put my hand on his arm and checked him for coldlight. He was lightly coated in it. I drew it to me, into me, left him clean and uncontaminated. He gave me a slow, half-lidded smile in response. Dimples. I'd never noticed them before. He probably didn't show them to just anybody.

'I'm fine,' he said. 'You?'

'Good.' I licked relish from my fingertips and examined the Secretariat in Oversight. It was rich in history, of course, but there was one floor in particular that radiated into the power spectrum. The Wardens floor. Not just the residue of all of the powerful that had come and gone through those doors, either; this was here-and-now kind of energy, being radiated at an intense level. 'Lots going on,' I observed.

'It's a busy day.' Laconic understatement from the master, as usual. *I'd like to see what actually panics you*, I thought, and then instantly knew that I didn't. No way in hell. 'Storm rolling in.'

I could feel charged fury in the air, particles churning and forming patterns and being flung apart by ever-expanding forces. The storm was out of control in the Atlantic, and heading this way. I turned out toward the sea and closed my eyes, drinking in the thick warm breeze, the muttering echoes of what was shaping up to be one hell of an early hurricane. At its present rate of growth, it was liable to come charging in to port packing wind speeds fast enough to blow the windows out of every shining building in its path. Experts said you couldn't bring down one of these skyscrapers with a storm, but they'd never seen the kind of power that was boiling out there.

Few people had, and lived to tell about it.

'Can't you do anything about that?' I asked. I felt genuinely spooked, every nerve stroked to a trembling edge by the touch of that wind.

'That? Sure.' Nothing happened. I looked over at him, but he was still focused on the building. 'What, you mean now?'

'It'll be a little late after it blows through here and Manhattan becomes the world's biggest junk shop.'

His dark eyes flashed toward the horizon, then back to me. 'I'm keeping it out to sea. Considering it's not the only damn thing going wrong, I think that's about the best I can do right now. Unless you think it's OK to turn the entire five-state area around Yellowstone into charcoal. Didn't anybody ever tell you that it's all about balance?'

Balance was great in theory. Not so great when you were having to make choices that would inevitably cost lives. I wasn't feeling up to godhood. 'What about California? Or are you just calling it a loss and hoping Disneyland will set up an undersea kingdom park off the west coast of Nevada?'

'Atlantis once had the best beaches.' He shrugged. 'Coastline changes are a matter of perspective. But no, actually. Lewis took care of that one. The earthquake's off.'

One crisis down. And speaking of Lewis... I

turned back to the building and studied it again, reading energy signatures. *Ah*. Of course.

'They've got him,' I said. 'The Wardens. Lewis is in there.'

'Yeah, I know.' Jonathan crumpled the cup and tried for a three-pointer in a trash can at least twenty feet away. Naturally, he made it. 'Considering that he's the only person who ever successfully stole from the Wardens' vault before, I was considering that a point in our favour. That is, if we can trust him.'

'Yes.' I didn't hesitate. 'Look, in all the time I've known him, Lewis has always been about the greater good. It's one of the reasons the Wardens want him so badly. First, he's so damn powerful that he can make things happen on a massive scale; second, they'd just like it a whole lot better if he was somewhere they could control him. Because they can't count on him doing things the way they want him to all the time.'

Lewis had never been ambitious, but if he'd wanted to, he could have snapped his fingers and made things happen in the ranks of the Wardens. For one thing, he could do the work of about a hundred of them, all by himself, and do it with compassion and control. Power like that, he didn't need the approval of the Senior Wardens, or the Council, or any damn body. He was of the live-and-let-live school of thought. Too bad the Wardens didn't feel the same way. They'd been afraid of him since the first day they'd realised what he was, and they couldn't be any less worried about him now.

Especially since he was bad-ass enough that he'd voluntarily given up three Djinn, just to make a point.

Something about the pulse and colour shift of that brilliant aura I was watching made me remember how I'd last seen him, at Patrick's apartment. 'I think he might be hurt,' I said. I remembered Kevin kicking him in the head. 'Maybe badly hurt.' Paul had said as much. Lewis had shown up at his house looking for information about Yvette – he'd remembered enough to know who had me, apparently. That still didn't mean he'd been functioning at peak efficiency. If he'd tangled with Yvette...

'Hurt I can fix.' Jonathan stretched, working out the kinks, and pulled a dull green baseball cap from his back pocket. He tugged it in place, one hand on the bill, one on the back. 'Ready?'

I looked down at myself and changed into business-ready mode. A black peachskin pantsuit was appropriate anywhere, even inside the UN Building. 'Do we have a plan?'

'You distract 'em, I get Lewis to open the vault, we boost David's bottle. Outta there.'

'Hell of a plan,' I commented dryly. It scared the hell out of me, actually.

His eyes were as hard as frozen flint, and the soft evening light did nothing to make him look any less frightening. He looked *serious*. 'It'll do. Move.'

* * *

We strolled right past security. I was reminded of the Empire State Building, and surprised myself by missing Rahel intensely; I had liked her. A lot. *And it's my fault she's...* What? Gone? Dead? Discorporated? The Djinn Formerly Known As...? I remembered her skin sloughing away, and couldn't control a sick tremor. The coldlight was intense now, up in the aetheric. Like a constant blizzard. Any Djinn – except, presumably, me or David – who went up there was doomed. Even Jonathan.

The Wardens Association floor required a card key for the elevator, which I didn't have, but it didn't seem to be any big deal for Jonathan; he just put his finger over the slot and got the green light and a lit-up button. The elevator was showing its age, and the trip was slower than usual. We didn't talk, just waited in that pocket-universe silence that people inhabit in elevators, until the door chimed and rolled back on a long, straight hallway lit with featureless pale squares of indirect lighting.

The Hall of Fame. Important-looking heavy plaques recognising Wardens for achievement above and beyond. They stretched in a row all the way to the end, most of them black-bordered to indicate posthumous awards. The place smelt of artificial vanilla, wood, and the faintest hint of flop sweat; it was a bad day at the office for everyone there. Except the Earth Wardens, presumably, who at least had the comfort of knowing Hollywood wasn't going to become a new coral reef.

The place was buzzing with activity. From a human perspective, it looked like any other busy New York office – smartly dressed people walking with purpose from one room to another, talking tensely to each other or cell phones, carrying reams of paper or folders or computers. No Djinn in attendance. I could see why, as I walked through the halls and dodged around unwary staffers; I was trailing blue glitter like Pinocchio's fairy.

It came to me finally that I was alone. I looked back, but Jonathan had vanished. *Poof*. Apparently that was part of the plan I wasn't privy to, up front.

I paused in the doorway of a huge round conference room and saw close to twenty of the most powerful Wardens in the world clustered there while a War Room map showed detailed schematics of weather patterns, real-time satellite imagery, infrared scans of the planet's surface to pinpoint hot spots. Yellowstone looked like a whiteout, but it wasn't the only one; there were fires raging in India, in Africa, and in Chile.

Paul Giancarlo was there, looking tired and stressed; he was arguing softly with somebody I didn't recognise, gesturing at the weather map and the Doppler radar display. From the hand gestures, I figured he was talking about the massive potential for hail. He was right, if that was where he was going; I could sense the ice forming up in the highest levels of the atmosphere, thick and grey and heavy.

Freight-train winds intercepted the ice on the way down, added moisture, tossed it back up to freeze again.

New York City was going to be pelted with a disaster of biblical proportions. This would make baseball-sized hail look like Styrofoam. I had power, but not much, and certainly not enough to disrupt a process with this kind of momentum behind it. There were thirty or forty Wardens still working on it, I sensed. But none of them had Djinn.

And none of them were going to be able to stop it. Not singly, not collectively. It was simply too big, and had too much control of its own destiny. Lewis could stop it, but even then, it would be a tough battle.

Paul's eyes swept over me without pausing as he turned away from the heated debate; his weightlifter-dense muscles were tensed under the soft cotton of his shirt. His tie was loose, his sleeves rolled up. I could feel the anger coming off of him, the metal-sharp smell of sweat.

He knew they were losing.

I wanted to say something to him, *anything*, but I didn't have the time and it was too much of a risk. I backed out of the doorway and continued down the hall.

Sandwiched between the main conference room and a smaller one just as frantically occupied was a recessed alcove with a bubbling fountain and a whole lot of names inscribed in marble.

The roll of the dead. I paused for a few seconds to look over the names.

Yes, at the bottom, sharp and new-cut: *Robert Biringanine. Estrella Almondovar. Joanne Baldwin.* There was something really final about seeing that. What was the old saying? It was set in stone. In a way, it was even more final than a coffin.

'Move,' a voice at my side whispered. I looked up to find that Jonathan had popped back out of whatever hole he'd gone into; he tugged my elbow in a way that definitely discouraged memory-laning. I walked with him down to the end, where the hallway split off into a T-intersection. We had to dodge an oblivious gopher with two overfull cups of coffee and a wildly scared look in his eyes; trainee, I judged, who was probably going to be begging for an assignment somewhere safe and peaceful, like Omaha, when this was all over. The building seemed to shudder underfoot, and I heard glass rattling in the windows.

The storm was starting to roll in.

'Can't hold it,' Jonathan said. His lips were tense, white rimmed, and set in a straight hard line. 'Faster we can do this, the better for everybody.'

As if to underscore the point, thunder boomed outside, unbelievably loud. This monster had come roaring in fast – too fast for natural forces to be the only thing going on. The blue sparklies were busy little critters.

In Oversight, just about every doorway glowed, due to the accretion of years of Wardens working here. Some were flickering madly, like magic lanterns in a high wind. One near the middle glowed especially brightly, and the power spilling out had a dense, almost gravitational feel to it.

Definitely Lewis, behind that door. I waited for Jonathan to make the next move, but he just put a hand on my arm and pulled me out of the way of another fast-moving clique of Wardens rushing to do damage control. Some of them looked white faced, on the very edge of panic. The pallid smell of L'Air du Temps mingled with the sharp organic aroma of fear.

Distraction, Jonathan said. *Keep them looking at you. Do whatever you have to, but keep their attention for at least five minutes. That should give me enough time to get Lewis and get to the vault.*

I nodded and opened the door. In the space of three seconds, I moderated my eyes to a demure dove grey, and replaced my black conservative pant-suit with my distraction outfit.

Thank you, Kevin Prentiss, for being such an inspirational little jerk.

French Maid outfit, a handful of colourful balloons, Shirley Temple hair, and a big fake smile. I strolled into the room and found it was an infirmary, full of sterile white room dividers and one occupied bed at the far end, with three people clustered around it.

My high heels clopped loudly on the linoleum, and one of the people leant out of the range of the curtains to take a look. He stopped, did a double take, and gave me the full-body X-ray scan. A middle-aged man, definitely not immune to the outfit.

'Hi!' I said brightly. 'I'm here to deliver a birthday wish—'

'What the hell?' Another man popped out, this one white coated and with a disapproving frown that said *doctor*. I didn't know him, but then I'd never spent any time in this particular part of the Association. 'How'd you get in here?'

I smiled at him and launched into a rousing rendition of Marilyn Monroe's version of 'Happy Birthday,' complete with the appropriate wiggles and breathy laughs, cosying up to the first man. He looked appreciative, if a little dazed. The doctor just looked apoplectic, and started to turn away to duck back behind the curtains.

I grabbed him and sat him down in a chair, straddled him, and began to do my very best impersonation of a lap dancer. Doctor he might be, but he was definitely a guy. And he was finding it hard to keep professional detachment in the face of my, ah, assets.

I finally attracted the attention of the third person, female, who resembled Nurse Ratched but had a far more generous sense of humour. She had a malicious glint in her eye that convinced me the doctor wasn't the most popular of all the guys on staff.

I presented the doc with the balloons and gave him a big lipstick-heavy kiss.

'Not my birthday,' he finally managed to rumble. 'Ahem.'

I stretched it as long as I could, then gave him another kiss, waved goodbye to the audience, and got a weak-wristed wave from the Warden, nothing from the woman, who was still laughing too hard. I clopped out again, swinging the big bow on the back of the apron with as much vigour as possible to hold their attention.

As soon as the door clicked shut, I misted away. I hadn't seen or felt Jonathan taking Lewis out; I just had to hope he'd managed it. I sped down the hall, past the fountain and my memorial inscription, past all of the heavy weight of the past, hit the floor running in my black pantsuit and conservatively straight hair. I wasn't trying to hide now, and startled staffers moved out of my way. 'Hold the elevator!' I yelled, and slid in behind two Wardens in suits and red power ties. We all exchanged weary smiles. I pushed the button for the ground floor.

Nothing happened. No lights. *Crap.* I didn't have a badge. The security not only wouldn't let me on the floor without a card key, it wouldn't let me off, either. I patted my pockets, looked bothered, and one of the nice gentlemen – neither of whom was heading to the ground – badged for me and pressed the button.

Nice people make things so much easier.

We stopped on the thirty-seventh floor, let one guy out, and were on the way back down again when the elevator shuddered to a sudden, teeth-rattling halt.

'What the—' the remaining Warden said, frowning, and pushed buttons.

A recessed speaker came alive in the wall. 'The building is now under a security alert. Please be patient. The elevators will restart momentarily.'

He slumped against the wall. 'Great. Again.'

'Happens a lot?' I asked.

He nodded, gave me a sideways look, and then a full smile, with teeth. 'Sign of the times, you know how it is. So. Visiting?'

'From Iowa,' I said. 'Des Moines office.'

'Not a great time to be here, huh? What with the weather.'

'Yeah, I thought it looked bad. Actually, I'm Earth, so any storm looks bad to me,' I said, and returned the smile tooth for tooth. 'You know, Earth...corn, peas, wheat...breadbasket of the USA?'

'Huh. Would have taken you for a weather girl. Stormy eyes.' Ah, romantic weather talk. In the old days, it might have even gotten him somewhere.

'My name's Ron.'

I said the first thing that popped into my head.

'Gidget.'

'Really?'

'Really.'

'Whoa.' Ron had dark thick hair, cut short, and eyes of no particularly interesting shade, but he knew how to focus. 'You in for meetings?'

'Actually, just finished. I'm on my way to the airport.' Lying wasn't just fun, it was a way to lay false trails. With any luck, they'd be chasing an Earth Warden named Gidget all the way to Des Moines for the next few hours. 'They're sending me out to the fire. Maybe I can do some good with animal rescue.'

Ron looked dubious. 'I wouldn't be trying to go anywhere, in weather like this. I'd just stick around, if I were you. We have a pretty secure storm facility. It doubles as a nuclear shelter, so I'm assuming it'll hold off a tornado if it has to.'

'Tornado?' I repeated, and tried to look like a dumb Iowan girl. 'You're kidding, right?'

'There's a lot of disturbance in the aetheric. You didn't know?'

'Well, sure. I just figured it was...' I made a vague gesture. Let him fill in the rest.

'Ah. Yeah. You must've heard we caught him.' When I stared at him, unmoving, he added the rest. 'You know. Lewis. Lewis Orwell?'

'Really?' I tried to sound impressed, and not ready to backhand him into next week for the way-too-satisfied tone he was taking. 'Was he here in the city?'

'Close by. New Jersey, as it turned out. All these years, looking for him, and he was right across the state line. Funny how things turn out.' Ron nodded sagaciously. 'They think he's behind this stuff.'

'What?' I didn't have to feign shock on that one.

'Sure. You think it's an accident that they get their hands on him, and all hell breaks loose on not one but three fronts? They've got the West Coast problem under control, but we're going to take a real beating from this storm. Not to mention those poor bastards out in Yellowstone.' He leant closer. 'They think he might have some kind of Demon Mark. Anyway, they're getting Marion Bearheart in here. I figure they're going to try to, you know...' He made a yanking-up-by-the-roots gesture. I literally staggered, caught by sick surprise.

'They're going to *neuter* him?'

He looked surprised at my reaction. 'Well, not...actually...I meant they were going to, you know, close off his connections. Make sure he couldn't do something like this again.'

I'd known perfectly well what he'd meant. Neutering was the right word for it. *Castration.* Ripping out the heart and soul of who he was. It was as horribly malicious as throwing acid on the Mona Lisa – Lewis was a treasure, a once-in-a-thousand-years goddamn *gift*.

They *could not* do this to him. I wouldn't let them.

I forced a smile. 'You're on Marion's staff?'

'Afraid so.' Ron tried for a sheepish little-boy cute look. It almost worked. 'I'm just in training, though. No way they'd let me even in the same room for a procedure like that. They're waiting for at least four other Senior Wardens before they even try anything.'

I smiled, nodded, and wished to hell that the elevator would start. Not that I couldn't mist out and get away, but I couldn't do it with Ron staring at me, not if I wanted to have any kind of chance for a clean escape. *God, Jonathan, you'd better have him.* I'd tear this building down one steel I-beam at a time if I had to, to make sure that they didn't carry through on their threats.

No wonder Lewis had been so paranoid all these years, running for his life. I'd have been catatonic, if I'd known what was waiting for me back here among my so-called *peers*.

Just as I was starting to wonder whether to seduce Ron or knock him out, the elevator jerked again and started sliding down. Fast. A red light on the panel read SECURITY LOCKDOWN.

'They're sending us to the ground floor,' Ron said. 'Looks like they'll be searching everybody.'

'Fun.' I rocked back and forth on my low-heeled shoes, ready for fight or flight, but when the elevator doors opened a navy sports coat type with the UN emblem over his vest pocket waved me impatiently out, along with Ron. I followed his pointing finger. It looked like a mob scene, which was great for fading away. You're never more alone than in a crowd of strangers. All Wardens, even better.

'Hey!' Ron was trying to keep up with me as I slipped between people, heading for the sealed and guarded exits. 'Um, Gidget! Wait up!'

I stepped behind two particularly bulky women who looked like they might have been part of a Russian delegation, and disappeared.

Jonathan? I sent silently. No answer. *Earth to Jonathan! Dammit, you'd better be there!*

Crap. Getting Lewis out of here without taking him through the aetheric was going to be next to impossible, but we had to find a way. We couldn't chance leaving him here.

I waved my hand through the air and watched it collect an insubstantial weight of blue fairy dust. I crushed it into nothing, but that didn't matter; it was a constant blizzard even here. The aetheric would be choked with it. No. We couldn't leave that way.

I caught sight of a familiar face in the crowd, and went cold. Marion Bearheart was here – had just made it in before the lockdown, by the look of it. Her brown suede jacket was spattered with dark drops, and water caught the light in tiny glints in her grey-and-black hair. She looked grim and haunted, arms folded over her chest. She was listening to an earnest stream of dialogue from Martin Oliver, who even now looked like the nattiest, most in-control man on the face of the world. He wasn't in control of much, today, but I still wouldn't have wanted to cross him. He reminded me of somebody…Ashan, Jonathan's chief rival back in the Djinn bubble. The same kind of severe, uncompromising confidence, and a kind of elegant, almost sexual grace.

I remembered, out of nowhere, a conversation I'd had back in college about a man I'd been thinking of dating. *Describe him*, my best friend had said. I'd giggled and said, *He's sweet*. And she'd looked at me very seriously, taken my hands, and said, *Corazón, sweet men are only sexy until you realise that they're too weak to hurt you.* I hadn't agreed with her – still didn't, in some ways – but there was no denying that dangerous men had a visceral attraction.

The woman who'd said that was on the Wardens' wall of the dead. Like me. I hadn't even had time to mourn her. I didn't even really know if I should, and that was the worst of it.

Marion's cool, strong gaze swept my direction. I quickly put out the *don't-notice-me* vibe. She scanned right past me, frowned, and turned to someone at her elbow. I focused on her lips. She was asking if he sensed anything strange. He shook his head, but she didn't look convinced.

Man, we needed to get the hell out of here. And I needed to get down to the vault.

A huge, rolling crash of thunder like the world's

largest pane of glass dropped from ten thousand feet made everybody in the room flinch and duck. Most clapped hands over their ears. Some, like Marion, turned toward the big picture windows, and the sharp white crack of lightning lit up their strained faces.

I heard the dull thump of the first of the hail hitting the street outside. Ice exploded like a bomb, scattering frozen white shrapnel for twenty feet. Before the debris had rolled to a stop, another piece of football-sized hail crashed down onto the roof of a yellow cab speeding by. It ripped a hole right through the steel.

The storm had shaken loose of any semblance of control, and now it had a target: the only people who had a hope in hell of stopping it.

Us.

I felt it drawing in, focusing around the building, and it was a sense so suffocatingly strong that I wanted to gag. Even as a Djinn, this was oppressive; I couldn't imagine what it would feel like to a Warden. I didn't need to imagine it, actually, all I had to do was look around. They were scared. Scared out of their minds.

'Down to the shelter!' That was Martin Oliver, who'd climbed on top of the security desk to address the crowd of several hundred milling around the lobby. 'Everybody! Quickly!' Even now, he looked controlled and calm. No wonder he was the guy in charge.

Security started directing people toward a grey door marked with a bomb shelter symbol; the crush got intense, quickly. I noticed that Martin hadn't joined the stampede. In fact, he stayed where he was, on top of the security desk, staring out at the street as rain started lashing the windows in thick, lightning-shot streaks.

More hail was crashing down. Cars had stopped moving out on the road, and drivers were abandoning their vehicles to run into any available cover. I felt power stirring, and knew what he was trying to do: cover the potential victims as they scrambled for shelter. I reached out and did what I could, which wasn't much; I was feeling weaker all the time, and the connection to David had shrunk to a tiny filament, sparkling silver but feeding me nothing but a trickle of power.

I felt the storm shift its attention, responding instinctively to the lash of power.

Oh boy, I thought. It was like being caught in the full glare of the biggest spotlight in the world. With a big target painted on your chest.

The storm lobbed a twenty-pound piece of ice sideways, into the windows.

'Down!' I screamed, and leapt. Djinn defiance of gravity let me carry the leap the last ten feet, and gave me enough momentum to impact hard against Martin Oliver and topple both of us back behind the desk, onto a bruising hard floor.

The window shattered with so much force that

fragments flew past to embed themselves in the teak-wood wall behind the desk. Some of them were bloody. I shoved Martin down when he tried to get up and risked sticking my head up. Wind was screaming through the jagged hole in the window. It instantly jerked my hair back straight as a flag.

There were at least twenty people down, some moving, some not. There was a lot of blood, more leaking out over the marble floor with every faltering heartbeat. The non-combatants, mostly UN staffers and delegates who'd gotten caught in the wrong place at the wrong time, screamed and jammed up against the exits. Marion was already heading toward the wounded against the tide of panic. As an Earth Warden, she'd be of a lot more use than anything I could do. Some of them could still be saved. She was the one to do it.

'Baldwin.' The name snapped my head around, and I was blinded by my wind-whipped hair until I clawed it back and held it fisted in my left hand. Martin Oliver had gotten to his feet and was staring at me with intense, grave concentration. 'Joanne Baldwin?'

I didn't have time for long explanations. 'In the flesh.' More or less, but it didn't seem the time to spill that particular bean. 'Sorry about that, sir.'

He rejected the apology with a sharp hand movement. 'Can you do anything about that?'

He gestured out at the monster looming grey-green outside. It was firing off lightning bolts every few seconds, and thunder was a continuous subsonic rumble. What could I do about it? What had he been smoking? And then I remembered. I'd been told before that I had more power than Bad Bob Biringanine, who had once faced down a certain hurricane by the name of Andrew and killed it before it claimed even more lives. Not that I'd ever believed such a thing…and yet Martin Oliver, one bad-ass Weather Warden in his own right, was looking at me as if I was the hope of the world.

And I had to say, regretfully, 'No, sir. Sorry.'

Maybe in my human days – maybe – but not now, at the ragged end of my Djinn powers and enslaved to a…

…I had an idea.

I held up a finger. 'Be right back.'

Now that I knew the coldlight wasn't damaging to me, I could travel fast. I rose up into the aetheric, was instantly smothered by a whirling hungry blizzard of the stuff, but I didn't need sight to feel where I was going, not in this case. Homing instinct.

I flew.

The glitter clung to me, built up like a thick snow coating, but I refused to let it slow me down. I didn't see or sense any other presences up on the aetheric, but if there were any, they'd have been blue snowmen like me, masked from contact. Any Djinn still trapped here were probably frozen solid – if not frozen dead. *Damn.*

I collided with something. Not anything solid – that wasn't possible, on the aetheric plane – but the pulling confusion was just as surprising and upsetting. I drifted, shook off as much coldlight as I could, and tried to see what it was that I'd hit. I had to wipe off sparkles like ice on a windshield, but I finally realised that I'd found a Djinn. Which one, I couldn't tell. It didn't matter.

I grabbed hold and towed it with me, fast, bucking the glitter headwind as fast as I could, and then falling, with a shocking sense of gravity, into…

…Patrick's apartment. It was just as I'd left it. Sedate, well furnished, kind of pallid in a *Better Homes and Gardens* kind of way.

Blood dried to a dull brown mat on the neutral carpet where Lewis had been taken down.

I looked over at the Djinn I'd brought with me as his eyes rolled back in his head and he collapsed in slow motion to the floor.

I'd brought Patrick home.

Even though there was no time, I couldn't leave him like this, with the coldlight eating its way through him like worms on speed. He was already screaming, skin bubbling and beginning to slough. I grabbed hold – tried not to think about the slick, greasy feel of his flesh – and called all of the coldlight to me. It spiralled eagerly, abandoning the feast and climbing my arms in a blue-white frenzy.

'Nice doggies,' I murmured, and as soon as I was sure I had enough of them, I went across the room and shook them off in a flurry of disappointed critters. They dropped into the carpet like invisible fleas. They'd eventually make their way back to whatever victim was handy, but with any luck, Patrick would survive. At least as long as any of the rest of us would.

'Sara?' Patrick's eyes were open, blue and blind. His glasses were gone. I went back to him, got on my knees, and leant over him. He slowly focused on me, and went pale. 'Oh. You.'

'Yeah. Nice of you to remember. By the way, this whole slavery thing…it's working out just great.' I resisted the urge to punch him while he was down.

His gaze sharpened. 'You're still alive.'

'Surprised?'

That woke up a weak smile. 'Pleased, actually. Help me up.' He held out his hand. I stared at it for a second, then took it. Warm skin, as human and real as my own. Whether or not it was as human and real as an actual living person was something else entirely. Patrick heaved himself to his feet, staggered drunkenly and used me as a cane for a few seconds. 'Ugh. I see you haven't changed your mind about the room.'

'Yeah, well, I admit, the retro trashy look had its charms, but right at the moment I'm more concerned with saving some lives.' I pointed up. Even inside of his apartment, I could hear the thunder and feel the electric snap of the lightning strikes. 'Gotta go.'

'Yes,' he agreed. He looked at me very seriously for a few seconds. 'Where is Sara?'

'At Jonathan's house.'

He looked ill. 'They'll destroy her.'

'Actually, they've got bigger problems to worry about just now. Like me.' I left him and moved around to the front of the couch.

Yep. There he was, my teen Nero-in-training, crashed out in a sprawl on the leather couch, mouth gaping to show poor dental hygiene. He was snoring.

Also smiling.

I leant over and whispered, 'Kevin? Wake up.'

No response. Damn. I'd drawn on his own power to put him in this trance. Was it something I could snap him out of? I hadn't been thinking that far ahead, I had to admit. I reached out, grabbed, and shook him. His oily hair flopped back and forth, and he snorkelled a breath. His eyelids fluttered.

Nothing.

'Kevin!' I screamed, and shook him again. 'Damn, what do I have to do? Wake up!'

He mumbled something, smacked at me ineffectually with a clumsy hand, and tried to turn over.

I grabbed him and kissed him. After the first few slack seconds, I felt him kiss me back.

Ewwwwwwww. Not that boys his age were great kissers in general, but he had a *lot* to learn. *No* style points. I broke free before the wiggling worm of his tongue got too far into my mouth and shook him again, for emphasis.

His eyes were open, but cloudy. Cleaned up, he probably wouldn't be half bad, but the fact was he wasn't cleaned up, or even clean. The body odour alone made me think of places without running water or inside plumbing.

'Wha?' The word was garbled, but still semi coherent. I yanked him up by the grimy T-shirt to a sitting position. '...gone.'

'Shut up and listen,' I said. 'I need your help.'

'...help?' He blinked slowly, like an owl. His pupils were way too large. 'Why?'

'Philosophy some other time. Just repeat what I say. Got it?'

'Repeat.'

'Very good.' I resisted the urge to pat him on the head, mostly because I really didn't want to get greasy. 'I order you to destroy the storm.'

'Mmmm?' His eyes were glazing over. I pinched him hard enough to make a welt, and he yelped and cleared up. 'What?'

'I order you to destroy the storm. Say it.'

Oops. I'd woken him up too much. 'Why?' The vague look was vanishing like snow under an Arizona summer sun. 'You. You...you tricked me.'

'Just say it.'

'Or?' His jaw hardened as muscles clenched. He was willing himself awake, and all of the nice happy thoughts he'd been dreaming were slipping away.

'You'll put me to sleep again?' I'd liked him better asleep. Who wouldn't? 'No. *I'm* your, ah, master. You do what *I* say.'

'Then tell me to destroy the storm.'

His eyes narrowed behind the pretty, girl-length lashes. 'Why should I? What's in it for me?'

'Oh, I don't know...survival? Can't you *feel* this?' But then I realised that of course he couldn't; for him, like for most people, the storm was just a storm. Bad, yes. A killer. But not sentient, not rabid and scenting fresh meat. Not *alive*. His talent was fire. 'Shit. *Please*, Kevin. Do one decent thing in your life. I'm begging you. Let me do this.'

He kept staring at me for a few seconds. My bottle was clenched in his fist, my soul in his control, and the lives of thousands hanging in the balance.

'Fine,' he finally said. 'Go destroy the damn storm.'

I was almost out of there when he added, 'And take me with you.'

I materialised back in the lobby at the Secretariat tower to find it mostly deserted. Martin Oliver was still there; so were some of the security guards. Earth Wardens were shouting to each other over the steady shriek of wind, and a continuous silver curtain of rain was slicing in through broken windows. Everyone on the east side of the building was out, now. The storm had been continuing its grenade attack. The marble was a minefield of ice and glass shards, water, and blood.

Kevin was whooping in my ear. He liked aetheric travel a little too much, even with the smothering blanket of coldlight – *ah, that's right,* I remembered, he couldn't see it. None of them could.

'That is so *cool*!' he crowed, and did a spastic little dance on the slippery floor. He stopped, stared around. 'Jeez. You weren't kidding.'

'No,' I said. I was boiling over with power now, rich red power that pulsed in time with my fast, adrenalised heartbeats. 'Stay here.' I walked over to the nearest broken window.

'Baldwin!' Martin Oliver yelled. I looked back at him and let my eyes flare silver. For the first time that I could remember, he looked outright surprised, but he recovered in seconds. 'Be careful.'

I raised a hand in thanks, or farewell, or whatever, and stepped out into the storm.

Different now than it had been, back in my just-plain-girl days. The storm was a delicate latticework of interconnecting forces, with the coldlight swarming around it like a bloodstream, feeding it, insulating it, holding it together. I didn't get a sense that the light itself was hostile – just mindlessly opportunistic.

The storm was alive, therefore it was capable of being parasitised. Eventually, the coldlight would probably grow out of control and consume too much energy and start the chain reaction that would remove the threat – but I had no idea how long that would take. Too long, probably. No way could I count on it to happen in time.

I spread my arms and rose into the clouds, trailing blue sparks like a comet trail. Where I went, the coldlight flocked. The storm sensed me immediately, and recognised a threat; lightning began to stab through me, millions of volts of electricity attempting to explode every cell in my body. I bled the charge off, used it to draw in more coldlight. An ever-increasing spiral of blue, with me at the centre.

Up, climbing the sheer grey tower of the anvil cloud. Up into the cold, the thin air, the mesosphere, where if the storm could be said to have a heart, the heart resided.

The storm responded by battering me with ice and more lightning. Plasma balls formed white-hot and flung themselves at me, but the command Kevin had given me was utterly straightforward and the power being pulled out of him was staggering. I just flicked the St Elmo's fire away, bent lightning bolts at right angles, and reached for the vulnerable beating heart of the beast.

A scream stopped me. A piercing, panicked cry that went right through me like a sword thrust.

My master's voice. 'Come back! Oh God, come back *now*! Right now!' Kevin sounded scared – worse than scared, horrified.

I could have gone, but I didn't have to. I had the

choice, because I hadn't fulfilled the first command he'd given me; the two commands effectively cancelled each other.

Free will. Go back and baby-sit Kevin, or kill this thing and save thousands – maybe tens of thousands...

I didn't think there was a choice. I ignored the screaming – even though it continued, sawing right through me, body and soul – and focused on the storm instead.

I reached in and grabbed the core process that was at the centre of the giant. It wasn't much, really; some overexcited molecules, a pattern of reflecting and replicating waveforms that perfectly reinforced each other. The tough part wasn't disrupting it, it was finding it and reaching it.

The Wardens couldn't see it, because it was built out of nothing but coldlight.

I reached in and took hold of it, drew the sparks to me, and consumed them the way they consumed others. *We are all born from death*. Patrick had told me that. I hadn't realised he'd meant it literally.

The winds continued to blow, but the waveforms fragmented and began to cancel each other instead of resonating. Clouds began to break apart instead of pull inward. Temperatures began to cool here, warm there, chaos theory taking over.

It would storm for a while, but it was just another freak weather story now, one of those things that would play on CNN and the Weather

Channel for the next few days, and be forgotten by everybody except a few cab drivers and weather conspiracy nuts who believed the CIA was behind it all. Rain, hail, lightning. The usual stuff.

I let the power of it soak into me, reviving me, and then slowly drifted back down toward the UN Building. It was hard to see through the swirling, choking mass of coldlight that was being pulled toward me but I could see the place needed about a hundred new windows. The people weren't so lucky. As I folded back into flesh, blood, bone, and all the necessary fabric accessories, I saw that there were still a lot of people down on a floor that was awash with inches of rainwater. There had been blood, but it had been diluted and flushed by the storm; now that the rain was abating, some of the wounded were leaking red puddles.

Some, more ominously, were not.

I completed the transformation back into human form, felt my hair fall silky and straight over my shoulders, and for the first time thought, *I have it right. Finally.*

And then I realised what I was looking at. I'd left Marion, Martin Oliver, and a few other Wardens tending to the wounded, trying to get them to safety...and there was nobody moving now.

Instead, there were more bodies.

I skidded to a stop next to a crumpled form in rain-soaked brown suede. Marion's hair looked dark and thin, pounded by the storm's violence; she was still and quiet and pale. I checked her pulse and found her heart beating, though slowly. Martin Oliver was down, too, all his grace and fearless strength stripped away. His shirt was soaked through pink, and underneath there was a raw, four-inch-long tear through his sternum. Glass. He'd been skewered.

He didn't have a pulse at all. Just a vast, echoing silence.

I looked up as lightning flashed white, smelt hot ozone and cooling blood, and realised that someone was missing, someone I'd left behind.

Kevin.

I misted and felt that gravitational tug, down and to the left – he was still in the UN Building, but somewhere at least a level below. I sank through concrete, steel, cold empty space, more concrete and steel...

...to a hallway that lit up in Oversight like Broadway. *Lots* of power rattling around in here, wild and barely contained; the place was a blizzard of sparkles. The barely felt tug of Kevin's presence led me down through the deserted corridor, around a corner, and I saw a sudden flare of auras ahead, so bright they even punched through the curtain of glitter. I pulled back, still in mist form, and tried to get a sense of where I was and what was going on.

Kevin was definitely up ahead. So was Lewis. I couldn't tell if Jonathan was there or not, Djinn auras were all over the place, like wildfire...

Where the *hell* was I? I slowly misted forward again, found a convenient recessed doorway, and came down into skin to take a look.

At the end of the hall was a huge shiny door, like the kind you see in the movies when there's something *really* cool to steal. It was standing half-open.

There was a body lying a couple of feet away, human, bleeding hideously into the carpet from what looked like a fatal slash to the throat. The security guard was still breathing, but just barely... As I watched, his eyes glazed over, and the last whisper rattled out of his throat.

I heard voices, and carefully moved out of the cover of the doorway, hugging the wall. Whoever was there, they were inside the vault.

Lewis's voice. '...don't have to do this. Let him go.' Lewis sounded calm, but I felt the effort underneath it. Something bad was going on, something worse than the head injuries I knew he'd already sustained. I could feel the pulse of his distress, mental and physical, across the empty space separating us.

I advanced slowly, one step at a time, wondering where the hell Jonathan was, where David was, what had gone so wrong about all of this. I couldn't believe Kevin had killed the people upstairs, or taken out the dead guard on the carpet. Then again, maybe I was underestimating his capacity for desperation, or fury...

By moving all the way to the right side of the hall, I could see a slice of the interior, beyond the open door.

There were more unmoving figures in there, down on the ground. One wore a UN Security blazer. I extended my senses and found they were both dead.

Lewis was standing, utterly still, with his hand wrapped around a blue glass bottle. It was still stoppered. *David...* Across from him, Kevin was on his knees, being held there by a hand around his throat. He looked unconscious. At the very least, he was too scared to fight.

The hand that held him was big, square, and covered with blood.

I moved forward, trying to get in, and came right up against a barrier, like a thick pane of glass. A Djinn barrier. I'd have to be in a bottle to pass through it, and once inside...*shit*. My bottle must be on the other side, with Kevin. Probably stuffed in his pants pockets, along with his condoms.

'Please,' Lewis said, and worked the glass bottle nervously against his pants leg. He looked awful. Bruises covered half his face like an elaborate tribal tattoo – courtesy of Kevin's kicks in the head – and where he wasn't bruised he was pale, with a sick oatmeal tinge. 'You have a choice. Don't choose to do this. There's no going back.'

'There never is.' The hand holding Kevin was a man's, right down to the hair on the wrist and the big, blunt fingers, but the voice was a woman's, and it issued from somewhere on the other side, where I couldn't see. I didn't need to. I knew who she was, that voice was never going to leave my nightmares. *Yvette*. Of course...if Lewis had been there, they would have confiscated David's bottle and taken Yvette in for interrogation, too. Which meant that somewhere in the confusion upstairs, she'd escaped and come down here to rifle the vault for her favourite slave.

Over my not-quite-dead body, bitch. I tried the barrier again, searching for a weakness, but it was slick and perfect. I didn't think any of them had noticed me. I was staying just out of sight, misting where I had to in order to stay unnoticed. Mist, solid, didn't matter. I wasn't getting through to the other side. I'd have to wait for them to come out.

She said, in a voice as sweet and hard as petrified honey, 'Give me the bottle, Lewis. I might just let you live.'

He kept rubbing the bottle against the side of his leg, and I figured out what he was doing. It had a rubber stopper. He was slowly working it out, giving David a chance to escape. 'Tempting.' His voice cracked, and he swallowed hard and wet his lips.

'Look, not that I don't think that as psychos go you're a really lovely woman, but the last thing I want to do is give you a Djinn. So I think you'd better think about—'

'Kill him,' Yvette said.

The hand holding Kevin clenched, and I heard bone pop with a crunch like glass in plastic. Lewis yelled, stretched out his hand, and white fire flared from him to bathe Kevin as he was allowed to fall limp to the ground. *Oh God.* His neck, that sound had been the kid's neck breaking.

I didn't feel any release. Kevin wasn't dead. Lewis was keeping him alive, at least for the moment, but Lewis only looked a shade or two better than a corpse himself.

The Djinn who'd just killed Kevin – even if it was happening in slow motion – moved to the side, and I saw his face.

It was Jonathan. He looked blank, hard, as impenetrable as frosted glass. Nothing there of the humour or assurance I'd come to expect...he was wiped clean. Made something else.

He'd been claimed.

Yvette came into view. She didn't look so fresh, either – bruised along the side of her face, hair disarranged. Her eyes had a werewolf shine, and she no longer was hiding behind that fragile pretty shell. She looked bone hard, tough, and ready to kill. Not that she'd had to get her French-manicured hands dirty. She'd used (*oh God*) Jonathan for that.

She was holding a small glass bottle in her hands, something all-purpose, cheap but sturdy. Jonathan's prison. I remembered David telling me that he'd never been claimed. What was it like, to be so powerful, so old, and have to submit to this? I could barely stand it, and I was just days old. For him, it must be like…

…*rape*, David had said. And it was. Just like that.

'Give it up,' she said to Lewis. 'Believe me, he's not worth it. He's a cheap, mean, arrogant little son of a bitch, and he'll never amount to anything. In fact, you'll probably be better off with him dead. Count on it.'

He didn't listen, or if he listened, he didn't stop pouring energy into the boy.

I might have been the only one who noticed the rubber cap of the blue bottle in his hand fall out and bounce away into the shadows…but no, I saw something in Jonathan's eyes, a shift, a kind of blind focus. He knew.

David was out.

Lewis was panting now, slicked with sweat; he was pouring his life out to keep Kevin alive. And he couldn't possibly keep it up.

Yvette was moving toward him with that same hunting-tiger grace she'd used against David, and I wanted more than anything in my life to rip my way through this wall, drill diamond-hard claws into her heart and rip it out.

Lewis shifted his gaze and looked right at me. Fierce, utterly committed eyes. My throat went dry.

'Go fix the rift,' he said. It looked like he was talking to me, but I knew he wasn't. It was a direct order, and it was given to a Djinn who'd just come out of a bottle and was still mist…a Djinn whose bottle he held in his hand.

I felt David begin to rise up through the aetheric. Leaving without me.

Yvette laid a hand on Lewis, and it was like watching a roach crawl across the face of the Mona Lisa.

He formed the word with his lips, silently, where she couldn't see. Still holding my eyes prisoner. *Go*.

He'd die if I left him. Hell, he'd probably die if I didn't leave him, but at least he wouldn't die alone, unwitnessed…

I felt the cord between myself and David stretch and grow thin under the strain.

Yvette's hand slid insinuatingly along Lewis's sweat-damp neck as he poured his concentration into keeping her last victim breathing.

Go.

Lewis didn't have my bottle. He couldn't command me. With Kevin all but dead, nobody else could, either.

I whispered, at a pitch I knew only he could hear, *I love you*.

And I shot up like a burning arrow into the aetheric, mourning.

I found David one level above the aetheric. No words. We melted, merged, our auras shifting and blending. I remembered what he'd told me once about making love as a gas, and felt a smile bloom sad and warm inside. Even in the disembodied state, he was as familiar to me as my human heartbeat had once been, and just as necessary.

Jo... A whisper through the empty spaces, a caress without skin or body or words. The purest form of love I had ever felt. *I'm so sorry. I couldn't let you die, but I didn't want to die, either. And that's the only way to make a Djinn. Through sacrifice. I tried to cheat. This is what comes out of it.*

He could feel the mourning in me, and the guilt, and the horrible weight of responsibility. His touch made it easier. Nothing could make it easy.

He was already moving again, rising, driven by the compulsion Lewis had placed on him to close the rift. So long as he was moving up, I knew Lewis was still alive. There was that, at least.

I went with him. The coldlight was almost solid now, energy made matter. The image came to me that it was antibodies, that we were the invaders here, and this excess of them meant the universe was sick, maybe dying.

Up. I don't know if there were other Djinn there, because all I could see was coldlight, a continuous blizzard of sparks surrounding us like a hot blue shell. I kept bleeding them off of David. They rolled harmlessly off of me.

Up.

We slowed and stopped, and although I couldn't see anything I knew we'd arrived. David's compulsion would have delivered us to the right place. When I stretched out my senses I could feel the rift, turning slowly like a slow-motion whirlpool as it sucked the coldlight from the demon reality into ours.

Get back, David said, and gently tried to push me away. I clung harder. *Jo, you have to get back now. I need to do this alone.*

'No.' I didn't even know if I could do it, or how stupid an idea it was, but I formed flesh. I was surprised it was even possible here, in this place, but I took on weight and dimension and artificial life. No air to breathe, but that didn't matter, not for a short while; I could manufacture an atmosphere good enough to sustain me for a while, out of the same primal material I'd just formed my body from.

A hot sirocco of wind whipped through the nothingness, blowing back my straight black hair, whispering close over my skin.

Hands closed around my shoulders from behind. They slid up my neck and combed hair away from my skin, and I shivered at the kiss that burnt right at the juncture of my neck and collarbone.

'*Jo.*' His whisper was as rough and unsteady as his fingers. 'I thought I'd never see you again. Not in any way that mattered.'

I turned. David was back to *my* David, hair slightly too long for neatness, warm copper eyes, kissable lips. I wrapped my arms around him and held him. There was too much tension in his body, but it felt *right*. At last. The coldlight was a continuous white-noise hiss of blue against the bubble I'd formed around us, but it didn't matter just now. I wanted to stay in his embrace forever.

And I couldn't. I knew I couldn't. Too high a price for that.

He kissed me, gentle and slow and warm, and the taste of him nearly made me weep. He cupped my face in both hands, and as he pulled back his eyes were luminous with peace.

'It's OK,' he said, and drew his thumbs over my lips in a caress that was as intimate as anything I'd ever felt. 'Jonathan knew. One of us has to go. I've had my time.'

'Wrong,' I corrected him, and put all my strength into a shove that sent him stumbling backwards. 'I'm giving you mine.'

I dove straight at the whirlpool.

David's scream followed me in, but it was too late, too late to even wonder what the hell I was thinking, because I felt the darkness on the other side of the rift and with it, a visceral surge of panic, and knew this was going to hurt, *badly*.

And then I hit the paper-thin cut between the worlds, and stuck there with an impact that shredded me back into mist. Pieces of me began to be sucked away, through that rift, and I had to fight to hold on against the intense black pressure.

Where the pieces of me went through, the rift sealed.

Oh God.

I understood now. I understood why Jonathan had been so reluctant to send David to do this, because he'd known what had to be done. The only thing that could seal this thing was my blood, or David's, because we'd birthed this thing, like some distorted child.

I let go. Let go of everything – all the fear, the pain, the anguish, the guilt. I felt the cord back to David break with a high, thin singing sound like a snapped wire, and his presence vanished from my mind.

I was alone.

I let go and let the Void have me, as much of me as it needed to seal the hole between our two worlds. It was like bleeding to death – a slow, cold unravelling, a sense of being lost one drop at a time. There was pain, but the pain didn't matter.

What mattered was that I sensed the rift drawing together, healing.

The flow of coldlight at the rift slowed, stopped. It drifted in a sparkling blue weightless dance around me.

What was left of me.

I felt the rift seal shut with a kind of vacuum-seal thump, and instantly the coldlight glowed white-hot around me, bright and brilliant as a million stars exploding, and faded off into darkness. It couldn't exist here without the rift, just as I couldn't exist without the umbilical to David.

There was not much left of me. Just enough to remember who I was, what I'd been. Faces in my memory, but I didn't know them anymore. It was all falling away.

Falling like snow into the dark.

The snow turned to light. Sunlight. I was standing in a meadow full of grass that was too green to be real, and there was a woman walking toward me through flame red flowers. Her white gown shifted in a wind that didn't stir the fields.

White hair like a cloud. Eyes the colour of deepest amethyst. Beautiful and cool and peaceful.

'Sara.' I didn't know where the name came from. 'I'm dead, you know.'

She reached out toward me. 'No,' she said, and caressed the satin of my hair. 'No, my sweet. Not yet. There is a part of you that remains. Humans are like that.'

I remembered a coal black hunger, ice-edged shadows. 'Ifrit?' I whispered.

'You would be,' she said. 'But there is another way. And perhaps we owe that to you.'

'We?'

When she pulled back, I saw she wasn't alone. There was a man with her, big and muscular, running a little to fat, with a Scandinavian-blond unruly shock of hair and eyes as blue as a Caribbean sea. I knew him, and didn't know him. He smiled at me, very slightly, and I saw pain in it. And courage.

'I've lived too long,' Sara said. 'I've stolen life from others. Patrick betrayed you to buy it for me. There is no honour in what I've become.'

I didn't understand. The wind that rippled Sara's dress touched my face, combed cool fingers through my hair. It was gentle and beautiful and peaceful, and I knew it wanted to take me with it, into the dark.

'I did this for Patrick. I started the rift. What David did for you only accelerated it. Do you understand?'

I didn't. It was all falling away, sliding into the shadows.

'We do the worst things for love,' she whispered. 'So Jonathan was created. So David created you. So I created Patrick. And none of us should exist. The balance is gone.'

If balance was required, I was restoring it. Going away…

'Stay,' she said, and touched my face with those cool silver lips. 'There is a gift only Patrick and I can give. One last gift, in return for what you have given us.'

Words drifted up from the darkness inside of me. 'What have I given you?'

Her smile was beautiful, and sad, and perfect. 'A way to be together. And now I offer you the same, my love. Take it.'

She opened her arms. I looked at Patrick. There were tears shining in his eyes, and he backed away. Afraid, after all.

I stepped into Sara's embrace.

'No,' Patrick gulped, and turned back. He flung his arms around us both and hid his face in the pale lace of Sara's hair. 'Both of us or nothing. As it always was.'

Something wrapped hot around me, like clinging tar, and I thought, *I should have said no*, but then the pain dug deep and I screamed.

And screamed and screamed and screamed, until the universe exploded in a silent dark *pop* like a shattering of glass.

It didn't feel like a gift.

It felt like a betrayal.

When I woke up, someone was holding me in strong, warm arms. I tried to burrow closer and felt the embrace tighten. 'Jo?'

I lifted my head and saw that it was David. We were sitting against a wall in a hallway, next to a giant brushed-steel vault door. I felt...empty. Clean, but empty. Exhausted and powerless.

I felt *wrong*.

He was stroking my hair gently, letting it curl around his fingers. *Crap*. Curly hair again. Something hadn't gone right...

'Easy,' he murmured when I tried to get up. He rose to his feet, still holding me, and set me down on shaky legs. 'Oh God, Jo. My God. You're alive.'

Sara. Patrick. It had seemed so real, hurt so

much... I drew breath. It felt...wrong. Clumsy. Mechanical. 'Maybe.' Memory slammed back with a vengeance and flooded me with alarm. I turned to look inside the vault.

It couldn't have been the hours it had seemed, up there at the top of the world. It had been seconds, minutes at most.

The confrontation was still going on.

Lewis was still standing, but even as I watched he swayed and collapsed to his knees. The white burn of energy I'd seen him giving to the motionless, broken body of Kevin Prentiss was almost spent, just flickers now, pulsing in time with Lewis's laboured heartbeat.

God, he was dying. I couldn't believe he'd held on so long, or that Yvette had *let* him...but then I saw the look on her face as she watched him, and I knew why she'd waited. He was suffering.

She liked that kind of thing too much to stop it prematurely.

Jonathan was more of an absence than a presence in the room – blank, stiff as a statue, no sense of the restless energy and power that had been as much a part of him as the sarcastic half-smile. Yvette could not be allowed to keep him. The damage she could do...

'We have to do something,' I said to David. He reached out, encountered the barrier, and slid his hand along it.

'I can't.' His voice was rough and low in his

throat; he hated being helpless, hated seeing Jonathan reduced to this.

I reached out, and my hand slid past his, into the barrier, through it without pause. I heard his intake of breath, but then I was committed, and I had to *move*. No time to think about things.

I threw myself forward, onto Yvette.

She was stronger than she looked, and softer. I'd caught her by surprise; she really hadn't believed any Djinn could get past that barrier. We hit the floor hard enough to make her scream and me gasp for breath, rolled, and fetched up in a tangle against some metal shelves that teetered precariously from the impact.

They were full of bottles.

Full of *Djinn* bottles.

Every one of them marked with a black seal.

These were the Djinn who'd been infected with Demon Marks, who'd been sealed away, never to be released again, because if a demon ever succeeded in taking over a Djinn, the power of that combination would be... Nobody even wanted to think about it.

It was the equivalent of a room full of nuclear bombs, rocking back and forth over our heads.

Yvette still held Jonathan's bottle, I hadn't succeeded in making her drop it. She opened her mouth to scream out a command. I punched her in the face, hard, felt my knuckles explode into white pain when they crushed her lips against her teeth.

'You,' I panted, and punched her again, 'don't say *anything*.'

She was still trying to mumble a command. I grabbed her shirt, tore it, and stuffed the blood-spattered satin in her mouth.

Jonathan hadn't moved.

His bottle was clenched in her right fist. While she battered at me with her left, I grabbed hold and smashed her right hand painfully back into the metal shelves. I saw blood and didn't let that stop me. I did it again. Her fingers loosened.

I grabbed for the bottle, but she clung to it like an octopus. She yanked my hair hard enough to bring tears to my eyes, then spat the gag out of her mouth to yell, 'I order you to—'

Panic gave me the strength of at least two, if not ten. I grabbed her right hand again, took hold of her index finger, and snapped it in two with a brisk, crackling sound.

She interrupted her command with a shriek.

The bottle rolled free. I grabbed for it, but she caught me with a wild swinging left hook, and tossed me off of her in a heap.

'Bitch!' she panted. Red blood drooled from her cut lip, and she looked savage, utterly crazed. 'I'm going to make you *suffer*—'

She devolved into cursing, scrambled after the bottle. I tackled her and pulled her back.

Right about that time, Lewis collapsed face forward on the floor. He was still holding David's bottle. He flipped over on his back, stared blankly up at the light fixtures in the ceiling, and rolled over again to crawl his way toward the half-open door.

I saw Kevin's limp body take in a shuddering, unaided breath.

He raised his head, and I was frozen by what I saw in his eyes... It was confused, painful and full of rage.

Lewis had *healed* him. What that had cost I couldn't imagine...to Lewis, or to Kevin. The fury in the kid was like nothing sane.

He lunged forward at the same time as Yvette for Jonathan's bottle, and got there first.

I saw the shift in Jonathan instantly as his loyalty shifted from mother to son.

Yvette pushed herself away and got to her feet, backing up as far as the room would let her. Kevin and Jonathan were between her and the door.

'Don't,' she said, and wiped blood from her face with the back of her hand. 'Sweetie, don't do this. You know you don't want to—'

'You,' Kevin said tightly, and looked at Jonathan. 'Kill Yvette. *Now.*'

Jonathan didn't hesitate. He leapt like a cat, cleared me as I rolled into a ball and covered myself, and on the way formed steel-hard claws from the tips of his fingers.

I felt a hot spray of blood on my face, and gagged on the taste. *Oh God, oh God*...not that she hadn't deserved it, but...

Kevin was watching his stepmother die with a blank, intense stare. When it was over, when the blood stopped and Jonathan stepped back with the claws red-misting away, Kevin transferred that stare to me.

God, those *eyes*. So empty. It was like looking into a grave.

'You left me,' he said. 'I told you to come back. I *screamed* for you.'

I didn't dare answer. Or move.

'You said you wouldn't let anything happen to me,' he whispered. 'I don't like liars.'

He had my bottle. He dug it out of his pocket and held it in his left hand – such a small thing, to rule everything about me, life and death – and smiled at me and said, 'I want you to burn. Burn yourself alive. Burn until I get tired of hearing you scream.'

I felt a flash of pure, nauseating fear, waited for the compulsion to take over, but...

...nothing happened.

I slowly uncoiled from my protective ball. Kevin looked furious. 'Did you hear me? I said *burn*, you bitch!'

I got up, flexed my right hand. It hurt. There were cuts in my skin from Yvette's teeth when I'd punched her.

'Sorry,' I said, with a kind of slow wonder. 'Don't think that works anymore.'

I looked up and saw David's face touched by the same sense of intense, odd awareness.

'You're alive,' he whispered. 'You're...human.'

And then his expression changed to utter horror, and he started to batter at the barrier between us.

I was human, and I was trapped in here with Kevin and the most powerful Djinn in the universe, who was completely under Kevin's control.

Trapped with a kid who'd just killed his stepmother without blinking.

Kevin echoed David's whisper. 'Human?' I didn't like the hard, wet shine in his eyes. 'Good. Maybe you can hurt the way you let *me* hurt.'

Lewis crawled over the threshold of the barrier, dragging David's bottle with him. David reached down and pulled him out of the way, crouched down and exchanged a look with him.

They both looked at me.

Lewis drew in a painful, hitching breath, and said, 'Do whatever you have to do, David, but get her out of here. Do it now.'

David blew through the barrier like it wasn't even there, slammed into Kevin from behind and sent him flying. Kevin, off balance, tripped over Yvette's bloody corpse and into the rows of shelves that were still trembling from their last hard slam.

They tipped.

Black-sealed bottles fell. Some broke, hitting metal edges or each other, and even though I couldn't see any Djinn I could feel them, swirling like a hot wet storm in the room.

David grabbed me. He pulled me past Kevin,

who was still squirming to get up. I tried to slow down, because I had the opportunity to grab Jonathan's bottle, but David's imperative was clear. Get me out. Don't stop for anything.

He shoved me forward, and I passed the barrier just a heartbeat ahead of him.

That was enough. His command was fulfilled, and the barrier slammed in place, knocking him backward. I reached out and touched him, but I couldn't pull him through, couldn't drag him to safety...

Kevin rolled over, still clutching Jonathan's bottle, and yelled, 'You! Kill him!'

'David, come here!' Lewis yelled, virtually at the same second. The barrier dissolved. David lunged through.

Jonathan grabbed, and missed.

Something was happening inside the vault. I couldn't see it, not with human eyes, but when I used Oversight it looked like hell in there – tortured, writhing bodies, Djinn fighting each other on the aetheric, Kevin and Jonathan blazing like a white star in the centre. I felt a chill of premonition and turned to Lewis, who was propped against the wall, looking worse than I'd ever seen him.

'I can't,' he whispered, even though I hadn't asked. 'I've got nothing.'

If he had nothing left, David had nothing. We all watched as the black-sealed Djinn, free of their captivity, started manifesting in the real world.

Nightmares. They looked horribly disfigured, half demon, and they made a terrible sawing noise like metal tearing. Screams. A kind of scream I never wanted to hear again.

'Get out of there!' I blurted, and held out my hand to Kevin. 'You have to get out, Kevin! Please! You don't know what you're doing!'

He could have. All he had to do was walk two feet forward, take my hand. Make the choice.

There was such a horror of devastation in his eyes. A dawning awareness that what he'd done had consequences, had a kind of history that was never going to let him go. Sin is like a stalker – you may learn to ignore it, but you can never hide from it.

He took one step, stopped, and gave me the emptiest smile I had ever seen. He said, 'Concerned about me now? Too late, *Joanne*. I'm not gonna be anybody's bitch anymore. Not hers, not yours... I'm gonna have power. So much power none of you can do anything to stop me.'

He looked past me, to Lewis. 'You're that guy. The one she was so afraid of. The one with the big mojo.'

Lewis didn't blink. 'Maybe.'

'Huh.' Kevin swept him up and down with a look. 'No shit. Thanks, man. For saving my life.'

'You didn't have to pay me back by killing her.'

Kevin's face flushed a dull, mutinous red. 'You don't know anything about it.' He turned to

Jonathan. 'Can you get me out of here?'

Jonathan's eyebrows quirked over his empty stare. 'Where do you want to go?'

'Anywhere.' Kevin, under the stress of the moment, was forgetting the rules. He looked at Jonathan, who stared back, waiting. 'Anywhere but here!'

'You have to be specific,' Jonathan said. And, as Kevin's mouth started to shape something – something I was pretty sure would have been *home* – Jonathan said, 'Might as well make it someplace fun. Disneyworld. Las Vegas. Something—'

'Vegas!' Kevin crowed. He looked pleased with himself for seizing on it. 'Hell yeah. Definitely Vegas.'

Jonathan, I thought, *what the hell are you doing?* He could have detailed the kid to death, could have asked him to define his designation down to a few square inches of ground, but I could see that he'd gotten what he wanted. 'You have to order me,' he reminded.

'Oh, right. Uh, take me to Las Vegas... Wait!' Kevin threw up a hand. 'What the hell are these things?'

He was looking at the barely visible Djinn swirling in the air. Jonathan didn't shift his gaze. Probably didn't want to look at them for long. I wouldn't have.

'Djinn,' he said. 'They're sick.'

'Yeah? Fuck me. Well, let them go, they're creeping me out.'

'No!' I yelled, and lunged forward. Too late. The barrier holding the Djinn back popped with an almost physical sensation, and the infected, tormented Djinn vanished. Kevin looked around the vault at all of the bottles lining the shelves. The ones on the right were all sizes and shapes, unsealed; the ones on the left were marked in black with the glyph that signified a demon infestation.

He grabbed some of the black-sealed bottles and stuffed them into his baggy pants pockets. 'Let's go,' he said to Jonathan. 'Vegas. Move your ass.'

Lewis said, very grimly, 'David, stop them from leaving.'

I was looking at David when he said it, and I saw the flicker of agony that crossed his face; Lewis didn't know what he'd just asked him to do. Fight Jonathan. Fight someone he had loved and respected for a thousand years or more.

Someone he knew he couldn't beat.

Kevin threw a sideways look at Jonathan, clearly realising that *Vegas, move your ass* didn't qualify as a proper command. Which meant David had the upper hand. 'You. Mojo guy. You think you can take me?'

Lewis said, 'I didn't save your life to arm wrestle with you.'

'But you're strong, right? Stronger than anything?'

'Not anything.'

'But almost anything.' Kevin looked sly, shot a

greasy look at Jonathan. 'Hey, I've got a better idea. We can do Vegas anytime.' He looked over at me, and the craziness in his eyes made me feel weightless and sick. 'You should've been nicer to me, bitch.'

I think I knew, somewhere deep inside, what he was about to say, but there was no way to stop him. No way any of us could have stopped him.

Kevin pointed at Lewis and said, 'Give me all his power. I want it all.'

A clear, unequivocal command, one Jonathan wouldn't have any choice but to follow.

Lewis cried out, arched forward, and a river of white light flooded out of him, slammed across the empty space and into Kevin's narrow T-shirt-clad chest. David, still held by the previous command, couldn't act, and this was so far outside of my area of expertise that there was nothing I could even think to say, much less do.

Lewis went utterly limp. Unconscious. Out of the fight. Which meant that David was powerless.

Kevin opened his eyes, and smiled. *Smiled.* Flexed his arms like a weightlifter striking a pose.

'Kevin, don't do this. You can't hide,' I said. My voice was shaking. I gathered Lewis's limp body in my arms and felt how hot he was, how fragile. How *human.* Like me. 'Kevin, they'll never forgive you for this. Humans or Djinn. They'll hunt you down. They'll destroy you.'

He lowered his arms and looked like a sixteen-year-old kid again, scrawny, nervous, arrogant. 'Yeah? Well, you tell them, they try it, I'll kick all their asses. Count on it.'

I just shook my head. He didn't know. He didn't understand.

Kevin snapped his fingers at Jonathan. 'Now. Today. Take me to Vegas. We've got some fun to be having.'

'Stop him!' I pleaded with David. He looked stunned, angry, and completely baffled.

'I can't. Lewis...' He looked down at the man I held in my arms. 'It's gone. All his power. There's nothing to draw from.'

Too late, anyway. A sensation of rushing wind, and Jonathan and Kevin were gone.

'Can you track them?' I asked. David crouched down next to me and nodded. 'Oh, God, David...can you *fight* them?'

'Not alone,' he said. 'Not like this.'

I closed my eyes and looked inside myself, felt the warm red swell of power. I'd been put back into human form with all my potential included, which meant that maybe I was the only one qualified to do this thing. The only one with enough raw energy.

But I had to do something I'd sworn I never would. And no matter what anybody said, it would change things. Forever.

As always, David knew me. He said quietly, 'You know you have to.'

I took the bottle from Lewis's limp fingers, and

felt the sudden rush of strength, the giddy sensation of David's allegiance transferring itself to me.

He looked at me with those copper eyes, smiled so warmly I felt the embrace of the sun fold around me, and said, 'It's about damn time. What took you so long?'

My lips parted as I felt the two halves of us knit together in a partnership like nothing I'd ever felt in my life. Equals. There was nothing subservient about the Djinn, not like this... He was me, part of me, more than me. And I was more than him.

I gently eased Lewis down to the carpet and stood up to face David. He reached out, put his hands on my shoulders and slid them up to gently cradle my face. Thumbs traced my lips and left a memory of fire. He was so damn beautiful it made me want to explode.

'We'll do this together,' he said, and kissed me.

A long, sweet kiss that fired me deep inside, a pilot light kicking in with enough force to make my knees go weak.

'Yeah,' I murmured into his open mouth. 'Can we win?'

His smile was a warm ghost against my lips. 'Don't know. But it's going be one hell of a good fight.'

I was warned by the clatter of metal and the creak of a heavy door at the far end of the hallway, but there was no point in getting flustered by the fact that the Wardens had finally dug themselves out of their chaos and come looking. 'Freeze!' somebody roared with the authority of a man with a big gun. I wasn't worried. I'd faced down worse.

I opened my mouth to give David my first command...

...and I heard a loud *boom*, loud as the world, saw David's pupils expand in shock, felt my body jerk hard against him.

Oh, shit, I thought.

They'd just shot me in the back.

I had time for one last command. David was already readying himself for battle, for killing, for more death.

'Back in the bottle,' I whispered, tasted blood, and saw David's eyes go even wider in anguish as the wind sucked him down, into the bottle.

I was crying when I slammed the stopper in place, and curled up on the ground, gasping for breath against the growing, howling pain with his bottle held in both hands, against my heart.

Some shadows leant over me.

Darkness.

I woke up slowly, to the beeping of machines and the dull mutter of voices.

I opened my eyes and focused slowly on the man who was sitting next to me, his large hand wrapped around mine.

'Jo?'

Not David's voice, not his touch. Dots of light

swirled and settled into the haggard outline of Lewis's face. Pallid, lined, textured by at least a day's unshaven growth of beard. Greasy hair.

'You look like shit,' I whispered, and his dry lips cracked into a smile. He was wearing a hospital gown, one of those designs that flatters nobody. So was I. There were tubes tethering my arms, and a dull ache in my lower back.

It came back to me in flashes, pieces. David's eyes. The sound of the gun. *Don't hurt them.* That brought a surge of adrenalin that forced back drugged calm. 'David – oh God please tell me they didn't take him—'

Lewis reached out, opened a drawer in a stand next to the bed, and took out a blue glass bottle. He handed it to me. It was stoppered.

'He's fine. I…' Lewis wavered and licked his lips. 'I kept him safe for you.'

'Some asshole shot me.'

'They didn't know. All they knew was that there were dead Wardens, and the vault was breached. They couldn't know.'

I made a not-convinced noise. 'Hurts.'

'I know.' He reached out and traced the curve of my cheek with his fingers. 'You've been out for two days.'

Time delay before the dread set in. Two days? *Two fucking days?* I struggled to sit up, but drugs and Lewis and weakness kept me down. 'Kevin – he took Jonathan—'

'I know.' Lewis's voice had that silvery calm that Martin Oliver had been so famous for. 'Jo, it's OK. We've got teams on his trail. We'll find him.'

'*Not* OK!' Lewis didn't understand. *Couldn't* understand. He didn't know what Jonathan was. What Kevin had at his command. The powers of the strongest Warden in the world, plus the monstrous power of the single greatest Djinn... They'd sent *teams*? They might as well have sent packs of Girl Scouts. 'Got to go. Get after him.'

His strong hands pushed me back. 'You're not going anywhere for a while.'

I clenched my fingers around David's bottle and, before he could stop me, dragged the rubber stopper out of the mouth.

Zero to sixty. David was there instantly, fast as thought, staring down at me from the other side of the bed. Still trapped in that instant of panic and fury, thinking I was dying.

His hot-penny eyes flashed to Lewis, to me, and then he reached down and gathered me up into his arms.

I hadn't known how cold I was until I fell into his warmth.

David was whispering words, but I didn't know them – languages long dead, but the music was universal. Love, and fear, and sheer relief. He kissed me, kissed me hard, and I let myself melt into him.

When he pulled back, I realised that Lewis was talking. Urgently. 'David, you can't be here. They don't know about you. You have to leave this to the Wardens now. She's getting the best of care—'

'Quiet.' David hissed it, and when I looked up I saw the two of them exchanging a full-force stare. '*Leave*. You can't do anything for her.'

Lewis's eyes betrayed him with a flicker, and I remembered that he'd been stripped of power. Emptied. He was no more than any other mortal out there, walking around oblivious. David meant it literally. Lewis couldn't heal me. Couldn't do anything but hold my hand.

I couldn't imagine how that felt, for someone like him who'd held the power of the world inside of him.

'Don't say that,' I said, and drew David's eyes back to me. 'He's my friend. Always.'

That eased some of the darkness in Lewis's eyes, at least. He gave me a very small, pale smile.

'So...as a friend...how much trouble am I in, exactly?'

He started to answer, but in the next few seconds there were footsteps ringing on tile, and then the white curtain around my bed got whipped away in a shriek of metal rings, and an entire delegation was standing there. I was, I realised, in a familiar room. The same one where I'd done the French Maid lap dance for the doctor – who was standing in the corner with his arms folded across his chest, looking none too happy. Next to him was a weary, bleary Paul Giancarlo. Next to *him* was Marion Bearheart.

David let me go and stood up. Shield and protector. I took his hand and squeezed it lightly. 'No,' I said. 'Relax, David. Friends.'

I wasn't sure of that, actually, but a battle wouldn't do any of us any good. David settled – outwardly – but I felt the tension in his grip on my fingers.

'Friends,' Marion echoed softly. 'I see. You assume a lot, Joanne.'

'I assume you wouldn't have saved me if you didn't think I was worth the trouble.' It was a long speech. I felt winded at the end of it.

Marion cut a look toward Paul, who slid his hands in his pants pockets and looked secretive. He didn't volunteer a comment, so she continued. 'The boy. Kevin. Do you contend that he was to blame for all of the…chaos?'

Boy, that was a loaded question. 'Blame is kind of a broad term. If you're asking, did he kill people, yes. He did. And he's got a very powerful Djinn under his control, not to mention a couple of bottles of quarantined ones.' I had to pause for a couple of breaths. The dull ache in my back was blossoming into something hot and immediate. 'He was on his way to Las Vegas. You know that?'

Marion nodded. 'We know. What we need to know is how powerful is he, exactly? Can you tell us that?'

I could. I wasn't actually sure if I should. My hesitation made Paul sigh and step forward.

'Jo, dammit, we've lost enough people. Not to mention a full fifteen Djinn. Don't screw around, here. I don't want a higher body count out of this.'

I felt a headache start pounding between my eyes. 'You lost a team already, didn't you?'

Nobody answered, and then Lewis said, quietly, 'Three people. We think they're dead.'

I sucked in a deep breath – it hurt – and nodded. 'You'll lose more. Pull them back. Track him, don't try to take him.'

'Somebody has to try,' Marion said grimly.

'Fine. I will.' I struggled to sit up. The doctor and Lewis and David all tried to stop me, but I wasn't having any. Screw internal damage. I had a fix for that.

'David,' I said. 'Heal me.'

I'd never understood what it meant, before, when that command was given. It wasn't just that the way opened for David to touch that deep well of potential… It was a path that moved both ways, a true and perfect union. Through him, I touched him. And something else. Something even greater.

He looked back at me with a dawning astonishment in his eyes. He reached out to take my other hand, holding both, staring down at me.

And the power that flooded through me, *God*, unbelievable. I knew it was my own, purified and refined through him, but the richness of it was staggering. There was pain, but more than that, there was *pleasure*. An amazing amount of it.

I gasped out loud, held on tight, and rode it out. When it subsided to aftershocks, I gasped, 'You ever felt that before?'

His smile burnt, it was so glorious. 'Never.'

'Me neither.' I yanked tubes out of my hand and swung my legs over the side of the bed. People made protests. I ignored them and put my weight on my feet, felt the world go steady and sharp around me. I looked down at my hospital clothes and felt a sad regret for my lost ability to design my own wardrobe. 'David? Clothes?'

Dark peachskin suit settled gently over my skin. A silk shirt, sharply tailored. On my feet, lethally beautiful shoes. I glanced up at David, who lifted a shoulder in a half-shrug.

'I learn,' he said. 'What now?'

The rest of them were silent. Nobody was trying to stop us. I looked from one of them to the other – Marion, Paul, Lewis – and finally at David.

'Are you ready for this?' I asked him. For answer, he let go of my hand and stepped back, and settled an olive drab ankle-length coat around his shoulders.

His copper eyes hid themselves behind human brown, and round spectacles. He looked mild and gentle, except for the strength of his smile.

'I'm ready,' he said. I turned to Paul and held up a hand. He echoed the gesture.

'Las Vegas?' he asked. 'Just so I know where to send the body bags.'

'You in charge now?'

'Until things get settled. This place isn't all that under control right now.'

'You'll do fine,' I said. 'Paul. Keep your people out of my way.'

Marion cleared her throat. '*My* people will help.'

'*Your* people will get killed,' I corrected. 'This is my fight. Mine and David's.'

'He's just a kid,' Lewis said. He hadn't gotten to his feet. Hadn't done anything but sit quietly, watching the show. 'Go easy.'

I looked at him in Oversight, and saw something terrible. Something I should have known all along.

Lewis was dying. The emptiness inside of him was like cancer, eating away at him; his aura was already pallid, turning necrotic. Kevin had already killed him; Lewis's body was just still fighting the inevitable. If there was any chance at all to save him, it had to be reclaiming his powers from Kevin.

This had to be done. For him. For Jonathan. Even for Kevin himself.

It just wasn't going to be as easy as, oh, fighting your average demigod.

'What do you need?' Paul rumbled.

I turned a smile on him, saw him warm in response, and said, 'Besides a vacation? I think I need a really fast car.'

Epilogue

For those who like this kind of DIY stuff, you can make your own *Heat Stroke* soundtrack with these cuts (but please, support the artists, buy the CDs!):

'If Heartaches Were Nickels'	Joe Bonamassa
'Gett Off'	Prince and the New Power Generation
'American Woman'	Lenny Kravitz
'Missionary Man'	Eurythmics
'Hella Good'	No Doubt
'A New Day Yesterday'	Joe Bonamassa
'The Stroke'	Billy Squier
'Coconut'	Harry Nilsson
'Wild Wild West'	Escape Club
'Stranglehold'	Ted Nugent
'(If You Were) In My Movie'	Suzanne Vega
'Jane's Getting Serious'	Jon Astley
'Battle Flag'	Pigeonhead
'Bed'	Semisonic

(Because people often ask what kind of weird stuff I listen to when I'm writing.)

Peace...

Rachel Caine

'Murder, mayhem, magic, meteorology – and a fun read'
Jim Butcher, bestselling author of The Dresden Files

ILL WIND

BY RACHEL CAINE

Joanne Baldwin is a Weather Warden. The Wardens Association has been around pretty much for ever. Some Wardens control fire, others control earth, water or wind – and the most powerful can control more than one element. Without them, humanity would be wiped off the face of the planet.

But now Joanne is on the run from another kind of storm: accusations of corruption and murder. Her only hope is Lewis, the most powerful Warden. Unfortunately, he is also on the run, having stolen three bottles of Djinn and become the most wanted man on earth. Joanne must find him, and find him fast, as some really bad weather is closing in...

CHILL FACTOR

BY RACHEL CAINE

Living, dead or Djinn, Joanne Baldwin just can't stay out of trouble. Now she's on a time-sensitive mission to Las Vegas to retrieve the world's most important Djinn from the world's most dangerous teenager...and she's doing it alone.

That's bad enough but having to deal with a past that's determined to buy her, and suffering from serious wardrobe shortages...well, that's over the line.

One thing's for certain, Joanne is gambling everything this time.

WINDFALL

BY RACHEL CAINE

You think you're having a bad day? Joanne Baldwin has lost her job as a Weather Warden and saving the world doesn't usually come with a decent pension plan. Burdened with a difficult sister in need of rescue, accused of weather-related murder, and finding herself in the middle of a Djinn civil war...well, Joanne's bad times are just getting worse.

With enemies approaching from all sides, not to mention mounting credit card bills (Manolos don't come cheap, you know) Joanne is praying for a windfall. But the mother of all hurricanes approaching the Florida coast isn't quite what she had in mind.

FIRESTORM

BY RACHEL CAINE

Rogue Weather Warden Joanne Baldwin is racing to New York to warn her former colleagues of the impending apocalypse. An ancient agreement between the Djinn and the Wardens has been broken, and the furious Djinn, slaves to the Wardens for millennia, have broken free of mortal control.

With more than half the Wardens unaccounted for in the wake of the Djinn uprising, Joanne realises that the natural disasters they've combated for so long were merely symptoms of restless Mother Nature fidgeting in her sleep. Now she's waking up – and she is angry...